KOSSUTH SQUARE

KOSSUTH SQUARE

ADAM LEBOR

HEAD of ZEUS

First published in the UK in 2019 by Head of Zeus Ltd

975312468

A catalogue record for this book is available from
the British Library.

ISBN (HB): 9781786692733
ISBN (XTPB): 9781786693280
ISBN (E): 9781786692726

Typeset by Divaddict Publishing Solutions Ltd.

Printed and bound in Great Britain by
CPI Group (UK) Ltd, Croydon CRO 4YY

Head of Zeus Ltd
First Floor East
5–8 Hardwick Street
London ECIR 4RG

WWW.HEADOFZEUS.COM

For Kati, Daniel and Hannah

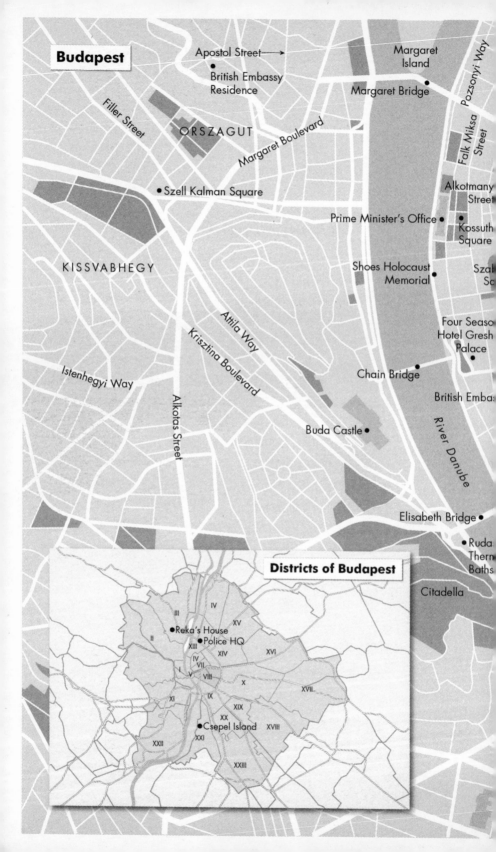

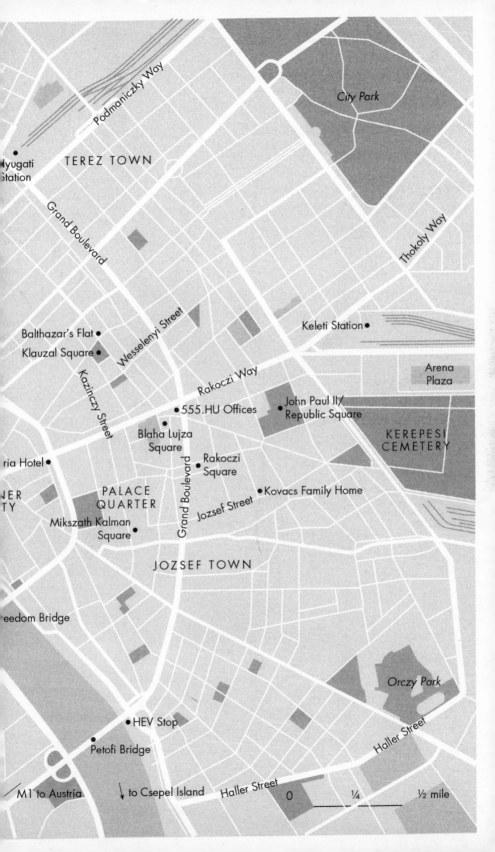

Podmaniczky Way

City Park

Nyugati
Station

TEREZ TOWN

Grand Boulevard

Thokoly Way

Wesselenyi Street

Balthazar's Flat •

Keleti Station •

Klauzal Square •

Arena
Plaza

Kazinczy Street

Rakoczi Way

• 555.HU Offices

John Paul II/
Republic Square

KEREPESI
CEMETERY

ria Hotel •

Blaha Lujza
Square

PALACE
QUARTER

Rakoczi
Square

• Kovacs Family Home

Grand Boulevard

Jozsef Street

NER
TY

Mikszath Kalman
Square

JOZSEF TOWN

eedom Bridge

Orczy Park

HEV Stop •

Petofi Bridge •

Haller Street

M1 to Austria

↓ to Csepel Island   Haller Street

0   ¼   ½ mile

There are such things as false truths and honest lies

—Gypsy proverb

PROLOGUE

Buda hills, 1995

She stood at the side entrance to the villa, watching her father's car head down the hill towards the Margaret Bridge, grey smoke trailing from the exhaust of the rusty blue BMW saloon. There were no other vehicles on the road. The house was painted a dark yellow and the walls glowed golden in the soft light of dusk. The party sounded inside: muffled voices, distant laughter, snatches of music. The air was fresh and cool, notably fresher than at home, even in the local park. She was sixteen years old and for the first time in her life, or at least as long as she could remember, she was alone. She looked around. A dog barked in the far distance but the pavements were empty. Where was everybody? Did people actually live in these houses? Her home in Jozsef Street, in District VIII, was barely twenty minutes' drive away, but she felt like she was in another world. It was a strange sensation, but not unpleasant. No little or big brothers or sisters jumping on her, demanding that she read to them or play games. No parents giving her chores. No meals to cook or clear, no plates to wash, no ashtrays to empty, no little ones to be washed and put to bed. No shouting, crying, laughing. No favourite cousin, either – well, favourite distant cousin, distant enough for everything to be proper – giving her secret smiles or those smouldering looks.

The BMW vanished from sight and she patted her long black hair again, needlessly. Freshly washed, it felt soft and silky under her fingers. A hair wash was a rare treat. There was no running hot water at home. Instead Anyu, *Mother*, and Marta *neni*, Auntie Marta, had filled the biggest pan in the kitchen and boiled the water on the cooker, washing her long tresses as she had stood over the sink, the suds running down her back. She turned to face the door. It was dark brown, thick and glossy with varnish. There was a heavy brass door knocker, polished and gleaming. She had never seen a house like this from the outside, let alone stepped inside one. There were two gardens and she could see them both: one in the front where a narrow path led between two manicured lawns. French windows opened on to a much bigger garden in the back, which had more lawns and flowerbeds. There was even a swimming pool. She couldn't swim; even shallow water made her nervous.

She was nervous now, of course she was. When she left, *Anyu* had walked downstairs with her, down all five floors – their building had no lift. That was something because *Anyu* was quite overweight, had to go back upstairs on foot, and didn't like to leave their flat. *Anyu* had cried a bit when she got into the car with her father, and she asked why but *Anyu* said it was only because she was so proud of her daughter and she was going to have a big adventure. The two of them had been to Buda before, window shopping at the new shopping centre where the security guards had followed them at every step, but they were used to that, of course. She had sung at a couple of bars around Moszkva Square with Roma Drom, her uncle Melchior's band, but she had never been this far up the hills. This was her first solo performance. No wonder her mother was proud. It was unusual, to be sure, for her to be allowed out on her own, to sing for strangers without Melchior, or any other male relative there to chaperone her. But her parents had arranged it, so she was sure it would be all right. And she would not be completely alone: *apu*, Father, had promised her that a couple of Melchior's musicians would be there to accompany her.

She looked herself up and down, pleased at what she saw. She was wearing her best outfit: a long black-and-silver skirt with a flower pattern, a plain black blouse, and a black–and–silver shawl over her shoulders, silver earrings with black gemstones. She glanced at her skirt, patted it smooth. The photographer that morning had said she looked beautiful. She had never been in a photographer's studio before and could not wait to see the pictures. If any man bothered her, she would swing her skirt over him, make him *mahrime*, unclean. That was one of the greatest shames in Gypsy culture. She frowned for a moment. Did *mahrime* work with *gadjes*, non-Gypsies? She was not sure, but even if it didn't, her brothers and cousins would deal with anyone who caused trouble. And she had big plans for the future, beyond singing. Hungary was a free country now. The old ways were changing, and not just for the *gadjes*. So far, only two people knew of her dream to be a teacher: her mother and her favourite cousin. The problem would be her father, she knew. But even he, she was sure, could be persuaded.

She savoured the moment, the air and the quiet and quickly looked herself up and down before she went inside. A touch of mascara highlighted her eyes, the colour of emeralds, *he* had once told her. She blushed at the memory, pulled the shawl tighter, for comfort, wishing he was there. But he had promised to take her for ice cream again, to celebrate once she was back. There would be so much to talk about. A bird trilled somewhere nearby, as if to approve.

She shivered for a moment, from excitement perhaps and also because the breeze was picking up and the air was starting to cool. The party, she could see through the windows, was in full swing. It looked very fancy: there were waiters and waitresses moving back and forth in black trousers and grey blouses, holding trays of drinks and snacks, and all the guests looked so elegant. One of the windows opened and a young couple stepped out. The sound of jazz drifted out into the summer evening. He was handsome, in his early twenties, looked almost familiar. She had seen him on television a couple of times, she remembered, talking about something or other. Her father had switched the TV off when he'd found her watching it, muttering about 'lying *gadje* politicians'. The woman, his girlfriend she guessed, as they were holding hands, was younger, a very pretty blonde wearing a black dress that would get the wrong kind of attention on Jozsef Street. The music ended and there was scattered applause, which meant it must be a live band. For a moment she frowned. Melchior's musicians did not play jazz.

Never mind, she told herself. They were probably having a drink and a cigarette somewhere, waiting for her. She would make it work, whoever she was singing with. Her real worry was how would she fit in at such a posh place, with such a posh crowd? Would they look down on her, the Gypsy girl from Jozseftown? Perhaps they would point and mutter, even snigger. She didn't care. She was used to that, and worse. And none of them, she knew, could sing like she could, with a voice that could soar like an eagle, whisper like a lover and stop dead every conversation in the room.

She touched her hair once more for luck, lifted the heavy door knocker and rapped it twice.

ONE

Loczy Lajos Street, 6.00 a.m., Thursday, 10 September 2015

The dead man was on his knees in the centre of the bed, naked and still bent at the waist. His backside pointed high in the air and his spine sloped down to a jowly face resting on one side. He had brown skin the colour of mahogany, and thinning black hair that seemed too dark to be natural spread across a shiny scalp. A dark urine stain had spread out underneath him onto silk sheets the colour of blood.

Balthazar Kovacs pulled on a pair of blue latex gloves, touched the side of the man's neck under his jawbone, waited for half a minute. Nothing moved. Even through the glove the man's skin was cold. He took out a ballpoint pen from his jacket pocket, slid it under the man's right arm where the palm joined the wrist, and lifted his hand. The palm drooped down, manicured fingernails dangling in the air. Balthazar lowered the pen, let the man's hand back down onto the bed and stripped the latex glove off his right hand, before holding his fingers in front of the dead man's mouth and nose. The air stayed still.

Balthazar put the glove back on, turned to the young woman standing nearby watching him. 'He's definitely dead.'

'Are you sure?'

He nodded. 'Very.'

'He's not just unconscious or something like that? Maybe he is in a coma,' she said hopefully.

'No. He's dead.'

Kinga Torok's grey eyes widened. 'Am I in trouble?'

'Not if you tell me everything that happened. Did anyone give you something to give him?'

He watched her carefully as she answered. She wore a blue silk robe over black lingerie. Her fine blonde hair was mussed and her mascara was smudged. But she held his gaze, eyes open and as innocent as they could be. 'No. Nothing. Really.'

'Drugs, powder, something to drink? It's much better if you tell me now, Kinga.'

'You mean, to kill him? Of course not. Why would I do that? I earn good money here. I send half of it back home. I don't want to mess that up.' Her voice was confident, almost disdainful.

Balthazar stepped away from the bed, looked at the dead man again. Was she telling the truth? The part about not wanting to mess things up, almost certainly. The dead man's arms were splayed, as though he had been trying to wave or call for help. A killer in the room would not have left Kinga alive. Death was probably caused by a heart attack or some kind of seizure. He glanced again at Kinga. She returned his gaze, unsettled certainly – who wouldn't be? – but not fearful or anxious. At first Balthazar thought the dead man might be a Gypsy. He was dark enough. Balthazar knew all the city's Roma power brokers and pimps, businessmen and wheeler-dealers who could afford a night with Kinga in the VIP salon. This was not one of them, but he could be from out of town.

Either that, or he was a foreigner. There were, he supposed, worse ways to go.

Balthazar asked, 'Do you know who he is?'

Kinga shrugged. 'No. An Arab, maybe. He told me to call him Abdi.'

Balthazar yawned, ran his fingers through his thick black hair, felt the weight inside him grow steadily heavier. Abdi, or whoever he was, was the reason why Eszter, the brothel's manager, had called him an hour ago, begging for his help. Balthazar knew that the brothel had dealt with a couple of dead punters before, overweight middle-aged men who had died of heart attacks. Only last summer a visiting German pastor had expired in the arms and legs of a pair of nineteen-year-old twins. Dead punters were always bad for business, but could be managed. Enough 20,000-forint notes would grease the wheels of officialdom to move the body out of the brothel, alter the reports to save reputations and relatives' memories. But a dead foreigner was much more complicated.

Balthazar asked, 'Abdi what?'

Kinga shrugged. 'Who knows? We didn't talk much.'

Balthazar glanced at the body on the bed. Abdi. Probably short for Abdullah. That could mean nothing. Rich Arab tourists were pouring into Budapest nowadays. The city's high-end brothels were doing more business than ever, few more than his brother Gaspar's place. But not all the Arab visitors were moneyed, able to afford a night in the VIP salon. Some were camped out at Keleti Station, travelling on fake papers as they steadily made their way to the west. Hungary's borders had collapsed, the prime minister had resigned in a corruption scandal connected to Gulf investors and the Ministry of Justice was entangled in a people-trafficking ring channelling Islamic radicals to the west. Perhaps Abdi, or his death, was telling him something.

Balthazar brought himself back to the room, turned to Kinga. 'So what did you do?'

She laughed. 'How much detail do you want?'

His question, Balthazar realised, could have been better phrased. 'I mean, was there anything strange, out of the ordinary?'

'No. At first, just the usual. He booked me for the whole night. Although he wanted... you know...' She paused, blushed, suddenly bashful, looked away for a couple of seconds. 'He offered me double, but I said I wouldn't do that. It hurts.'

Kinga Torok was twenty-two, a slender, pretty blonde, recently arrived from a tiny village near the Serbian border. Her father was unemployed and her mother worked as a cleaner. Smart and very ambitious, Kinga spent her daylight hours studying law at Budapest's ELTE university. At night she earned more in a few hours than her mother took home in a month, especially when she was the queen of the VIP salon. The room was the most expensive in the house. It had wall-to-wall dark-purple carpeting, near full-length mirrors on both sides of the bed and a further mirror on the ceiling. The bed was a rococo extravaganza with a carved, oversized gilt footboard and headboard, both upholstered with crimson padding that matched the sheets. A small matching cabinet stood next to it, its surface piled high with freshly laundered thick, white hand towels. An antique Biedermeier wardrobe stood in one corner, where the client and his company could leave their clothes. Facing it stood a black-lacquered Japanese cabinet with a built-in fridge, with the remains of the night on top: two bottles of Moët et Chandon champagne, one empty, one unopened, two flute glasses cut from Bohemian crystal, one almost full, one empty, and a packet of blue, triangular pills.

The room might be luxurious, but it stank: of sweat and semen, spilled alcohol and urine and the slow ripening of a dead body. Balthazar stepped aside and opened the window. He breathed deeply as the cool, fresh air of a Buda morning seeped inside, then walked over to the cabinet, glancing up at the ceiling as he went: the minimalist overhead lamp, with six sprouting metal arms, each with a steel bulb on the end, was oddly modern and did not fit with the rest of the baroque decor. Balthazar picked up the strip of pills: two empty blisters. Enough for a night, he supposed, assuming that they were indeed Viagra.

Balthazar turned the pills over in his hand, still wearing the blue latex glove.

'How many of these did he take?'

Kinga shrugged. 'Dunno. Just the two, I think.'

'Food? Did you or he eat anything?'

'Nothing. He drank most of the champagne. But I saw him open it.'

'Did you have any?'

'Just a few sips. We are not supposed to drink.'

'Which is yours?'

Kinga pointed at the glass that was three-quarters full.

'Sure?' asked Balthazar.

'Positive. It's too dry for me.'

Balthazar thought for a moment. It would be difficult, but not impossible, to adulterate the champagne. But then Kinga would have been affected as well. 'How do you feel? Dizzy, weak or anything?'

'I'm fine. Really.'

'Did he take anything else?'

He watched her as she spoke. 'No,' she said, 'nothing,' but this time she looked to the left and her pink tongue flicked over her upper lip for a second. Balthazar walked over to the cabinet. Amid the party debris there were several patches of fine white dust. 'Come here, Kinga,' he said. She walked over. 'What's this?' he asked.

She shrugged. 'Talcum powder?'

Balthazar turned to her. She still carried the smell of sex, a musty tang overlaid with sweat. He could see her body move under the flimsy gown, the top of a lacy black bra. He tapped his forehead. 'Do you see anything here?'

She looked puzzled. 'No.'

'Does it say "stupid" or "dumb cop"?'

'No. Of course not.' Kinga looked down for a moment then met his gaze. 'It was only a couple of lines. He took it.'

'Yours or his?'

'His. I don't have any. I don't like it. It makes me jittery. And Eszter told me no drugs, especially tonight.'

Balthazar took out an evidence bag, held it open over the edge of the cabinet and swept the white powder inside. He sealed the bag, then placed it in his back pocket. 'And the rest?'

Kinga shrugged. 'Dunno. Maybe he used it all.' Her voice brightened. 'Perhaps that's what he died of.'

'Nice try. Where's the bag, or box, or whatever it was in?'

'I told you. I don't know.'

'Try again.'

She pulled her robe tighter. 'What's this about? I thought you were here to sort things out. Not accuse me of taking drugs. I already told you, I don't like it,' she said, her voice rising in indignation. 'Look, I know what you think of me.

I'm only doing this for a couple of years, to help my family and get some money together. Then I'm moving to London. Lots of my friends are there already. I'll get a proper job, with a law firm.'

Balthazar stepped nearer. Kinga was a bad liar. 'I'm sure you will. But meanwhile, I know someone who got six months for having a single joint in their sock. Coke is at least double that, probably triple. And if there's enough to deal, then it's years.' He paused, looked her in the eye. 'And you can forget any ideas about a legal career.'

She glared at him, walked over to the top drawer of the cabinet, reached inside to a corner at the back, took out a small transparent bag, silently handed it over. He weighed it in his hand. At least ten or twelve grams, about €1,000 worth of cocaine. The cost of a night in the VIP salon, half of which went to Kinga. He placed the bag on top of the cabinet next to the Viagra pills. 'Anything else you want to tell me?'

Kinga shook her head, trying hard to meet and hold Balthazar's gaze. Far too hard. He looked at the dead man again. Something about him... he stepped nearer the bed and looked again at the man's right hand. He took out his pen again, lifted the wrist and looked closer. He was right. The flesh on the middle finger was indented at the bottom, a pale strip a quarter of an inch wide.

Balthazar lowered the dead man's wrist and turned around. Kinga was watching him. He asked, 'Really? From a dead man?'

She blushed. 'But I didn't...'

He held his hand out, said nothing. She reached inside her gown pocket, handed him a large gold ring, with an onyx stone mounted in the centre. 'Who would know? Maybe it fell off. We could sell it, split whatever we get.'

Balthazar stayed silent, tilted his head to one side, his hand still outstretched. 'Trying to bribe a policeman? That wasn't your smartest move, Kinga, especially for a law student. That ring is evidence. Your prints are on it now.'

Her face fell. 'Oh. I hadn't thought of that. Can't you wipe it down?'

'Maybe. Tell me again what happened,' said Balthazar. 'And no more BS.'

Kinga shrugged. 'OK. It was just the usual stuff. He took the pills, snorted the coke. We did it for a while, nothing special. Then he slept for a couple of hours. So did I. He woke me up and we started again.' She gestured at the bed. 'Like that. He just went on and on. I was getting sore. So I did the ripple. That usually does the trick. He was shouting, so I did it tighter. Then he started groaning and shaking. I thought that was it. I was relieved. My back was hurting.'

'And after that?' asked Balthazar.

'At first I thought he had, you know… finished. He stopped moving. But completely. He felt really heavy. When I turned around, his head was resting on my shoulders. He wasn't saying anything and he had gone all floppy. I slid out from underneath. He fell forward and he stayed like that.'

She smiled and looked him in the eye, let the wrap slide open an inch or two. 'I saw you on the Internet. Arresting that Arab terrorist on Rakoczi Way. That was amazing.'

'No it wasn't. That's my job. Let's focus on the here and now, Kinga. A man died underneath you. Was he nervous? Agitated?'

Kinga saw that her flirting was not working. She pulled her robe closed. For a moment Balthazar saw her for what she was: a village girl alone in the big city, where her sexual appeal had drawn her into deep and potentially dangerous waters. 'Did I kill him?' she asked nervously. 'Am I in trouble now? I've never killed a punter before. What do you think?'

'I think you should stop talking. Go and clean yourself up and put some clothes on.'

He watched Kinga walk out, glanced again at the dead man and the damp patch on the bedsheets, lost in thought. After three years in the Budapest police murder squad he had seen his share of corpses: shot, bludgeoned, poisoned, half-crushed. He had once found a torso with all four limbs sheared off. The indignity of death, the sudden hollowing-out of a body, the rushing greyness, the void where there was once life but now only stillness, still unsettled him. He looked at the dead man again, had a powerful urge to ease him down onto the bed and straighten his body out. The dead man's skin was already turning purple, his lips and fingernails going pale as the blood drained away. Balthazar glanced at his watch. It was 6.10 in the morning. Eszter, the brothel's manager, had called him an hour ago. That meant Abdi had been dead at least that long. In three hours or so rigor mortis would set in. Abdi had to be moved out before then, before his body locked and the smell, bearable now, became overpowering. But where?

For now, though, he needed to find out who Abdi was. The brothel, obviously, did not take its punters' names and most paid by cash. But most people carried some kind of ID. Balthazar opened the wardrobe door. A blue single-breasted suit was hanging on a clothes hanger, a shirt on another. He ran his fingers through the trouser pockets. There was no sign of a wallet. The fabric had an expensive sheen but Balthazar did not know much about business attire. He had one suit, purchased from Zara for his university graduation, worn at his police coming-out ceremony, his wedding, then more or less untouched. But it was clear from the smooth feel of the dark-blue cloth, the way it rippled through his fingers, that this was an expensive piece of tailoring.

He opened the jacket to see a discreet silk panel on the inside advertising a Savile Row tailor, smiled to himself. Definitely not a Gypsy then: his people preferred well-known labels to advertise their wealth, would wear them like badges or shoulder patches if they could. But there was something stiff inside the jacket's breast pocket. He took it out and stepped away from the wardrobe. The booklet was a passport, maroon in colour, embossed with Arabic script. He looked at the dead man then back at the photograph page. Abdullah al-Nuri. Born in Saudi Arabia, citizen of Qatar. He looked again at the dead man. It was him, there was no doubt. Balthazar exhaled hard. Mr al-Nuri was bad news. He meant consulates, diplomats, foreign governments who were not bribable. And what if there had been foul play? That meant sealing the room, a proper autopsy and crime scene investigation, sending the evidence for testing. That could not be done on the sly. And that, in turn, meant drawing the attention of the Hungarian authorities.

The door opened a few minutes later and Kinga walked back in. She wore a pink T-shirt and loose blue cotton trousers, her hair loose around her shoulders, her face wiped clean of make-up. The courtesan was gone, replaced by a pretty girl from the countryside. She looked young and innocent, which was, he guessed, part of her appeal.

He asked, 'Have you been with him before?'

'No.'

'Have you seen him before?'

Kinga twisted her wet hair, stepped nearer. She smelled of soap and shampoo. 'Not here.'

'Where?'

'You won't tell them, will you? That I also work here?'

Balthazar said, 'Not if you stop talking in riddles.'

Kinga's face creased in concern. 'Cause I really don't want to lose that job. It's very well paid. And there I don't have to do anything except smile and serve drinks.'

Balthazar's voice turned hard. 'Kinga. Listen to me. There is a dead man in this room. You were the last person to see him, to be with him, while he was alive. If this turns official that will make you a suspect. The prime suspect, actually. So tell me, where did you see him before?'

'A suspect? But I didn't do anything.' Her voice turned tearful. 'It's not my fault. They said you would fix everything. And now you want to arrest me.'

Balthazar stepped forward. 'Please, calm down. Just tell me what happened.'

'But I did,' she said, almost pleading. 'That's it, everything I know. I promise. Do you know who he is?'

She was, Balthazar thought, telling the truth now. He had seen Kinga lie about the cocaine and she was not very good at it. And she was scared. 'Yes. His name is Abdullah al-Nuri. So the more you tell me what you know, the faster we can sort this out. Where did you see Mr al-Nuri for the first time?'

'Last Friday. I was a hostess.'

'A hostess?' That word, in Budapest, Balthazar knew, had a multiplicity of meanings.

'Yes. A proper hostess,' said Kinga, her voice stronger now. 'Making conversation. Chatting to people. I can speak English. And French. It was at a reception for Arab investors.'

'Where?'

'The Royal Palace, at the Buda Castle.'

Balthazar's feeling of dread intensified. There was only one person who could use the historic site for entertaining. The call to the ambulance and forensics would definitely have to wait. 'Who was holding the reception?'

Kinga smiled proudly. 'The prime minister. The other one. Pal Dezeffy.'

TWO

Several hills away from the brothel, in a home gymnasium on the crest of Bimbo Way, Attila Ungar was pounding a heavy black punch bag suspended from the ceiling. The slashing guitars, angry lyrics and pounding drums of Arpad, Hungary's premier *nemzeti* (national) rock band, filled the room as the bag swung back and forth. The more the singer shouted about the traitors of Trianon, who had taken more than two-thirds of Hungary's territory in the 1920 eponymous treaty and the filthy *komcsis* – slang for Communists – the harder Attila punched the heavy bag.

This morning he was working on multiple distance training: a lightning-fast combination of jabs and crosses with arms fully extended, then moving in for some close-quarter hooks and uppercuts, before spinning left and right to deliver a fusillade of high roundhouse kicks, a single one of which would fell most adults. He finished with a barrage of elbow strikes that left the bag swinging back and forth like a hanged man in a windstorm. Panting, drenched in sweat, he stepped back, wiped himself down with a towel and drank almost a litre of water.

Attila had been divorced for more than five years. He lived alone in a spacious flat on the top floor of a four-storey modern development in one of Buda's most upmarket quarters. The flat cost far more than he would have been able to afford on a policeman's salary or even that of a Gendarme commander, but nobody was asking awkward questions. The white-walled gym was in the smallest of the three bedrooms. His was the largest, with a king-sized double bed, one half of which was rarely used, except when he called an expensive escort agency. There were two smaller guest bedrooms, one complete with a large flat-screen television and an Xbox, and several drawers full of designer clothes for a sixteen-year-old boy. But Henrik, Attila's son, rarely visited and had never stayed overnight. Monika, Henrik's mother, had sent him to a progressive, German-run school that did not believe in disciplining errant pupils. Attila had bought Henrik an iPhone. But the last time they met, briefly in a park, he was still using an old Nokia. To Attila's horror, he was wearing a rainbow flag T-shirt. He often did not take his father's calls, and rarely called him back.

A shelf of free weights stood in the opposite corner of the gym, a treadmill on the other side of the room. A small sink and work surface stood near the punch bag. Attila ran the cold tap, cupped his hands under the water, then splashed his face and neck, before towelling himself down again. He glanced at the blender on the work surface, its glass jug a third full with brown, slithery chunks slopping around in a white liquid with pale, floating shreds. The breakfast smoothie – chicken liver and oatmeal in milk and yogurt – could wait.

Much of one wall was taken up with an oversized reproduction of a poster that had appeared around the city a couple of months earlier when the government announced that the Gendarmerie, the pre-war national police force, was about to be reconstituted. The black-and-white poster showed a group of Gendarmes on horseback, wearing their trademark hats with cockades, rounding up a group of Jews in a village in the spring of 1944. The Gendarmes were laughing, the Jews looked terrified. Overlaid on the photograph, in heavy black ink, were the words: 'No return to 1944, no to the new Gendarmerie'. But the poster, part of a campaign by activists and opposition politicians of all political stripes, had not worked. The new Gendarmerie had been on the streets for a month or so, and complaints were already pouring in from human rights groups about their heavy-handed tactics. Few expected the complaints to have much traction – the Gendarmerie, with its hazy mandate to 'protect national order' and 'guard the dignity of the government and Hungarian nation' reported directly to the prime minister. The usual oversight bodies – the ombudsman, Parliament's human rights committee – had no power over the new force.

Attila filled up a water bottle and walked out onto the long wrap-around terrace that encircled most of the flat. He stood there for several moments with his eyes closed, enjoying the cool fresh air, waiting till his heart slowed and his breathing calmed. The modern brutalist blocks of Deli, Budapest's southern station, sprawled in the centre of the low ground, further downtown, the railway tracks splaying out like the limbs of an octopus. For a moment he was an eight-year-old boy again, taking the train from Deli to Siofok on the south shore of Lake Balaton, excited and overjoyed to be going on his first family holiday with his parents and younger brother. Until the memory slid, as it always did, into a vision of his father, Zeno, drunk at the hotel, screaming abuse at the government, the Communist Party, the whole stinking system, smashing his plate against the floor and the manager threatening to call the police unless they paid and left immediately. They did and returned home to Csepel Island on the outskirts of Budapest. There were no more holidays after that. His father was arrested at dawn the next day. They did not see him for six months, only heard rumours that he had been spotted at one of the villas high in the hills where political troublemakers were taken. Zeno returned home a broken man. Within two years he had drunk himself to death. And if his parents had lived, Attila wondered, had been there for him? If he had grown up in a home, even a meagre panel flat, instead of a state-run orphanage, would there still be such a rage burning inside him? He watched the early morning traffic flow into the city, drinking the rest of the water, when his mobile telephone rang. He quickly walked back and grabbed the handset. The call was short, perhaps thirty seconds long. Attila nodded as he listened, then wrote down an address and walked across to the blender. There he turned the switch to pulse, watching as the brown lumps exploded, sending bursts of blood again and again against the glass, red threads trickling down the sides as the liquid turned into a smooth brown slurry.

Loczy Lajos Street, 6.30 a.m.

Balthazar turned as the door to the VIP salon opened and Eszter walked in. The brothel's manager was a Roma woman in her fifties whose long black hair was shot through with silver-grey. She wore smart navy trousers and a sky-blue business blouse and carried herself with the brisk assurance of a bank manager about to refuse a loan application. Her deep-brown eyes had seen too much to be shocked any more at the vagaries of human nature. She looked at the dead man on the bed, pursed her lips, then exhaled. 'He's still there,' she said, her voice throaty from years of cigarettes.

Balthazar said, 'He's not going anywhere.'

'No. I didn't think so.' She walked around the bed, considering the dead man from several angles. 'Shouldn't we straighten him out? It's not very... dignified.'

Balthazar shook his head. 'No. Definitely not. Don't touch him. We don't know what he died of yet.'

Eszter was a former *oromlany*, joy girl, herself. Unlike many of her peers, she had not taken drugs or slipped into a life of petty crime. She was used to handling crises. Given the nature of the business, and human nature, they were to be expected. Threats, sneak thievery by the working girls, punters who tried to evade their bills and complained about the service, even occasional outbursts of violence, all these could be managed, hushed up, smoothed away with wads of banknotes, offers of free return visits, violence, or threats of more violence. But a dead man was much trickier, especially if he was a foreigner.

Eszter turned to Balthazar. 'He's not one of ours, is he?'

Balthazar shook his head. 'No. Not a Gypsy or a Hungarian.'

'So who is he?'

'His name is Abdullah al-Nuri. A Qatari.'

Eszter grimaced. 'That's a problem.'

The door opened again. A large Gypsy man stepped inside, quickly followed by another, who was even more overweight.

'*Jo reggelt kivanok, batyam* – good morning, my older brother,' exclaimed Gaspar Kovacs in a voice like gravel as he embraced Balthazar. Balthazar breathed in Gaspar's familiar smell: sweat and tobacco smoke, overlaid with the *kajszibarack hazipalinka* – home-distilled apricot schnapps – that a relative made for them in the countryside, then stepped back and looked him up and down. Gaspar had probably been up all night but looked like the evening was just beginning. His long black hair was slicked back. He wore his trademark black silk shirt, open almost halfway to his midriff, hanging loose over his substantial belly, a thick gold rope chain and black, shiny track pants over red-and-white Kanye West trainers that cost €500 a pair. His brown eyes, set deep in a doughy face, were clear apart from a faint redness around the rims.

The two men kissed four times, twice on each cheek, as the second man watched. Gaspar pointed at the dead man. 'Not a bad way to go.'

Balthazar said, 'That depends.'

'On what?'

'If someone helped him along the way. That's why we asked you to come and have a look.' The two brothers' eyes met. 'Thanks, *batyam*,' said Gaspar, his voice serious now. Gaspar turned to Eszter and Kinga and greeted them, this time accompanied by a small bow. Fat Vik, Gaspar's consigliere, also wished the women good morning and turned to Balthazar. The two men clasped hands and quickly embraced. Fat Vik was dressed in his usual oversized white T-shirt and grey track pants. He was even bigger than Gaspar, with a bald head that shone with a faint sheen of sweat. Both men were breathing heavily. Apart from the occasional brawl, neither had exercised since they left school. The house had no lift and the VIP salon was at the top, on the third floor.

Kinga yawned and turned to Balthazar. 'Do I need to stay?'

He shook his head. 'No. You can go home. But don't go anywhere far and keep your phone on.' The four of them waited until Kinga had left.

Gaspar looked at Eszter. 'What's all the fuss about? We've had punters die on the job before. That's why we pay retainers to the ambulance service and the paramedics.'

'Because I thought he was a foreigner, and I was right,' said Eszter. 'If we lose a foreigner here, you need to know.'

Gaspar shrugged. 'OK, so he's a foreigner. That makes it more complicated.' He turned to Balthazar. 'How long do you think this will take?'

'That depends.'

'On what?'

'On what "this" is. Why, *ocsim*, my little brother – are you in a hurry?'

Gaspar glanced at his watch, a gold-plated Rolex. 'Actually, yes.'

'And why is that?' asked Balthazar, although he suspected he already knew the answer.

Gaspar shrugged, 'Busy day, *batyam*.'

Balthazar asked, 'How many?'

'Enough. Enough to make it worthwhile. Don't worry, Tazi. Everything's set up. The border's open now. It's a clear run all the way to Vienna. *Nem lesz semmi baj*. There won't be any problems.' Gaspar turned to the dead man. 'Meanwhile, we need to sort this out.'

Balthazar turned to Eszter. 'You have the CCTV footage?'

She did not reply immediately, shot Gaspar a questioning look. He nodded. Eszter said, 'Yes. The usual. The front of the house. The entranceway.'

Balthazar asked, 'With timings? Correct timings?'

Eszter nodded. 'Yes.'

'The corridors? The rooms?'

Balthazar watched a faint tinge of pink appear on Eszter's cheeks. She looked down for a couple of seconds. He looked back at Gaspar, who still said nothing. Balthazar held his younger brother's gaze. A memory flashed through his mind. They were boys, barely in their teens, mucking around at the playground on Republic Square, not far from where they grew up in the Gypsy ghetto in District VIII. Balthazar turned away for a moment to watch a girl he liked as she walked past with her sister. When he turned back, two neighbourhood toughs had Gaspar face-down in the sandpit. His brother was fighting and struggling, but there were two of them, both bigger and more powerful. Balthazar swung around and kicked one in his ribs, leaned over and punched the other on the side of his head. They slid away from Gaspar, yelping in pain, and ran off. That was more than twenty years ago. His younger brother was now the most powerful pimp in the city, running a string of brothels – some upmarket, like this one, others less so – several lap-dance bars and a network of streetwalkers. But neither he nor Eszter could lie to Balthazar. Partly because the fierce Roma code of family loyalty did not allow it, but also because Balthazar would know immediately.

Gaspar smiled. '*If* we did film there, why would you need it?'

Balthazar gestured at the dead man. He thought it was highly likely that the rooms had concealed CCTV. Several local police officers and a couple of councillors enjoyed occasional free use of the palace. Filming them in action would be the best insurance against any future difficulties. 'I am a detective in the Budapest murder squad. That's my job. Don't you want to know if someone is killing your punters? And why they might be?'

Eszter said, 'I certainly do, Gaspar.'

Gaspar turned to Balthazar. 'How much do you need?'

'The last twelve hours.' He yawned again, winced as a sharp ache shot across his jaw, and quickly closed his mouth. The pain from the beating at Keleti the previous Friday was easing, but at times like this, when he was tired, it flared up. Technically he had been up an hour, but in reality he had barely slept. The dream was back, had been every night since the events of the previous weekend. As he lay in bed on his back, watching the first smears of dawn lighten the sky, Eszter's call had almost been a relief.

'OK.' Gaspar turned to Eszter. 'Give it to him.' He rubbed the back of his neck. 'I need a massage.'

Fat Vik laughed. 'You are in the right place, *brat*.'

Gaspar rolled his head in circles, back and forth. 'Not that kind. A proper massage.'

Eszter said, 'Actually, we do those as well.'

Gaspar laughed, 'Thanks. But I'm in a hurry today.' He looked at Balthazar. 'That footage. It won't be going anywhere, will it? Because you are already all over the Internet. I don't want this place to be.'

Balthazar said, 'Of course not, *ocsim*. Where is the camera?'

Gaspar looked up at the lamp.

'Which one?'

Gaspar pointed at one of the steel arms. Balthazar looked up. There was nothing to distinguish it from the others. 'Clever.'

'Now what?' asked Gaspar.

'I'm thinking.' Balthazar walked over to the window, closed his eyes, took great lungfuls of the clean autumn air, breathing through his nose. The breeze was scented with the smell of burning leaves and cut grass, the last days of summer. A buzzing noise sounded in the distance, rising and falling over the hum of distant traffic, but then faded away. He rubbed his eyes and opened them. Buda stretched out before him, rolling green hills dotted with red-roofed villas, once stately mansions now chopped into flats, sleek new apartment buildings with solar panels on the roofs. The city was split in two by the river. Flat, urban Pest on one side and leafy, green Buda on the other. He was born and lived all his life in the same city, but lush Rozsadomb, Rose Hill, was another world to the narrow alleys, dark courtyards and backstreets of Jozsefvaros, where he grew up.

He looked again at the dead man. Abdullah al-Nuri, a dead Qatari. Now, after some time in the room, the scene had settled in his mind. Balthazar's instinct was telling him clearly that none of this was a coincidence – and nor was it good news. If someone had wanted al-Nuri dead, they had gone to a lot of trouble to make sure he died in Gaspar's brothel.

Balthazar turned around. His brother and Fat Vik were standing looking at him, as though he held the key to making complications and difficulties vanish. Sometimes he did. But he also knew the limits of his networks, his ability to game the system, make inconvenient things disappear or re-appear somewhere more suitable. There was one person, he knew, who would definitely want to know about this, and might be able to help.

Gaspar asked, 'Now what?'

Balthazar said, 'I make a call.'

THREE

The police officer slid his passport into a machine reader and stared at the monitor for several seconds. Marton Ronay looked around as he waited. Until today, the furthest east he had been was Berlin. That city was much nearer Poland than he had thought, but was still part of Germany, the civilised, western half of the continent. Now he was in the east, in a land that bordered Ukraine and Romania, almost in the Balkans. He thought for a moment of his great-aunt in New Jersey, the stories she told of the 'old country': the wartime siege and hunger, the feral youths roaming the city, nights ripped apart by gunfire, the brother who went out for bread in the winter of 1944 as the Russians advanced and never came home.

But that was more than seventy years ago. Communism had collapsed in 1990. Hungary was a democracy now, a member of NATO and the European Union, but still, this pristine modernity was not quite what he had expected. The arrivals hall had a polished cream marble floor, white walls and a row of glass booths where the police officers sat. One illuminated billboard showed a sequence of photographs of Hungary – he recognised the chain bridge and Lake Balaton. Another showed attractive young people chatting on their iPhone Xs

29

or joyfully moving money around on Internet bank accounts. Even the toilets, which he had just used, were spotless. The immigration queue moved swiftly, at least in comparison to every American airport he had ever passed through. And then there was the man flicking through his passport. The policeman was probably in his late twenties. He wore a light-blue uniform shirt, nicely filled by broad shoulders. Floppy brown hair fell over cool, assessing hazel eyes. Marton looked at the name on his shirt: Szilagyi Ferenc, written in the Hungarian fashion with the family name first. Welcome to Hungary, indeed.

Ferenc almost made up for the delay. He was certainly better-looking than the fat Mexican or whatever guy who had pulled him out of the line at JFK, taken him into a filthy side room, made him turn out his pockets and daypack and asked him what felt like a hundred questions about why he was going to Hungary.

Marton felt the policeman's glance on him, stifled a yawn. He was exhausted. He had transferred at Frankfurt, expecting a short, hassle-free flight of an hour. The flight had left and arrived on time, but once they'd landed at Budapest all the passengers had been held up for more than half an hour on the tarmac. Some problem with getting a staircase, the captain had said. Marton had watched from his window seat as the luggage was unloaded from the hold and placed onto trolleys before being driven away, although he could not spot his case among them. He rubbed his eyes and stifled a yawn. The pressure was building now behind his eyes, the band of tension spreading. It was definitely the start of a headache, hopefully not a full-blown shooting-stars-and-explosions migraine.

The policeman removed his passport from the reader, still holding it. 'What is the purpose of your visit, Mr Marton?' he asked, clear eyes holding his. 'Business or pleasure?'

Marton tried to read his look. Brisk, polite, professional. Was there a flicker of something else underneath? Did they have gaydar in Hungary? Surely. It was a universal mechanism. 'Both. I have some meetings. But I will also be doing some tourism,' he replied in fluent Hungarian. He paused, smiled hopefully. 'Maybe you can recommend a guide?'

The policeman continued staring at Marton's passport, his handsome face impassive. Marton smiled, gathered his courage. Even if he got it wrong, what was there to lose? He leaned forward. 'Or perhaps you have some free time. It's always so much better when a local shows you their favourite places.'

The policeman did not smile back. 'There is a tourist information booth in the arrivals area. They can help you.'

Marton nodded. A strikeout. But he had only been in the country for less than an hour. There would be plenty of other opportunities, he was sure. Ferenc continued speaking. 'You speak very good Hungarian. Your family name is Hungarian. You have relatives here?'

Marton paused for a second. Yes, he did, although none that he wanted to admit to and he was certainly not about to tell Ferenc that, no matter how good-looking he was. 'My parents left in '56. We spoke Hungarian at home. I still have some distant cousins here,' he said. 'You know us Magyars. We are everywhere. Conquering the world.'

That at least brought a glimmer of a human response. Ferenc seemed about to smile but then thought better of it. He moved back from the glass, turned away for a second as he scribbled something on a notepad. He turned back to Marton, stamped his passport and slid it under the glass. 'Welcome in Hungary, Mr Marton.'

For a moment Marton thought of correcting his grammar, then thought better of it. In any case, the next passenger was already moving forward behind him. He took his passport and walked through to the baggage arrivals hall. A cascade of luggage – overstuffed rucksacks, suitcases wrapped in clear plastic to deter light-fingered baggage handlers, black executive trolleys, cardboard boxes wrapped in duct tape – was tumbling onto the second carousel. The hall was crowded with families, businesspeople tapping on smartphones, lone travellers, a group of Korean tourists being marshalled by their guide who held a small Korean flag. A baby started howling. After a minute or so, Marton saw his bag, an expensive black-and-brown TUMI trolley, slide down the belt onto the carousel. Marton slid past several Koreans, took his luggage, extended the handle, and walked through the green customs channel, behind a bald, lanky businessman in a black suit. There were large two-way mirrors attached to each side of the wall. A poster warned against bringing in undocumented pets, plants or meat products. He kept his pace steady, tried to ignore his racing heartbeat.

A bored-looking customs guard, a tall man in his fifties with sloping shoulders, watched the businessmen walk by. He turned and looked Marton up and down. Marton returned his glance for a couple of seconds, then looked ahead. The exit was to the right, two glass doors that opened automatically. Breathe, he told himself, you are nearly there, and you are not carrying anything illegal. The dangerous stuff is in your head, and there are no customs guards in the world that can get to that. The doors opened. A low brushed-aluminium barrier marshalled the exiting passengers into the arrivals area. He walked into the throng and the tiredness hit him. A young couple fell on each other and kissed hungrily, a mother in her forties embraced a lanky, embarrassed-looking teenager, hugging him and crying. They had told Marton that the driver, a man called Laszlo, would be waiting for him, would recognise him and would take him straight to the flat. A wiry man in his late twenties, wearing a badly fitting denim shirt, with a nose that looked like it had been broken, walked up to Marton. He smiled confidently, showing a row of crooked teeth. 'Welcome in Hungary. How was your flight?' he asked in strongly accented Hungarian.

Marton asked, 'Are you Laszlo?'

'Laszlo, yes, yes, Laszlo,' replied the man. 'You must be much tired. Don't worry, I will arrange the all. Hotel, everything.' Marton paused for a moment. What was this talk of a hotel?

'I don't need a hotel. I'm going straight to the apartment,' Marton said.

The taxi driver nodded, reached for Marton's bag. 'Apartment, yes, yes. All is arranged. Very nice place in the downtown.'

Marton was about to hand over his luggage when he saw the badge on the man's chest. The 'Official Taxi' badge had obviously been printed at home, with a blurry photograph of the man in the kind of plastic cover used by conference delegates. The name underneath was Kiss Sandor. Marton kept a grip on his bag, shook his head. 'No. No thank you.'

The taxi driver's smile faded. He pointed at his badge. 'What is problem, Mister? I am official taxi.'

He reached for Marton's bag again. Marton pulled it away, stepped back, adrenalin cutting through his fatigue, and was about to start arguing when another man appeared. He was older, in his forties, with buzz-cut steel-grey hair and blue eyes. He wore a well-cut brown leather jacket and a black woollen poloneck and clean jeans and moved with a confident ease. The first taxi driver looked him up and down, considering his options. The man in the leather jacket leaned forward and spoke in a low voice. The first taxi driver immediately stopped talking and moved away, scanning the hall for easier prey.

The man in the leather jacket put his hand out. 'Mr Marton. Sorry about that, this place is full of jackals. I'm Laszlo. But you can call me Laci.'

Neither of them noticed the tall businessman watch their exit, and then make a telephone call.

Loczy Lajos Street, 7.20 a.m.

Balthazar, Gaspar and Fat Vik stood behind Eszter at her desk, her fingers gliding over her silver-and-white Apple keyboard as she called up the program that controlled the in-house CCTV system. The office stood at the end of a corridor on the ground floor with a view out on the large garden. Eszter's workplace was tidy and homely. The walls were painted a light shade of pink and the floor was covered with narrow parquet slats laid in a diagonal pattern. A pale cream sofa took up most of one corner, with a rainbow-patterned throw covering its back. A tall yucca plant stood in the other corner. The window was open, and a breeze blew in. The garden was only used by Eszter and her *oromlanyok* between clients, but was still well maintained, the edges of the lawn neatly trimmed and lined by rose bushes. Three wood-and-rattan recliners stood in the middle of the lawn around a low coffee table. A framed photograph, its colours fading, showed two boys, perhaps eight or nine years old, both dressed in green-and-white strip of Ferencvaros, one of the city's best-known football clubs, as they grinned at the camera.

Eszter's two sons were nineteen now: one, Miki, was in prison, after he was caught picking pockets on the number-two tram. The other, Pal, was still at high school, had never been in trouble apart from a couple of playground fights after being taunted, and was about to graduate. High school graduations among Roma teenagers were still rare enough to occasion a huge family party. For a moment Balthazar wondered if he would be invited. Eszter, he was sure, would be glad to see him. So would his mother, Marta. The problem was his father, Laszlo. Laszlo had cut off all relations with Balthazar after he joined the police. The two had not spoken directly for more than eight years, although various relatives were occasionally used to send messages about family affairs, and Alex, Balthazar's twelve-year-old son.

Balthazar watched Eszter as she worked, his eyes moving over her desk. A mug held several pens and pencils, and a stack of three trays was filled with neatly filed paperwork. The brothel operated as a legitimate business, a day spa, although Eszter kept two sets of books. The first set was maintained on the computer with standard office software. Eszter recorded around half the house's earnings on the Excel spreadsheets and paid tax on them. The second set of accounts, that recorded the actual movements of money, were handwritten in a ledger that was kept locked in a safe that was built into the floor. The brothel even took credit cards, although not surprisingly most customers paid in cash.

Eszter sat back and stared at the monitor for a moment, her face creased in puzzlement.

'What's the matter?' asked Gaspar.

She tapped the keyboard again, several times. 'Nothing, I think. The program is just sticking. Wait...'

The left side of the monitor suddenly filled with feeds from half a dozen cameras. Yellow numbers at the bottom of each marked the current date and time. The cameras covered the entranceway, the pavement outside on the street, the foyer, the internal corridor, the rear of the house and garden and inside the VIP salon. Balthazar looked at the screen for several seconds – all the cameras seemed to be working. The VIP salon camera showed a rumpled bed, now empty, another the foyer. He glanced at the camera covering the street outside: a jogger bounded past, heading downhill – a skinny, balding man who looked to be in his fifties, wearing a white Nike T-shirt and grey shorts.

The private ambulance had arrived soon after Balthazar made his call.

They had all watched silently as the ambulance men had worked quickly, as if suddenly aware that the slack skin, lolling limbs, gaping mouth and dead eyes had just a couple of hours before belonged to a living, breathing person. The ambulance men straightened al-Nuri out, zipped him into a body bag, slid him onto a trolley and wheeled him away.

'Can you rewind the footage an hour or so back? For all the cameras?' asked Balthazar.

Eszter nodded. 'Of course.' Her fingers slid across the keyboard. For a couple of seconds the six screens carried on showing the same images. Then they blurred and turned black.

Eszter leaned forward, frowning. 'That's strange.'

'What is?' asked Gaspar. He stepped nearer, tapped the monitor. Balthazar's brother was hopeless with technology and could barely operate his smartphone. He had left school at the age of fourteen and was only haltingly literate. But his instincts for trouble – and potential trouble – were razor-sharp. They kept the Kovacs family businesses in profit and its members safe. 'Why isn't it showing anything?'

Balthazar lifted his brother's hand away. 'Leave it, *ocsim*. And let Eszter do her work.' Gaspar shrugged, stepped back. Eszter tried again but nothing moved. The six monitors stayed black. Balthazar said nothing, but watched with a growing sense that this morning was becoming a larger and larger problem, even though it was not yet 7 a.m.

Eszter moved the cursor back to the camera covering the palace. She rewound the footage by an hour or so, to 5.30 a.m., when Kinga had alerted her that the client had collapsed. The CCTV frame stayed black, the computer silent.

'I don't understand,' said Eszter. 'We checked the system this afternoon, before we opened. Like we do every day. All the cameras were fine. Working perfectly.'

'Try the other cameras,' said Balthazar.

Eszter went through the same routine with all six cameras. The result was the same every time.

Balthazar watched with a growing sense of foreboding. 'What time did we leave the VIP salon?'

Fat Vik glanced at his watch. 'Around 6.40 a.m.'

Balthazar said, 'Try the room at that time.'

Eszter did as he bade. The screen stayed black. She turned around in her chair, her eyes wide with anxiety. 'I don't understand. This has never happened before.'

Gaspar ran his fingers back through his hair. 'We've never had a dead Qatari before.' He looked at Balthazar. '*Batyam?*'

Balthazar was about to answer when the screen flickered. All six feeds suddenly lit up. Each showed the same image: Balthazar, Gaspar, Fat Vik and Eszter standing in front of Eszter's desk, staring at the monitor.

FOUR

Three miles away, on the Pest side of the Danube embankment, in an imposing corner office on the third floor of the neo-Gothic extravaganza that was the Hungarian Parliament, the country's first female prime minister stood by the window looking down onto Kossuth Square, a cup of coffee slowly cooling in her hand. The workday for many started at 8 a.m. and a stream of commuters were walking quickly across the grey granite flagstones on their way to the nearby ministries, as well as the numerous law firms and companies that kept offices nearby, all making sure they kept close to the hearth.

Reka Bardossy watched the yellow-and-white number-two tram roll along the front of the square, past the almost equally imposing National Ethnographic Museum. Three guardsmen stood by the enormous flagpole on the edge of the square, still as the Queen's Life Guards outside Buckingham Palace she had once seen in London. The guardsmen wore olive-green uniforms and peaked caps. They looked very smart, but they were also extremely capable: each was a highly trained officer in the National Counterterrorist Force. Security had been stepped up over the last few months, since Budapest had become the epicentre of Europe's migrant crisis.

Reka glanced at her fingertips. The dirt was long gone and her manicurist had done amazing work. But several of the nails were still irregularly shaped and one, which still throbbed occasionally, was only an eighth of an inch long. She slowly exhaled, placed the coffee cup down on a nearby table and called her husband, Peter, for the third time that day. This time, he picked up.

'It's me,' she said, tersely. 'When are you coming back?'

His voice was emollient. 'I'm sorry I couldn't talk before. I was in a meeting with the Qataris. I told you darling, I can come back when I am finished out here. We're nearly done, hopefully. It's so hot here, it's unbearable. About forty degrees in the shade.'

Reka had no interest in the weather. 'How is it going? Will they invest? Will they go ahead with the project?'

'They are making encouraging noises. They are not saying no. Things move slowly here, lots of elaborate formalities before we get down to business.' His voice turned affectionate. 'I cannot just break off in the middle and fly back to Budapest – even if my wife is now prime minister.'

Reka tapped her fingers on the table, the pace speeding up as she spoke. 'I am under siege here. I need you here, Peter. Not in Doha. I don't know if I can do this on my own.'

'Of course you can. We've been planning for this for years. You will be fine. What time is he coming for the meeting? They are waiting here for his report back, once he has seen you.'

'At eight o'clock. In a few minutes.' She paused, took a deep breath, the words tumbling out of her mouth, 'Peter, someone tried to...'

'Tried to what?'

Tried to kill me. But I killed him instead, she almost said. But that was not a conversation for an open line on a mobile telephone. '...To, oh it doesn't matter. There's so much going on. Too much.'

Noise sounded in the background. It sounded like a female voice. It was a female voice. Peter said, 'I know. I'll be there soon for you. I'm sorry. I've got to go now, darling. They are calling me back. I'll call you tonight. Promise.'

She hung up and looked out again, watching the water shimmer as it flowed across the wide moat that lay behind a row of concrete cubes, both protecting the Parliament from car bombers. Despite the migrant crisis, compared to other European capitals, Budapest took a relaxed approach to the *orszaggyuleshaz*, the national meeting house, as the Parliament was known. Almost all of Kossuth Square, apart from the areas by the entrance to Parliament, was open to the public. Until recently, protestors had been allowed to gather, even set up protest camps on the green area to the side of the main gate. Pal Dezeffy, her predecessor, had forbidden such gatherings, claiming they were a security risk. Which they were, Reka supposed – but one of her first acts had been to rescind that decree. Kossuth Square was the symbolic heart of the country. It had, in a way, brought her to the prime minister's office. The Social Democrats had taken power after riots and protests in Kossuth Square in the autumn of 2006, on the fiftieth anniversary of the failed 1956 uprising, an event seared into every Hungarian's consciousness. The rickety right-wing government had collapsed, in circumstances that still remained unclear, and Pal Dezeffy had been appointed prime minister, which he had remained until he had resigned last week.

The square had been recently renovated: the Socialist-style statue of Lajos Kossuth, the leader of the failed 1848 revolution against the Hapsburgs, had been replaced by a

gleaming ultra-realist, kitsch new version. As a child of the
1970s – she was thirty-nine years old – Reka preferred the
previous version. Now the man many regarded as the greatest
Hungarian in history glowered down at the white stone steps
in front of him, his companions looking positively lachrymose.
Kossuth's look matched Reka's mood. Her marriage had long
been an arrangement of convenience, a union of political
and economic interest between two powerful families rooted
in the old, Communist regime. There had been lust at the
beginning – Peter was a handsome man – and some affection
too. But after a couple of years of watching a succession of
ever more gorgeous 'personal assistants' trail through Peter's
office, Reka's on-off affair with Pal had been rekindled. It
had started when they were teenagers, had flared up and
faded away for years. Once Pal Dezeffy took office as prime
minister, it reached new heights. Power, she had learned, was
an aphrodisiac and nowhere more than in this room.

Reka tried to disentangle her competing emotions. Two
were the most powerful: exhilaration and fear. Exhilaration
– that she had finally taken possession of the room for which
she had hungered since she was a teenage girl. Fear – that she
had only been in office for four days, and if the combined
secret services of the United States, Britain and her own
country made good on their threats, might be out again in
as many. After fear and exhilaration came a third emotion:
determination – that she would stay in the office which her
father, and grandfather before him, had promised her. Long
enough, at least, to redecorate.

The room was half-lined with dark-wood panels, above
which the walls were painted a light shade of ochre. Her
predecessors glowered out from their portraits, from the
grandees of the late nineteenth century, through the grey men

of Communism to the last in the line: Pal Dezeffy, each in a heavy gilt frame under a polished brass lamp. Only one was missing, Pal's grandfather, Gyorgy Kiss, the prime minister in the early 1950s, the time of the worst Stalinist terror. Csontvary's masterpiece, *Roman Bridge at Mostar*, was hung over a white marble fireplace, bringing a blaze of colour to the room. That, at least, would stay. Perhaps the desk too. It was dark and heavy wood, with a green leather panel in the middle. She smiled for a moment, recalling how she and Pal had celebrated his ascension to power on his first evening in office, how her skirt had slid back and forth across the leather. But her smile quickly faded when she remembered the small silver memory stick that she had been handed at the start of the week, and the consequences if the video footage it contained were released.

Outside the fountain nozzles hidden in the granite tiles suddenly erupted, breaking her chain of thought, spurting gusts of white mist over the square, catching a gaggle of young female Japanese tourists by surprise. Each wore a different fluorescent-coloured rain jacket. They laughed with delight, quickly pointing their telephones at each other as the water droplets slicked off a riot of wet, bright colours. Reka half watched a tall, well-built man walk across the green area, avoiding the mist and Japanese girls, towards the statue of Ferenc Rakoczi on the side of the square, vaguely noticing that he was carrying a long, narrow package. The number-two tram continued on its journey, winding around the corner of the Parliament area towards the Ministry of Justice, her most recent workplace, then rolled on, parallel with the embankment towards the chain bridge. On one level, she knew, it was a minor miracle that she was still free at all, let alone occupying the highest public office in the land. The ministry

– she herself, as former minister of justice – had been deeply implicated in the country's most explosive political scandal since the change of system in 1990. Hungarian passports linked to the ministry had been sold to people-traffickers, who in turn had passed them on to Islamic radicals, who had used the migrant crisis and the collapse of Europe's border controls to reach Hungary through the Balkan route and then travel westwards. Several of the Islamists had been detained at airports in London and the United States, where suspicious border officers had quickly established that the supposed Hungarian citizens could not speak a word of the language or name two or three other cities apart from Budapest, which they also mispronounced.

Reka had not only known about the people-traffickers; she had been taking a cut of each deal. But she had not known about the terrorist connection, in part, she admitted, although only to herself, because she had deliberately not asked enough questions. After the airport arrests she had been called in by the Budapest station chiefs of the CIA, the British Secret Intelligence Service and an officer in Hungary's own Allami Biztonsagi Szolgalat (ABS), the domestic security service, to a safe house in the Buda hills. The three spooks had threatened her with a lengthy term in an American super-max prison for her involvement in facilitating the movement of terrorist suspects. The toughest had been the ABS officer, an athletic-looking woman in her early thirties, with dark-blonde hair pulled back in a ponytail.

The three spooks wanted something, of course: information. Reka had put on the performance of her life, claiming that Pal Dezeffy was to blame for the passport racket. She had known nothing about any terrorist connection. Pal, she explained, had cut a deal with shadowy figures in the Gulf:

in exchange for a multi-billion-euro investment scheme that would transform the country, he would allow the would-be terrorists to pass through Hungary and give them passports. Hungary would be a transit point, a gateway to the west, a chance for the sclerotic monarchies to rid themselves of their Islamist radicals. Every bomb attack in Europe meant one less in the Gulf. Reka knew her best chance, her only chance, was to claim that she was running a sting operation. Reka said that she had allowed the passport-selling to continue only to draw out the traffickers' networks and their Islamist contacts. Once they were sufficiently mapped, she was planning to hand everything over. That had bought her some time, a week, to be precise, some of which she had spent angrily asking herself why she had not dug a little deeper into the Gulf connection instead of buying more designer handbags that she did not need.

Reka sipped her coffee, feeling the caffeine buzz course through her. Her dismay at her conversation with her husband was fading. Perhaps he was right. The most important task at the moment was to get the new Gulf investment package. A clean one, with no murky middle-men or passports slipped across a restaurant table. Everything flowed from that. Then she could drag Hungary into the twenty-first century. She was working on that here in Budapest while Peter focused on Doha. And what use would he be here anyway, running around with yet another 'assistant'? Reka told herself she was not jealous, not at all. She glanced back at the large antique desk. She almost believed herself. Just as when she told herself that she did not miss Pal Dezeffy and had no choice but to bring him down.

The sound of a ringing telephone suddenly filled the room. Reka walked across the room, sat behind the desk, and picked up the landline's handset. She listened while her secretary said a name, then hung up. She looked around the room once more, taking in the gloomy decor, glanced at the reminder she had written to herself on a yellow sticky note: 'Rainbow Gallery, Brody Sandor Street', then pressed a button at the side of the desk. The double doors opened and a youthful man walked in carrying a black leather briefcase. He had short light-blonde hair, wore skinny navy trousers and a slim-fitting sky-blue linen shirt that matched his eyes. Akos Feher, formerly an assistant state secretary in the Ministry of Justice, now the chief of staff to the Hungarian prime minister at the tender age of twenty-eight. Akos's appointment had triggered a sour envy among his older colleagues and had immediately alienated a whole class of apparatchiks whose support Reka would need if she were to stay in office, let alone implement any new policies. Neither she nor Akos fully trusted the other. But they were bound together, each knowing the other's darkest secret.

Akos stood in front of Reka. *'Jo Reggelt kivanok miniszter elnok asszony.* Good morning, Prime Minister.'

'Hallo, Akos. Did you bring it?'

Akos nodded.

Reka gave him a brief smile. 'Then it will be a good morning.'

Loczy Lajos Street, 7.30 a.m.

Balthazar walked down the white gravel path that led from the villa's front door to the gated entrance, his shoes scrunching on the loose stones. The path through the large front garden was a new addition, Gaspar's idea. It looked smart, but the gravel was also noisy and made it difficult for people to sneak in and out. The brothel was hidden behind a high fence of grey metal panels topped with metal spikes, with a sliding electric door in the middle. The 1940s modernist villa had once been home to a dynasty of industrialists, from Hungary's Schwab, ethnic German, minority, most of whom had been expelled after 1945. The Muller family had managed to stay but lost everything after the Communist takeover in 1948, and fled for good during the 1956 uprising. The property had been nationalised. But like most assets appropriated by the one-party state it had not been returned to its original owners, even after the change of system in 1990. Those were the years known as *vadkapitalizmus*, wild capitalism. Wild capitalism essentially meant that when the state owned lucrative assets, and that state no longer existed, everything was up for grabs at bargain basement prices – at least for the well connected. Balthazar had never bothered to check, but Gaspar had told him that the house was now owned by a property company incorporated in the Cayman Islands. Balthazar's enquiries as to who owned the company had been met with a shrug and '*mindegy*' – whatever.

He turned back to look at the villa before he stepped outside. He had never liked this place. Gaspar had recently spent a small fortune renovating the building, adding a jacuzzi, steam room and sauna. It was one of the most upmarket brothels in Budapest. There was even a chef, lured from one of the city's Michelin-starred restaurants, although few of the clients were interested in eating. The faded yellow walls had been repainted a light blue, but the paintwork had been shoddily executed and here and there on corners and by the roof, the yellow was still visible.

A line of plane trees planted in the garden loomed over the fence, their branches poking out over the wall. Balthazar waited for a moment as he pressed a small red buzzer on the side of the gate. A few seconds later the heavy panels slid open, rusty wheels squeaking on the rails underneath, and he stepped through onto the pavement. For a second or two he heard the buzzing noise again, before it faded away. The sun was up now in a clear blue sky and the air was already warming. He closed his eyes, stretched his arms upwards, his fingers interlinked. Perhaps he should move to Buda, find a nice place with a garden. And perhaps one day he would not have to spend half his waking hours clearing up his youngest brother's mess. Neither was likely. He and Gaspar were far more similar than they were different. Balthazar's life path could easily have slid into the grey area between crime and legitimate business, if not full-on criminality. His other three siblings at least lived comparatively normal lives.

Balthazar's second brother, Melchior, was a successful musician and was often abroad, playing with his group Roma Drom – Roma Way – at international festivals. Balthazar had not seen him for several months. One sister, Ildiko, still lived in the family building on Jozsef Street, and kept the books – one to be presented to the authorities and another that showed the actual movements of money – of Gaspar's businesses. Flora, Balthazar's youngest sibling, ran a hipster art gallery in the downtown part of District VIII that was rapidly gentrifying. But he and Gaspar were bound together, he knew, slotting into each other's lives like the symbols of yin and yang. For a moment he thought of his parents: his father, Laszlo, who would no longer acknowledge his existence, and his mother Marta's pain at their estrangement.

As Balthazar stepped through the gate and onto the pavement his telephone rang. He checked the number and smiled. It was true, surely, what they said about Gypsy women: they could see into the future, read people's minds. Especially those of their own blood.

He stopped walking and took the call. 'Hallo, Mama,' he said. It was a brief conversation. Marta wanted to see him, which was fine by Balthazar. They agreed she would come over around 2 p.m., and bring him some food. Which was especially welcome as there was nothing to eat in the house, except a half-full packet of Gyori biscuits.

He ended the call. Both he and Marta knew not to discuss the events of the morning on the telephone. And she would hear everything soon enough when Gaspar and Fat Vik returned to Jozsef Street. As Balthazar continued walking, a skinny man in his fifties with short grey hair, wearing grey shorts and a white Nike T-shirt jogged past. He was panting and glanced quickly at Balthazar as he ran uphill. How many middle-aged male joggers with grey Nike T-shirts were running around this part of Buda at 7.30 in the morning? It was the same man he had seen on the CCTV monitor on Eszter's computer, Balthazar was sure. Sure too, that this was not a coincidence, especially after his telephone call. Balthazar wished the running man a good morning. Hungarians were extremely polite, greeted each other in most personal encounters. Strangers wished each other *Jo etvagyat*, a good appetite, in restaurants, said hallo and goodbye when entering and leaving lifts.

The man did not answer, stared straight ahead, carried on running. Balthazar was mildly irritated. Every Gypsy had dozens of stories like that, and many far worse. He watched the man jog away, before looking up and down the street. Balthazar, Gaspar and Eszter had a much bigger problem. Someone was inside the CCTV system – and wanted Gaspar and his brother to know it. All four of them had stood watching for about half a minute, staring silently at the miniature images of themselves on Eszter's monitor. Eszter had been about to switch the computer off, when all six feeds suddenly started working properly again. But only from that moment. Eszter had tracked back through the timer again to the time when the VIP salon had been occupied, then to the arrival of the Qatari, tried all of the cameras, in fact – everything had been wiped from half an hour before his arrival shortly after 11 p.m. the previous day.

Balthazar watched as twenty yards away a black Mercedes 520 with tinted windows was pulling in on the other side of the road, sliding into a space between a white Toyota SUV and a navy BMW saloon. Such a vehicle might raise eyebrows in District VIII – unless it belonged to Gaspar or one of his business rivals – but was less unusual in this rich part of the city. Even so, Balthazar took a quick mental note of the car as he started to walk up a narrow stairway, before turning left onto Filler Street. The thoroughfare stretched from Rozsadomb down to Szel Kalman Square, the main transport interchange on that side of the Danube. For decades the square had been called Moszkva, after the Russian capital, and most Budapesters still called it by its old name.

If it wasn't for the events of the previous two hours, Balthazar might almost have enjoyed his early-morning stroll in one of Budapest's most pleasant neighbourhoods. Filler Street, like its neighbours, was lined with trees in front of houses, small shops, villas and low-rise apartment blocks set back from the pavement. The British ambassador's house, a gorgeous cream-and-white art nouveau villa, stood a few minutes walk away, on the corner of Filler Street and Lorantffy Zsuzsanna Street.

Balthazar walked to the brow of the hill, looking down towards the ambassador's residence. A grey pillbox stood outside the house with slit windows on three sides. Under Communism a member of the secret police had been stationed there twenty-four hours a day, monitoring the ambassador's movements and those of his family, taking note of any visitors. Nowadays the pillbox was manned again, watching for potential terrorist threats. The house was surrounded by a black iron fence and landscaped gardens. Another jogger passed Balthazar by, heading uphill, this time a woman in her thirties, wearing skin-tight pink lycra leggings, white wires trailing from her ears, oblivious to his presence.

Balthazar smiled at the memory of his first time at the residence, twelve years ago, when he had been invited to a reception to honour graduating Roma police officers, and how nervous he had been. Balthazar had seen some of Hungary's grand historical homes before, on school trips, or occasional family excursions to the countryside, but never something like this that people actually lived in. A uniformed maid had taken his coat, then directed him to a leather-covered guest book, where he scrawled a shaky signature. A few seconds later a waiter appeared with a tray of drinks. Balthazar rarely drank alcohol, but had taken a beer, about half of which he downed in a couple of gulps, before stepping into the marble-floored reception room. A waitress in a black-and-white uniform had offered him a shrimp canapé. He had never eaten seafood before and could still remember the burst of salty flavour exploding in his mouth. The reception room's walls had been lined with works of art and opened onto a landscaped garden with a small swimming pool. The ambassador and his wife had been very kind, chatting with everyone, making sure they felt at ease.

Another few yards downhill, just past a small ABC grocery shop, where the road curved on its slope, Balthazar saw a familiar profile: a woman in her early thirties, with an athletic build, dark-blonde hair pulled back in a ponytail, a strong, intelligent face. She wore skinny dark blue jeans, a white T-shirt and a blue hoodie, and was leaning against a nondescript grey Skoda, reading that day's edition of *Magyar Vilag*, a pro-government newspaper.

She waved at him, put down the newspaper and beckoned him over, waiting until he crossed the road. 'Good morning. You're up early today, Tazi.'

He smiled. 'Likewise.' He looked at the car, then back at her. 'And you're not on your bike.'

'Not today. This is a very steep hill.'

Balthazar gestured at *Magyar Vilag*. 'What's news?'

'I was hoping you could tell me that, Tazi.' She opened the car door, gestured inside. 'Jump in. I'll take you home.'

FIVE

Balthazar climbed into the car, sat down and looked at Anastasia Ferenczy. 'At least you say "Good morning".'

She frowned. 'I don't know what you mean.'

'Your jogger.'

A glimmer of a smile flickered on her lips. 'What jogger?' she asked, turning towards him, her eyes wide and faux-innocent.

'How many have you got? Skinny, balding, probably in his fifties. White Nike T-shirt, grey shorts that matched what was left of his hair. He didn't look like he was enjoying himself. And he could change his route. He keeps running up and down Loczy Lajos Street.'

'Oh. Him. He's a grumpy old fart. Sorry. I'll pass the word on.'

'Good. Why was he watching me?'

'Well, he wasn't watching you, exactly. More the place where you were and the people coming in and out of it. We were already keeping an eye on al-Nuri. Did you bring them?'

Balthazar handed her al-Nuri's passport and the packet of blue pills. 'Thanks for sorting that out. The ambulance came quickly. When will we get the forensics?'

'We're on it. Our guys will go back in an hour or so, take swabs and samples from the room. So tonight, with a bit of

52

luck. Thank you for the tip-off. Meanwhile, Tazi, we have *so* much to talk about. Maybe over breakfast? There's a new cafe on Falk Miksa Street I really want to try. Café Habsburg. It's Austrian–Hungarian fusion.'

'Breakfast yes; Falk Miksa Street, no.'

Falk Miksa Street was a stately, tree-lined thoroughfare of art nouveau apartment buildings, tourist-priced antique shops and several fancy bistros, popular with politicians and their retinues, in the heart of District V. It ran from the side of Kossuth Square to the Grand Boulevard just before the start of Margaret Bridge. The street was also home to one of the headquarters of the ABS. That, and its proximity to Parliament, meant that it was widely believed that the cafes there were bugged.

Still, the mention of food made Balthazar realise that he was very hungry. He had eaten nothing since Eszter's dawn telephone call, just drunk a glass of water and a coffee.

Anastasia continued talking, the car still stationary. 'You and I are quite safe. Café Habsburg has only been open three days. We won't get to it at least until the end of the week.'

'No. No Falk Miksa.'

'Why not? Are you scared to be seen with me?' Anastasia asked, her voice gently teasing.

'Not at all. I'm very happy to have breakfast with you. Just not fifty yards from your office.'

'OK. Let's get going. I'll try and persuade you on the way.'

'And you,' Balthazar asked. 'What's news with your family castle?'

Anastasia laughed. 'It's not a castle.'

The Ferenczys were one of Hungary's best-known aristocratic dynasties, Transylvanian nobility whose history mirrored that of Hungary. Every schoolchild knew their name. Balthazar too had been somewhat star-struck when he first met Anastasia a week ago. The Ferenczys had taken leading roles in the 1848 revolution against Austria, for which several had been executed. After the 1920 Treaty of Trianon that had seen two-thirds of historic Hungary handed to its neighbours, the family, and their palace outside Timisoara, had found themselves in Romania. The Ferenczys had moved to Budapest. Several had been sent to concentration camps after they were caught hiding Jews in 1944 after the Nazis invaded. More Ferenczys had taken part in the 1956 uprising against the Soviets for which they had again been executed or exiled. During the reign of Nicolae Ceausescu, Romania's half-crazed Communist leader, the family's palace had been turned into a holiday home for the party elite.

Balthazar had recently read a story on 555.hu that the Ferenczys were trying to reclaim their historic home. 'Palace, then.'

'Country mansion. Maybe. If we can raise a big enough bribe.'

Anastasia started the engine and began to drive. She had barely gone ten yards down Filler Street when a blue Volkswagen Golf began to pull out in front. She braked, waiting for the car to drive off. Balthazar shot her a sideways look. She looked good in profile, he thought, not for the first time. You wouldn't describe her as pretty, exactly, but she was definitely striking, slim but with the requisite curves; large, clear eyes the colour of emeralds; straight nose; a wide, full mouth and slightly pointed chin, the result of centuries of well-planned breeding, perhaps with the odd German noble and Jewish trader thrown in to spice the mix. He smiled for a moment, almost laughed as he remembered the verdict of Eva *neni*, auntie Eva, his neighbour and surrogate Jewish mother, after Anastasia had left an envelope with Eva the previous weekend to pass on to Balthazar. *'Nice teeth, spoke very well. No slang. Quite classy, I would say. You could do a lot worse.'* Maybe she was right.

Anastasia looked sideways at Balthazar. 'What's so funny?'

'I was remembering how Eva *neni* described you.'

'And how was that?'

'Don't worry. She liked you.'

'And I liked her.'

The vw Golf driver finally manoeuvred his vehicle out into the road and drove off, orange hazard lights flashing a quick 'thank you'.

Anastasia carried on driving. 'So how is the hero of Rakoczi Way?'

Balthazar looked around the vehicle before he answered. It was very different to every police car he had been in. Apart from the copy of *Magyar Vilag*, now on the back seat, it was empty. There were no crumpled coffee cups, fast food wrappers or empty plastic water bottles. Instead of the odour of stale tobacco or fast food there was a faint scent of soap and shampoo. Anastasia Ferenczy, Balthazar was sure, smelled better than he did. 'Don't,' he said.

'But you are a hero. You took down Mahmoud Hejazi. I hear our new prime minister is going to give you a medal. And a reception at Parliament.'

The Budapest police headquarters on Teve Street was full of rumours that Balthazar was to be publicly honoured by the new prime minister. Sandor Takacs, Balthazar's boss, had made several jokes about getting his suit dry-cleaned. The prospect of a public ceremony filled Balthazar with horror. It was bad enough that Eniko Szalay, his former girlfriend and the star reporter at 555.hu, was all over the news. Eniko seemed to have an incredible source at the highest level of government, who was feeding her all sorts of details about the passport rackets and terrorist connections. Balthazar just hoped that Eniko kept his name, and what she knew about him and his family, especially Gaspar, out of her reports. She had already elliptically referred to Gaspar in one of her stories last week, before all the weekend's excitement, mentioning a 'well-known figure in Budapest's underworld'.

Balthazar said, 'I really hope not.'

'Really? Why? You are a good role model.'

'You mean a good *diszcigany*,' he said, his voice wry.

A medal, a reception and no doubt lots of media attention – especially about his Roma origins – were the last thing he wanted. Firstly, because he had no desire to be a *diszcigany*, a decorative or token Gypsy, paraded before the cameras to show the Hungarian establishment's supposed but actually token commitment to equal rights. But more than that, his survival sense, honed over centuries, passed down through his ancestors, urged that the less attention he received, the better for him and his family. Especially at the moment.

Anastasia said, 'Do you remember that Roma boy, Jozsi, the one you met at Republic Square last week, when you were looking for the body of Simon Nazir, the dead Syrian?'

'Of course.' Jozsi had been a younger version of himself, Balthazar thought. Dressed in hand-me-downs, light-brown eyes, tawny skin, street-smart, wary.

'I told you I think that Jozsi told me that he had never been to a hamburger restaurant. The security guards always turned him away. I thought that was so sad.'

'He has now. I took him on Sunday to that new burger place on Oktober 6 Street. He loved it. We had a great time. There were three of us. We went with my son, Alex.' There should have been four, he almost said. He glanced again at Anastasia. Maybe he should have invited her instead.

Anastasia smiled with genuine pleasure. 'That's great, Tazi. I'm really pleased.' She shot him a sideways look. 'And how proud do you think Alex and Jozsi would be if they saw you getting a medal from the prime minister? What message would that send about hope and opportunities and breaking down stereotypes?'

Balthazar raised his hands in surrender. 'OK. I'll think about it. How's that?'

'Better.'

Maybe Anastasia had a point. Even if he did not want to be a role model, it seemed he was one. Perhaps that did bring some responsibilities. A *diszcigany* in Parliament, decorated by the prime minister, was still better than no Gypsies there at all. Meanwhile, he had enough to think about, and the day had barely started. The first time he had encountered Anastasia – it was not exactly a meeting – she had been sitting on a park bench near the municipal bicycle rack on Klauzal Square, near his flat in the heart of the old Jewish quarter in District VII. He had sensed she was watching him, a suspicion confirmed when soon afterwards a mobile telephone arrived in an envelope, one which she had used to make contact. Over the last weekend Balthazar and Anastasia had worked intensely together, especially on the fateful Sunday when Hejazi had been shot.

Anastasia asked, 'You remember what I was doing at Keleti, Tazi?'

'Sure. You were the world's most stationary taxi driver.'

She laughed. 'Something like that.'

Anastasia, Balthazar had learned, had been working undercover at Keleti during the migrant crisis, posing as a taxi driver, although one who had never had any fares and whose vehicle remained permanently parked. Her real job was to watch the migrants and keep a lookout for the dozen or so most wanted Islamic radicals whom her boss and his colleagues in London, Washington DC and other capitals, believed were using the chaos in Europe's borders to transit through the Balkans then westwards through the chaos at Keleti. Number one on the most wanted list was Mahmoud Hejazi

She continued talking, 'That story is not over. Not by a long way. The borders have collapsed, tens of thousands of people, many of them from Middle Eastern war zones with fake or no papers, including friends of Hejazi, are still using our country as a staging post and we have no idea who they are. Keleti is filling up again. I'm glad you called me this morning, Tazi, and not someone else.' She turned and smiled at him. 'I think we make a good team. I like your approach. Very unorthodox. But effective. Let me know if you ever want to move on from the police.'

Balthazar said nothing as he quickly ran through the events of the previous weekend, any of which could end his career and several of which could still lead to a prison sentence: taking home evidence – the SIM card he found on the ground near Simon Nazir's body – and failing to safeguard it; attending an illegal cage fight with a high-ranking member of the Serbian mafia; publicly tasting cocaine with the city's most notorious gangster; injuring two Gendarmes in a car crash; destruction of state property; illegal use of a flash bomb; assault; dangerous driving... the list went on and on. And that was without Gaspar's business activities, which were quite enough to end Balthazar's police career forever.

'We do what we have to, Tazi,' said Anastasia, as if reading his mind. 'You don't do anything for personal gain.'

Balthazar glanced up at the driver's mirror. There was a single car behind them: a black Mercedes. 'I think we're being followed.'

'I would be surprised if we weren't,' she replied, completely unperturbed. 'How about that breakfast? We have a lot to talk about.'

'Like what?'

Her voice turned serious. 'Abdullah al-Nuri, for starters. After that, we can talk more about last weekend. Hejazi was just the start. We need to unravel the network that brought Hejazi here, find his contacts, follow the money trail.'

She was right, of course. Hejazi's death marked the start of his investigation, not the end. And the more he thought about it, the more likely it seemed that Abdullah al-Nuri's death was somehow linked.

Anastasia continued talking. 'We both know that this is about much more than a man being shot dead on Rakoczi Way.'

'Or another found dead in Gaspar's villa,' said Balthazar. He glanced into the mirror again. The black Mercedes was still following, thirty yards behind them now. He looked at the number plate: MEH-025. A government car. MEH stood for Miniszter Elnoki Hivatal, the prime minister's office. Only one law enforcement agency had access to the prime ministerial vehicles.

SIX

Reka led her chief of staff to the corner of her office, her leather portfolio in her hand. She sat in one of two Biedermeier chairs that faced a heavy round mahogany table, and gestured for him to do the same. The furniture, like the decor, was not to Reka's taste. The Biedermeier style dated from the mid nineteenth century. Its ornate curved woodwork and plush upholstery striped in gold and green indicated prosperity, stolidity and good bourgeois values, as did the elegant Zsolnay coffee set, gold-rimmed with a dark-green glaze, laid on the table. Her office, like the building, was ridiculously oversized. She could still remember the statistics recited by the guide on her first visit here, when she was a teenager: twenty-seven gates to serve a complex of 691 rooms that was almost 300 yards long, fanning out in two symmetrical wings from the central hall. Reka planned to redecorate and refurbish the prime minister's suite, replace the whiskery old men on the walls with modern works by young Hungarian artists, the old-fashioned chairs and tables with pieces by local designers. She made a mental note to check out the trendy art gallery she had recently discovered on Brody Sandor Street, in the part of District VIII they now called the Palace Quarter. What was the owner's name? Flora... Flora something. The gallery

60

was called Rainbow. It had some very nice pieces by young local artists. Assuming, that was, that she could get through the next few days.

Reka poured them both coffee and waited for a moment while Akos helped himself to milk and sugar. He lifted the cup, looked at it for several seconds, then at Reka. 'Dark green. You got here at last.' There were four colours among the ministries and civil servants: plain white, for junior and middle-ranking officials, light blue for senior officials with the rank of assistant secretary of state, as Akos had held, dark blue with gold trim for actual secretaries of state, and the dark green with gold that was reserved for the prime minister's office.

'Yes,' said Reka. 'And I intend to stay for a while.'

'I'm glad to hear that,' said Akos. 'Last week I was being threatened with prison. For following your instructions.' He looked around, nodded to himself, 'Now I'm helping to run your government. Quite a turnaround. May I speak frankly?'

Reka nodded. 'Of course.'

'I was surprised when you asked me to be your chief of staff.'

Reka let a glimmer of a smile flicker over her face, tried to stifle a yawn. Not because she was bored – on the contrary, this had certainly been the most *interesting* week of her life – but because she was exhausted. Running a country was more work than she had ever imagined and especially when she was fighting for her political life.

'Why?' she asked.

Akos raised his eyebrows, thought for a moment before he answered. 'Well, we do have quite a... history.'

She sipped her coffee, grimaced slightly. It was tepid and slightly bitter, the old-style Hungarian institutional blend. She really would have to bring in her own, a mix of Ethiopian and Colombian that was ground for her in a small shop near her home in Obuda, on the other side of the river. 'Yes. We do, in the Ministry of Justice.'

'Which means that I don't have my own roof here, in the prime minister's office.' Roof was slang for protection.

Reka smiled, wider now. 'But you do, Akos. You do.'

'Apart from you.'

Reka nodded. There would have to be a wholesale purge, sooner or later, of Pal Dezeffy loyalists, she knew. But that could wait for now. She leaned forward as she spoke. 'Akos, you are smart and capable enough to make this work.'

He nodded slowly. 'I hope so.'

The truth was, she had no other options. She and Akos could each bring the other down. But it would be a mutually assured destruction. It was in both of their interests that she survived in office. And the Bardossys had faced testing times before. The Bardossys, like several Hungarian noble families, had hailed from present-day Slovakia before moving to Budapest in the mid-nineteenth century after the failed revolution of 1848. They had rapidly built themselves into the political world, but mostly as advisers behind the scenes, rather than public figures. Her ancestors had stood in this room, dispensing counsel, whether to the ardent revolutionaries of the short-lived Soviet-style workers' republic of 1919, under the quasi-democracy of the dim-witted Admiral Horthy who ruled Hungary until the Nazis invaded in 1944, and a succession of Communists, right up to the wily reformers of the late 1980s. Of all the Communist parties in the former Soviet bloc, the Hungarians had moved fastest. The wily Magyars had long realised that Communism was doomed, simply because the Soviet-backed state-controlled economy did not work. It was human nature to trade, turn a profit, improve one's lot. Janos Kadar, Hungary's leader after the failed 1956 uprising, had followed the advice of Reka's great-uncle Geza that social peace and stuttering economic progress was best assured by turning Leninism on its head, under the unstated motto of 'those who are not against us are with us'. That was still good advice, she knew, especially for a prime minister under siege, as she was. Reka opened her portfolio and skim-read the agenda. 'Akos, we have a lot to discuss. I assume you want to continue working together.'

Akos warily sipped his coffee. 'Of course, Madame Prime Minister.'

Akos had been the point man in the passport scam, liaising between the Ministry of Justice and the people-traffickers. A week ago, Akos had been summoned to the British embassy by a diplomat called Celestine Johnson. She had presented Akos with evidence of his involvement – and young mistress – and had tried to blackmail him into spying on his colleagues, including Reka. Now that Reka was prime minister the equation had changed. The pressure was on her. Both the British and the American ambassadors had paid a courtesy call earlier in the week, congratulating her on her appointment. Amid the usual courtesies and promises of future cooperation and encouragement for investors, both ambassadors had dropped subtle references to the deadline next Monday for Reka to hand over the information she had about her husband's role in the scandal that had brought down Pal Dezeffy and the flow of dirty money from the Gulf to Hungary. Information that would certainly bring her down as collateral damage.

But she was running Hungary, not the Americans or the Brits. Or so she told herself.

For a moment she back inside Buda Castle at Pal's grand reception last Friday, speaking to the Qatari business development director. They had spoken for a few minutes, much of which he had spent looking at her breasts. She glanced at her watch. Her mother's Patek Philippe had gone back into her jewellery box, replaced by a minimalist Skagen that looked sleek but cost a fraction of its predecessor. The Qatari was due here at 8 a.m. As for Pal, he was gone now, at least from public life. He had resigned four days ago, on Monday morning. But Pal was a graduate of the same political school as Reka: two children of the former Communist dynasties that had ruled Hungary for decades. After the change of system in the early 1990s, the party had desultorily purged a few hardliners and renamed itself the Social Democrats. But the networks of power politics and finance, the Pal Dezeffy and Bardossy dynasties, had first endured then grown rich and even more powerful. Pal, she was sure, would fight back as hard as he could. Because not only had she destroyed Pal's career, removed him from public life and cancelled every government contract with his companies, she had also exiled him from her bed.

Reka reached into her folder and slid a sheet of paper towards her chief of staff. 'As we agreed. It clearly states how everything you did for me in relation to the passports was done on government orders, as a means of gathering intelligence about the network and its connection to the people-traffickers and Islamists. You are given retrospective diplomatic status – *solely* in regard to this matter – and legally absolved from any potential sanctions.'

Akos read it once, quickly, then again, slowly. 'It's not signed.'

Reka sat back. 'I will sign it. Once you hand over what I asked for.'

Akos reached inside his briefcase and took out a clear plastic bag containing a narrow black oblong, four inches long, broken at one end and tapering sharply at the other. He slid the bag across the table. Reka glanced at the shiny sides, grimacing as she saw a patch of something brown, thick and matted around the tip. She picked up the bag by one corner, walked over to her desk and placed it inside a drawer, next to the silver memory stick. She signed the paper, added an official stamp from the prime minister's office – no piece of paper in Hungary, anywhere in central Europe, had any weight without a stamp of some kind – and handed the document to Akos. He looked it up and down, nodded and put it away in his briefcase. They both sat back and the atmosphere eased.

Akos said, 'Thanks. I'm glad we finally got that out of the way.'

'So am I. Now to today's business. What time is he due here?'

'At 8 a.m. We offered him a breakfast meeting, in one of the private rooms, but he said coffee would be enough.'

A few seconds later, Reka's mobile rang. She looked at the screen and took the call. Akos watched as she listened, saying nothing until the caller had finished speaking. '*Where?* What was he doing in a place like that? OK, don't answer, it's obvious.'

Reka ended the call, placed her handset on the table, closed her eyes for several seconds before she spoke.

Akos asked, 'What's obvious?'

'It doesn't matter. He's not coming.'

'Why?'

'Because he is dead.'

Filler Street

Balthazar watched in the driver's mirror as the Mercedes drew nearer and a brief toot sounded. He turned around to see a familiar near-shaven head and tattooed neck at the wheel of the car. A few seconds later he felt his telephone ring in his pocket. He took out the handset, glanced at the screen which displayed *Unknown number*. He looked in the mirror again. Attila Ungar was holding a mobile telephone to his ear.

Balthazar answered the call, put it on speaker. 'It's illegal to drive while holding a handset.'

Attila laughed. 'Then come and arrest me.'

'What do you want?'

'A chat about old times, Tazi? We are recruiting. Salaries at least twice what the cops pay. Triple, for you, as we go back such a long way. Plus bonuses. We pick up all sorts of things along the way. State-of-the-art equipment. Legal immunity. Fantastic canteen, steak every day. Hot waitresses. Sports centre. Thai masseuses. What more could you want?'

'Nothing, from you.'

Attila's voice turned hard. 'Your choice, Tazi. Tell your friend to pull over.'

'Why?'

'You've seen the plates on this. It's armoured. If you don't pull over I'll ram you.'

Balthazar glanced at Anastasia. She shrugged. They could, he supposed, take the risk and ignore Attila. But his former partner was not only prone to bursts of violence – which was why Sandor Takacs, the commander of the murder squad, had finally advised him to leave before he was sacked – he was also extremely dogged and blessed with a powerful sense of street cunning. So it was easier to get this, whatever it was, out of the way. He nodded at Anastasia and she pulled onto the side of the road, fifty yards from the end of Filler Street. There was enough space for two cars.

Attila parked behind them. He got out of the car, a squat, heavy figure, about five feet six tall, with a shaven head and oversized biceps. He carried a large-screen Samsung mobile telephone as he walked towards the Skoda. He was out of uniform and wore black jeans and a tight white T-shirt that emphasised his overdeveloped musculature. A tattoo of black talons crept up the side of his neck. '*Jo reggelt*, good morning,' he said.

Anastasia stared at him. 'It was. We're going across the river. I can drop you at the Four Seasons Hotel if you like.'

Attila's face twisted in anger. His body stiffened and his fingers waved in the air as though seeking something to squeeze and knead. The previous Saturday night he and a squad of Gendarmes had tried to arrest Reka Bardossy and Eniko Szalay in the foyer of the hotel. But Sandor Takacs had despatched a small army of regular police to protect them. First the police had destroyed the Gendarmes' vehicles parked in the hotel forecourt, taking sledgehammers to their windscreens and slashing their tyres. Then they surrounded the Gendarmes in the foyer. Attila and his men had left empty-handed. The CCTV footage of the Gendarmes waiting outside the building, their vehicles half-destroyed, until more were despatched, had been leaked and quickly went viral on the Internet. Attila closed his eyes, recovered his composure. 'No, thanks. I have my own car.'

Balthazar said, 'So we see. What do you want, Attila?'

'I told you. To help.'

'I'm waiting,' said Balthazar.

'Here? On the street?' said Attila. He glanced at Anastasia. 'Don't you want to do this in private?'

Balthazar said, 'This is private enough.'

Anastasia said, 'Get in.'

Attila opened the door and sat on the back seat. He smirked at Anastasia, caught her eye in the mirror. 'The Duchess and the Gypsy. A real Hungarian scene. Someone should paint you both. It would make a lovely picture.'

'Shut it, Attila,' said Balthazar. 'And get on with it.'

Attila reached forward, extended his arm and let Anastasia's hair slide over his fingers. He sniffed as he spoke, 'Mmm, that smells good. Better than you ever did, Tazi.'

In one seamless movement Anastasia pulled away, opened the glove compartment, extracted a Glock 17 pistol, whipped around, the gun in her right hand, and pointed it at Attila's head. 'Sit back. Hands up.'

He did as she ordered, his palms high in the air, facing the sides of his head. 'Whoa,' he said, his small eyes flitting from the gun to Anastasia and back. 'Take it easy, Duchess.'

Balthazar watched, saying nothing but impressed with the fluidity of her movements. Anastasia's face was calm but he could see the cold fury in her eyes as she spoke. 'Be careful, Attila. Guns can go off accidentally.' She moved her hand up and down and the weapon rose and fell. 'A few inches here can make a big difference at your end.' She let the gun point downwards, at Attila's groin.

'Message received. I'm going to reach into my pocket now for my telephone. Please be careful with the gun.' Attila's voice was calm as he spoke, his body language open and unthreatening.

Anastasia relaxed slightly for a moment, responding to his apparent surrender. At that instant he leaned to the right, away from the weapon. His right hand shot out, grabbing the barrel of the Glock. He bent his wrist back and pushed the weapon up against the roof of the car, his arm locked, the gun now pointing at the top of the rear windscreen. Anastasia raised her right fist, ready to slam it into the crook of his elbow. Such a blow would bend, even break the joint and give her a chance to take back control of the Glock. But they both knew the inside of a car was no place for a struggle over a firearm.

'Go ahead. But things could get very messy in here,' said Attila. 'And you are holding the gun. So you would have a lot of explaining to do.'

Balthazar said, 'How about if I take the pistol? Then Attila can show us whatever he wants to show us, and we can all get on with our day.'

Attila and Anastasia both nodded. Balthazar reached for the Glock. Attila's arm relaxed and Anastasia let it slide out of her hand.

Attila pressed a button on the mobile telephone screen and held it up so Balthazar and Anastasia could watch. The telephone showed a frozen image of Balthazar among a crowd of people inside a grimy, dilapidated industrial building. Balthazar pressed play. The images began to move, tinny sound leaking from the telephone's speaker. He was standing by a dark-skinned man in his forties, who wore a tight black vest and black jeans. The sides of his head were shaven and the hair on top was gathered into a backwards triangle, tied together by a topknot. Tattoos of eagles covered his arms and hands and the back of his neck.

An attractive young blonde woman in a red dress, with her hair pinned up, walked up to him holding a silver tray, on which three lines of white powder were laid out next to a silver tube, then walked off-screen. The tattooed man asked Balthazar if he would like to join him. Balthazar said no. The tattooed man picked up the silver tube, bent forward and sniffed up a line of white powder, then another. He offered the remaining line to Balthazar, who declined. The two men talked some more, the sound fading in and out. But the next part of the video was clear enough. Balthazar dipped a finger into the white powder and dabbed it on his tongue.

'Tut, tut,' said Attila. 'A coke-tasting session with Black George, the city's most notorious gangster. At an illegal cage fight for migrants.'

The film was bad news, Balthazar knew, but was not a surprise. In the age of near-ubiquitous CCTV and mobile telephones it was safe to assume that almost everything, especially anything potentially compromising, was being recorded. 'Who says it was coke?' He paused for a moment. 'It tasted quite sweet. I think it was some kind of sugar. Icing sugar, maybe?'

Attila laughed. 'Sure. Because we all know that Black George is in the icing sugar business. The type that goes up your nose.'

Balthazar shrugged. 'You got nothing, Attila. No evidence of anything except me putting a finger in something then tasting it. In any case I was undercover. And I needed to do that to maintain my cover.'

Attila laughed. 'You were working off the books, Tazi, on a completely unauthorised operation, consorting with criminals at an illegal gathering.'

That much was true. Sandor Takacs had given Balthazar the go-ahead to investigate the death and disappearance of Simon Nazir, but unofficially, and that part of the investigation had no authorisation. It was only on Sunday, when the Budapest police had gone into action across the city to find Mahmoud Hejazi in the mass exodus from Keleti, that Balthazar was back on the books. Until then everything he did was under the radar and unsanctioned. But he was not about to admit that to Attila. 'Whatever. Tell me something new.'

'Here's something new. So new it's barely a few minutes old,' said Attila, his fingers gliding over his phone. He called up a second video clip, pressed play and held the handset out so Balthazar and Anastasia could watch. The film showed Abdullah al-Nuri entering Gaspar's brothel, an ambulance arriving, two paramedics wheeling out a trolley on top of which was a black body bag, then Balthazar greeting Anastasia in the street. Attila slid across the rear seat and opened the door. 'Have a good day – and remember Tazi, my offer is still open, at least for now.'

SEVEN

Eniko Szalay held her iPhone to her ear and spoke sotto voce. 'I *did*. I already told you. I sent him an SMS apologising on Sunday evening, saying I was really sorry, I couldn't make it, and they shouldn't wait for me. Then another one apologising on Monday morning. And two emails after that. He didn't reply. How rude is that?'

'Not as rude as not turning up,' said Zsuzsa Barcsy. Eniko sighed, glancing across the Margaret Bridge while she listened to her friend. Zsuzsa, she knew, was right. Eniko could see a long, dark, yellow number-four tram slowly advancing, curving around from Margaret Boulevard, onto the bridge, slipping past the dense morning commuter traffic heading into town from Buda and the outlying suburbs. Even everyday scenes were shot through with the city's beauty. The Buda hills rolled away on the other side of the Danube, lush and verdant. The river flowed smooth and clean, the morning sunlight glittering on the grey-green water. A blue sky was dotted with tendrils of white clouds, although in the distance, a thick, grey mass promised a summer rainstorm.

Eniko continued speaking, 'Yes, I called him last night. He didn't pick up. That's six times I tried to talk to him, and I don't know how many texts and emails.' She watched the

72

tram advance down the boulevard. The tracks ran down the centre, bisecting a two-lane road on either side. Margaret Bridge had recently been renovated. Lamp posts in art nouveau style, decorated with delicate ironwork, stood every few yards. The tram tracks were flanked by yellow tiles, and a row of half-globes designed to stop cars sneaking into the space to cut past the traffic. 'What's done is done. Are you in today?' When Zsuzsa answered yes, Eniko said, 'Good. Because there's something I need to talk to you about. No, not on the phone. Gotta go now, Zsuzsika; the tram is almost here.'

The lights changed and a flurry of pedestrians crossed from the other side of the boulevard and walked onto the tram stop. For a moment she thought one of them looked familiar: a young, athletic-looking man in his late twenties, with short dark hair, a boxer's fluid walk and alert eyes. He wore a black T-shirt and brown cargo trousers. Had she seen him before? Perhaps hanging around at Blaha Lujza Square, near the 555. hu office? He walked away, and Eniko watched the tram approach the bend in the middle of the bridge. Margaret Bridge was almost V-shaped, with a sharp angle in the middle. A spur led off the bridge down to Margaret Island, the green lung of the city. The tram stopped there and disgorged more joggers, a flurry of brightly coloured lycra, then continued towards Jaszai Mari Square. The square was a major intersection – a few yards away the number-two tram started its journey at a right angle to the main boulevard, running parallel with the Danube, next to the squat, modernist building known as the White House, which housed MPs' offices.

Kossuth Square and Parliament were a tram stop or a short walk away, down Falk Miksa Street. This part of downtown had recently been renovated. A statue of Peter Falk, a distant relative of Miksa Falk, stood at the end of the street, dressed as his best-known role, the rumpled Detective Columbo, his dog standing by him expectantly. Columbo had his hand to his head in his signature gesture of puzzlement, usually a sign that he was about to deliver irrevocable proof of guilt to a lying suspect. A middle-aged lady, neatly dressed with a bob of brown hair, was setting up the Jehovah's Witness stall next to the statue, while two Gypsy men in tracksuits leaned on the bonnet of a white Opel parked by the side of the BAV shop, the state antique emporium. The shop would not open for a while, but they were staking out prime position to approach customers with something to sell before they stepped inside. Before the refugee crisis this had been Fat Vik's regular spot and Eniko often waved hallo to him as she waited for the tram. Today, however, none of the men looked familiar. Eniko turned and looked away. She did not see one of the Gypsies watch her carefully, take a mobile telephone from his pocket and make a call, his eyes still on Eniko.

Eniko glanced at the McDonald's on the ground floor of the apartment house on the corner of the boulevard at Jaszai Mari Square. It was already busy with the first customers drinking coffee and eating breakfast sandwiches on the chairs and tables outside. The building was carefully restored and looked gorgeous – this was prime riverside property – but still gave her the creeps. She remembered a story her grandmother had once told her – after the Arrow Cross coup in October 1944, the Hungarian Nazi militia had taken over the building. The House of Vengeance, as it was known, was usefully located near the edge of what was known as the International Ghetto, the maze of streets around Pozsonyi Way where some apartment blocks were under the protection of neutral embassies like Sweden and Switzerland. But as the Russians advanced, the protective papers lost their power. Those Jews like her grandmother's cousin Endre, who were taken down to its cellars to reveal where they had hidden their valuables, did not usually emerge alive. It was a warm morning and the sun promised more heat on the way, but Eniko shivered for a moment.

She looked away from the building, towards the stream of joggers and cyclists who were heading onto the bridge from the end of Pozsonyi Way towards Margaret Island. Part of her wished she was joining them instead of waiting to step into a crowded tram before another twelve-hour day, even if she was the most-read, if not the most famous, journalist in the country at the moment. Eniko knew she was a good reporter: fast, sharp and diligent in her sources and fact-checking. But her reputation rested on one source. And she knew that if she used the information she had received that morning that source would be blown forever. She glanced around again. Something, or someone, was making her uneasy. Was she being watched? Or maybe it was knowing too much about the apartment house opposite. The man in the black T-shirt had disappeared, but the hairs were prickling on the back of her neck. She looked back at the BAV shop. The two Gypsy men had disappeared. The middle-aged lady at the Jehovah's Witness stand was engrossed in conversation with a tall man in a dark-blue suit, carrying a briefcase. Maybe she just had an over-active imagination.

Eniko was used to men's attention. Her face emphasised some distant Slavic ancestry, or perhaps the first Magyars who had ridden in from somewhere in Asia, with sharp cheekbones, and blue-green eyes. Her long brown hair was straight today, like most days, swept back in a ponytail. She wore very little make-up, just a touch of mascara. Her only jewellery was a single silver hoop in the top of her left ear, a small homage to bohemia, which she touched when she was nervous – like now. She was pretty, she knew. Not head-turningly beautiful, but attractive. Her nails were painted in a rainbow of colours and she wore blue, red and white Tisza training shoes, a retro brand that was very popular with her crowd of twenty- and thirty-something hipsters, skinny black jeans, a light-blue T-shirt and a cropped denim jacket. She smiled for a moment as she remembered a line she had read by Henry Kissinger: 'The presence of paranoia does not prove the absence of plots.' A teenage boy, perhaps sixteen or seventeen, standing nearby, caught her eye and smiled back.

Eniko told herself to stop worrying. This was her week. Or at least it was supposed to be. Her scoop for 555.hu on Sunday evening had brought down the prime minister, Pal Dezeffy. His fall had in turn been covered by the international press, many of which quoted her story. Most of the major newspapers and TV stations had already set up shop in Budapest, many around Keleti Station, which had become the epicentre of Europe's refugee crisis. The flow of people continued up from the Serbian border, but only a few dozen were camped out at Keleti now. After the mass walk to the Austrian border on Sunday the frontier had stayed open. Hungary was once again a transit zone, rather than a destination point. But the fall of Pal Dezeffy meant that Hungary was still the lead story on many international bulletins. So far she had been interviewed by CNN, BBC, NBC, ABC, Russia Today and all the main news agencies.

Eniko's main source, Pal's successor, had fed her further snippets during the week about the corrupt network that had reached from Pal's office to rich Gulf investors, which had produced a further stream of stories. But as well as pride

Eniko felt a growing sense of unease, for two reasons. For a moment she was back in the bar at the Four Seasons Hotel, last Saturday night, hearing Reka Bardossy's question: *'As I understand it, the time to frame a story, to shape how it is covered, is when it is first reported. Is that correct?'* Eniko had agreed, explaining that the initial projection was what stayed in people's minds, although it could go in different directions later. *'Once it's out, it's impossible to control,'* Eniko had explained.

Except it seemed that this story, of Pal Dezeffy's perfidy, was not impossible to control. A steady stream of leaks from Reka to Eniko – all of which made perfectly legitimate stories in their own right – had ensured that media coverage, both domestic and international, had focused on the disgraced former prime minister rather than Reka Bardossy, his former minister of justice, whose officials, including her new chief of staff, had overseen the corrupt sale of passports to people-traffickers who had passed them on in turn to Islamic radicals. Eniko had been used. Some might even say that she had been bought, and they might be right. Not with anything as crude as money or other financial benefits. But with information. And now she had information that could help destroy Reka Bardossy. It was not a pleasant feeling to think that she had become a convenient, pliant conduit in a high-stakes political battle, even if her career was soaring.

And she was starting to think that there may be a price to pay. Her telephone rang at odd times of the night and day from blocked numbers. She sometimes felt that she was being followed, although she had seen no evidence of it, and in truth, did not really know how to tell. She would never admit it to anyone, but one reason why she really wanted to talk to Balthazar was that she felt... not exactly scared, but certainly nervous. She was, she knew, swimming in very deep waters. Attila Ungar had already taken her off a suburban train last Saturday and interrogated her in a cold, damp, abandoned building on Csepel Island, in a remote part of Budapest where she had never been before. Attila had threatened Eniko and her mother. He had eventually let her go, and now Eniko had the prime minister as her roof, her protection. But these were febrile, turbulent times. Reka Bardossy could lose her office and position as easily as she had gained it – especially if Eniko used the information she now had. The smarter move would have been to turn up on Sunday night and meet Balthazar, even if it stirred up turbulent emotions again. Balthazar could handle himself. And if he needed back-up there was a whole tribe of cousins to call on for help. It would be good to know that he was around to help, if she needed it.

The tram stopped in front of her, interrupting her train of thought. The four and six, which curved through the heart of the city along the Grand Boulevard, were the modern, German model, with huge windows and long, walk-through carriages. The double glass doors slid open, and half a dozen teenagers stepped out, chattering happily. She moved aside and waited until they passed her, then stepped into the carriage, a stream of commuters following her.

Eniko stood by the door, hemmed in by the crowd. It was only five stops until they reached her destination, Blaha Lujza Square, and the office of 555.hu. The tram advanced along the boulevard, stopping at Nyugati Station. A few passengers stepped off but more got on board. Eniko stepped back against the wall of the carriage, watching Nyugati slide by as the tram pulled away. Budapest's western terminus was not as grand as Keleti, but it was more beautiful, a graceful construction of glass and blue-painted wrought iron, designed by Eiffel's studio in the late nineteenth century. Two Gendarmes stood on the steps. One had his head cocked and seemed to be speaking into his shoulder radio. A thin young African man sat on the floor next to them, his hands bound behind his back, a blue rucksack at his feet.

The tram passed Oktogon, the eight-sided plaza where the Grand Boulevard met Andrassy Avenue, Budapest's most stately street, and the start of Kiraly and Wesselenyi Streets, which opened into District VII, the city's historic Jewish quarter. The next stop would be hers, Blaha Lujza Square.

Eniko felt a presence behind her. She turned around to see someone standing close to her. Too close for comfort – the man in the black T-shirt and cargo trousers. Her heart began to beat faster. He was staring at her. She tried to step away, but the carriage was too crowded.

He stepped nearer. 'I think you dropped this,' he said, his right palm open.

Eniko looked down, saw a small black memory stick with a silver cap in the man's hand. She shook her head. 'No, I don't think so.'

He smiled. '*Kedves holgyem, biztos vagyok hogy leejtetted.* My dear lady, I am sure that you dropped it.'

She looked him in the eye, covering her nervousness. 'Do I know you?'

'No. You don't. But I know you. And your work. I think you will find this useful.'

'Why?'

He leaned forward with the memory stick between his thumb and forefinger, the end of the stick just a couple of inches from her face. She could see the rough stubble on his chin. '*Csak.*' Csak, pronounced 'chuck', literally meant *only*, but in slang it meant *because*, as a parent might say to a child.

The teenage boy she had smiled at was watching, picking up on the man's menacing vibrations, despite the two white wires leading from his ears. He caught Eniko's eye, as if to ask if she needed help. But he was standing several yards away, and two elderly ladies were gossiping about their medicines in front of him, oblivious to what was happening. In any case the tram was almost at Blaha Lujza Square and she did not want to make a scene.

Earlier that week Eniko had persuaded the editors of 555. hu to buy her another iPhone, which she used purely for work. She had changed the number on her older phone and given it to a small group of friends and contacts. The work mobile had a red case, the personal one a blue case. Each phone was in a front pocket of her jeans. She felt the right side buzz and vibrate. She took out the handset: a text message had arrived to her personal phone. She looked down at the screen. The display read *Unknown number*.

The man in the black T-shirt said, 'Read it.'

Eniko looked at the screen. The message said: '*Take the memory stick.*'

Bajnok bar, Mikszath Kalman Square, 8.30 a.m.

Anastasia looked at her watch. 'There's an empty place at Reka's breakfast table.'

Balthazar frowned. 'I don't understand.'

'Al-Nuri was due to have breakfast with the prime minister. She was lobbying him to keep the Gulf investment package in play. But without the passport racket.'

'Was he interested?'

'Like a lot of men, he was definitely interested in her. But yes, he had agreed to talk about it.'

'Oh. That explains a lot.'

'Everything, I would say. Unless he really did have a heart attack. The question is, why was he killed in your brother's brothel?'

Balthazar thought for a moment before he answered. 'It was the easiest place to get the job done, I guess. A shooting or a hit and run on an important foreigner would draw too much attention. But how the hell does Attila have the video footage of him entering, leaving and us meeting?'

'The Gendarmes are on the war path. Especially after last weekend. They have all sorts of new equipment. Even drones. They are filming everything. And they will be leaking it whenever it suits them. All they need to do is post it on YouTube.'

For a moment Balthazar was back on the pavement outside the brothel, listening to the distant buzzing sound before it faded away. 'That explains it. I kept hearing a noise this morning like a swarm of bees in the distance.'

Anastasia nodded. 'That was the drone. Or drones. This is going to get really dirty, Balthazar. It's not clear who will win.'

Balthazar smiled. 'We will.'

They were sitting waiting for breakfast at a corner table in the front room of Bajnok, a gloomy bar on the corner of Mikszath Kalman Square in the western part of District VIII that bordered District V, the centre of the city. Csongi, the owner, was in the kitchen cooking them both breakfast. Csongor Falusi was a former flyweight boxer and childhood friend of both Balthazar and Gaspar. He had bought the bar more than a decade ago. It had been redecorated once, in various shades of cream and brown, and been untouched since. The colours, which had now merged into one, were stained with years' worth of nicotine. Csongi's trophies were lined up on a small shelf above the bar and the walls were decorated with framed, faded clippings of his fights. A red-and-blue paper tablecloth covered the surface of the Formica table. A plastic bread basket stood in the middle, next to two small ridged-glass salt and pepper shakers.

Balthazar looked out onto the square as he reached for a slice of bread then shook some salt over it, childhood memories running through his mind. When he was a kid, growing up on Jozsef Street, a ten-minute walk away, this part of District VIII was as rough and run-down as his neighbourhood, a place of grimy tenements and streetwalkers, several run by his father. The patch of grass was rough and untended, the apartment buildings dark and crumbling. He had come here on one of his first dates – if *date* was the word for an hour or two stolen from both their parents' monitoring. They had sat on a rusty bench with cracked wooden slats and eaten ice cream. Balthazar closed his eyes for a moment. The face of a Roma Madonna. Eyes you could dive into. Fingers that slid so easily into his. He could still remember the look on her face, the beautiful innocence, as she talked about her childhood dream, to be a teacher. In most families, that was an everyday ambition. But their families had different plans. Then another memory filled his head and he closed his eyes for a moment, trying to banish it.

Anastasia touched the back of Balthazar's hand. 'Wake up, sleepyhead.'

Balthazar blinked. 'I'm not asleep. I'm thinking.'

'OK, thinker. What about?'

Those memories were not for sharing. An edited version would do. 'I used to come here as a kid. It was a quarter of an hour's walk, straight down Jozsef Street, across the boulevard. Near enough to get to easily, but far enough not to bump into friends or relatives.' He pointed at a balcony on the first floor of a pristine apartment building, newly painted cream. 'See that?' The balcony was a mix of marble and delicate wrought ironwork.

Anastasia looked where he indicated. 'Yes. It's beautiful now. I think that building belongs to the church.'

'It did. They sold it. That's a 750-square-foot flat behind the balcony. How many people used to live in it, do you think, until the developers moved in?'

Anastasia shrugged. 'I don't know. At 750 square feet, probably two bedrooms and a lounge. Four, five, six?'

Balthazar laughed. 'Twenty-six. Three generations of one Gypsy family. Parents, children, grandchildren. They were part of the Lakatos clan.'

Anastasia was amazed. 'Where did they sleep?'

'They managed. We have a different concept of personal space.'

'How different?'

'It doesn't really exist. But now look – we are in hipster central.'

They looked out at the square for a moment. In one corner a large statue of Mikszath Kalman, one of Hungary's best-loved writers, looked out onto his eponymous square. The ground was neatly tiled and a curved island, topped with a lush garden, stood in the middle, all bordered with rounded bricks. A young woman in her late teens, wearing a black miniskirt and a pink halter top, sat by the base of the stone statue. Two young mothers, tending pushchairs with sleeping infants, chatted by a tiny espresso bar in a caravan, beside a small double door at ground level that was firmly bolted.

He tapped the table. 'Apart from Csongor, who is still holding out.'

Anastasia raised her coffee cup. 'And long may he do so.'

'Did you ever go there?' asked Anastasia, pointing at the closed entrance.

Balthazar laughed. 'Tilos Az A? I tried, once, but they would not let me in.'

'Because you are a Gypsy?'

'No. They didn't care about that. Because I was barely fourteen.'

During the early 1990s, when the city's young people were still intoxicated with freedom, but starved of decent party places, the doors had opened into a cellar club that was the centre of bohemian nightlife.

'I tried as well,' said Anastasia.

'And?'

'I got in. I had just turned sixteen, but I looked older.' She smiled, looked wistful for a moment, her eyes alight. 'That was another world in the 1990s. We were all so hopeful, almost high on freedom.'

'Yes, we were. Even the Gypsies,' said Balthazar.

Balthazar had graduated from Fazekas High School, itself a rare achievement for a Gypsy boy from the backstreets of District VIII, and had then won a place to study law and politics at Budapest's Eotvos Lorand University. His education had divided his parents. His father, Laci, had angrily dismissed Balthazar's studies as a waste of time. His first son, he insisted, would anyway follow his father and his grandfather into the family business of pimping and running girlie bars. But Balthazar's mother, Marta, had other ideas.

When Laci raised his hand to her, she batted it away, stopped cooking for him and made him sleep on a sofa in the lounge. He soon relented. Balthazar had then taken a Masters degree in Nationalism Studies at Central European University, a small but well-renowned graduate college in downtown Budapest.

His telephone rang and he looked at the screen. It was Sarah, his ex-wife.

Anastasia said, 'Aren't you going to take that?'

Balthazar nodded.

'Work or personal?'

Balthazar gave her a wry smile. 'Sarah. My ex-wife.'

'I've leave you to it, then. I'm going to wash my hands,' she said, stood up and left.

Balthazar took the call, wondering what Sarah wanted so early in the morning. Something from him, that was for sure. Balthazar had met Sarah Weiss while they were both students at CEU. She was a pretty Jewish girl from New York, but her brains and self-confidence had attracted him as much as her looks. They quickly fell in love, quickly moved in together, and got married. Balthazar started his doctorate on the Poraymus, the devouring, as the Roma called their Holocaust. The work went well and after a couple of years his supervisor had strongly hinted that he was in line for a junior lecturer's position, and would, if that went well, rapidly be granted the holy grail of academia: tenure, a job for life. He and Sarah had a child, a boy named Alex. Life was good: they lived comfortably in a large flat on Pozsonyi Way in District XIII. Sarah also started a PhD, in Gender Studies, focusing on the inner dynamics of Roma families. But as he and Sarah discovered that passion and finding each other exotic were not enough to build a life and home, the marriage wobbled, then collapsed. Sarah decided she was a lesbian and left Balthazar for a German postgraduate student from Tubingen called Amanda. Balthazar left academia and joined the police force, to the horror of Sarah and her uber-liberal friends.

Sarah usually called just before Balthazar was due to have Alex over or take him somewhere, with some kind of reason – usually fictitious – why the meeting had to be postponed or cancelled. Power and control were very important to Sarah. At one stage she had been so obstructive that after two weeks of not seeing Alex, Balthazar had been reduced to borrowing an unmarked police car and parking outside the American school in Nagykovacsi, a village just outside Budapest, that Alex attended, just for a glimpse of his son. This week, though, she had been more amenable than usual and had brought Alex to meet Balthazar the previous Sunday, and even let him stay over. This was, he thought, in large part because she needed something.

They exchanged greetings. Balthazar paused and did not say anything. Sarah blinked first. 'It's about Saturday, Tazi.'

For a moment Balthazar's stomach flipped. Surely she was not going to cancel? He, Sarah and Alex had arranged a day trip, leaving at 8 a.m. on Saturday morning to Nagyszentfalu, a village just south of Budapest where a group of Gypsy women had set up a weaving collective. It was precisely the kind of project that Sarah needed to write about to finish her PhD. And without Balthazar she would have no means of communicating with the weavers. Sarah had, at most, a few dozen words of Hungarian, and knew none of the Roma dialects. Best of all, because she needed Balthazar, Sarah had agreed that the trip would not be counted against his monthly time with Alex of two overnight weekend stays and one evening a week.

'What?' asked Balthazar. 'It's all planned, everything is set up for you. Don't tell me you're cancelling.'

'No, of course not. It's about Alex. He just told me that you bought him a burger on Sunday. And a milkshake.'

Balthazar frowned. 'I did. Teenage boys like burgers. Is that a problem?'

'Actually, potentially, yes. Do you know the provenance of the beef?'

He closed his eyes for a few seconds. From a dead cow, he wanted to say. Like most beef. Instead he answered, 'No. Should I?'

'Ideally, yes. We only want Alex to eat organically reared beef. And the roll is a problem. And the milkshake.'

'Really? Why?'

'We think he might be gluten and lactose intolerant.'

'We?'

'Amanda and I. You know we're both vegan now. We don't approve of him eating meat.' Amanda was in awe of her partner, and felt guilty about the whole tangled German–Jewish relationship and so acceded to whatever Sarah wanted. But Amanda was not the issue.

Balthazar sighed. Coming back to this part of town was stirring a lot of memories today – memories and emotions. That and the events of the morning. And the weight of his family. His brother, again. Gendarmes on his trail. And now he had to deal with his ex-wife's obsessing about Alex's non-existent food intolerances. 'Alex wolfed it down. And he loved the milkshake. No complaints afterwards, no tummy ache, nothing. He even wanted another burger afterwards.'

'You didn't,' said Sarah, her voice alarmed.

'No. Of course not. But sure, next time I'll ask about the beef, or find somewhere organic.'

'Vegetarian would be better. Or even vegan.'

'Leave it with me. Anything else I can help with?'

'Thanks. I wanted to ask something about Saturday.'

'Go ahead.'

Sarah, Balthazar knew, was angry and frustrated that her academic career was stalling. Gender Studies was a new and modern discipline, sneered at by some as an artificial construct to keep sub-par academics employed by critiquing each other's work. Her mistake had been to choose a specialisation – the role of women in Roma family dynamics – into which, without Balthazar, she had no point of entry. That had worked fine when they were together. Balthazar had introduced Sarah to his family, of course, taken her around the slums and tenements of Districts VIII and IX, out to the settlements on the edge of villages, where Roma families lived in shacks with no running water or electricity. But once they had split up, Sarah had no means of entering that world, which was closed and suspicious of outsiders. Apart from Balthazar, she did not know any Gypsies, and his family, obviously, were not going to help her. Which for Balthazar was a good thing, as it gave him some leverage in what was otherwise a very unequal battle for access to his son.

Sarah said, 'My new supervisor has asked me to look at the question of transitioning in the Roma community. He says it would add a whole new dimension to my thesis. And you know there is this associate professor post coming up in Gender Studies. It's a brilliant opportunity for really original research. Do you know any Roma people who are transitioning? It would be so helpful.'

Transitioning. For a moment he heard the voice of Eva *neni*, after Balthazar had explained to her what Sarah did for work: *'From this she makes a living?'* The memory made him laugh, but kept his voice deadpan as he answered.

'Yes, of course. I've met several. It's popular now. Lots of people are trying.'

He could hear Sarah's excited intake of breath as she answered, 'Oh, that's so amazing. Do you think they would talk to me?'

'Sure, why not?'

'Will you ask them?'

'Sure.'

'Thanks, Tazi. Thanks so much. Were they successful, the transitions?'

'Not usually, no.'

'Oh. Why not?'

'Because as much as they self-identified as a *gadje*, tried to behave like one, even if they were light-skinned, everyone still knew they were a Gypsy.'

Sarah's voice became tight. 'Very funny, Tazi. We'll see you on Saturday morning.'

Sarah hung up and he put the telephone down. Anastasia appeared and sat back down. 'You're laughing. Good phone call?'

Balthazar smiled. 'Sarah wants me to find a Gypsy who is transitioning from one gender to another. Apparently it would help her with her PhD thesis.'

'And can you?'

'Probably not. I told her I knew a lot of Gypsies who were trying to be *gadjes*. She didn't think it was funny. You know us Roma. Our family models are still pretty traditional. We are quite behind the curve.'

'Not always, Balthazar. And not all of you,' said Anastasia, with a smile that reached her eyes.

'Thanks. I've been thinking, as we are working together, there's something else you might be able to help me with.'

'Such as?'

'There's an old case I might re-open.'

'How old?'

'Twenty years or so.'

'That's a very old case. Why now?'

'I'd rather not say for the moment. I'm still thinking about it. But if I do... your service has a much wider repertoire available than us plodding cops.'

'You mean we can break into places and bug telephones?'

'Yes. That's exactly what I mean.'

'Are there any national security implications in this case?'

Balthazar shook his head. 'None.'

Anastasia asked, 'This is personal, isn't it?'

'Yes. Very.'

She gave him a knowing, almost affectionate look. 'In that case, of course. Whatever you need or want.' They shook hands, her palm cool in his. 'Now, back to business.'

EIGHT

'I still don't get it, Eni. Why didn't you go?' asked Zsuzsa
Barcsy. 'I thought you really wanted to. You could have finally
met Alex as well. That's a big thing that he asked you along
with his son. You never met him while you were together.'

Eniko and Zsuzsa were standing on the corner of the
wrap-around balcony of the imposing sixth-floor apartment
that served as the offices of 555.hu. The balcony reached
higher than their waists, its pale stone wall thick and wide,
topped with a curved granite lip overlooking Blaha Lujza
Square. Eniko looked down, did not immediately answer her
friend. The city was spread out below them. Behind them,
Rakoczi Way stretched to Keleti Station; in front of her, it
crossed the Grand Boulevard at Blaha Lujza Square, before
slicing through downtown towards Astoria and the Elizabeth
Bridge.

'I couldn't, Zsuzsi,' said Eniko. 'I was working.' Even as
she heard herself articulate the words she thought she did not
sound very convincing. She watched the traffic lights change
colour as the traffic slowed then stopped on Rakoczi Way,
before the vehicles began to move along the Grand Boulevard,
driving through Blaha Lujza Square. It was hard to imagine
that just a few days ago this downtown plaza had been the

centre of every news bulletin, not just in Hungary, but around the globe.

Now Blaha Lujza Square looked as it did on an everyday Budapest morning. Pedestrians and commuters rushed back and forth between trams, buses and the entrance to the metro. Eniko's favourite pensioner, Maria *neni*, who came into town each day to sell flowers from her village outside Budapest, was in her usual place by the entrance to the metro station. Today she was selling daisies, rather than her usual bluebells, for 300 forints. The sandwich man advertising the Bella Roma pizzeria was walking up and down, handing out flyers and smiling widely at passers-by, many of whom kept a wide berth – smiling at strangers was regarded as very suspicious behaviour. The only sign of the previous weekend's events was a small noticeboard on the other side of Rakoczi Way, on the corner of the Grand Boulevard, with a photograph of Mahmoud Hejazi, requesting anyone with information about him to contact the police.

Zsuzsa looked at her friend, her eyebrows arched. 'Really?' she asked. 'You filed your story by early Sunday evening. It was online twenty minutes later. It's three stops on the metro from here to Kossuth Square. They were going to a burger bar on Oktober 6 Street, which is another five minutes' walk away. And even if you had to come back to work, how long does it take to eat a burger?'

Eniko did not reply. She had no good answer. Why hadn't she gone to have dinner with Balthazar and Alex? Instead she had sent an SMS apologising that she could not make it, and had sat in the office, reading and re-reading her story after it was filed, when there was no need to make any more edits, then planning the next day's follow-ups. She had spent the rest of the evening standing on the same balcony, with a couple of colleagues and a can of warm beer for company, watching the column of migrants slowly proceed down Rakoczi Way. Was she really so scared of what she had rediscovered the previous weekend about her feelings for Balthazar? However much she tried to deny it, maybe she was. It was certainly starting to look that way. She was behaving like a teenage girl, running away from her emotions.

'Do you think he will invite me again?' asked Eniko.

Zsuzsa laughed, her wide blue eyes alight with humour. 'After you dumped him then stood him up? What do you think?'

'Probably not.'

'And then there's all the other stuff.'

'What other stuff?'

'He is a Gypsy. He let you into his family, introduced you to his brothers, sisters, the whole clan. Family is everything for them. And then you said no thanks, and walked away. He won't forget that. And neither will they.'

Zsuzsa was right, Eniko knew. She had enjoyed the Kovacs clan's riotous gatherings more than she had ever imagined: the music, the warmth, the tables laden with food, the endless flow of every kind of drink.

Eniko shot her a wry look. 'What's happened to you? I thought you were supposed to be my friend.' Eniko glanced at her watch. 'And why are you in so early?'

'Because I've got a lot to do. And I am your friend,' said Zsuzsa brightly. 'But sometimes you need to hear the truth, Eni. You dumped Balthazar. Then you stood him up, even though he is probably still interested. Then last week you didn't want to go out with the best-looking actor in the city because he is boring. Half the women in this city would have elbowed you out of the way to eat sushi with him.'

'Tamas Nemeth is boring. He just talked about himself the whole evening.' She took off her trendy tortoiseshell spectacles and began to polish them needlessly on the end of her T-shirt. Should she tell Zsuzsa about the encounter on the tram and the memory stick? The more she thought about the events of the morning, the more unsettled she felt. She might have been followed from her flat on Raoul Wallenberg Street, in the heart of District XIII, to the tram stop on Jaszai Mari Square. And they – whoever *they* were – also had her new, personal telephone number.

'A man who talks about himself. Imagine that,' said Zsuzsa, dryly.

Hungary had been a member of the European Union for more than a decade, but was still a very conservative society, especially outside Budapest. There were barely any women in public life, apart from a few celebrity reality TV stars and sports champions, and only a handful of women MPs. The passport scam aside, that ingrained sexism was another reason why many commentators thought Reka Bardossy's administration would last a couple of weeks, if that. But the culture clash was growing between Eniko and Zsuzsa's generation and their elders. Even at 555.hu, which was the country's most liberal and irreverent website, the executives, most of whom were male, still dispensed a stream of compliments and remarks on their female colleagues' appearance, to their increasingly vocal annoyance.

Zsuzsa peered down into Blaha Lujza Square, her hand to her forehead, turning from side to side. 'Do you see a line of Hungarian men down there, all waiting eagerly to go out with an independent-minded woman coming up to thirty, with a career and income of her own? Because I don't. And if there was, that would be the biggest story in 555's history.'

'No. I don't. But we can live in hope. What's got into you this morning?' She looked at her friend for a moment. Zsuzsa was a pretty, clear-skinned countryside girl, born in a small village on the *puszta*, the great plain. Her round, intelligent face was framed by long, wavy auburn hair. Several inches shorter than Eniko, she was slightly plump, and self-conscious about her figure.

Zsuzsa's voice softened. 'I'm sorry. I know you've got so much to think about at the moment. I just don't want you to be left on the shelf.'

Eniko said, 'Well *you* won't, Zsuzsika, looking like that.' Eniko had noticed Zsuzsa's new look when they met in the office ten minutes ago, but had still been shaken up by her encounter on the tram. Now she was on home territory again and had relaxed a bit, she gave her friend the once-over again. Zsuzsa usually wore loose, baggy clothes. Today she was wearing a knee-length denim skirt and a black scoop-neck close-fitting top. Zsuzsa usually smelled of soap and shampoo but Eniko could smell some kind of perfume, almost musky. And she was getting more and more assertive. In Eniko's experience such transformation usually had one cause: a new man. In any case it was time to move the conversation on from her own disastrous personal life.

Eniko said, 'I like your new look. It suits you. Almost vampy.'

Zsuzsa's confidence wobbled. She frowned, looked down at her cleavage and tight top, as if surprised at herself. 'You don't think it's a bit... OTT?'

Eniko laughed. 'Absolutely not. We gotta use what we got.' She looked Zsuzsa up and down. 'And you are.'

Zsuzsa blushed and swallowed. 'Thanks.'

'So why the new look?'

'*Csak.*'

Eniko smiled. 'Who is he?'

Zsuzsa blushed. 'Nobody... someone.'

'What are you working on? Can you tell me that?'

'Sure. Migrants, mostly. I'm going to Keleti later. Wanna come? I need to do some research but I'll do that later. The Internet is incredibly slow this morning. I could barely get onto the website.'

Zsuzsa was a general news reporter, although recently, like much of the staff at 555.hu she had been working on the migrants story. This was her first proper journalistic job. She had graduated from Eotvos Lorand University with a degree in English and media studies and had worked as an intern at several newspapers and websites before starting at 555. hu. She was several steps below Eniko in the newsroom's hierarchy, especially after Eniko's recent scoops, but Eniko had taken her under her wing, given her a crash course in writing, interviewing and reporting. Thanks to the migrant crisis, and her talent and dedication, Zsuzsa's career was progressing rapidly.

Eniko said, 'Good old Keleti. My second home. I've been off that story for a couple of days.' For a moment she felt almost nostalgic for her time at the station – was it really just a week ago? – doing some actual reporting, speaking to real people, crouching down in the heat and dirt and dust, hearing human stories. 'I've been too busy being Reka Bardossy's de facto press officer as she drip-feeds me snippets about Pal Dezeffy.'

Zsuzsa looked shocked. She knew journalists were cynical, of course, but this world-weary? 'But your stories are going around the world. She's an incredible source.'

'An incredible source with an agenda. Let's not talk about

that.' Eniko's voice brightened. 'I'll come to Keleti with you if you tell me who you're meeting.'

Zsuzsa looked down from the balcony, suddenly intensely interested in the commuters and shoppers striding across Blaha Lujza Square. 'Nobody. I'm not meeting anyone.'

Eniko knew that Zsuzsa had broken up with her childhood sweetheart, Huba, a month ago. Huba was an engineer who hated Budapest, almost as much as he hated Zsuzsa's job, and the idea of her going out and meeting an endless stream of strangers, some of whom were men. Once Zsuzsa had turned down his proposal of marriage, there was nothing more to say. He had moved out the next day and returned home.

Eniko laughed, 'Mr Nobody? Come on, Zsuzsika, you can tell me. First date?'

'Second.'

'Oooh. Lunch or evening?' said Eniko, pausing for a moment, raising her eyebrows. 'Evening, I guess.'

'Early evening. Six o'clock. Cocktails.'

Eniko laughed, gently mocked her friend. 'Cocktails. Fancy.'

'Yes. I know. Actually, I've never been to a cocktail bar.' She frowned for a moment. 'What should I order?'

'Nothing strong. Vermouth or Campari soda. Where is it?'

'A new bar. I've never heard of it. Zuma.'

'When did you meet?'

'On Monday.'

'That's only four days ago. And you are already on your second date. Serious. How did you meet Mr Nobody?'

'We just got chatting.' Zsuzsa pointed down to Blaha Lujza. 'We were both waiting for the 4/6 tram.'

'Name? Age?'

Zsuzsa smiled, enjoying the moment. For once, Eniko was grilling her about a man. 'His name is Adorjan.'

'And what does Adorjan do?'

'He's an adviser. Something to do with politics. He promised to tell me more tonight.'

Bajnok bar, Mikszath Kalman Square, 8.45 a.m.

Csongor appeared from the kitchen, carrying two white, oblong plates laden with food. He placed them down on the table with a flourish. Csongor was in his early thirties, of medium height, wiry and muscular, with a wide forehead, a boxer's nose that bent leftwards and a thin scar above both of his grey eyes.

'Thanks, Csongi,' said Balthazar. 'I didn't know you could cook.'

Csongor smiled. 'Neither did I. It's my first breakfast. The wife usually does it but she's away this week. What do you think?'

Balthazar looked down at the plate. A pile of small fried sausages stood next to two fried eggs, spattered with paprika and two dollops of red and brown. The smell of the food was making Balthazar's mouth water. 'I think it looks great.'

'Good.' Csongor pointed at the coloured splashes. 'Ketchup. Mustard. *Jo etvagyat*, I wish you a good appetite.'

Anastasia laughed. 'I've got one.' She speared a sausage as Csongor walked back to the kitchen, bit the end off and chewed slowly.

Balthazar realised he was ravenous. He ate most of the meal in a couple of minutes, then dipped the end of a sausage in an egg yolk and watched the golden liquid flow around the fried meat. Could he and Anastasia really work together? She was smart, tough, perceptive. But the ABS and the police were wary colleagues at best. They had different mandates and different agendas. The security service had far more powers than the police, had more technical and manpower resources. The ABS also had an annoying habit of letting the police do the hard work of investigating a murder or high-profile robbery then walking in and taking the case.

On balance, though, he thought yes. He needed to find out how and why al-Nuri had died. If, as he was starting to suspect, the worst case was likely – that he had been deliberately killed at the brothel to target Balthazar and Gaspar – then he would need some help. It was conceivable that al-Nuri had simply died of a heart attack. It was not conceivable that the brothel's CCTV system had failed, then reversed itself to show Balthazar, Gaspar and the others. That was clearly a message. Someone was inside the system. But who? The ABS, he was sure, had the means to do that. As did the Gendarmerie.

Balthazar said, 'Something weird happened this morning at the brothel.'

Anastasia gathered more food on her fork. 'You mean weirder than a dead Arab who might have been poisoned while pleasuring himself with one of your brother's *oromlanyok*?'

'Yes, even weirder than that,' said Balthazar, as he gave a quick account of the CCTV malfunction.

'That is strange,' said Anastasia.

'Was that you or your people?'

'No. It was not. And we don't send signals.'

'So who was it?'

Anastasia glanced outside before she answered, then pointed. 'Them, I guess.'

Balthazar followed her finger. Two black Gendarmerie vehicles had taken up position on the opposite corners of the square: one by Revitsky Street and another by Krudy Gyula Street. Each had tinted windows covered by black wire mesh. A white globe mounted on a stick on the roof slowly rotated, filming the square and its surrounds.

'Attila's keeping an eye on you,' said Anastasia. She turned for a moment and waved through the window, before facing Balthazar again. 'Meanwhile, I have something else to show you.'

'Another video?' asked Balthazar, as he demolished a fried egg. 'Is anything in this town not being filmed?'

'Not if it might be useful ammunition. At least this was not filmed by the Gendarmerie.' Anastasia glanced down at Balthazar's half-eaten breakfast. 'I will show you once you have finished that. This one is not pleasant viewing. And if it ever gets out, as these things usually do, it's the end of Reka Bardossy's brief term as Hungary's first female prime minister.'

Balthazar smiled. 'I'm a detective in the murder squad. I've seen plenty of actual bodies, many of which met a nasty end. But none of which were connected to Reka Bardossy, so now you have me really intrigued.' He pointed at her telephone. 'Show me, please.'

'It's an actual killing. A messy one. I'd eat up if I were you.'

Balthazar speared the remaining sausages and ate them, before mopping the rest of the egg yolk with a piece of bread. Once the breakfast was gone, he looked at Anastasia and nodded. 'Ready when you are.'

Anastasia called up a video file on her telephone, pressed play and passed Balthazar the handset. He watched Reka Bardossy walking by ramparts of the Buda Castle, a man approaching her, Reka throwing something in his face, the two of them grappling on the ground, Reka's right hand frantically scrabbling in the dirt, grabbing something and slamming it into the side of the man's neck. The man froze, then toppled to the side, a dark pool leaking from his punctured skin.

Anastasia was right. The footage was unsettling. The dim lighting and grainy quality gave it the look of a low budget horror film. Watching a recording of someone dying was as disturbing as being near an actual dead body. Many of the corpses he had encountered in his work were often already cold by the time he arrived. Nor was the sight of al-Nuri dead on his knees a pleasant start to the day. But Balthazar had not seen him die. Now he had watched a man twitch and jerk in his death throes. And a man, he realised, who looked familiar.

Balthazar pressed play again and watched the film for a second time, stopping the video several times and zooming in on the frozen shots of the fight, especially the scenes where the dead man toppled over with the object in his neck.

'He is dead?'

'Very.'

'What did she stick in his neck?'

'The heel of her Louboutin. Designer shoes. They cost hundreds of euros a pair.'

'Who was the dead man? I think I've seen him before.'

Anastasia reached inside her bag and took out a plastic folder containing several photographs. She slid them across the table to Balthazar. 'You have.'

The photographs showed the head of a burly male, probably in his early thirties. He had a knife scar under his right eye. Balthazar nodded. 'Sure. It's one of the Gendarmes who beat me up at Keleti last week.'

'That's what I thought. His name is Jeno Katona. An old friend of Attila's, from their time as part of the ultras, the hard-core violent football fans.'

'Where is his body?'

'We don't know.'

'Who was Kaplan working for?'

'That's where it gets even more interesting. Pal.'

'How do you know?'

Anastasia tilted her head to one side. 'We know all sorts of things. That's what we do.'

'Pal Dezeffy wanted to kill Reka Bardossy? But weren't he and Reka...?'

'Lovers, friends, yes, they were both children of the party elite. They grew up together in those lovely mansions in the Buda hills. But while Pal was dealing with the Qataris he and Reka also had a side operation, selling Hungarian passports to traffickers. Unfortunately the traffickers then sold them on to the Islamists, who kept getting detained at British and American airports. The CIA and MI6 were on it. It looked like the whole thing was about to collapse. Pal thought Reka was about to go down, and would take him with her as collateral damage. So she had to go.' Anastasia tapped the screen of her mobile telephone. 'But she had other ideas. And there's more.'

Somehow, Balthazar knew what was coming next. 'This is what you wanted to tell me?'

'Yes.'

'Gaspar?'

'Yes. He's mixed up in this.'

'He's not in that league. He just dresses up migrants in Gypsy clothes then drives them across the Austrian border. It's a straightforward business deal.'

Anastasia looked down for a moment, as if deciding how to phrase her next sentence. 'It's much more than that, Balthazar. Did you give him my message?'

Anastasia had told Balthazar the previous weekend when they met for the first time to tell Gaspar to 'get out of the travel business'.

'I can't remember. I think so.'

Anastasia smiled. 'You're a terrible liar, especially for a cop. Don't you know that the most important thing is to take a position and stick to it? So that means no. You didn't tell him.' Her voice turned serious. 'Listen to me now, Tazi, and please pass this on. Your brother is way out of his depth. He really does need to get out of the travel business. Especially after last weekend. When is the next group due to leave?'

'Today. I'm not sure when.'

Anastasia looked doubtful.

'Really, I don't know. This morning I think. They change the times, don't decide until the last moment.' For a moment he could hear his brother replying to his question:

'Why, ocsim, are you in a hurry?'

Gaspar glanced at his watch, a gold-plated Rolex. 'Actually, yes.'

Balthazar said, 'They leave from—'

'We know where they leave from, Balthazar.'

'Then why don't you stop them?'

'We aren't in the immigration-control business. And we are not the police. We are not interested in crime unless it's organised, international and affects or threatens national security.'

'And Gaspar is doing that?'

Anastasia leaned forward. 'Yes. He has been. I keep telling you this. I do wish you would listen. And Pal had plans for you. Nothing good, I'm sorry to say. This is him talking to Attila Ungar, last week while he was still prime minister.'

Anastasia picked up her telephone and played a sound file: Pal's voice sounded. 'What matters is that you get rid of him. Make it look like an accident. Use a knife. They like knives. Everyone will think it's some kind of Gypsy feud.'

NINE

Marton Ronay looked down at the flyer he had just been handed. It was A5 in size, printed on heavy glossy paper in full colour. A racist cartoon version of a black man groping a young, frightened-looking blonde-haired white woman filled most of the page. The headline across the top declared 'Defend our homeland' in large letters, while written underneath in smaller type were the words *Magyar Nemzeti Front*, Hungarian National Front.

Marton put the flyer down, trying to keep a straight face. 'O-*kaay*,' he replied, his Midwestern American accent stretching out the second letter. 'Talk me through this,' he said, making sure to keep his voice neutral.

Pal Dezeffy nodded enthusiastically. 'Sure. It's a leaflet. As it says, for the Hungarian National Front.'

'And what, exactly, is the Hungarian National Front?'

Pal smiled, pointed at the flyer. 'That. More or less.'

'So there is no actual, functioning organisation of that name?'

Pal shook his head. 'No. Is that a problem?'

'No. Not all,' said Marton, telling himself to be grateful for small mercies.

Pal picked up another flyer from the small pile on the table in front of him and started reading the words on the bottom half. '"Stop the migrant flood – join the patriots' revolution." What about that? I wrote it,' he said proudly.

Marton replied, 'The slogan is good. You define the problem and offer a solution.'

'And the picture,' said Pal. 'It's effective, no?'

'It's…' perfect for Alabama in the 1930s, Marton almost said. Instead he paused for a moment while he searched for the right words, '… certainly very direct.'

'But?' asked Pal. 'I hear a "but".'

The former prime minister, Marton could see, was starting to get irritated.

'The picture is…' he paused, looked for the right words, 'a bit old-fashioned. Does the MNF have a website?'

Pal shook his head.

'Twitter? Instagram feed?'

'No. Only an email address.'

That was something, Marton thought. The less of the MNF there was, especially in cyberspace, the better. He asked, 'Does the email address work? Is anyone monitoring it?'

Pal replied, 'Yes. We are building a database of contacts.'

'That's useful,' said Marton.

Pal tapped the pile of leaflets. 'So will we use these? We still have thousands of them.'

For kindling, maybe. Or confetti, Marton felt like saying. But he had to be careful how he answered. Firstly, because these guys were the client, paying him $1,500 a day plus accommodation, a generous per diem and other expenses. And secondly, he knew how proud and prickly a certain type of Magyar could be, especially when on the defensive. And this guy, who had been prime minister a week ago, who had been humiliated in the national and international media, portrayed as an aider and abetter of terrorists, and who faced an uncertain legal future, was very defensive. 'Explain to me, please, Mr Dezeffy. What exactly is the purpose of the leaflet?' Marton asked.

'To make people nervous, scared. So they welcome the new Gendarmerie,' said Pal. 'To create fear, not just of the migrants, but the consequences for society as a whole if they come, a potential breakdown in law and order.'

'Well,' said Marton. 'Instilling fear is an effective technique. The question is how you do that so that people want the solutions you are offering. They have to be scared, but not too scared. It's a quite delicate balancing act.'

Marton watched Pal as he considered his reply. Understanding, he saw, was slowly dawning. Pal said, 'So you don't like the leaflet.' He looked down again at the flyer. 'You think it's crude.'

Crude is one word, thought Marton, but did not say so. 'It's not about what I like. It's about what works.'

The picture, Marton knew, was a total disaster. The aim was to bring over the undecided, not pander to mouth-breathing Neanderthals and scare everyone else away. But he could not say that. He needed to get Pal to realise it himself. A bit of flattery always helped. Marton leaned forward. 'Mr Pal, you are an experienced and very sophisticated politician. You have won two general elections for the Social Democratic Party. You have steered this country through difficult times, transitioning from one system to another. You know how to manage such dramatic transformations, how to guard the nation's interests. You have always been a patriot, someone true to the interests of his homeland. What's not being reported in all the distortion about the Gulf investors is what that money would mean for Hungary. How much good it could do.'

Pal's voice rose in excitement, 'Exactly. We need to rescue that deal. So we can bring Hungary into the twenty-first century.'

Marton watched Pal as he spoke, trying to take the measure of the man. The former prime minister had just turned forty. Trim, apart from an embryonic paunch, he wore a white open-necked shirt. He had regular, even features, brown eyes, and short black hair trimmed with grey. He was a handsome man, but the strain of the last few days was etched on his face, in the deep lines around his eyes and mouth, while his skin, under the remnants of a tan, had an unhealthy pallor, all too familiar to Marton, of someone who spent too much time indoors, mainlining coffee, if not other stimulants as well. There was a pale raised line of flesh on the right side of his neck, Marton noticed, some kind of scar, he guessed. Sitting next to him was a younger man who looked to be in his late twenties. Adorjan Molnar – call me Adi, he had said – had been introduced as an 'adviser'. Adorjan was slimmer, and wore a tight black polo shirt that showcased a muscly build that must have cost many hours in the gym. He had wide-set blue eyes, spiky hair so blonde it was almost white, and sensual lips, and exuded an easy charisma.

Marton continued, 'So, Mr Dezeffy—'

'Call me Pal, please.'

'Pal, we – the world – are now in transition between two systems, two ages. This is the dawn of the digital age. It is reshaping politics and the world in ways that we could not imagine a few years ago.'

'We are aware of that,' said Adorjan. 'That's why we have brought you here. We have seen your work in the United States. Your record is impressive.'

Marton nodded. 'Thank you. Let's look back for a moment. Who did you and your party target in those successful electoral campaigns? Party loyalists, who will vote for you anyway, or undecided voters?'

Pal said, 'Undecided voters, of course.'

'And where are they?'

'On the centre ground.' Pal paused, looked down again at the picture. 'Well, perhaps it is a little... direct.'

'Perhaps,' said Marton.

That was something at least, thought Marton. He looked down at the crude caricature. 'Are there many black people among the migrants?'

'A few,' said Pal, 'but they are mostly from the Middle East or Afghanistan.'

Marton frowned. 'That's what I thought. I've seen a lot of the coverage from Keleti. Most of the people seem to be from Syria or Iraq. I'm curious – why the focus on black people? Shouldn't that be someone dressed as an Arab, or wearing a headscarf? That would be much more relevant, surely?'

Pal shifted in his seat, looked momentarily uncomfortable, before recovering his composure. Because you don't shit on your own doorstep, he thought, especially when it is covered with golden tiles. Instead he replied: 'The leaflet, as I said, was part of a campaign to spread fear, build support for the Gendarmerie. But we have moved on from that. The Gendarmerie is established. And now we have a very different *political* situation.' For a second, anger flashed in his brown eyes. 'As you know.'

There were four of them in the conference room, sitting in expensive chrome-and-leather office chairs around a long, black mahogany table: Marton, Pal, Adorjan and a gaunt older man, with straggly grey hair and a nasty flaking skin problem, who looked like he was well into his seventies. His beige shirt, with a large, fraying collar and brown jacket with wide lapels looked like they were either long-owned items of 1970s clothing or had been bought in a job lot at a jumble sale. He sat watching at the other end of the table, like a vulture waiting for its prey to finally expire while he took notes in a yellow legal pad, between taking drags on a disgusting-smelling cigarette. The brand, Marton saw, was called Sopianae, something local, he assumed. The old man had not asked anyone else in the room if they minded if he smoked. Marton did – a lot, in fact. But something about the man's manner, his hands that were like yellow talons, most of all the way Pal and Adorjan kept glancing at him, made Marton sense that he should grin and bear it.

The conference room was a large space, on the top floor of a modern office building on the corner of Szabadsag Square, in the very heart of the city. The walls were a brilliant shade of white, decorated with a series of photographs showing some of the foundation's projects: redecorating a ramshackle school in a remote village in eastern Hungary; a summer holiday camp for underprivileged children, many of them Roma, on the south shore of Lake Balaton; a soup kitchen in Budapest, where Pal and others served hot meals to a line of the homeless and destitute. A large flat-screen television was mounted on one wall.

The windows looked out onto the landscaped gardens of the square where, at the far end, the Soviet war memorial to the liberation of Budapest stood next to the highly fortified

American embassy. Szabadsag Square – the name meant Freedom – was one of the most important in the city, second only to the nearby Kossuth Square.

Pal continued speaking, 'So if you don't like the leaflet, then how do you suggest that we proceed?'

Marton's voice was emollient. 'May I speak frankly?'

'Of course.'

Marton glanced at the end of the table. The old man was watching him intently, smoke trickling from his nostrils. Marton thought quickly. This discussion, where he set out his thoughts and tried to guide clients into the twenty-first century and the digital age, was often difficult. It was certainly best conducted when he was reasonably alert and not numbed from travel. But it had to take place, and if it was going to be a deal-breaker, then better to know that now. And the main principle was very simple. He started to speak: 'Our aim is simple: to sow doubt. Doubt and confusion. Doubt as to why Reka Bardossy is sitting in your chair, in your office. Confusion as to why someone deeply enmeshed in the recent' – he paused – '*events* is now running the country.'

Marton glanced at Pal, who nodded in agreement. 'Then we provide the answer.'

The man at the end of the table spoke for the first time. 'How?' he asked, his voice raspy from cigarettes. 'How do you suggest that we do that?'

Marton said, 'We destroy Bardossy's credibility, shred her image. But we don't target her directly. That would be too obvious. People would dismiss it as more politicians' infighting.'

Pal leaned forward, his gaze locked on Marton. 'So who do we target?'

Marton replied, 'So far, Bardossy's media strategy has worked very well. She is using Eniko Szalay to frame the story. Szalay's reports, that Bardossy was running a sting operation to catch the Islamic radicals, are the main source for the international press. Much of the domestic press is also following her lead.' He sat back for a moment, nodding slightly. 'As a professional, I must say that it's a highly effective approach. So far the story has been framed to Reka Bardossy's advantage. We need to stop that. And we can, because Bardossy's strategy has a serious weakness. It rests on the credibility of one person: Eniko Szalay.'

Pal smiled. 'If we destroy Eniko Szalay, we take Bardossy down with her.'

Marton said, 'Precisely. Once we have unsettled Eniko Szalay, made her scared, she will start to make mistakes. Then we strike. You have followed my suggestions?'

Adorjan nodded. 'Of course. She received the footage this morning. We messaged her personal phone as well, which will unsettle her even more.'

'Good,' said Marton.

A tentative knock on the door sounded. Marton watched as Pal glanced at the grey-haired man, who nodded. Adorjan stood up and opened the door. A young woman walked in, holding a tray of coffees. She was notably pretty, Marton saw, her light-brown hair pinned up in a bun, wearing a cream blouse with a high collar and a black tailored business suit with a short skirt that highlighted her shapely legs.

'Thank you, Csilla,' said Adorjan, as she placed the tray on the table. 'Csilla is an intern here at the foundation,' he continued, his hand resting on her lower arm. She turned to smile. 'Csilla might be working with us, depending how we go forward,' said Adorjan. 'She's developing the foundation's social media strategy. She's very talented and up to speed on the digital world.'

Marton said, 'That's good to know,' wondering if Csilla could actually speak for herself. He asked her, 'What do you find works best here?'

Csilla turned to Marton, her eyes quickly assessing him. Marton sensed immediately that she seemed smart and capable. She said, 'That depends on the age of the target audience.'

'Under thirties,' said Marton.

'Same as everywhere. Instagram and Twitter. We have a Facebook page, but it's quite lame. Facebook, websites, they are for old—' she paused, blushed slightly before continuing, '... a different generation. That's what I have been explaining to my colleagues.'

'Are they listening?' asked Marton.

Csilla said, 'I hope so.'

'Me too,' said Marton.

'We are,' said Adorjan.

This was something, thought Marton. At least there was one person plugged into the twenty-first century. Csilla handed each of the men a white porcelain coffee cup, except the grey-haired man who shook his head. She looked around, asked, 'Do you need me for anything else?'

Adorjan replied, 'No, thanks. We'll catch up later.'

Marton watched Adorjan's eyes on Csilla's backside as she walked out of the door. Csilla, he thought, probably had a month or two at most in Adorjan's bed until the next intern arrived. Then things would get messy, especially if he and Csilla were working together. But he would deal with that if and when it happened.

Marton stifled a yawn as he reached for his coffee. The jet lag rushed over him again like a sucker punch. He looked down at the flyer. The picture aside, a *leaflet*? Really? In 2015? What were these guys thinking? There was a lot going on here, a lot to process. He needed time to think, to formulate a proper plan and strategy. But meanwhile all he wanted was to go to sleep, had done since he'd landed and struck out with Ferenc the handsome policeman. Instead he had been taken straight to his apartment by the driver who met him at the airport. He had been given ten minutes to drop off his luggage at the apartment on Alkotmany Street and quickly freshen up, then was brought here. Luckily the two places were very close to each other.

Pal's voice broke Marton's reverie. 'We are taking some other measures as well.'

'Which are?' asked Marton.

'Some virtual, some physical, in the real world.' Pal glanced at Adorjan, who picked up a remote control and pointed it at the large flat-screen television. The screen filled with the first frame of a video. Adorjan pressed down and the images began to move. A group of skinheads ran into the forecourt of Keleti Station, shouting abuse, kicking and punching wildly among the migrants. Many cowered in fear but several fought back, and eventually enough of a crowd had formed to drive the skinheads out of the station and into the traffic on Thokoly Way, where the brawl continued, cars and buses flowing around the fighters, pedestrians scurrying away.

A squad of police cars and vans arrived and swept up the brawlers. A slow montage followed, of news clips about the violence on state and private Hungarian channels, as well as the BBC, CNN, French, German and other international channels. Many featured a short interview with the government spokeswoman, a stern-looking woman in her thirties, with short-cropped brown hair. She blamed the migrants for provocations and starting the violence, and promised strong measures would be taken to keep the streets safe.

The news clips finished, and the video then showed the police vans parked in a large courtyard. The skinheads and the migrants piled out, many of them laughing as they slapped each other's backs and shared cigarettes around. Each one presented himself to a man with a clipboard, who checked his name, handed him an envelope containing 30,000 forints, around £80, then ushered him across the courtyard to where several long tables were piled with food and drinks.

Marton said, 'Impressive. They were all yours?'

'Every one,' said Pal. 'A few were hired for the day.'

Marton smiled. This was more like it. 'Whose idea was this?'

Pal glanced at the grey-haired man at the end of the table. Something passed between them, Marton sensed, but he could not quite figure it out. Pal said, 'Does it matter? It worked.'

'Yes, it did,' said Marton.

'Better than the leaflet?' asked Pal.

'Much,' said Marton. 'We can do a lot with video. What else have you got? Stuff that can go public?'

Pal picked up the remote control and called up a menu on the screen. A new video file appeared. 'Speaking of Eniko Szalay...' The first frame showed Reka Bardossy and Eniko sitting in the bar of the Four Seasons Hotel.

Newsroom of 555.hu, 9.30 a.m.

'Where's the sandbox, Vivi?' asked Eniko.

Vivien Szentkiralyi kept staring at her screen while she waved her left hand at the pile of computer equipment at the side of her desk. 'Dunno. In there somewhere.'

The systems manager of 555.hu sat at an enormous right-angled desk, which took up most of a corner of the newsroom. There were two monitors facing her, angled together in a wide V-shape, and another to the side. The part of Vivien's workspace directly in front of her chair was comparatively tidy: a single keyboard and chipped mug of the green tea that she seemed to mainline all day. The left side of her desk was piled high with ancient laptops, cables, keyboards and wi-fi routers, CDs, DVDs, empty cans of energy drinks and pizza boxes, several of which still contained rock-hard, desiccated crusts.

In the middle of the chaos on the left side of Vivien's desk, under two other laptops was a black, old-fashioned IBM ThinkPad, at least fifteen years out of date. Eniko reached for the IBM, careful not to start a cascade of computers, parts or pieces of pizza. The IBM was 555.hu's sandbox. Purchased unused, still in its original box, when the website had launched a couple of years ago, the sandbox had never been connected to the Internet and could not be. The laptop was so old, it needed a special card to connect to wi-fi. There was no wi-fi card – Vivien had filled the wi-fi slot and the cable ports with epoxy glue that was now irremovable. That also prevented the sandbox from ever being connected to 555. hu's main network or server. The USB ports, however, had been left functional to receive memory cards or sticks. The IBM's original operating system had been wiped and replaced by Linux. That system, favoured by techies, was regarded as the safest as almost no viruses for Linux were written. The sandbox was a secure space for viewing questionable or unknown files, or opening email attachments from unknown senders, somewhere for the journalists and techies to play around. The sandbox's hard drive was also divided into several partitions, each firewalled from one another. Even if one was infected by a virus, the others would remain uncontaminated. Eniko planned to use the sandbox to take a look at the memory stick she had been handed on the tram that morning.

Eniko levered the sandbox out, feeling its weight in her hand. 'Can I take it?' she asked Vivien. The systems manager nodded. 'Sure. But bring it back.'

Vivien was a tall, pale, almost gangly woman in her late twenties, with short-cropped jet-black hair and a silver nose ring. Today, like every other day Eniko had seen her, she was dressed in a black T-shirt and black skinny jeans that were ripped at both knees. Vivien was never especially chatty or friendly, never socialised and nobody knew anything about her personal life, if indeed she had one. But she was extremely good at her job and had several times rescued Eniko from computer disasters, and recovered files she had thought were lost forever.

Eniko thanked her, and turned to go. Apart from Eniko and Vivien, the newsroom was quiet. Zsuzsa had gone out for coffee and the other reporters were either not in yet or were scrolling through Hungarian and foreign news websites. Distracted by Zsuzsa's new look and evening date, Eniko had for a moment put aside her anxiety about the events of the morning and the memory stick the man had had given her on the tram. Now Eniko had the sandbox, she could at least safely view the contents of the memory stick. But for that she would also need somewhere private.

This was Eniko's third job in journalism. Her first was on a local paper in the south of the country, near the Serbian border. After that she had worked for a respected business weekly, investigating the links between politicians in the ruling Social Democratic Party, the new class of oligarchs and their companies. Then the weekly was bought up by one of the same oligarchs, all the investigations were shut down and the staff given a choice of stay and receive a six-month bonus or resign by lunchtime. Eniko and about half of her colleagues had left. She had joined 555.hu soon afterwards, and had never felt as at home anywhere else.

Eniko looked around the newsroom. This had been the salon of the once-magnificent art nouveau apartment that was now home to 555.hu. Unlike most *polgari*, or bourgeois flats, it had somehow escaped being chopped up into smaller units during Communism. The apartment's grandeur had faded, but it had still kept a sense of the old Budapest a century ago, when the Hungarian capital had been the epicentre of a literary and cultural renaissance, spearheaded by its writers. The high-ceilinged rooms were still decorated with plaster cornices, although they were now grey and chipped. The windows rattled in their paint-peeling wooden frames whenever the wind blew hard or the tram passed by underneath, and the varnish on the light-wood parquet slats had long since worn away, but somehow the ramshackle surroundings perfectly suited the website's irreverent energy. And while the large black marble fireplace might be chipped and cracked in places, it was still the centrepiece of the newsroom, topped with awards that 555.hu and its reporters had won. A poster of H. L. Mencken, a famous American journalist, added to the bohemian atmosphere. Underneath the photograph of his face was his most famous quote: 'The relationship between the journalist and the politician should mirror that of the dog and the lamp post.' 'Especially in Hungary' someone had added in pen. Eniko looked ruefully at the poster, as she had done every day this week. Mencken's advice was not an accurate representation of her relationship with Reka Bardossy.

Eniko was about to go, when she heard Vivien exclaim, '*Bassza meg*! Fuck it.'

She glanced at Vivien and the monitor in front of her. The screen showed lines of code rapidly flowing downwards, while another, smaller window on the lower right-hand side showed a terminal command line, that gave access to the operating system. The screen to her right was open to Gmail. The screen to her far left showed the 555.hu website, with a ticker showing the number of visitors. Eniko did a double take when she looked at the numbers the ticker was displaying. The numbers were spinning so fast they were a blur of pixels.

'What's happening, Vivi?'

Vivien tapped rapidly at her keyboard. 'DDOS.'

'From who?' asked Eniko.

'I wish I knew. A whole army of zombie bots, coming in from all around the world. Way beyond the normal stuff.'

A Distributed Denial of Service attack meant that someone was using a massive network of computers – many of which had been surreptitiously hijacked and so were known as zombie bots – to bombard the 555.hu website with requests to view its pages. The website could not handle that number of contacts and crashed. A DDOS was the simplest kind of cyber-attack to organise – programs to run one could be easily downloaded from the Internet. And they were almost impossible to trace.

'Can you beat it off?' asked Eniko.

'I'm trying. We are usually under continual attack, but those are pinpricks, nothing our firewall can't handle. I've never seen anything like this before.'

At that moment a paunchy, balding man in his late forties strode into the newsroom. Roland Horvath, the editor in chief, was indignant. 'Vivi,' he demanded in a loud voice, 'why is our website down?'

TEN

Sandor Takacs was standing by the window, looking out at the city, deep in thought, when Balthazar stepped into his office. He breathed in the warm, stale air, was about to sit down in their usual corner alcove where two easy chairs stood next to a small coffee table, when Sandor turned around and said, 'Don't bother, Tazi. We're going out in a few minutes.'

Balthazar frowned. 'Listen, don't get me wrong, boss, but why did you call me in just to go straight out? We could have met wherever we are going. Somewhere with AC or a breeze.'

Sandor's office was like an overheated bathroom. The only thing missing was a large tub of hot water. The large picture windows showed a panoramic view of the Danube and the city, but did not open. The usually humming air-conditioner mounted on the wall was silent. A small fan stood on Sandor's desk, rotating back and forth, but merely churned the sticky air. Balthazar continued talking, 'Haven't they fixed your AC yet?'

'No. They haven't. Missing part, apparently,' said Sandor as he turned around, his forehead coated with a light sheen of sweat. 'And we can't meet where we are going. We need to arrive together.'

'Sounds exciting. Destination where, exactly?'

'You'll see.'

Balthazar walked over to Sandor's desk, which was unusually tidy. Several case folders were arranged in a neat pile on one side, while that day's issue of *Magyar Vilag* lay over Sandor's keyboard. Instead of the customary king-size ashtray full of shredded cigarettes, there was a small white dish next to his keyboard, containing several thin sticks of raw carrot. Sandor's office was a large corner room. The walls were painted a light blue, the floor was a plastic laminated parquet. The Budapest police headquarters were located next to the national police headquarters, in a complex of glass and steel buildings in the rougher end of District XIII. The walls of the room were lined with pictures of Sandor at the headquarters of the London Metropolitan police, the New York Police Department and the FBI, as well as an array of framed certificates from the courses he had completed there. A separate display showed Sandor with every prime minister since the change of system.

Balthazar was about to ask about the carrot sticks when he scanned the newspaper headline: 'More Questions over PM Bardossy's Passport Connections'. *Magyar Vilag* was usually a reliably pro-government newspaper. Under Pal Dezeffy's administration the newspaper, once a venerable institution, had been turned into little more than a propaganda rag for the ruling Social Democratic Party and the government, generously subsidised with lucrative state advertising contracts. He picked up the newspaper and quickly read the article. The story, which had no byline but which was attributed to '*Magyar Vilag* reporters', was a skilful mix of assertions, insinuations and hypotheses dressed up as fact, backed up by quotes from anonymous sources about Reka Bardossy's connection to the passport scandal that had brought down her predecessor. The article was a mishmash but its message was clear enough: Hungary's new prime minister was not as squeaky clean as she claimed to be.

Balthazar put the newspaper down and turned to Sandor. 'Pal?'

Sandor nodded. 'Of course. He won't go down without a fight. And even if he does, he will try and take Reka down with him. Pali *bacsi*, Uncle Pali, has still got plenty of supporters. There were lots of happy passengers on his gravy train. And now it's stopped, it's not certain that they want to take a trip with Reka instead.'

Balthazar looked down at the white dish. 'Speaking of gravy, you on a diet, boss?'

'My wife thinks so.' He gestured at the dish. 'Help yourself. As many as you like. If I eat any more carrots I will turn orange.'

Balthazar reached down, took a carrot stick and bit into it. It was crisp and surprisingly tasty. 'Thanks. This is pretty good.'

'I'm glad. We grow them in our garden. But that's not why I called you in.' Sandor gave Balthazar a knowing look. 'We need to talk.'

'We do.' Balthazar had a strong sense, not for the first time, that Sandor knew far more about his doings than was ideal.

The commander of Budapest's murder squad was of medium height, and stocky build. He had a fox's quick and alert small brown eyes, and thinning grey hair that every morning he carefully combed over a bald spot that was only spreading as he moved into his early sixties. Lately, Balthazar had noticed that his boss would smooth the tendrils back into place when he was anxious or mildly stressed about something. Born in a small village in the south of Hungary, near the Croatian border, Sandor might well have joined many of his relatives in the smuggling business, or eked out a living on a smallholding after graduating from high school.

But Communist officials were then on the lookout for smart countryside boys – and, occasionally, girls – to bring to the capital as part of the ruling party's social engineering project, to build a new and loyal cadre of state officials and functionaries. For the first time in Hungary's history, it had been a plus to be born poor. Sandor had been put through police training school and rapidly promoted to detective, then rose steadily through the ranks until he was appointed commander of the murder squad. Unlike in most Western European capitals, this was not an especially arduous job. The advantage of one-party dictatorships was that they usually kept crime under control. Sealed off behind the Iron Curtain, Hungary had been almost free of organised and international crime, especially because other than antiques and paintings, there had been little worth stealing. The currencies of the Soviet bloc, Hungary's included, had been almost worthless in the west. Most murders had been domestic, or bar fights that had gone wrong. Sandor's easy manner, and countryside accent, meant that most criminals – and many colleagues – had not taken him seriously at first. They had soon learned to, as had Balthazar.

Balthazar gave Sandor a resume of the events of the morning: how he had found the dead Qatari on his knees, the private ambulance, the drugs he had given to Anastasia Ferenczy to be analysed and the way the brothel's CCTV had been remotely wiped and then reversed to show Balthazar and the others in Eszter's office. 'How worried should I be? Is my family being targeted?'

Sandor looked thoughtful. 'A dead man in your brother's brothel. Someone inside the CCTV system. And they want you to know about it. I would say that's a yes.'

'I had breakfast with Anastasia. She says the Gendarmes are filming everything for some kind of final showdown.'

'She's right. Pal will fight back. As hard and dirty as he can.'

'Maybe Gaspar's CCTV system just went berserk. Computers do that sometimes. Maybe al-Nuri died of a heart attack.'

Sandor picked up a carrot stick, bit it in half and chewed thoughtfully while he looked Balthazar up and down. 'You're right. This is pretty good. Maybe I'll grow organic vegetables when I retire. But meanwhile, I still don't believe in coincidences. Al-Nuri was supposed to meet Reka Bardossy this morning. All the Gulf investments are up in the air now. That was Pal's deal. Pal certainly had the motive to get rid of al-Nuri. And he probably had the means. Pal is down but he is certainly not out. And he still has plenty of friends in high – and low – places. Such as our old colleague Attila.'

'What did the PM want with al-Nuri?'

'To get the investment deal going again, but openly and transparently. That money can transform this country.'

'And if she can get the money, she is secure as prime minister,' said Balthazar. 'All those wavering politicians in her party and the opposition, wondering how long she will last, will start to support her. She beats off any threat from Pal trying to wreck her from behind the scenes and takes Hungary into the twenty-first century.'

Sandor smiled. 'That as well. You should go into politics, Tazi, if you ever leave the force. Or with your specialist knowledge and experience, you could be one of her advisers. I'll put in a good word for you. But not for a while, please.'

'I'm happy on the streets.' He paused for a second. 'You know Reka?'

'Since she was a baby. Her father was an official at the ministry of the interior when I moved to Budapest as a young policeman, back in the 1970s.' He smiled for a moment, lost in a memory. 'Reka's father brought me to the big city. We hit it off. He took me to their house quite often.' Sandor paused. 'What a place. We had a toilet in the garden and no running hot water when I grew up. They had six bathrooms.'

Sandor reached for the carrot sticks, picked one up, shook his head, put it down, then reached into a drawer of his desk and pulled out a packet of Sopianae cigarettes, a cheap, rough Hungarian brand, now barely available. He opened the packet, took out a cigarette, held it to his nose and inhaled deeply, closing his eyes for a moment.

'I thought you had given up,' said Balthazar.

'I've given up smoking them and I've given up pulling them to pieces. This is all that's left now.'

Sandor took one last sniff, put the cigarette down on his desk and gestured for Balthazar to follow him to the window.

Balthazar had never met anyone more skilled at navigating the complicated currents of political and economic interests, while still keeping his integrity, than Sandor Takacs. Ever since they had arrived in Europe, around 1,100 years ago, the Magyars had suffered centuries of invasion and foreign domination: Tatars, Turks, Austrians, Germans and Russians had all occupied and ruled the country. The collective memories of foreign overlords had nurtured a special skill in reading the runes and working out the best way forward. All of that depended on contacts, especially contacts who could open the *kiskapu*, the little gate that gave a path around officialdom. Sandor's network was unrivalled, and reached into the other law enforcement agencies, the security services, across the political spectrum and the new class of economic oligarchs. Which was one reason why Balthazar had decided to come clean about the events of the morning. His boss would hear about the dead Qatari sooner rather than later and it was preferable if he got the news first-hand.

Balthazar and Sandor looked out at the concrete sprawl of Robert Karoly Boulevard, an eight-lane highway that spanned the city's drearier suburbs and led onto Arpad Bridge. The bridge was a brutalist concrete span that had none of the charm of the Margaret Bridge or the Chain Bridge further south and downriver. Two orange number-one trams rolled along the middle, passing each other on the way. Teve Street, home of the police headquarters, reached through the middle of District XIII. The riverside quarter was one of Budapest's larger ones. It bordered District V at Jaszai Mari Square to the south, and District IV, known as Ujpest, New Pest, to the north. The southern end of District XIII, known as Ujlipotvaros, New Leopold Town, was a middle-class, liberal area with a substantial Jewish community dubbed 'Lippy' by young hipsters, where Eniko Szalay and her mother lived. But gentrification had not reached Teve Street and its surrounds, which were home mostly to drab tenements, basement bars and boxy concrete government buildings.

Balthazar watched a white police launch race downriver, white water spilling in its wake. There were no other craft in sight and the boat's pilot swerved from side to side, bouncing on the water, clearly enjoying himself. 'That looks like fun. Maybe I should put in for a transfer to the river police.' He turned to Sandor. 'You would give me a reference, wouldn't you?'

Sandor smiled. 'Can you pilot a boat?'

'Not exactly. But I'm sure I could learn.'

'Which is the stern and which is the bow?'

Balthazar thought for a moment. 'There's one at either end. Of every boat,' he added hopefully.

Sandor laughed. 'Standard buoyage distance within the city limits?'

'Erm... can I get back to you on that?'

'Sure. Meanwhile we can talk about your knowledge of tides, currents, whirlpools, how to read the water...'

Balthazar brightened at this. 'I know that the most dangerous place is by the stanchions of a bridge, because the same volume of water keeps flowing but gets forced into a narrower area so the currents there are much faster and stronger. That's where most people drown, because they get sucked under. Like that case we had a year ago. The bankrupt banker whose creditors threw him off Margaret Bridge. So if you fall in, head for the shore as fast as you can.'

Sandor gave him a sideways look. 'It's a start. Swot up on the rest and I'll let you know next time the river police are recruiting. Meanwhile, try not to fall into the water. Especially not before your reception.'

Balthazar watched a jogger in a lime-green vest running along the pavement of Arpad Bridge, braving the traffic fumes, before turning off onto the spur that led down to Margaret Island. 'The reception. That's one of the things I wanted to talk to you about, boss. Do I really have to—'

'— turn up, in your best suit and represent the Budapest police force while Reka Bardossy hands you a medal in a nice presentation box and then power-schmooze whoever she has invited? Yes. You do. You even get to choose some of the guests.' Sandor raised an eyebrow. 'Carefully.'

Carefully, Balthazar knew, meant no Gaspar or Fat Vik. 'But—'

Sandor said, 'Sorry, Tazi, but nothing. Anyway, what's the problem?'

'You know. Family stuff. It will draw a lot of attention. To them, as well as me. I might be a good role model. But they aren't.'

Sandor's voice softened for a moment. 'Look, Tazi. I understand you don't appreciate the limelight. And I understand why. But you are already bathed in it. You're all over the Internet. Budapest is packed with reporters from every major newspaper, television channel and website from around the world. Hungary and immigration are the story of the moment. And you are the centre of that story, like it or not. The heroic cop who took down the world's most wanted Islamist while he posed as a refugee at Keleti Station. So let's find a way to make this work, for all of us. And, there is the whole... er...' Sandor paused, as he walked over to his desk and picked up a carrot stick, bit off the end and ate it slowly.

Balthazar smiled, knowing full well what was going through his boss's mind. 'Gypsy thing?'

Sandor stopped chewing. 'I wouldn't put it like that, exactly.'

'How would you put it, boss?'

Sandor smiled and looked upwards for a moment, as though remembering some lines recently learned. 'Positive role models are one of the most effective ways to break down unhelpful stereotypes. The Budapest police is an equal-opportunity employer, equally committed to advancing all of its officers' careers, including those from the Roma minority.'

Balthazar laughed. 'You mean if I accept the medal and the reception it shows that we are not all pimps and prostitutes?'

Sandor flushed red. 'That is *not* what I meant. And that's not fair.'

Balthazar smiled. 'I know, boss. Cheap shot. I'm sorry.'

Sandor nodded. 'You're forgiven. If you go to the reception.'

Sandor had been Balthazar's patron throughout his time in the Budapest police. He had supported him from his time on the street, as he rose up through the ranks to become a plainclothes detective in the murder squad. The path had sometimes been bumpy. Balthazar's colleagues reflected wider Hungarian society. Many officers, whose only encounters with Roma were when they arrested them, were suspicious of Balthazar. A few were hostile, openly racist. The more far-sighted were helpful, keen to show that law enforcement could offer a stable career and integration for a minority that was too often excluded and marginalised. Others were indifferent to Balthazar's origins, which was how he best liked it. They judged him like any other colleague: on the quality of his detective work. The Budapest police force was trying hard to move with the times. Sandor had recently spent several days in London on a diversity training course, and the force had recently started its own training programme to make its officers more aware of how Roma society worked, and of the unbreakable bonds of family loyalty that shaped their interaction with the wider world. But for all his support, and seminars in London, Sandor was still a man who had spent his formative years under Communism, in a society sealed off from western ideas of anti-racism and minority rights. However loyal and supportive he was to Balthazar, and however hard he tried, older, more ingrained ideas still endured. Police work, by its very nature, involved contact and interaction with criminals. Most of the Gypsies Sandor had met had been lawbreakers – as was a large part of Balthazar's family.

Balthazar's voice turned more serious, 'But it is a fact that my brother is the biggest pimp in the city. And my father used to be. And Gaspar runs a brothel where...'

Sandor held up his hand. 'One thing at a time. The reception is also an honour for us, the Budapest murder squad. We can always use a few more tiles in our roof. Especially ones from the prime minister's office.' He paused, about to play his trump card. 'In any case, Nora has already picked her outfit.'

Balthazar surrendered. 'OK. Case closed.'

Sandor walked over to his desk and picked up a silver-framed photograph of himself as a much younger man in his police uniform, with a proud, pretty girl with curly brown hair on his arm. Among the police Sandor was a rare example of a man who was still happily married; he had three children and nine grandchildren, a good number of whom appeared at the family home for lunch every Sunday afternoon.

'How many years now?' asked Balthazar.

'Forty next month.' Sandor put the photograph down, his round, pudgy face softening in a smile. 'Speaking of ladies, how's your friend, Eniko?' he asked, mischievously. 'She's a busy girl, bringing down the prime minister, giving non-stop interviews to the international press.'

Balthazar scowled. 'I don't know. And she's not my friend. She's my ex-girlfriend.'

'Last weekend she was overnighting in your flat when we had to arrange protection for her. Haven't you seen her this week?'

'No.'

'Shame. I always liked her.' Balthazar had brought Eniko to a couple of social events at work. Most of his colleagues had shied away from her as she was a reporter. Sandor had not. He said, 'She was smart and didn't try to milk me for information. Chance of a reconciliation?' Balthazar's boss, like every Hungarian over the age of fifty that he was close to, made no secret of his opinion that he should remarry and have more children as soon as possible.

'I don't think so. I invited her to have a burger with me and Alex and Jozsi, the Gypsy kid who was with me at Republic Square, last weekend.'

'That's a good start.'

'Doesn't look like it. She said she would come, then didn't turn up. She sent a text message saying she could not come.'

'Shame. And Sarah?'

'Actually, she's being a little less difficult than usual. She brought Alex to meet me on Sunday and was quite friendly.'

Sandor's shrewd eyes narrowed. 'What does she want?'

'Help with her dissertation. She's worried she won't get tenure at CEU.'

'What's the dissertation about?'

Balthazar concentrated hard for a moment. 'I think I have this right. "Gendering the domestic bio-space: a study of inter-familial power dynamics in Roma society".'

Sandor nodded slowly. 'Which means?'

'Gypsy women run the show in Hungary.'

Sandor laughed. 'Not only Gypsies. And not only in Hungary. Maybe I should be a professor. And don't worry about Eniko. She was probably busy working. Anyway, now that you're famous, the girls will be lining up. There are plenty more *fogas* in Lake Balaton.'

Sandor squeezed Balthazar's shoulder for several seconds. Balthazar closed his eyes for a moment, a wave of emotion, completely unexpected, breaking over him. He had never missed his father as much as in these last few days. The two men had not spoken for years. Laszlo Kovacs was so enraged when Balthazar had joined the police that he demanded that the Kris, the Roma communal court, rule that his son be ostracised. Such a punishment, the most severe in the Gypsy code, would have severed all of Balthazar's connections with his family. For a Roma ostracism was a virtual death sentence. As a child Balthazar had heard stories, a mix of fact and fable – it was impossible to know which was which – about Gypsies, generations back, who had been ostracised, walked into the forest and had never been seen again. But Marta, Balthazar's mother, had petitioned for him. Eventually the Kris had ruled that Balthazar could see his male relatives and return to the courtyard of the family's apartment block on Jozsef Street whenever he liked, but female relatives, including Marta, could only meet Balthazar with Laszlo's permission. Balthazar was banned from family events and needed his father's permission to enter the actual family home.

All of that was manageable, more or less. Gypsies were not known for sticking to the rules, especially when close family was involved, even where the Kris had issued a ruling. Marta and Flora, Balthazar's gallery-owner sister, met him away from Jozsef Street. Laszlo knew, of course, but his anger had mellowed over the years. And as Marta reminded him occasionally, like many Roma men, he had no idea how to cook or run a household. Recently several birthday parties had been organised in restaurants or the homes of friends and relatives, ostensibly for space reasons as the Kovacs clan grew in numbers, but everyone understood it was mainly so that Balthazar could attend. At the most recent celebration, for Fat Vik's birthday a month ago, Laszlo had acknowledged his son with a terse nod, which Balthazar guessed counted as progress. The trickiest part, especially on days like these, was that the Kris had ruled that Balthazar would never share any information with the police on any investigation into criminal activity that was connected to his family. If that rule was broken, full ostracism would follow.

Balthazar swallowed, and tried to keep his voice light as he replied, 'Sure, and those *fogas* have all got very sharp teeth. Boss, can we talk about something else? I am sure you didn't call me in to discuss my marriage prospects. Because that's a very short conversation. And we need to talk about...'

Sandor's voice turned serious. 'We will, I told you. Just be patient. So, the reception is settled.'

Balthazar looked again at the line of photographs of Sandor with the country's prime ministers. Pal Dezeffy was still there, grinning with his arm around Sandor's shoulder. Sandor was smiling, holding out in front of him a small, velvet-lined box that contained the Cross of the Merit medal, a great honour.

Balthazar looked at the photograph of Pal, then at Sandor. 'There's something I need to tell you about Pal.'

'I'm listening.'

Balthazar took out his mobile telephone and played the sound file of Pal ordering his murder.

Sandor exhaled. '*Micsoda kocsog.*' *Kocsog* literally meant 'jug', but in slang roughly translated as 'prison bitch'. It was probably the worst in the very colourful litany of Magyar swearwords. Sandor's face, usually jovial, hardened and his eyes narrowed. 'So he wanted to kill one of my officers. We'll see about that. The fake police officers who tried to take you in are still in hospital, that private place out near Huvosvolgy.' Huvosvolgy was a rich suburb of Buda. 'They must be working for Pal. They refused to give any identification or information. We cannot get to them. They are in a private room, and there are two Gendarmes on the door, twenty-four hours a day.'

For a moment Balthazar was back in Goran Draganovic's Lada Niva, on a dark lane in the back of District X, heading back to the city after the cage fight last Saturday night when they had been stopped by Gendarmes driving Toyota SUVs who were pretending to be police officers. A car chase had ensued, resolved when Balthazar and Goran used thunder flashes and stun grenades to make sure the Toyotas crashed into each other.

'So what are we going to do about it? Can't we arrest Pal?' asked Balthazar. 'Conspiracy to murder. All here, captured on a sound file.'

Sandor shook his head. 'No. It's a start, but it's not enough. It's digital. His lawyers will shred it. Nowadays anything can be faked. Where did you get it?'

'Where do you think?'

'Anastasia.'

'Of course.'

Sandor said, 'Be careful of her. She's very charming and helpful when she wants to be, but she and her bosses have their own agenda. It overlaps with ours but it's not the same. We want to arrest the bad guys and put them away. They want to turn them, play games, plot with their friends in the CIA and MI6.'

'So what are we going to do?'

'For the moment, nothing, while we consider our options. The person we are going to see will be very interested to hear your recording.' Sandor glanced at his watch. 'Gyuri will be here in a couple of minutes. Let's go.'

ELEVEN

Eniko stepped through the door and closed it gently behind her, the IBM laptop in her right hand, her iPhone in the pocket of her jeans. At first glance, the circular room – the inside of a small turret above the roof of the building – looked exactly the same as usual. The walls, once white, now a dirty shade of cream; the trio of closed, curved windows that looked out onto Blaha Lujza Square, their cracked frames shedding shards of white paint like a snake renewing its skin; a single light bulb dangling from the ceiling; and the small, brown 1960s armchair that Eniko had carried up the stairs one weekend when nobody was around, in its usual place, by the centre pane. This was her favourite place, an architect's folly reached by a narrow, winding staircase, an eagle's eyrie over the city, her private refuge. Somewhere she could admit, even if only to herself, that she was nervous and may even be out of her depth.

As soon as Eniko took a couple of paces and stepped into the room she knew that someone had recently been there. She had a sense for places, could pick up the vibrations of what had happened there. In somewhere like Budapest, where too much had happened, that was a curse as well as a blessing. The air in the room felt heavy, almost oppressive, charged with something. She breathed in slowly through her nose. The smell banished any doubts. The room's base odour – dust, rusty pipes – was still there, but today there was something extra: a whiff of sweat and cigarettes. Only a faint trace of a man, but definitely there.

Eniko reached for the old-fashioned light switch that was mounted on the wall near the door frame: a small black peg, perhaps half an inch long, poking out of a round black Bakelite holder that dated back to the 1950s, if not before the Second World War. The switch was untouched, still caked in dust, but that meant nothing.

Eniko was about to switch the light on, when some sixth sense told her not to. If she was right, if someone else had been here, then why send a signal that she was now? The windows were covered with lace curtains, unwashed for decades – she often wondered who had placed them there, a pair of lovers, she liked to think, meeting secretly in the daylight hours – thin, but enough to mask her movements. Eniko walked over to her armchair and sat in it, closed her eyes for a moment. The chair was low, barely a foot off the ground. That male tang was definitely stronger here, as though whoever had been inside the turret had spent more time by the windows, perhaps by even this window.

She opened her eyes, took out her iPhone, tapped out her passcode and opened WhatsApp. Three photos had arrived that morning, sent from 'A friend'. Eniko had tried several times to call the number that supposedly sent the photos, but each time it was unobtainable. One showed the man she now knew was Mahmoud Hejazi, the Gardener, entering a modernist villa somewhere in Buda; another pictured him leaving the same place. The third showed him standing inside the house, talking to a woman. The woman's face was clear: Reka Bardossy. None of this was proof of anything. The photographs, she knew, could be faked, or photoshopped. Nowadays the tools to create fake news, including fake images, were easily available. She could easily ask her colleagues in the photo department to take a look at the files and also check the metadata that was usually included in any digital image, that recorded the type of camera used and the date and time that the photograph was taken. But Eniko was reluctant to have the photographs leave her possession until she decided how to proceed. And in a way, nowadays it mattered less whether the images were genuine: in the age of the insta-smear they would be explosive, no matter how strong Reka's denials. Eniko smiled for a moment, remembering once again her conversation with Reka in the Four Seasons Hotel: *'As I understand it, the time to frame a story, to shape how it is covered, is when it is first reported. Is that correct?'* The story would be that Hungary's new prime minister had met at home with one of the world's most wanted Islamic radicals. And Eniko had it first. Now what?

She could – should – show the photographs to Reka and ask her if they were genuine. In any case Eniko would have to give the prime minister a chance to comment if 555.hu was going to use them. Or, she could show them to Roland Horvath, the editor, and let him decide how to proceed. But Roland, Eniko knew, also had an agenda. Roland had been appointed by Sandor Kaplan. Like his friend and business partner, Pal, Kaplan had been a leader of the Communist Youth organisation in the 1980s. After the change of system, during *vadkapitalizmus*, both men had used their party connections to swiftly buy up valuable formerly state-owned property and companies for almost nothing. By the early 1990s both Pal and Kaplan were dollar multi-millionaires. So Roland, as a Pal ally, would push Eniko to use the photographs as soon as possible. He had already been putting her under pressure to find something on Reka, complaining that Eniko's stream of scoops were too one-sided. Well, now she had found something on Reka without any effort – there it was, sitting on the screen of her iPhone. And part of Eniko knew that whatever Roland's agenda, he was right. By any standards, even the ultra-partisan ones of the Hungarian media, these photographs were news. There was a chance, she guessed, that the photographs had been sent, or would be, to other journalists. But for the moment at least Eniko was the biggest name in Hungarian journalism, and they would have the most impact under her byline. She ran her fingers through her hair, rolled her shoulders and stretched. Reka's photos, she decided, could wait another hour or two. Meanwhile, there was something else she had to deal with.

She was about to fire up the IBM and insert the memory stick when her telephone rang. She took it out of her pocket and looked at the screen, which displayed 'PMO', short for prime minister's office. Eniko had already received several calls from Reka's staff and a couple of times from Reka herself, asking her to come in for a meeting. Eniko took the call and listened while Akos Feher spoke. Yes, she was free this afternoon at one o'clock, she said. Yes, she could come to Parliament. But why? Akos did not answer, except to say that an entry pass in her name would be waiting for her and that she should be on time.

Eniko shrugged. 'Sure, OK. I'll be there.' To get my lines, while Reka feeds them to me, she almost said. Instead she hung up, put the sandbox on her lap, and inserted the memory stick into one of the USB ports. A small window opened up showcasing the video file and she pressed play. An acid flush filled her stomach. The clip showed Eniko leaving her apartment that morning – she was wearing the same clothes – walking down Pozsonyi Way to the tram stop near Jaszai Mari Square, and standing waiting for the number-four tram. The threat was clear: we know who you are, where you live and what your routines are. None of this was exactly hard to find out, but it still chilled Eniko to know that she had been tailed and covertly filmed.

For a moment she heard Attila Ungar's voice, as she sat in front of him in the cold, damp, abandoned building somewhere on Csepel Island last Saturday, a female Gendarme at the door. After a long pause, Attila had claimed that the woman at the door was called Tereza.

Te-re-za. One of our Christian saints.

Tereza was Eniko's mother's name. She took out her telephone, started to call Balthazar before remembering that he was not taking her calls. Her hand was shaking, her fingers sliding over the screen. She stopped for a moment, breathed deeply several times and forced herself to stay calm. She waited fifteen seconds, blocked her outgoing number and called Balthazar again. His telephone rang and rang unanswered. She was about to hang up when she heard his voice.

'Hi, Tazi, it's me,' she said.

'Eniko? It says unknown number.'

'I blocked it. I'm getting some weird calls lately. But nothing from you. Aren't you talking to me any more?' she asked, trying to keep her voice light and cheerful. She felt the handset tremble slightly against her ear, hoped he could not sense it in her voice. 'I'm so sorry I couldn't make it on Sunday. How were the burgers? How's Alex?'

'Fine. Him too.' Balthazar's voice was terse.

'I tried to call you a few times. How's your head?'

'Good, thanks. No more headaches. I've been busy. Not as busy as you, though. Congratulations on all your stories.'

'Where are you? You sound like you're outside.'

'I am. So what's new? Can I help you with something?'

Eniko took a deep breath. What did she expect? At least she finally had him on the line. It was time to apologise, to try and rebuild, at least a friendly relationship. Then she could tell him that she was scared and really wanted to see him. 'Tazi,' she said, looking for the right words, 'I'm a bit… Look, I'm really sorry about Sunday. I wanted to come. I was excited to meet Alex. I'd just really like to…'

'Really like to what?' asked Balthazar, his voice softening a fraction.

She was about to answer when she glimpsed something on the floor by the window, a round metal cylinder with a pointed tip, about half an inch wide and four inches long, its case a dull brown colour. She crouched down. Her eyes widened. Was it what she thought it was? She had never seen one in real life. The silence stretched out as she stared downwards.

Eventually Balthazar said, 'Eni, what's happening? Are you OK?'

She reached forward with her left hand, her nervousness now morphing into excitement as she picked up the slim, brassy cylinder, rolling it between her fingers. It *was* what she thought. 'Nothing. I'm fine. Tazi, I'm really sorry, I've got to go. I'll call you back later.'

Parliament, 11.40 a.m.

Gyuri Balazs, Sandor's driver, was waiting for Balthazar and his boss a couple of hundred yards away, parked outside a nondescript apartment block halfway down Csongor Street. Fresh graffiti by the entrance proclaimed *Migransok haza*, Migrants go home. As Balthazar walked towards the vehicle – an Audi, he guessed – he looked at his iPhone screen as though Eniko might be hiding behind it. Shaking his head with irritation, he then put it back in his trouser pocket. Despite everything that had happened, the sound of Eniko's voice had rekindled a tiny spark of hope. For a moment he thought that she sounded genuinely contrite and that she still wanted to see him. Perhaps she had a good reason for not turning up on Sunday. He should at least take her calls, hear her out. They were adults, after all. They both had a lot going on in their lives, especially at the moment. Then, just as he was thawing, something else had beeped on her radar, something far more important, obviously, and he was dismissed. What more do you want? he asked himself. You fell in love with her, introduced her to your family, were about to ask her to move in and she dumped you. The only reason she calls or wants to see you is to advance her journalistic career. That's why she blocked her outgoing number, because that was the only way to get you to take her call. And her career is doing just fine. He could still hear Eniko's voice in his head. He knew the cadences and timbres of her voice. She sounded nervous. There was something almost pleading about her tone: 'I was excited to meet Alex. Tazi, I'd really like to...'

Balthazar stepped aside to let a weary-looking elderly lady holding a carrier bag filled with carrots and potatoes pass by. Really like to what? It didn't matter and he had enough other things to think about. And not all of them were doom and gloom – for instance, there was the trip he had planned this Saturday with Alex and Sarah. He had not seen his son since their burger outing the previous Sunday, although they had texted each other during the week, and he had even managed a quick conversation when Alex was for once out of sight and earshot of his mother. Balthazar was no longer in love with Sarah – Eniko had at least chased away that ghost – but the end of his marriage still pained him. Even as their relationship faded away, he had tried to fix things, to make it work, if only for Alex's sake. But Sarah had been insistent. She had fallen in love with a woman, and they were moving in together. A part of him had hoped that Sarah would be a bridge, help him span the chasm between his two worlds: of the Gypsies and the *gadje*. That had not worked out, but at least he had a son. Only one, and no daughters. By Gypsy standards, for a man in his mid-thirties that was considered a meagre result – and especially meagre when Sarah still used Alex as a kind of control mechanism, restricting Balthazar's access even when it was his turn to have the boy over, or take him out for the day. On Saturday, at least, on the trip to Nagyszentfalu, Balthazar would be in control.

Sandor, who had diplomatically walked on ahead while Balthazar spoke to Eniko, was already sitting inside the vehicle when he reached it. Balthazar's guess was right. The car was a black Audi A6 with tinted windows, the preferred mode of transport for high-ranking government officials and politicians – as well as oligarchs and mafiosi who wanted the appearance of respectability. The paintwork shone like polished obsidian and the chrome door handles glinted in the bright summer sunlight. The car sat low on wide, thick tyres. It was a much fancier vehicle than usual. Sandor's driver usually drove his boss in a Volkswagen saloon. Gyuri stood waiting by the side of the Audi. He had worked for Sandor for more than twenty years. They both came from the same village in the south of Hungary and Gyuri was married to one of Sandor's cousins. Gyuri was in his late fifties, balding, with small blue eyes, round shoulders and slightly bowed legs. He was barely five feet six tall, but his unprepossessing appearance was deceptive: he was an instructor on the police service's advance driving course and could handle any car under the most extreme conditions. He held the door open as Balthazar approached, exposing a beige leather shoulder holster and the dull metallic grip of a Glock pistol.

'*Tisztelettem*, Lieutenant Kovacs,' said Gyuri. Hungarians were generally very polite. There were three levels of formality in everyday speech. *Tisztelettem*, which meant 'I honour you' or 'I respectfully greet you' was the most polite. Gyuri held the rank of captain, more senior than Balthazar, but still used the honorific.

Balthazar returned the greeting, looking the Audi up and down as he did so. 'Nice car. What happened to the vw?'

Gyuri shrugged. 'Came to the end of its useful life.' He leaned forward and ran his hand over the bonnet. 'I like this one better.'

Balthazar looked at Gyuri's holster, which was now exposed. Hungarian police officers were usually armed with a FEG PA-63 pistol, a clone of the Walter PPK. The FEG was a cheap weapon, mass-produced under Communism, and still in service. Gyuri's holster held a Glock 17, a heavier-calibre gun that did not jam and had serious stopping power. Balthazar asked, 'Are we expecting trouble, Gyuri?'

He smiled, revealing a row of small, neat teeth. 'I hope not,' he replied, as he opened the door. 'Shall we...?'

Balthazar slid into the vehicle next to Sandor and Gyuri closed the door behind him. Balthazar could feel the weight of the door as it swung back into place. Gyuri scanned the street in both directions, swiftly moved into the vehicle and started the engine, which barely sounded. The seats were covered with soft, light-brown leather, divided by a large armrest with a deep indentation that contained three small bottles of chilled mineral water. The passenger compartment was separated from the driver's area with a partition, also covered in leather, that reached up to the height of the window. There were two small screens on either side of the partition, with a touch menu offering television or Internet. The remainder of the space was filled by a tinted glass partition. Balthazar tapped the car window on his side with the joint of his forefinger. The glass felt much thicker and more solid than usual.

'Should I be worried, boss?' he asked. 'It's armoured. The windows are bulletproof. Gyuri is armed.'

Sandor laughed. 'No. And we can talk here. It's probably safer than my office. That's swept for bugs every morning and evening, but nowadays you can never be sure.' He turned to Balthazar. 'You said you wanted to talk. I'm listening.'

Balthazar looked out of the window as the car turned on to Papp Karoly Street, another small side street, then turned again onto Robert Karoly Boulevard, heading towards the river. The driver drove fast and smoothly, navigating a swift path through the traffic, then turned again onto Vaci Way. The road was a wide thoroughfare that led north to Vac, a small town outside Budapest from where it took its name, and south to Nyugati Western Station. The car turned south, zipping down the bus lane.

Balthazar asked, 'Where are we going?'

'The very heart of the city. There is someone who very much wants to meet you. She's really looking forward to it.'

She. An Audi kitted out like this, and a driver with a gun and an earpiece heading downtown. That was a clear enough answer. Perhaps he could talk her out of this reception idea. He had another proposal instead. Balthazar sat back for a moment, his mind drifting through the events of the morning. The dead man was bad enough, but beyond that, the visit to the house had unsettled him, as it always did. Balthazar's family had taken ownership of the property almost twenty years ago. He could still remember his parents arguing about it, his mother shouting that they did not want that damned house, did not need it, his father's terse replies. Both his parents had fallen silent when Balthazar had walked into the kitchen to ask what the matter was. His father walked over to the fridge, opened a beer and drained half of it in one go, then walked out the room. His mother had busied herself chopping onions and garlic for the family's dinner. Marta had wiped her eyes, sniffed loudly and brushed off his questions about why they were shouting. His father had refused point-blank to talk about it. This was the second time the house had been redecorated, but however much paint was slathered over the walls, however expensive the renovation, however fancy the redesign of the garden, the house had never felt comfortable, and not just because of the business it hosted.

Perhaps it was haunted. Enough buildings in Budapest were. There were legions of ghosts drifting through the city: dispossessed aristocrats lingering in their palaces up and down Andrassy Avenue; middle-class Jewish families in the art deco apartment blocks of District XIII; long-vanished Schwab traders lurking on the hill named for them in Buda. There had once been a small prayer room in what was now the Kovacs family apartment building on Jozsef Street. Before the war, the area had been home to a substantial Jewish community. The space was now used for storage, but there were still brown marks on the paintwork where the benches had been fixed to the walls. At night in his childhood, when he could not sleep, Balthazar had more than once heard distant voices chanting in a strange language. He had asked his mother if she had heard anything. She shook her head, told him he had an over-active imagination, but the look on her face told her she had. And there was his own ghost. She did not speak to him, but sometimes he felt her presence.

He closed his eyes for a moment, banishing the memory of the white coffin in the parlour of her family home, wishing himself back more than twenty years to Mikszath Kalman Square, eating ice cream in the sunshine of an early summer's day, stolen moments in a new world bursting with possibilities, even for Gypsies. Today his ghost was especially persistent. He didn't mind, welcomed her back, in fact. Almost without realising it, he had taken a decision, one long overdue, at least since he became a policeman. He could feel her approval, or so he liked to think.

The trick would be getting Sandor on board. Opening a cold case was never welcomed, especially one with a personal connection. But his stock was high at the moment. And if Sandor refused, or made things difficult, he would find a way. In Hungary, there was always a way. The *kiskapu* led everywhere. It was just a question of finding the right *kapu*, and the entrance fee, if need be. Balthazar watched the shop fronts and stores of Vaci Way slide past, feeling more settled now. The shops here, like much of Budapest, were being replaced with the kind of stores, restaurants and coffee chains to be found in any European city. Old apartment buildings were being knocked down, replaced with uniform steel-and-glass office blocks. There was so much money sloshing around the city now, a good part of it, he knew, ending up in his family's businesses.

The car pulled up at the traffic lights by Nyugati Station, under the Ferdinand Bridge, another concrete monument to Communist-era brutalism that blocked the view of Nyugati and reached over the Grand Boulevard. Across the other side of the boulevard, an ugly 1970s concrete shopping centre loomed over a small piazza and an underpass that led to the station. An enormous version of the now-familiar poster showing Pal and his associates linked with a spider's web and draped in red was hung over one side of the shopping centre.

Sandor and Balthazar both looked at the poster. '*Kirugjuk a komcsikat*. Let's kick out the commies. Who's paying for these?' asked Balthazar.

Sandor said, 'I don't know. Someone on the right wing, I guess. A frustrated oligarch, or would-be oligarch.'

'Are there still Communist-era networks? It's twenty-five years since the change of system.'

'Who won the last election and the one before that?'

'The Social Democrats.'

'Successors to?'

'The Communists. But there were proper elections,' said Balthazar. 'We are a democracy now. Upright members of the EU and NATO. Wouldn't they be worried if it turned out there'd been no real change of system after all?'

Sandor patted Balthazar's knee. '*Kedves Tazikam*. Yes, of course there were proper, free elections. The system's changed.' He gave his protégé an affectionate look. 'But you know the old saying, the more things change, the more they...'

Balthazar said, '... stay the same.'

'Exactly. The *elvtarsok*, the comrades, have always known how to give themselves a helping hand: in the media, doling out nice state tenders, in other, less visible ways. Once a group of people run a country for decades, they make sure that even if they have to give up power they will still have influence behind the scenes.' He paused. 'More to the point, when will you get the forensics results from Anastasia?'

'Soon, I hope – tonight.'

'What else, Tazi? I can see there's something else on your mind.'

Balthazar's voice turned serious. 'Boss, there is something else I want to talk about.'

'I'm listening.'

'I want to re-open an old case. I'll be honest with you. It's personal.'

TWELVE

Eniko had just handed the IBM laptop back to Vivi when she saw Roland Horvath looming over the front of her desk. 'Can I see you in my office, please?' he asked.

Eniko said, 'Sure, I just need to finish typing up my notes.'

He shook his balding head. 'No, you need to come now.'

Eniko glanced at Zsuzsa, who sat at a desk nearby, well within earshot. Zsuzsa shrugged and gave her a quizzical look. Eniko said, 'I'm on my way.'

Eniko followed Roland across the newsroom to his office, the loose parquet rattling under her feet. He closed the door firmly behind him after they walked in. The space was the largest room in the former apartment, but sparsely furnished. The white walls were bare, as was his desk, apart from a computer, a keyboard, that day's newspapers and a framed photograph of Wanda, his teenage daughter. On the other side of the room half a dozen chairs were arranged around a plain brown wooden table, where the senior editors gathered for conference. A silver laptop was open on Roland's desk, its screen facing the editor. Sitting in one of the chairs was Kriszta Matyas, the news editor. Like her boss, she had recently arrived from the state media. Roland had worked as a political reporter for the state television channel, where he was known mainly for the softball questions he respectfully asked of ministers and government officials. Kriszta, a thin brunette in her forties, had worked on the foreign desk of the state news agency, churning out dutiful copy about the visits of foreign dignitaries and the latest trade deals. She was dressed in a formal blue jacket and skirt and wore heavy make-up, which made her quite out of place among the irreverent bohemians of 555.hu. Roland was dressed in his customary baggy jeans and an ill-fitting white shirt which ballooned out at the sides. Eniko and her news editor were not allies. Eniko spent much time rebuffing Kriszta's demands to include ever more and longer quotes from officials in her stories, especially when they had embarrassed Pal Dezeffy or his government.

Roland led Eniko to the table and bade her sit down in front, while he and the news editor sat facing her. Printouts of her stories were piled up in the centre of the table. This was not, she knew, good news. Eniko tried to force herself to concentrate, which was difficult with a used cartridge in the front pocket of her jeans. It was about five or six centimetres long and tapered at the end. Eniko did not know anything about guns, but she had seen enough films to guess that this was a rifle bullet, not pistol ammunition. Was this the actual cartridge of the bullet that had shot Mahmoud Hejazi? She guessed so, for there had only been one shot. It was a strange feeling to have something in her pocket that had taken a man's life. Eniko realised now that she had almost certainly found the nest of the sniper who had shot Mahmoud Hejazi the previous weekend. What was surprising was it seemed nobody else had been there. Presumably it was not hard to work out the trajectory of the bullet. The slug, she knew, had passed through Hejazi's body and become embedded in the tarmac, from where a forensics team had later dug it out. The 555.hu building was the only one in the neighbourhood with a round mini-tower above the roof. Video footage of Balthazar's dramatic takedown of the Islamist terrorist had gone viral around the world. Eniko, like many reporters, had tried to follow up and find out more about the shooter but had been stonewalled. The city morgue had no record of the body arriving. All the police would say was that their enquiries were continuing. Her political contacts had nothing to add and quickly shut down the conversation when she started to probe further. How could the dead body of one of the world's most wanted Islamic radicals just disappear after being shot dead outside her office? It all smelled strongly of a cover-up. She needed someone who operated among the police and officialdom and Budapest's underworld. But only one person fit that bill, and she had to use subterfuge so he would take her calls.

Meanwhile, judging by the stern looks on the faces of her editors, and the printouts of her stories, she had more immediate issues to deal with. Although she was not sure why. Thanks to her scoops about Pal Dezeffy and his resignation, 555.hu was the most-read news website in the country. Traffic was up to record levels and advertisers were pouring in. Some of her stories had been translated into English and there was even talk of launching a smaller, English-language version of the site. So why did her bosses look so severe this morning? If this was an ambush she had better go on the offensive. She sat up, smiled and said, 'You both must be pleased. More readers, more traffic, means more advertising and more revenue. We're doing well.'

'Yes. But our website is not,' said Roland. 'It's been out for most of the morning. And now there's this.' He turned the laptop around to face Eniko. 'This is our home page. Or what you get if you try to reach our home page.'

Eniko looked at the screen. Black letters on a white background that filled the screen proclaimed: 'Stop the lies and propaganda. Tell us the truth about Reka Bardossy. #honestreportingHungary'.

'I am telling the truth about Reka Bardossy,' said Eniko, trying to sound as convincing as she could, but now feeling even more unsettled. First the film of her going to work, then the bullet, and now this: a website hack aimed straight at her. The hashtag was an especially smart move, she thought.

'Are you?' asked Kriszta. 'Are you really?'

She began to read from the top sheet of printouts: 'A sting operation to catch Islamic radicals. Ms Bardossy is said to be fully cooperating with Hungarian and international authorities.' Kriszta put the paper down and picked up another printout: 'Western intelligence services confirm that Pal Dezeffy had direct links with Gulf financiers directly linked to Islamic radicals.' Kriszta then read from a third sheet: 'A source close to the government confirmed that the police are investigating Pal Dezeffy's financial links to the Gulf.' She put the papers aside. 'We are not in the PR business, Eniko. This is a news website. You are a reporter, not Reka Bardossy's spin doctor. If you want that job then why don't you apply? I'm sure you'll get it. She needs a new press chief. And then maybe we will get our website back.'

Eniko felt a dull anger rise inside her, partly because Kriszta's barbs had hit a nerve. But they would not go unchallenged. She stared at Kriszta as she spoke, 'Spin doctor. One who manipulates the news, glossing over inconvenient truths.' She picked up her mobile phone and quickly flicked through her emails until she found the one she wanted. Before Kriszta had arrived from the state news agency, Zsuzsa Barcsy had compiled some articles that she had edited. Eniko started reading, 'Pal Dezeffy welcomed Abdullah Nursultan, the president of Uzbekistan, to Hungary, and said he was looking forward to further deepening political, economic and cultural cooperation between the two countries, before presenting him with the Cross of the Republic. Have you ever read an Amnesty International report on Uzbekistan, Kriszta? They boil dissidents alive.'

Kriszta shrugged, 'Sadly, we don't live in a perfect world. Hungary is a small country and does not have the luxury of choosing its trading partners. And your reporting is far from perfect.'

Eniko looked at Roland for support. He flushed pink and looked down at the table. Eniko then fixed her gaze on Kriszta as she spoke. 'OK, let's talk about my reporting. Have you ever been taken off a train by plainclothes Gendarmes in the pursuit of a story for this website, held and interrogated?'

Kriszta blinked first and looked away. 'No.'

'Have you had members of your family threatened while working for 555.hu? Needed police protection?' Been sent a video of your movements this morning, she was about to add, but then thought better of it, fighting to keep her anger under control.

'No,' said Kriszta.

'Then please choose your words more wisely.'

Roland began to speak. He was visibly nervous now. Roland was notorious for his hatred of confrontation, which had left a notable power vacuum on the editorial floor. A vacuum, it was now clear, that had been filled by Kriszta. He was also perhaps, Eniko thought, remembering their uncomfortable encounter the previous week at Retro-kert, a ruin pub in District VII, where he had insisted on meeting Eniko for a drink, before offering her the position of editor of szilky.hu, a gossip website. Roland tried to take a more conciliatory tone than Kriszta. 'Eniko, we know how much traffic your stories have pulled in, and how our advertising revenue is up, in large part thanks to your reporting.' He paused for a moment, re-arranged the sheet of printouts, then patted them. 'There is some excellent work in here. But Reka Bardossy was minister of justice while this was going on. The jihadis' passports came from her ministry, were supplied by her officials. Whether or not she was running a sting operation, she knew about it. There was a lot of money sloshing around. She was probably getting a cut. We need that as well.'

Kriszta leaned forward. 'Exactly. Take her for more gin and tonics. Find out how much. You're a reporter. It's your story. Get digging.'

Roland said, 'We want something to run on Monday next week. Or...'

'Or what?' asked Eniko.

Kriszta said, 'Szilky.hu still needs an editor.'

Now Eniko felt like pulling the cartridge out of her pocket and standing it on the table, its tip pointing at the ceiling, and saying, 'Here's something I found in our roof this morning. The bullet that killed Mahmoud Hejazi. You can run that next Monday.' That would shut both of them up. She was furious inside at the open threat, especially because part of what they said, about letting Reka off the hook, had an element of truth. But there was no need to show it, not yet. Instead she nodded, looked first at Kriszta, then at Roland, acknowledging the new power dynamic. 'You're right. I'm on it.'

★

On Vaci Way, approaching Nyugati Station, 11.50 a.m.

Sandor asked, 'How old is this case?'

The car stopped at a pedestrian crossing. Balthazar watched a woman in her mid-thirties cross, holding a toddler by the hand. About the age she would have been by now. 'Twenty years ago. The summer of 1995.'

'That's a long time ago. I'm not even sure the files will still exist. Which one?'

'Virag Kovacs.'

Sandor blinked, looked out of the car window for several seconds before he answered. For a moment Balthazar thought he stiffened, but when he spoke, his voice was casual. 'Opening a cold case that's more than two decades old is a big hassle, Tazi. Why?'

Balthazar knew that for now at least, after the events of the previous weekend, he had some credit. It would be very hard for Sandor to refuse his request. Especially when he explained why he wanted to re-open the case. 'Virag Kovacs was my cousin. She drowned in the swimming pool at a villa in Buda.'

'Your cousin? Whose party? Whose villa?'

Balthazar looked at his boss as he replied. Sandor's hand was gripping the arm rest, his fingers tight against the leather. Something was going on here. But what? These were the obvious questions and Balthazar had tried to answer them several times over the last few years. So far he had found out nothing concrete. It was almost as if the party had never taken place. The coroner's report was barely more than a couple of paragraphs long and had said Virag's death had been an accident. It did not even include the address where she had died, which was a basic error of omission. Balthazar would have liked to ask the coroner for more information, but he was long dead. All Balthazar knew – had heard, really, and could not confirm – was that the party had been some kind of society event, hosted by up-and-coming young politicians in the Social Democrat Party, which had recently won its first election. Balthazar replied, 'I don't know. That's why I want to re-open the case.'

Sandor lifted his right hand, ran it across his scalp, looked away for a moment. 'Virag Kovacs. 1995. OK, I'll look into it.'

The car pulled up at the traffic lights by Nyugati Station. Two trams crossed in front of them, one heading to Margaret bridge, the other towards Oktogon. Four Gendarmes stood by the stairs that led into the station, checking passers-by and their papers. The Audi's indicators were not on, so Balthazar knew that the driver would continue straight, down Bajcsy-Zsilinszky Way, and most likely make a right turn onto Alkotmany Street, into District V, home to most of the government ministries and Kossuth Square. He was right. The car soon turned onto Alkotmany Street, past rows of grandiose apartment buildings, an upmarket designer dress boutique and a shop with a tank of live lobsters in its window. Parliament stood at the end of the street, the green, red and white banner flag of Hungary rippling gently in the breeze.

A block before Kossuth Square, the car turned right onto Vajkay Street, looping around behind the Ethnographic Museum, then turned left onto Szalay Street, a much wider thoroughfare. A black Gendarmerie van was parked on the left side, by the corner of the museum, two Gendarmes leaning against it, smoking and chatting. On the other side of the street stood a grey police van. Three male officers and one female police officer stood around the vehicle, warily watching the Gendarmes. One of the Gendarmes flicked his cigarette butt at the police, then gave the female officer the finger, raising his chin in her direction, as if to say 'Come and get me if you dare'. Sandor and Balthazar watched as she was about to walk across the road, when one of her colleagues shook his head and gently held her arm to hold her back. She had bright red hair, Balthazar saw. She stopped and gave the Gendarmes the finger back twice, one from each hand. Balthazar smiled as she mouthed something that looked very much like *fasz* – prick.

The long-standing hostility between the two forces was now barely contained. Both sides knew that open conflict was now inevitable.

Sandor told the driver to stop for a moment, pressed a button so the window slid down. The police officers were suspicious and alert, and started walking over, but smiled when they saw Sandor's face. The red-haired officer saluted Sandor and Balthazar, then asked, 'How much longer do we have to put up with this, sir? I thought this was sorted out last weekend, at the Four Seasons.'

Sandor smiled. 'Not much longer, I hope. We are working on it, but we are not there yet.'

Sandor glanced at the Velcro name tag attached to her tunic: Takacs. It was a very common name in Hungary. 'Are we relatives?' he asked. 'May I ask your first name?'

'Veronika, sir. You can call me Vera.'

'Then probably not. But be careful, Vera.'

'Yes, sir,' she said, saluting again.

Sandor nodded, closed the window and the Audi turned right onto Falk Miksa Street, past the ABS headquarters, until it could finally turn left onto Balaton Street, then left again onto Balassi Balint, where it followed the number-two tram line until Kossuth Square. Here too the street was lined with grand apartment blocks along one side of the tram lines, facing the river, garlanded with cherubs smiling and gargoyles leering from the roofs, corners wrapped in ornate balconies. On the other side a smart wooden fence, interspersed with stylised concrete reliefs of athletes, marked the Olimpia Park. Balthazar often came here with Alex who loved to climb around the new, modern playground. A gaggle of Chinese tourists stood outside the Amata shop, staring at the array of dark-wood art deco furniture in the window. The shop, run by an affable Russian, was substantially cheaper than its competitors a block away on Falk Miksa Street, and Balthazar had bought several items there over the years. A few yards away, on the other side of Marko Street, a security guard walked out of the high-end grocery store on the corner, carrying half a dozen shopping bags and loading them into the boot of a 7-series BMW saloon.

A tram rattled by on the other side of the road, towards Margaret Bridge, as the Audi headed towards the edge of Kossuth Square. Entrance here was restricted to government vehicles and those on official business. Behind the statue of Lajos Kossuth, a wide ramp sloped underground towards a car park for the use of MPs and government officials. Balthazar watched the two Parliamentary guardsmen standing on either side of the slope, clearly waiting for the arrival of the Audi. A small blue tent had been pitched on the green area in front of Kossuth's statue. On the other side of the square tourists laughed and skipped as a cool white mist suddenly gusted up from the nozzles buried in the flagstones and rolled past the entrance to Parliament. One of the guardsmen touched the radio attached to the jacket of his olive-green uniform as the car approached, dropped his head down towards his shoulder and began to speak. Balthazar turned to Sandor. 'Look at them: we're really getting the VIP treatment.'

Sandor smiled. 'That's because you are one now, Tazi.'

The guardsmen stood watching as the Audi slowed down but headed straight towards a single black cylinder that controlled entrance to the underground ramp. Balthazar watched, wondering which would be more damaged, the car or the bollard, if there was a collision. A couple of seconds later the cylinder smoothly slid down into the ground. The Audi descended into the underground car park. The bright lights reflected off the dark-grey walls. Balthazar noticed CCTV cameras in every corner. He turned around to watch the cylinder slide back up behind them.

The driver parked the Audi by the doors to the lift. Balthazar and Sandor stepped out of the vehicle. A slim young man with blonde hair, wearing a close-fitting blue suit, was standing by the entrance. He stepped forward to greet them. 'Welcome to Parliament. My name is Akos Feher.'

ABS headquarters, Falk Miksa Street, 11.55 a.m.

A hundred yards or so away, Anastasia Ferenczy sat in her office watching her computer monitor as the CCTV feed over Kossuth Square showed the Audi carrying Balthazar and his boss disappear into the underground car park. That was a police channel and easy to access. But now the vehicle would be out of view. One of Reka Bardossy's first acts was to close the Parliament CCTV network from all outside connections and greatly reinforce its security. It was impossible to access. That was a smart move by Reka, but one which this morning made Anastasia's life more difficult. The beleaguered prime minister was getting good advice and Anastasia had a pretty good idea who was supplying it. Anastasia opened a new window, entered the personnel directory and called up the file for Antal Kondor. His photograph showed a tall, broad-shouldered man with a shaven head and deep-set blue eyes. Antal was forty-two years old. Born in Nagykanizsa, a medium-sized town in the west of Hungary, he had studied law at Budapest University but had not graduated. Instead, he had joined the ABS, or rather one of its many previous incarnations. The name of the service seemed to change with every new incoming government, but its structure and mission, to protect national security, remained the same.

Antal had worked for the operations division, whose staff were out on the streets, bending the law when necessary. Most of Antal's career had been spent in counter-intelligence, finding and monitoring foreign agents operating in Hungary and their sources, and disrupting those relationships. Antal's file was surprisingly sparse on details. Anastasia was fairly sure she had seen him once or twice at Keleti Station that spring and in the first part of summer, and in the side streets around the area. That would be natural. The mass influx of refugees was top of the ABS's agenda and of great interest to its partner services. Anastasia and her colleague knew each other by sight, of course, but had never acknowledged one another. After twenty years' service or so in the ABS, a few months ago Antal had left quite suddenly and had joined the Ministry of Justice, while Reka was in charge, as a 'security adviser', in effect her personal chief of security, a position he still held now that Reka was prime minister. Most of the staff who had worked for Pal Dezeffy, especially at high levels, or those involved in policy development, had now been sacked. The concept of an impartial civil service, serving whoever won an election, had not taken root in Hungary, at least at higher levels. Reka Bardossy was right, Anastasia thought, not to trust Pal's people to guard her political or personal wellbeing. Plus, the migrants were still coming, there were surely more revelations about Reka's connections to the passport scam yet to be revealed and now there was this extraordinary video footage of her despatching her would-be killer with the heel of her shoe. It was only a matter of time, Anastasia was sure, before the footage appeared on YouTube.

Anastasia's instinct – and Antal's CV – told her that whatever was unfolding in her homeland, Antal was a player. But what, exactly, was he up to? She needed to know more. Anastasia read through the sparse personal details once again then called up more information about him. The screen flashed: 'Access denied – you have insufficient security clearance.' She sat back for a moment, reading the words again. Maybe there was a mistake, a glitch in the system. She tried for the second time to access Antal's file. The same message flashed up. This was unusual. Anastasia was cleared for everything but the highest level of security, which was reserved for the director and his two deputies. She could ask to see the files, she supposed, but that would be a loud and clear signal of her interest in Antal. Her request for access would already be logged. Something told her to hold fire on making an official request. One thing she did know about Antal was that he was a crack shot with a pistol and had almost made Hungary's Olympic team. There had been rumours – never substantiated or, as far as she knew, properly investigated – that between university and joining the ABS Antal had served as a mercenary in the Yugoslav wars, enlisting in a Croatian army battalion for foreign volunteers that was implicated in war crimes against civilians.

Anastasia opened the video clip of Reka killing her would-be assassin at the Buda Castle again. This was a new, longer version circulating around the ABS, one that showed not just the killing but its aftermath. She fast-forwarded through the action until the end, when the dead man lay in the dirt, a dark stain leaking from the heel in the side of his neck. Akos Feher appeared, holding some kind of rod or bar in his hand. He and Reka spoke, then he pulled the heel from the side of the dead man's neck. Reka made a call. Anastasia fast-forwarded through the next few minutes, which showed Reka and Akos dragging the dead man out of sight, then sitting waiting. Soon afterwards, a tall, broad-shouldered man appeared. He wore black clothes, a hooded top and a dark baseball cap which he kept pulled low over his head. He removed a pistol, fitted with a long suppressor, from his pocket. He carefully aimed and fired. The CCTV feed shook for a second then turned black. All of the CCTV cameras along the castle walls had been quickly destroyed soon after the first. She rewound the footage, watching again. It was Antal, she was sure.

Anastasia sat back, closed her eyes for a moment, stretched and yawned. She had put through the cocaine and Viagra Balthazar had given her as a top priority and the forensics results should be back by the end of the day. There was a chance that they might come up clean, but her instinct told her that al-Nuri had been murdered. His death and the hack of the brothel's CCTV system in the same hour were too much of a coincidence. And after ten years' service in the ABS, she no longer believed in coincidences, especially in the middle of the migrant crisis. To her surprise, she suddenly found herself missing Keleti Station. Despite the squalor and the human misery, at least there she had been in the centre of the action, among human beings. There were real people to watch, to talk to, a sense that she was doing her duty for her country. She felt a pang of regret, almost grief for the death of Simon Nazir, an innocent Syrian who had come here with his wife to make a better life for both of them and was then brutally murdered. Here she was stuck inside her office, a small, narrow room at the end of a long corridor on the fifth floor of the ABS headquarters. It was a dreary space, barely lightened by her attempts to humanise it: light-grey walls, a pot plant by the window whose leaves, she saw, were once again sagging in the thick heat of the Indian summer, a couple of posters by Picasso and Mondrian.

From the outside, the building was a fine example of late Communist-era functionalism: a main block covered with narrow grey concrete window frames, a car park in the front and a small rotunda where the security guards sat. Anastasia had once visited the headquarters of the British SIS on the corner of Vauxhall Bridge Road, marvelling at how hard it was to enter the building. Visitors had to walk through a round cylinder to get in, an armoured, high-security version of the kind of revolving doors used by hotels. The whole building was protected by high walls. Here, the ABS headquarters had a wire fence, painted an incongruous shade of turquoise, and two metal barriers.

She walked over to the window and looked out. An elderly lady was feeding the stray cats who lived in the front car park, her hand passing titbits through the wire fence. A few yards away a homeless man with a bandaged leg sat talking to a smiling teenage boy, who handed him a bag of groceries. For a moment Anastasia was back in the CIA safe house on Filler Street the previous Saturday evening, sitting with Celeste Johnson, the MI6 Budapest station chief, and Brad Miller, the CIA station chief, as they demanded that Reka Bardossy hand over everything she knew or could find out about her husband's involvement in the passport scheme. Reka had agreed, of course. But then she had not been prime minister, just a minister under threat of imprisonment or extradition.

Would she survive? It was now Friday lunchtime and she had until Monday morning to hand over the details. The terms of the agreement still stood. Anastasia, too, had played hardball. All three of them had threatened to go public with what they knew about her involvement in the passport scandal, followed by arrest and even extradition. Hungary's anti-terrorism legislation had a wide latitude for interpretation. Reka had protested that she knew nothing about the terrorist connections to Hejazi, which may even have been true. But her husband certainly did and there was enough on Reka to bring her down as well. Reka could perhaps survive the footage of her fighting and killing the man sent to murder her. Any half-decent lawyer could make a case for self-defence. The new footage, showing the aftermath, was something else. Instead of calling the police, Reka, Akos Feher and Antal Kondor had run an illegal clean-up operation and disposed of a dead body.

Anastasia watched the elderly lady gather up her bags and wave goodbye to her feline flock. The cats looked indignant at her departure, then quickly dispersed across the car park. One ran under the director's Audi. Anastasia took a piece of chewing gum from a packet in her pocket and crunched into the white coating while she considered her next move, the mint flavour flooding her mouth. The political situation was still febrile but had stabilised somewhat over the last few days, at least compared to the weekend and Monday when Pal had resigned. Reka had almost made it through her first week in office. She was planning to appoint her first cabinet next week. She had received messages of support from London, Paris, Berlin and Washington, among others. Western leaders knew that the migrant crisis was not over. Hundreds of refugees were still pouring in across Hungary's non-existent southern borders. Hungary's allies needed stability in central Europe. That was the big picture.

The smaller one, being considered in Anastasia's drab office, was that her agenda was not the same as Celeste Johnson's and Brad Miller's. They were British and American intelligence officers. They were in the information business, especially information about terrorism and terrorist connections. They cared little where it came from or what the consequences of withholding would be. After 9/11, 7/7, and the other terrorist attacks in London and Europe, that was entirely understandable. But Anastasia was Hungarian. Yes, terrorists had passed through Hungary en route to the west, disguising themselves as refugees. Yes, corrupt officials in the Ministry of Justice had sold passports which had ended up in the hands of Islamic radicals trying to enter Britain and the USA. Reka had argued that her involvement in the passport scam had been a sting operation, to draw out the traffickers' and Islamists' networks. And she was certainly spinning the media like a veteran – thanks in part to Eniko Szalay's reporting, even the international press were buying that line. But there was certainly enough evidence to bring her down and send her to prison.

Now though there was a new question to consider. Did Anastasia really want to depose Reka Bardossy, just a few days after she had taken office? And send her to be arrested, even put on an airplane to the US? Democracy here was barely twenty-five years old. There were still plenty of powerful and influential people, many in Parliament and one or two even in her building, who longed for the firm hand and certainties of the old regime. Pal was out of public life. For the moment he was down, but he was definitely not out. He was a street fighter behind the scenes and would be working hard to depose Reka, ready to step in the moment she was out of power. There were broader issues to consider, of political stability and national security. Reka might have won her battle with Pal Dezeffy for now, but she lacked a political base and a cohort of loyal staff. Anastasia was not sure that Hungary could afford to lose two prime ministers in less than two weeks and still keep functioning. And who would be the most likely beneficiary of the subsequent chaos? Pal Dezeffy. Behind the scenes, Pal's *komcsik* still had powerful networks.

Beyond that, there was the question of Mahmoud Hejazi's companions. Hejazi was dead but his two associates had disappeared. They may have gone west in the chaotic mass exodus last weekend. Or they may still be in Budapest. Perhaps they were hiding out nearby. It was impossible to know. The two men, both known Islamic radicals, had disappeared. The CCTV footage had been checked but there was no sign of them in the crowd as it poured down Rakoczi Way, over Elizabeth Bridge and out of the city towards the Austrian border. That did not necessarily mean anything – wrap-around sunglasses and baseball caps pulled down over the faces would be enough of a disguise. But what if they were still here? And plotting revenge for the death of Hejazi? That was possible, perhaps even probable. Anastasia picked up the telephone on her desk and buzzed her assistant, told him to bring the files on Hejazi's companions and anything new on them.

A minute later a knock on the door sounded. Szilard Dudas poked his head around. Anastasia beckoned him in and gestured for him to sit down. Szilard was in his mid-twenties, pale, tall and lanky with short brown hair, and almost stooped from years sitting at a desk in front of a monitor. He wore a black T-shirt with a gothic dragon and black stovepipe jeans and was carrying two files and a memory stick. Szilard was a computer expert, who spent too much of his spare time playing complex multi-player fantasy games. He was unusually animated, Anastasia could see. 'So what have we got?'

'A lot. None of it good. Let's start with this,' he said, handing the memory stick to Anastasia. 'Security found it in your car.'

'The Opel?' asked Anastasia, puzzled. She had checked the car only that morning after meeting Balthazar. There had been nothing there.

'No, it was in the taxi. The one you never drove at Keleti. In an envelope in the driver's side pocket.'

Anastasia frowned for a moment, thought back to the last time she had seen the vehicle. It was last Friday morning, a week ago, just before she had tried to tail Simon Nazir. She realised that she had not driven it since, had forgotten about the vehicle completely in the excitement of the previous weekend. Luckily someone in the ABS had remembered it and brought it back to the service's vehicle pound.

'What's on it?' asked Anastasia.

'Open it. IT security has already checked it. You'll see.'

Anastasia plugged the stick into her computer and opened the video file. The clip lasted around ninety seconds. Her day, she realised, had suddenly become even more complicated. 'Is it genuine?' she asked.

Szilard nodded. 'As far as IT can tell. It hasn't been doctored or edited. It's raw footage.'

She exhaled. 'For a dead man, Mahmoud Hejazi is causing a lot of complications.'

Szilard slid two brown folders across Anastasia's desk. 'Indeed. And it only gets worse. The two other men with him...'

Anastasia held up a hand for a second, signalling that Szilard should wait. 'Hold on a moment. Let me catch up myself.' She picked up the top file and leafed through the first file. A photo showed a stocky man with brown eyes, his round, pudgy face topped by curly grey hair. She rapidly skimmed the first couple of pages, reminding herself of the details. 'Adnan Bashari. Born in Baghdad in 1968. Former member of Saddam Hussein's elite Republican Guard. Fought against the Americans in the invasion of Iraq in 2003. Sacked from the Iraqi army, joined the resistance and eventually signed up with Islamic State, before heading west. Last seen at Keleti Station, a week ago.'

There was other background material on his work and life history, but nothing new since she had last looked a couple of days previously. She picked up the second file and skimmed the first couple of pages. Omar Aswan, born in Basra, southern Iraq, in 1958, was thinner, with black eyes, sharp features, grey hair and a neatly trimmed salt-and-pepper beard. Like Adnan he had been a Saddam loyalist, then transferred his allegiance to the Islamic State. Anastasia looked at Szilard. 'The new stuff?'

'It's not collated yet, so there's nothing written yet. The analysts are still working on it. But you need to hear this. It seems Adnan is Omar's bodyguard.'

'Why does he need a bodyguard?'

'Omar is a scientist. An expert in his field.'

'Which is?'

'Chemical and nerve agents. He was part of the planning group for the Halabja attack.'

Anastasia grimaced with distaste. The Halabja attack in 1988 was one of the worst atrocities of the Iran–Iraq war. The Iraqi air force attacked the city in Kurdistan with chemical and nerve agents, killing and injuring thousands of civilians. She could still remember the grim television footage of the civilians lying in the street, the dead mothers still holding on to the bodies of their children, their faces frozen in pain and terror as they tried to flee the deadly mist.

Szilard said, 'It gets worse.'

'How much worse?'

'Considerably. There is a very strong Hungarian connection. That may be why they were, or are, here. They both studied in Budapest – chemical engineering at the Technical University. Omar Aswan in the late 1970s, Adnan Bashari ten years later. They were part of an exchange programme run by the Ministry of Education. They both speak Hungarian. The course was taught in Hungarian, so they had to become fluent, at least in the technical stuff.' He paused for a moment. 'Can I try and find them?'

Anastasia smiled. After months of steady, sustained pressure, Szilard had finally had his transfer from analysis to operations authorised. He had just finished his basic training in surveillance and counter-surveillance. His computer expertise meant he was allowed to skip the classes on data research and cybersecurity. Instead he had extra firearms training, at which, to everyone's surprise, including his, he had excelled. Years of video games had sharpened his reflexes to a level far above the average, especially facing multiple opponents in a confined space. 'No, Szili. We need you here for this. But you'll be out in the field soon, I promise.' She looked down again at the photographs from Halabja. 'We taught them how to gas people?'

Szilard raised his eyebrows. 'Maybe. Part of the course was run by the military then. It was restricted to a handful of specially chosen students and highly classified. We were in the Warsaw Pact, and Moscow had an extensive biological and chemical weapons programme.'

'Let's get the records. Maybe there's something there about these two. Ask the Ministry of Defence for access.'

'I already did.'

'Great. What did they say?'

'First they said there was no such programme. Then I pushed harder and they said all the records were destroyed. Back in the 1990s. Before we joined NATO.'

'Do you believe them?'

'Of course not. Nothing is destroyed here. Everything's potential future leverage.'

Anastasia leaned back and stared at the ceiling. Something was nagging at her. She looked at Szilard. 'Who was minister of defence in the 1970s and 1980s? Didn't they call him the Magyar Gromyko, like the Soviet foreign minister who was always in the government? What was his name?'

'Zoltan Pal.'

'Father of Pal.'

'The very same.'

THIRTEEN

Reka Bardossy's office, Parliament, 12.00 p.m.

Attila Ungar: What about the Gypsy?

Pal Dezeffy: Keleti didn't work. He met someone from the ABS this morning.

Attila: Who?

Pal: Someone. It doesn't matter who. What matters is that you get rid of him. Make it look like an accident. Use a knife. They like knives. Everyone will think it's some kind of Gypsy feud.

Reka Bardossy pressed the pause button on the digital recorder and looked at Balthazar. 'I received the sound file this morning. But it isn't news to you.'

Balthazar shook his head. 'No. It's the second time I've heard it today. The boss has it as well.'

'What do you want to do?' asked Reka.

Sandor Takacs said, 'Take down Pal, obviously. We've talked about this with Balthazar. It's something, but it's not enough on its own to arrest him.'

'No,' said Reka, 'it's not. But he's crossed a line and there will be consequences. When we take him down, and we will, he goes down for good.'

Sandor replied, 'That's fine with me. But in the meantime I

have a detective in serious danger. What are you – we – going to do about it?'

Reka said, 'Firstly, of course, I am concerned about Detective Kovacs's personal security. That is the priority. These are the measures we will take.' She looked at Akos, who started writing as she spoke, then back at Balthazar and his boss. 'It's clear you are being followed, by someone working for Pal. We will make it clear to Pal that if anything happens to you, involving knives or anything else, this recording will be publicly released by the prime minister's office, together with a statement that we are assured of its authenticity. Even if Pal denies it, the damage will be done. I will also make sure that the funding which has been arranged for his think tank and comfortable life in political exile will evaporate – and that he knows that. You are probably right that it is not enough to arrest him. But it is enough to shred his reputation and destroy any attempt at a political comeback. We will also share it with our allies.' She glanced at Akos again, who was writing rapidly. 'Akos, make sure that Celeste Johnson at the British embassy and Brad Miller at the US embassy get copies of this recording.'

Akos stopped writing for a moment. 'The Germans, French, Israelis?' he asked.

Reka thought for a moment. 'Yes. Give them all a copy. They should know who they have been dealing with. We will also share it with Anastasia Ferenczy, if she does not have it already. The ABS need to up their game, improve their counter-surveillance. She should have spotted that the two of you were being watched when you met last week. Where did you meet her, by the way?'

'Kadar, on Klauzal Square.'

Kadar was a Budapest institution, decades old, still

serving traditional Jewish food on red-and-white chequered tablecloths, washed down with soda from old-fashioned heavy glass siphons. Reka's face brightened with pleasure. 'I love that place. It's like time travel. We went there all the time when I was a student. I'll take you there for dinner, once this is all over.'

Balthazar started with mild surprise. Was the prime minister flirting with him? He was certainly getting a lot more attention from women, he noticed, since the footage of him taking down Mahmoud Hejazi had gone viral on the Internet. 'Sure. As long as nobody has used a knife on me,' he quipped.

Reka's voice turned serious. 'That is *not* going to happen.'

There were four of them in the room: Reka, Akos Feher, Balthazar and his boss, all sitting at the end of a long mahogany table. A Zsolnay set of a coffee pot and gold-rimmed cups and saucers stood in the middle, together with a crystal jug of iced water, and two large plates of small cakes and *pogacsas*, small savoury scones, without which no Hungarian meeting was complete. Despite her determination, the prime minister looked exhausted. Her hair was dry and stiff and her face was pale. Small crows' feet shot out from the sides of her eyes, and her blue eyes were rimmed with red. She wore a plain black business suit, with a cream blouse, a tailored jacket, a below-the-knee skirt and flat Gucci loafers. A grey silk scarf covered the base of her neck. Yet despite her wan appearance, Balthazar could see that she was still an attractive woman.

Reka caught Balthazar's eye and smiled, as if reading his mind, paused for a moment, then looked around the room, a politician in complete charge of her brief. Balthazar watched her with growing interest, sensing the steel core that brought Reka Bardossy through a career in politics, to its very summit

– and her determination to stay there. Reka continued speaking, 'But connected to that are also wider issues, matters of national security. Solving one will take care of the other.' Reka turned to Sandor, leaned forward and rested her hand on his arm. 'But for that I will need your help, Commander Takacs.'

Sandor smiled. 'So formal, Madame Prime Minister. How can I help?'

Reka said, 'Sanyi *bacsi*, Uncle Sanyi, can you please lend me Detective Kovacs for a special mission?'

Balthazar's eyes met those of Akos, whose eyebrows almost imperceptibly moved upwards. The same thought went through both their minds. Sanyi *bacsi*?

Sandor sipped his coffee for a moment, knowing full well what the two men were thinking, enjoying the moment. 'Prime Minister, it is kind of you to even ask. I could not say no, even if I wished to. And I don't. But perhaps you could tell us a little more about what you have in mind.'

Reka looked around the room, at each man in turn. Could she trust them? In fact, she had no choice. Normally she would deploy Antal Kondor for this kind of work, but for all his skills, his very appearance had 'state or government operative' written all over it. Balthazar Kovacs, she was sure, could get into places that Antal never could, and talk to people who would run a mile from her head of security. Reka began to speak. She explained how she and Balthazar had a common interest in finding whoever had killed al-Nuri. Balthazar because the Qatari had died in his brother's day spa, as she delicately put it, and she because al-Nuri was trying to negotiate a new investment package from the Gulf, one with no strings attached or requests for passports for Islamic radicals, one that would allow her to modernise

Hungary's parlous infrastructure and healthcare system. Al-Nuri's death would eventually reach back to Pal, she was sure. Pal, more than anyone, benefited from the Qatari diplomat's death. It would be Balthazar's job to find and document the connections. Then they could arrest Pal, charge him with conspiracy to murder. Reka would issue Balthazar with a special warrant, issued by the prime minister's office, that provided legal immunity from anything he needed to execute his mission – apart from killing people or causing serious bodily harm or injury, she hastened to add, unless in self-defence.

'We have your word on that?' asked Sandor.

'Not just my word.' Reka turned to Akos. 'Please show him the draft warrant.'

Akos opened his folder and slid a piece of paper across the table to Sandor. He read the document slowly. 'OK,' he said as he passed it to Balthazar. There were three paragraphs filled with long sentences of turgid legalese and a large round stamp underneath with Reka's signature. The stamp, he knew, was the most important thing. Balthazar skimmed the text, which seemed fine, but he was not a lawyer. If it was good enough for Sandor it was good enough for him. He put the warrant back on the table. 'Is this dangerous?'

'Quite possibly.' Reka paused and looked him in the eye. 'But the truth is you are already in danger, Detective Kovacs. Pal and Attila Ungar tried to kill you once. You are unfinished business. We will warn Pal off, as I said. And I have other plans for Attila, for the whole Gendarmerie, in fact. But Pal does like to tie up his loose ends. Thankfully, he does not always succeed.'

Balthazar said, 'May I speak frankly, Prime Minister?'

Reka nodded, 'Please do.'

'A cynic might wonder if you are exploiting my personal connection to this case to use me to ensure that your rival can never return to the political stage.'

Reka's blue eyes locked on to his. 'A cynic might. But a realist might say that we both have a community of interest in ensuring that, ideally, Pal is put away for a long time and, at the very least, leaves the Hungarian political scene for good.' She gave him a bright smile. 'So why not work together?'

She was completely right, thought Balthazar, but he was not about to agree so quickly. Things acquired easily were never properly valued. 'Can I think about it, Prime Minister?'

'OK. But not for too long. I would like your answer today. Or else I will have to make other arrangements.'

'I'll need a weapon. Something more powerful than the usual police-issue.'

Reka nodded. 'Sure. That won't be a problem.'

Balthazar sipped his coffee for a few seconds, just enjoying the moment. He glanced at his watch. A week ago, around now, he was being knocked to the ground and punched senseless at Keleti Station by a group of Gendarmes. Now he was drinking coffee out of gold-rimmed Zsolnay crockery with Hungary's first female prime minister, who wanted to task him with a special mission. He was not exactly licensed to kill, but he was authorised to get the job done. Balthazar reached for a *pogacsa*. 'Prime Minister, I am honoured that you have asked me here to talk about this. I will certainly respond by the end of the day.'

Reka said, 'Thank you, Detective Kovacs.'

Balthazar took another *pogacsa*, suddenly hungry, and looked at the row of portraits of the prime ministers, the stern old men staring at him. What were they thinking? he wondered. Who is this Gypsy and what's he doing here in the inner sanctum? Or, your government is requesting your assistance, Detective Kovacs, we hope you will wish to help? He knew his answer, of course. He had already spent a decade in public service as a policeman. He knew his duty as well as anyone. But he also knew enough to leverage something back. 'However, if I did accept, I would have one condition of my own. Two, in fact.'

Reka said, 'I expect you do. I'm listening.'

'I'm flattered that you would like to give me a medal and a reception for my work last weekend. I don't really like being in the public eye. But I am, so there's nothing to be done. However, I suggest that we postpone this medal ceremony until the current events are resolved. It's a little early to be celebrating, especially if I am to accept your mission. That's the first condition.'

Reka nodded. 'That makes sense. And the second?'

'A reception is a good idea. I will attend. But one not for me, but for deprived and socially excluded children. A good number of whom will naturally be Roma.'

Reka glanced at Akos, who shrugged as if to say, 'Why not?'

Reka said, 'A party? Lots of kids running around, shouting and having fun? Sure. Let's do it. This place is far too stuffy anyway.'

The telephone on the desk rang twice before Akos picked it up. He listened for a moment, then replaced the receiver. He turned to Reka. 'Madame Prime Minister, your next appointment is ready.'

The four of them rose and walked to the door. Reka turned to Balthazar and shook his hand. 'I look forward to hearing from you,' she said, holding his hand for longer than was perhaps necessary as they walked through the door. She gave his palm a quick squeeze before she released it. As Balthazar stepped into the ante-room for a second he did a double take. Sitting on a sofa, leafing through a news magazine, was Eniko Szalay.

The sight of Balthazar and Reka Bardossy walking out of the prime minister's office hand in hand into the ante-room threw Eniko completely. She put her magazine down as she stared at them from the sofa. Reka gave Eniko a brief nod of greeting, then turned around and returned to her office. Balthazar and Sandor greeted Eniko and she managed to mumble a reply as the questions tumbled through her head. What were they doing here? What was going on? Why was Tazi holding hands with the prime minister? Despite Eniko's consternation, the biggest surprise was how pleased she was to see Balthazar, her pleasure shot through with a distinct sense of relief. At least here, in person, he would have to acknowledge her. Eniko stood up. Normally she would greet both men with a kiss on each cheek but she quickly sensed that this was not the right place or time for such informality.

At the same time Akos was watching all this with great interest, she saw, instantly sensing that there was some backstory here, trying to work out the personal connections. Sandor was as friendly as ever, but Balthazar was reserved, making sure to keep his distance. He actually took a small step away from her, Eniko noticed, feeling a sliver of hurt. One part of her wanted to say, 'Sorry I had to hang up on you, but someone's secretly filming me and I'm scared and guess what, Tazi, I found a sniper's bullet cartridge in the roof of our office building.' Another wanted to tell him simply, as a sophisticated woman would, that it was a pleasant surprise to see him and that she would call him. Instead, to her annoyance and growing embarrassment, she stood there like a gawping teenager.

At that moment a pale young woman in her late twenties with a bob of black hair and finely sculpted eyebrows walked in from Reka's office. She introduced herself as Kati Tolma, the prime minister's personal assistant, and beckoned Eniko forward. Eniko turned, mumbled a goodbye as Akos escorted Balthazar and Sandor out. Kati guided Eniko into Reka's suite, then left.

Eniko fixed a smile on her face, pushing thoughts of Balthazar aside, trying to take control of her emotions as she looked around the room. This was not the 555.hu office, the bar of a ruin pub or some dusty eyrie overlooking Blaha Lujza Square. She had been summoned by the prime minister of Hungary. For some reason she kept thinking about the spent cartridge. Eniko had remembered to put it away, in the back of one of the drawers of her desk at the office. But had she wiped it clean of her fingerprints? In all the excitement of the morning she could not remember. She would do so again, as soon as she was back at the office. She could only imagine what would have happened if she had arrived at Parliament with a piece of used ammunition in her handbag. Whatever. She would deal with it later. Now *be professional*.

Reka was sitting at her desk and rose to greet Eniko. She gave her a quizzical look. 'You look a bit frazzled, Eniko, but it's still too early for gin and tonics. So I can offer you tea or coffee.'

Eniko tried to clear her mind of bullets, snipers and videos of her journey to work. She looked around the room, taking in the row of portraits, the wooden panelling, the heavy furniture, the spectacular view over the river and Buda. It was her first visit to the prime minister's private office and she forced herself to smile, hopefully naturally. 'Tea, please.'

Reka pressed a button on the telephone on her desk and put it on speakerphone. 'Some tea, please, Kati.' She looked around the office. 'So what do you think of my new work quarters?'

Eniko wondered how to answer. The room was overwhelmingly male and very old-fashioned, all dark wood and walls and glowering old men with luxuriant moustaches. But she could probably speak her mind. It was not as if Reka had decorated it herself. Previously Eniko had met the prime minister at her house on Remetehegyi Way in Obuda, ushered in through a side entrance in the garden. Rather like Mahmoud Hejazi, she thought, suppressing a smile. Reka's house had been much more to Eniko's taste: light and modern with some stylish designer furniture. She would answer honestly, Eniko decided. 'It's fine for a British gentleman's club in Piccadilly, I guess. All you need is some old *bacsi* in an armchair sleeping off a good lunch. Or for Hungary a hundred years ago.'

Reka laughed. 'You are so right. I want to redecorate the place, and the ante-rooms. Bring Parliament into the twenty-first century.' She gestured at the row of portraits. 'They've got to go. I might keep Lajos Kossuth, but that's it. There's plenty of room in the National Museum for the others. What else would you do?'

Eniko frowned. Had the prime minister called her in to discuss interior decorating? Maybe she needed a woman's input. Lord knew, there were few enough of those around the Hungarian Parliament. She looked around the room, walked across to the desk and rested her fingertips on the wood. 'I'd keep the desk. It's a symbol of power and continuity. It positions you as the latest in a series of prime ministers. But I'd get some modern rugs, get rid of the portraits, as you said, find some works by young Hungarian artists, get some decent lamps. Lighten the walls. Basically, bring in whoever designed your house. They did a pretty good job.' She paused, her voice puzzled. 'But Prime Minister, why are you asking me this?'

Reka smiled. 'Because I have a proposal for you. Perhaps a request would be a better word. And if you accept, which I very much hope you will, not only for my good but for that of our country, I would like you to feel at home in your new workplace. But first, why don't we sit down,' she asked, guiding Eniko to the corner nook.

A few minutes later, Eniko sat sipping her tea as she pondered Reka's offer, trying to process what she had just heard. Acceptance would bring every journalist's dream: a ringside seat at the epicentre of power and unrivalled knowledge of how it was exercised. But at a high price: of no longer being a journalist. It would be a kind of sweet torture. Knowing so much, but never being able to write about it. Perhaps in thirty years, she could get clearance for her memoirs, but nothing until then. 'I'm flattered, Prime Minister. Really, I am.'

'But? I hear a but.'

'We call it going to the dark side,' said Eniko. 'Controlling information, instead of disseminating it. PR companies, governments, whatever.'

Reka said, 'Eniko, tell me, why did you become a journalist?'

Eniko looked down into her teacup for a moment, smiling to herself, as though it contained a younger and more idealistic version of herself. 'To expose wrongdoing. To do good. To make a difference, I suppose, all those things that naïve young reporters believe in. And to be on the inside track, enjoy the gossip that most people never get to hear.' She stared into the distance, as though seeing something fade away in front of her. 'That feeling when you are on a story, the adrenalin's pumping, the deadline's pressing, the editor's yelling and you are the only person in the world who can write it. When you press the send button, and there it goes, it's out there and soon afterwards, the whole world can read it. And maybe, just maybe, it will make a difference.'

Reka leaned forward, her voice, her body language almost entreating. 'You can have all of that here. You can do good. Make a difference, be on the inside track. Just think of me as your new editor, controlling what you can and cannot say. You can enjoy the spectacle – why not? Just on the other side. Instead of asking questions at press conferences you will be answering them. It's not such a big difference. Eniko, I'm offering you a six-month contract. If it doesn't work, you can go back, of course you can. We can spin it, you were temporarily seconded during a period of national crisis, or something. We already have a mutually productive relationship, don't we? This is just the next step.'

For a moment Kriszta Matyas's voice echoed in Eniko's head. '*You are a reporter, not Reka Bardossy's spin doctor. If you want that job then why don't you apply?*' Now it seemed she did not even need to apply. The job was being offered to her on a Zsolnay plate. She paused for a moment, her eye falling on a portrait of Jozsef Antall, Hungary's first prime minister after the change of system, an old-fashioned conservative and a fundamentally decent man. Antall stared back, frozen in time. 'That next step is a very big one. It would be the end of my career as a journalist. There's no going back.'

Reka leaned forward. 'Really? I'm not sure about that. Lines are blurring nowadays. Just take a long holiday afterwards.

Or move abroad for a while. Or become a media consultant. You will have very valuable inside knowledge.'

One part of Eniko listened, almost ready to be persuaded, another watched with detached, professional interest at a very skilful operator at work. Reka continued speaking, 'There is no dark side any more, Eniko. Only varying shades of grey. We are all in the information business. We all want to control the flow. You do the same and so do your editors. Your website has an agenda, to provoke, be rude and irreverent as well as inform. That's fine. I also have an agenda. To bring this country into the twenty-first century. To modernise government. To update the infrastructure. I'm not asking you to work for a tobacco company or an arms dealer. I'm asking you to work for your government, to serve your homeland.' Reka leaned forward, her voice urgent now. 'Eniko, this is a national crisis. Terrorists are using us, this city, our country, as a gathering and transit point. We have to stop that. Journalism is a form of public service. So is being my communications chief. Somebody has to manage that relationship, with the public and with the media. I think you would do it very well.' She paused. 'The truth is, I need your help. There's nobody else I can trust. And Pal won't go down without a fight.' She looked at Eniko. 'Can you fight, Eniko? Because it's going to get pretty dirty. Pal's people are still in charge of state television, radio and the state news agency. He went to school with Gergely Matics, the editor in chief.'

'Why don't you sack him? Pal sacked his predecessor when he came to power.'

Reka looked thoughtful for a moment. 'I have thought of that, of course. But so far Matics has steered a fairly even course. He's waiting to see how events play out, and who wins. In any case, I don't have a suitable successor lined up yet. There will be a lot of empty desks if I start purging everyone who worked for Pal.'

'Matics doesn't control the Internet. There's 555, all the other websites.'

Reka laughed. 'Eniko, why would they bother? You all do great work at 555, but how many people outside downtown Budapest are reading it? What does the most recent reader survey show?'

Eniko and her colleagues knew that most of their readers were in the capital, but still the results had come as a shock. 'Almost seventy per cent are in Budapest. The rest are divided between the big provincial cities and foreign countries, especially Britain and Germany.'

Reka nodded. 'Where much of your generation has moved to. So you can expect some unpleasant coverage. But it will pass.' Reka continued talking, sat back and looked around the office as she spoke, gestured at the portraits of the prime ministers. 'But more than that, these gentlemen have had their turn. Now it's ours, don't you think?' She looked down at her desk. 'Would you excuse me for a few moments, Eniko, while you think things over? I have some pressing things I need to deal with.'

Eniko nodded as Reka turned to some paperwork. Reka was surprisingly passionate and convincing. But more than that, there was her own self-interest to consider. Journalism was a very fickle trade. Eniko was a star now, yes, but much of that rested on the migrant crisis and her access to Reka. The migrants would eventually stop coming, especially once the new border wall was built. Eniko knew that if she said no to Reka's offer the prime minister was unlikely to keep feeding her the information that made her stories the most popular on 555.hu. Sooner or later she would have to leave 555.hu and start anew, somewhere else, not an easy prospect in Hungary's shrinking media landscape. And there was the whole question of her personal security. Reka already knew that Attila Ungar had taken her off the HEV, the suburban train, last Saturday. Afterwards she had had to take refuge in Balthazar's flat while Sandor sent police officers to protect her mother. At first, she had thought that with the death of Mahmoud Hejazi the crisis had passed and she would be safe. But she was still being followed and filmed. Maybe Reka should know that. It was already getting dirty. At least if she was on the staff here she would get security.

Eniko took out her telephone, making sure that she called up the video of her movements, which she had transferred earlier in the day, and not the photographs of Mahmoud Hejazi leaving Reka's house. Eniko asked, 'Prime Minister, may I show you something? It's already getting dirty.'

Reka put her pen down. 'Of course.' Eniko slid her iPhone across the table and pressed the play symbol on the video file.

Reka watched the clip until the end. 'That's a threat. Do you have any idea who sent it?'

'Not precisely. The Gendarmes, or someone connected to them?'

'If it was Attila and his boot boys, we'll soon know. If you give me a copy of the file I will hand it to our security people, see what they can find. You will get the results, whatever you decide. If you do come on board, I can't guarantee your safety here, but I can certainly greatly improve it. And if you don't, we can also take measures to keep you safe.'

Eniko thanked her, put her iPhone away and watched Reka write a note to herself. She could try it for six months. Reka was right. If it didn't work out, she would take a holiday, maybe move back to London. Either way, former head of communications for a prime minister was certainly better on her CV than editor of a gossip website. She looked around the room at the row of beards and moustaches. Perhaps Reka was right. Now it was the women's turn.

Eniko asked, 'What terms did you have in mind?'

Reka smiled. The conversation was moving in the right direction. 'They are generous, but not extravagant. The position is paid according to a civil service grade. A million forints per month salary, five weeks' paid holiday, plus all public holidays, use of Parliament's gym, holiday home at Lake Balaton, subsidised canteen and a car. All the free tea and coffee you can drink. But I'll be honest with you, Eniko. This is not an eight-to-four job. You will be on duty or on call 24/7. There are no guarantees, even if you are on holiday. As you know, being in the news business.'

Eniko thought for a moment. One million a month, about 3,000 euros, was more than double her current salary. She could save a deposit for a flat. Her mother's arthritis was getting worse. The doctor had recommended a stay at a thermal spa in Heviz, but they didn't have the money. If she took the job, they could afford it. 'If I accepted, when would I start?'

'Ideally, in a couple of hours. But tomorrow morning is fine. We open for business at 8 a.m.'

Eniko started with surprise. 'That soon? That barely gives me time to clear out my desk. How about next Monday?'

Reka shook her head. 'No. We are making an announcement tomorrow, which I expect will cause quite a stir – and mark the start of a new era. So either you are here for that, or not at all.'

Eniko smiled to herself. Reka was already taking control. 'Can I know what the announcement is?'

Reka tilted her head to the side for a moment, made an unnecessary adjustment to her silk scarf and thought for several moments. She nodded to herself, reached into her portfolio, took out a sheet of paper and slid it halfway across the table, keeping her hand on the sheet. 'I have your word that if you do not take the job I won't read about this on 555. hu. Or anywhere else.'

'Of course not,' said Eniko. Reka lifted her hand and let Eniko read through the paper, once, then twice.

Eniko sat back and looked at Reka. Working for the government already looked more exciting than she had imagined. 'I'm in.'

Twenty minutes later, soon after Eniko left Reka's office to be escorted out of Parliament by her assistant Kati, the double doors to Reka's office opened unannounced. An elderly man slowly walked in. He wore a beige shirt with a large, fraying collar and a brown jacket with wide 1970s lapels, flecked with large scales of dandruff, that hung loosely from his bony shoulders. His cheap plastic shoes were worn and scuffed. A half-smoked cigarette dangled from his lips.

He walked over to the two easy chairs in the corner, sat down and beckoned Reka over to sit with him. 'Hello, Doshi. Did she accept? I assume she did. There was something wrong with the sound system. I couldn't hear your conversation.'

Reka hated being called Doshi, especially by the man in her office, whom she wanted out of her workspace, out of her life and out of Hungarian political life. The smell of his cigarette made her feel sick. So did his very presence. But that battle would have to wait, until she had consolidated herself and had mustered enough forces to rout this relic of the old system. She stayed where she was, standing, leaning against her desk. 'Sorry,' she said, not sounding very sorry at all. '*Technikai okok miatt*, because of technical reasons.' That catch-all phrase in Hungarian covered everything from a catastrophic power failure to running out of coffee. In this case it included Antal Kondor that morning removing and destroying the hidden microphones that fed from the prime minister's suite to the Librarian's room in a far corner of the building. 'Yes, she did accept.'

The man known as the Librarian fixed Reka with his watery blue eyes. 'Why?'

'She's scared. Attila and his thugs are tracking her. She thinks she will be safe working here.'

'And will she be?'

Reka's voice hardened. 'Yes. But she would be safe whether she is here or working somewhere else. Even if she leaves after a week. This is Budapest. Not Moscow. There are limits. Are we agreed on that? I have your word that you'll pass that on?'

The Librarian smiled, revealing two rows of yellow, angled teeth. 'Yes, Doshi. I'm touched at your concern. But you have my word. She is safe.' He walked over to the large desk and tapped the leather inlay. 'I trust you are not letting your history with Pal cloud your judgement. It's winner takes all now. There is no room for sentiment.'

Reka shuddered inside. Had he heard them having sex on the desk? She guessed so. She and Pal had both known the room was bugged. Somehow that had made it even more exciting. For a moment she felt a flash of guilt, until she remembered her husband's legion of 'assistants', the female voice in the background this morning and his reluctance to return home from Qatar. In any case her affair with Pal had taken place in another life. She looked down at her broken nails. 'Pal sent someone to kill me. I have very strong feelings about him. But they are definitely not sentimental.'

'Good. When will Eniko Szalay start?'

'Tomorrow. We will announce it tonight. She asked for the rest of the day to tell her colleagues and clear her desk. Are you sure this is such a good idea? I had Miss Szalay under control. The media narrative was being shaped just as we wanted. Now someone else will take over the story.'

'That would not have lasted for much longer. She's restless, been making noises about feeling used. Her editors want more critical coverage of you. She would have broken out, written something critical, just to prove her independence. Then you would have to find another pet reporter. We think we know who her successor will be. A naïve girl from the countryside. We can manage her.'

'I hope so.'

'I told you. We have it under control. Did she show you the video clip?'

Reka nodded, part of her feeling almost ashamed. 'Was that really necessary, to follow her, to frighten her? I think I could have brought her on board anyway.'

The Librarian's voice hardened. 'You think. You think you could have. But what if you could not have? And what if she wrote up a story today with the photos of Hejazi waltzing in and out of your house that she received this morning? How long do you think you would stay in this office? And how long before the Brits and the Americans had you on an aeroplane to who knows where, with an extradition warrant signed by Prime Minister Pal Dezeffy?'

Reka exhaled, looked down at her desk. She had always planned to recruit Eniko as her head of communications as soon as she was appointed prime minister. But not like this. It was all very grubby. 'But whoever sent her those photos can send them to anyone else. There are dozens of journalists who would love that story.'

'Doesn't matter. We can shoot that down, say they are digital forgeries, photoshopped, whatever. They have the most effect if Eniko Szalay uses them. She owns this story.' He drew on his cigarette for a moment. 'Much better to have her inside the tent. It would have been... difficult if she had refused. Things might have got quite unpleasant. But now, thankfully, we don't have to.'

Reka looked up. 'Meaning?'

The Librarian laughed, a hollow sound. 'I don't have to spell it out, do I?'

'I'm not comfortable with this.'

'Boo hoo. What do you think this is? Where do you think you are? In a therapy session where you talk about your feelings? Your comfort, or otherwise, is irrelevant. Do you understand what is at stake here, Comrade Bardossy? Pal is not sitting there, through his own greed and stupidity. So now you are. But that too can change. If scaring Eniko Szalay is the only difficult thing you need to do to stay there you can consider yourself very fortunate. And put the microphones back.'

He paused, his pale-blue eyes glinting. 'It would be a mistake to think of me as a fool, Doshi. Your dear father could explain that to you, if he were still with us.'

Reka felt a chill course through her. Was this a threat? Her father, who had served as minister of the interior in the years before and during the change of system in 1990, had been killed in a skiing accident in Austria the following year. The cause had never been properly explained. For some reason, Hunor Bardossy, normally a very cautious man, had gone off-piste where he had crashed into a tree. Reka's mother had never recovered from her grief and had died of a heart attack two years later.

The Librarian picked his cigarette from his mouth, looked around the room. 'Have you got...?'

'An ashtray. No. There's no smoking in here any more.'

'Really? No smoking,' he said, his hoarse voice full of wonder. He smiled, a smile that did not reach his watery eyes, drew hard on his cigarette, then blew out a stream of smoke. 'You know, Doshi, the problem with newly appointed generals?'

Reka coughed and shook her head, although she had an idea what was coming. 'No. But I guess you are about to tell me.'

'They are too eager. They want to fight on too many fronts at once. They spread themselves too thin, and they cannot control their territory.' He fixed her with a cold gaze. 'We both know what's coming, Doshi. The new versus the old. The upstart protégé turning against the elderly master.'

Reka stepped away from the smoke, 'I don't know what you are...'

The Librarian laughed. 'Let's not waste each other's time, Doshi. I welcome it. One generation fades away, another advances.' He coughed, a wet rattle deep inside his chest. 'That's how we move forward. I don't know how much longer I have. But let's make it worthwhile. A proper fight. So here's some advice, for free. Power must be acquired before it can be used.' He stepped closer. 'Marshal your forces, Doshi. Then you can go into battle.' He wiggled the cigarette in his fingers. 'Until then…'

Reka looked around. The cups from her meeting with Eniko were still on the occasional table. She walked across the room, picked up one and handed it to the Librarian. He dropped his cigarette into the slops at the bottom.

FOURTEEN

Balthazar's flat, Dob Street, 12.40 p.m.

Reka's driver dropped Balthazar on the corner of Dob Street and Klauzal Square. He sat for a moment on a bench just outside the park, stretched his legs and yawned, wincing at the dull ache that still coursed through his jaw. The concussion from last week's beating at Keleti had more or less worn off and his headaches were fading away. But his back and shoulders still ached from the blows he had taken. Add the stress levels of the last few days, especially the events of this morning, and it was no wonder that a tidal wave of exhaustion was hitting him. He had been woken at dawn, seen a dead body and watched it taken away, in a house that always gave him the creeps; sensed for certain that his brother Gaspar was somehow up to no good and there was more family trouble ahead; had breakfast with an operative of state security who was tracking his movements; and had then been taken to see the prime minister, who had issued him with a special warrant. A warrant to find enough evidence to bring down Pal Dezeffy – a former prime minister who had tried to have him killed, who still had powerful friends – once and for all. Oh, and on top of that, he had an uncomfortable surprise encounter with his ex-girlfriend. Who, to his weary acknowledgement, still made his heart beat a little bit faster

– and judging by her bumbling behaviour, he still had some kind of effect on her.

Klauzal Square, and his apartment building on the corner of Dob Street, suddenly felt very welcoming. Here his only task was to close his eyes, stretch out his legs, breathe in the smell of the park, feel the warmth of the sun and the late-summer breeze on his face and enjoy a few moments of peace. A dreadlocked hipster in a pink T-shirt and ripped jean shorts swished by on an extra-long skateboard. Two teenage boys on BMX bicycles spun wheelies up and down the path. Vera, Eva *neni*'s niece who lived nearby, stood gossiping with two other young mothers while their toddlers played in the sandpit. A male tourist in his early twenties, tall and blonde, walked slowly down the side of the square, staring at the map on his telephone until he saw the entrance to the Kadar restaurant and stepped inside. The sound of children's laughter drifted over from the park. For a moment Balthazar was back in the playground on Szabadsag Square the previous Sunday evening, watching Alex and Jozsi clamber over the wooden locomotives. The high point of the evening was taking the two boys for a burger at a nearby restaurant on Oktober 6 Street and the look of sheer wonder on Jozsi's face as he bit into the food.

Balthazar looked at the balcony of his fourth-floor home. The sight of his building always gave him a small surge of pleasure. Budapest was a city that well rewarded its residents and visitors, if they raised their eyes. Many of its apartment houses were urban works of art, decorated with carved figures, friezes and glistening tiles. His six-storey flat-fronted apartment building was an art deco period piece, recently declared a protected national monument. The central facade was decorated with modernist reliefs of workers and families, a different scene on each floor. Curved balconies stood on either side. Rezso Seress, the composer of 'Gloomy Sunday', the 1930s song immortalised by Billie Holiday, who had once lived here, was commemorated with a plaque by the front door.

Klauzal Square and Dob Street were the very heart of the old Jewish quarter. During the Second World War the area and its surrounds had been walled off. Tens of thousands of people had been crammed into the ghetto's narrow streets in the freezing winter of 1944–45. Eva *neni* had told him chilling stories of those weeks, when the Russians were advancing block by block and the frozen ground of the square was filled with bodies stacked like logs. Feral Arrow Cross militiamen had roamed wild, killing on a whim, rounding up the frightened, starving Jews before marching them away to be deported to forced labour, digging fortifications on the Austrian border, or to be shot into the Danube. Nowadays this part of Budapest was the liveliest part of town, known as the *buli-negyed*, or party quarter. The surrounding streets were crowded with *rom-kerts*, ruin pubs, in the courtyards of dilapidated apartment buildings, hipster eateries and artisan coffee shops. It was all a world away from the city in which he had grown up, where most restaurants were state-owned with a centrally planned menu serving dreary high-calorie fried food – if even that was available – and the most common refrain of the bored, surly wait staff was '*Sajnos, nincs*' – sorry, there isn't any – because they and the cook had sold off the ingredients on the sly to their friends and relatives.

But even with dreadlocked skateboarders, Klauzal Square was still holding out against gentrification. The buildings around the square were an architectural jumble, mostly of three- or four-storey apartment houses, with the kind of old-fashioned shops that were rapidly vanishing in the more upmarket parts of the city: a proper butcher, where manual and office workers gathered at stand-up aluminium tables for a lunch of home-made sausages and bread, an electrician's, a watch repairer's, a covered market. The park was encircled by a tidy grey metal fence, and each side was lined with trees. Inside there was a playground, a basketball court and manicured gardens. A bank of Bubi-bikes, green municipal bicycles, stood on the corner, complete with a solar panel pointing skywards to charge the electronic booking system.

For a second Balthazar's nostrils twitched as he realised that the breeze was carrying the acrid smell of burned hemp. He looked across the playground to see two teenage boys passing a long joint back and forth between them. One of them caught his eye and quickly nudged his friend, who looked at Balthazar. The friend, Balthazar saw, was called Denes and was the son of a local politician. Balthazar and the boy watched each other for a few seconds. Balthazar could go over and arrest them both. In fact he was duty-bound to do so. And they both knew what would happen next. Denes's father would be on the telephone to Sandor Takacs, asking for the case to be cancelled. The request would likely be granted, as Sandor banked a useful favour to an up-and-coming politician. And Balthazar would have wasted several hours on pointless paperwork. He smiled to himself for a moment. Except he now was a man on a special prime ministerial mission, which did not include dope-smoking teenagers. Still, he was a cop and had to take some kind of stand. He caught the boys' eyes, shook his head slowly and mimed taking the joint and flicking it away with his thumb. The two boys conferred rapidly. Denes dropped the joint on the ground and squashed it with his foot. He raised a hand in greeting, which Balthazar acknowledged with a nod, and the boys quickly left. Balthazar looked across the street to see Csaba, the pot-bellied owner of the ABC grocery store, laughing about the brief episode.

A few minutes later Balthazar walked into Eva *neni*'s kitchen to see his neighbour deep in conversation with his mother, Marta. The two women rose to greet Balthazar as he entered. He bent down and kissed Eva *neni* on each cheek, then embraced his mother, breathing in her familiar smell of home cooking and lavender perfume.

'Does he know you are here?' asked Balthazar, his hand still entwined in his mother's.

Marta laughed, a deep, throaty sound. 'Your father knows what's best for him. And that's enough.'

Eva asked, 'How was breakfast?'

Balthazar frowned, puzzled for a moment. 'Fine, thanks. Why are you asking?'

Eva gave him a knowing look. 'She's got class, that girl. I always thought so. Dinner soon, I hope. Then who knows?'

Balthazar laughed. 'Who does?' The *neni*-networks reached across the city, none more than Eva's. And it was not very far from Klauzal Square to Mikszath Kalman Square. Eva was the sentinel of their corner of Klauzal Square and Dob Street and ferociously guarded her territory. She was barely five feet tall, but her survival instinct had got her through the Nazi invasion, liberation by the Soviets and decades of dictatorship. Nothing of import happened without her knowing and she had played a minor supporting role in the previous weekend's events. On Friday Eva had accepted a delivery from Anastasia, an envelope containing a burner telephone that she used to contact Balthazar. Two days later Eva had brought up a plate piled high with her famous *turos palacsintas* – sweet-cheese pancakes with lemon zest – for Balthazar, Anastasia and Eniko, when Eniko had taken refuge in Balthazar's flat.

Entering Eva's kitchen was like time travel back to the 1970s, when it had last been furnished. The cupboards were dark orange with circular brown handles. A wall-mounted electric boiler delivered hot water into a white enamel sink. The two women sat at a small, brown Formica-topped table that overlooked the corner of Klauzal Square, drinking coffee from white cups with red bands around them and a red star on each side. The room smelled of the freshly baked chocolate biscuits that sat on a plate between the two women. A Liszt piano concerto played softly from a transistor radio on a shelf next to framed pictures of Eva's family – faded black-and-white shots of childhood siblings, parents and grandparents, and modern colour photographs of her only daughter and granddaughter, who lived in London.

Marta looked her son up and down, her maternal instinct instantly awakened. Balthazar could see her thoughts playing across her face: *What friend?* Marta was in her mid-fifties – she had given birth to Balthazar, her eldest son, at the age of eighteen, an age considered late for her generation of Roma women. Notably pretty in her youth, with thick, dark-brown hair, a wide, full mouth and big, bright grey eyes, she was now heavyset; her hair, still long, was shot through with grey streaks, but she remained a handsome woman. She wore a long black skirt and a grey silk blouse with a silver pendant. Like Eva, Marta had no qualms about making it clear that it was more than time for Balthazar to settle down, marry again and produce more grandchildren. '*Mondd, fiam. Egy chaisi? Ki az?* Tell me, my son. A girl? Who is she?' Marta walked over to the kitchen window, pulled the curtain aside, and peered out at Klauzal Square as though a potential bride was waiting to be noticed. 'And where is she?'

'So many questions. You should be a cop, Mum. And she is a colleague, nothing more,' he said.

'I've been hearing stories about your teenage years,' said Eva *neni*. 'All the fights you got into, protecting your brother.'

Marta smiled proudly, 'Jozsef Street was a rough neighbourhood then. Tazi was a tough guy.' She gripped his arm. 'Still is. Look at that muscle. We Roma are like Jews. Family, first and last.' Marta looked at Balthazar, holding his arm even tighter, her voice heavy with meaning. 'Right, *fiam*? Nothing comes between us.'

Nothing except a dead man in your brother's brothel, him dressing migrants as Gypsies then running them across the border, not to mention the Kris telling you that you cannot step foot inside the place where you grew up, he almost said. Still, nobody ever claimed that the *Roma drom*, the Roma way, was an easy one. So instead he looked at the table, where three white, round plastic pots for transporting food were held together by a red wrap-around handle. He walked over and lifted the edge of one lid. 'Nothing, Mum. Not even your *csirke-paprikas*.'

Marta said, 'I hope you are hungry.'

'I am now.' Chicken paprikas, cooked in a creamy, spicy sauce, served with home-made noodles, was his favourite dish. It smelled delicious. For a moment he was transported back to his childhood, sitting at the kitchen table with his father and siblings while his mother brought a steaming tureen to the table. Those days of eating together at Jozsef

Street were gone, probably forever. But at least his mother was here with him now.

'Good.' Marta picked up the food containers, then turned to Eva *neni*, thanking her for the coffee and biscuits. She and Balthazar kissed Eva goodbye, then walked into the foyer towards the lift. One of Balthazar's neighbours, a stooped and elderly man who had formerly taught at the Liszt Ferenc music academy, was waiting for the lift. Balthazar and his mother greeted him and the three of them rose upwards in silence, until they reached the fourth floor.

Balthazar had bought his flat five years ago for the equivalent of £30,000 soon after he and Sarah split up. District VII's rebirth as the party quarter, its central location and the renovation of the building meant his home was now worth almost three times that. The flat had two bedrooms, one decent-sized, which he used, a balcony overlooking Klauzal Square and a smaller space, originally the maid's accommodation, where Alex slept on the rare occasions that Sarah let him stay over. With a wife at his side, and a growing son, Balthazar had coped with his rupture from his father. But the double whammy of losing both his father and Sarah, and only seeing Alex for a few hours a week, had sent Balthazar into a depression. Unable to face long evenings alone in a silent, empty flat, he returned to District VIII, started to drink and frequent the bars of his youth. These were not the trendy ruin pubs around Klauzal Square, but smoky dives for hard-core drinkers, where cheap beer and rough wine washed down industrially distilled spirits, where the wrong word or even look was enough to trigger violence. It was Gaspar who had helped to save him from himself, pulling Balthazar off his bruised and bloodied opponent in a bar fight, after he lined up a punch that would have broken the man's cheekbones. Gaspar had then paid every bar owner within a square mile to ban Balthazar. The most he was allowed was a coffee in the morning. Gaspar's medicine, and a stern warning from Sandor Takacs, had worked. Nowadays he rarely drank.

Part of Balthazar thought that his career choice had helped to drive Sarah away. Once the passion and excitement had worn off their relationship and they tried to build an everyday life together and raise a child, he realised how her supposed liberal thinking was really just another ideological straightjacket, as rigid in its way as the Communist system under which he had grown up. Their dinner-party talking points demanded set responses. Any deviation from the party line brought bemusement at best, insults at worst. Sarah and her friends were horrified that he had joined the police, instead of taking up the path that had been set out for him, of an academic career. Balthazar had tried to brush it off, to put on a brave face when he and Sarah split up. But the truth was that the fact that Sarah had left him for a woman was somehow worse than if his rival had been another man, an emotional haymaker that struck at the very core of his masculinity. For all his time at Central European University, his travels abroad and worldly sophistication, Balthazar was self-aware enough to know that part of him was still a traditional Roma male. He knew how some in his community looked at him, the scandalised whispers about the Roma cop who could not keep his *gadje* wife, who now found her satisfaction with a woman.

Marta shook her head when she looked around the lounge and the bedroom. The coffee table in the lounge was covered with newspapers, news magazines and an empty pizza box.

Three half-finished mugs of coffee stood next to an empty bottle of beer and a crisp packet. She walked across to the French windows and opened them onto the small balcony, then bustled around, tidying up. 'Tazikam, it's not good for you to be alone. You need a woman. Forget these modern girls, journalists and professors. They are not for you. Gypsies and *gadje*,' she said, shaking her head, 'it never works. Leave it to me. I'll find you someone. Someone to look after you.'

Balthazar smiled, said nothing in reply, a part of him – surprisingly large – wondering if maybe his mother was right. What was he doing here, far from his family, eating alone every night? Perhaps it was time to shut down his one-man mission to straddle two worlds and return to the one where he could be himself. If and when he ever resigned from the police the Kris would immediately rescind its judgement. He could go home, for good. And who wanted more than that?

He glanced around the room as his mother bustled back and forth. The flat looked the same as the day he moved in, albeit more run-down. The walls, once white, had faded further. The narrow parquet slats had long lost their shine. Some had worn loose over the years and clattered when walked over. The dark, heavy sofa and armchair pre-dated the Second World War. The 1980s kitchen was only slightly more modern than Eva *neni*'s. Once the raw pain of his split with Sarah wore off there had been a couple of brief flings, but it had taken him a long time to let another woman into his life. He had neither the drive nor interest to renovate the flat. Eventually his depression had lifted, and after Eniko had virtually moved in he began to think seriously about sharing his life with a woman again. They had talked about redecorating, even bought some home magazines to look at designs and colour schemes. But then Eniko too had left. Balthazar's brief flurry of interest in interior design had vanished in her wake. The main addition was that one wall of the lounge now had fitted bookshelves, which were crowded with academic tomes on Roma life and society, and death in the Poraymus, classics of Hungarian literature, a handful of airport thrillers, and several reference works about forensics and modern police practice and procedure. A handful of photographs had been framed: Alex as a young boy, on a swing in a park in District VIII; Balthazar, his parents and siblings at his high school graduation; another with his mother when he graduated from university. In the centre was a silver-framed photograph of a pretty young Gypsy woman, with long, raven hair and a heart-shaped face. She wore a plain black blouse, a black-and-silver shawl and silver earrings with black gemstones.

He glanced at the photograph then picked up the pizza boxes. 'Thanks, *Anyu* but there's no need. I'm taking a break for a moment. Then I'll find someone myself.'

Marta took a step towards him, her grey eyes locked on his. 'Do that.' Message delivered, she walked over to the bookshelf and picked up the silver-framed photograph. 'I remember when this was taken.' Her voice turned sombre. 'The day of her concert. How beautiful she was. Is this new?'

Balthazar nodded. 'Yes. I had a small photograph, then I had it enlarged and framed. I don't know why, but lately she's been on my mind.' Even in Marta's hands, Virag's eyes seemed to follow him around the room. Perhaps if he had trusted his instincts, had insisted on going with her that evening, she might still be alive.

Marta put the picture back down. She wiped her eyes then was silent for several seconds, as though coming to a decision. 'Mine too. Go,' she said, pointing at the bathroom, 'have a shower, I'll tidy up, make your lunch.'

Marta bustled around in the kitchen until ten minutes later when Balthazar emerged from his bedroom in a clean white T-shirt and loose summer trousers. The flat had filled with the smell of the chicken paprikas and he realised how hungry he was. He sat in the kitchen at the small table by the window with his mother, suddenly aware of how much he missed his parents and simply having company while he ate. The meal was delicious, the tender chicken falling off the bone in a thick, creamy sauce flecked with paprika, and his mother's home-made noodles rich with egg.

His mother did not eat, just drank the coffee she had made herself and watched Balthazar work his way through the food. He looked up to see her eyes on him, put his fork down and held her right hand for a moment. There were patterns on the lower part of her four fingers, a rough, uneven dark blue above the knuckles, as though there had once been letters there that were later inked out. There was a story there, he knew, had done for years. But he and his mother were rarely alone, and he could never ask when relatives were around. Now there were just the two of them. 'Who was he, *Anyu?*'

Marta looked down at her hand resting on his and shook her head. 'Nobody, *fiam*. There is only your father. There was only ever your father.'

Balthazar traced the patterns on her skin. 'I don't see L, A, C, I there.' He peered closer, looked up at her, his voice mischievous. 'Maybe a J? Was there a Jozsi? Or maybe it's a T, for Tomi.' He frowned, looked closer. 'Actually, it looks like it was an S. Simon? Szilard? Solomon?'

Marta snatched her right hand back, placed her left on top of it as if to hide her fingers. '*Stop*. It was a long time ago and doesn't matter any more.'

He sat back, surprised at the vehemence in her voice, looked up to see his mother staring at him. 'Tazikam,' she said, swallowed hard, then paused. He watched in amazement as she wiped her eye.

'*Anyu*,' he asked, 'why are you crying? We'll fix it with Dad. He actually nodded at me in the courtyard the other day. He saw me from the balcony.'

Marta said, 'I'm so proud of you, son. Not just what you did on Sunday with the terrorist.' She looked around. 'Of everything. You've made a life for yourself. Broken the cycle. I always wanted you to be out of the family business.'

'So why are you crying?'

Marta looked down at the table, then out of the window. Balthazar waited. He knew all the signs of an impending confession: the nervous agitation, the inability to meet his eye. It built and built, the pressure rising until it could no longer be contained. He stayed silent.

Marta said, 'I should have told you years ago. But your father and his brothers would not let me.'

'What?' asked Balthazar, although his sixth sense already knew the answer.

Marta wiped her eyes as Balthazar passed her a piece of kitchen paper. He still had not said anything, but just waited for the story to come out, as he knew it would. She blew her nose and started talking. 'I didn't want her to go. I said it wasn't right. She was so young and beautiful, to be there without a chaperone.'

He knew immediately what Marta was talking about. 'Neither did I. But she was so excited. I should have gone with her. But Dad would not let me. I should have disobeyed him.'

'I know. But you were sixteen. And that would have brought severe consequences. It's not your fault.'

'So whose fault is it?'

Marta closed her eyes and shook her head before she spoke. 'All of ours. All of theirs. It was a birthday party. A very fancy occasion. All the politicians and businesspeople were there. He was a very powerful man. He wanted her there, to sing for him, he said. He'd seen her sing in a bar once, he said. It had to be her. It was hard to say no. In those days, twenty years ago, it was the same people in control. They said there had been a change of system but they still ran everything. We said no, she was too young. Our people don't do that, let young girls out on their own. They threatened us with the police, with all sorts of authorities. We had no choice, so we let her go. And he promised us, all he wanted was for her to sing. Just that, and then he would put her in a taxi.'

'But I thought a couple of the guys who played with Melchior were supposed to be there as well, to look after her.'

'That was the plan, Tazikam, but they never showed up. I don't know why.' Marta stood up, started clearing Balthazar's plate away.

He took her hand, 'Please, sit down, *Anyu*. Tell me what happened.'

Marta sniffed. 'I know what you know: they found her in the swimming pool, face-down. She was always scared of water. I remember when we all went to Lake Balaton that summer, to Siofok, she wouldn't go in the water, even though it barely comes up to your knees on the shore.'

'There's something else.' Marta took a deep breath. 'There's a reason you two were so close, why you loved being together, loved each other so much.'

'Which is?'

She started crying again, looked up and down, stretched out her hand, placed his fingers on hers, traced the patterns inked on her knuckles. 'My clever boy. His name *was* Sandor. Sanyi. We fell in love. Sanyikam, my sweet Sanyi.' She looked into the distance for a moment, lost in the memories. 'He was a few years older than me. That didn't matter. But he was a *gadje* and my parents forbade me to ever see him again.' She looked down at the table. 'We used to meet in secret. Until my father and your father paid him a visit one night. After that he moved away, left Budapest for a while. Sandor never knew, but I was pregnant. My parents wanted me to have an abortion but I refused. So they sent me to the countryside. I came back and we gave the baby to some cousins who were having trouble conceiving. It was all hushed up and then your father married me, instead.'

Balthazar's mind was racing – and then he understood. His heart thumped as he spoke. 'So Virag was not my distant cousin.'

Marta blew her nose, her face still wet with tears. She shook her head. 'No, she wasn't. That's why we made it difficult for you to meet her. I'm so sorry, *fiam*. Virag was your half-sister.'

Balthazar stood up and walked over to the kitchen. He stared down into the inner courtyard, could not speak for several seconds. A weight bore down on his chest. His knees felt weak. Virag. His favourite cousin, an ice cream cone in her hand on Mikszath Kalman Square. Virag, his half-sister. The shock of the news triggered other unwelcome memories. For a moment he was back on Rakoczi Way, Mahmoud Hejazi's body jerking underneath his shoe, sliding across the tarmac as the sniper's bullet hit, the blood oozing from his side. Balthazar started to shake, closed his eyes and held on to the edge of the sink, his breath shallow and ragged.

He opened his eyes, inhaled slowly several times, brought himself back under control, turned to see his mother staring at him.

'*Fiam*, are you OK? I didn't want to upset you. Come here. Sit down – you look pale.'

'I'm fine, *Anyu*. Just give me a minute. It's a lot to process.' Balthazar kept staring into the courtyard. Every building, every flat, every brick in Budapest had a story to tell, Eva *neni* had once told him. But none like this, surely. Part of him wanted to scream, to shout, upend the table and hurl the plates across the room. But that would only frighten his mother, which would achieve nothing. Instead he asked: 'Tell me how she died.'

'You already know. She drowned, *fiam*. She fell in the swimming pool. In the deep end. There was nobody around. She couldn't swim.'

Balthazar thought before he answered, questions flying around his head. 'She was at the party to sing. So what was she doing near the swimming pool when she couldn't swim and was scared of the water?'

'She was running. She slipped.'

'Running from who? Why?'

'We don't know.'

Balthazar sat back down, took his mother's hand. 'Why are you telling me this now?'

Marta looked down at the table. 'She comes to me sometimes. When I am asleep. In my dreams. She told me to tell you.' Marta looked at Balthazar. 'And because it's time.'

'I told Sandor Takacs I wanted to re-open the case. This morning.'

'So you see. She was right.' Marta paused for a moment, wiped her eyes. 'I'm so sorry, *fiam*.'

'So am I. I loved Virag, but I thought she was my cousin. We were so close. Now I know why. I remember, after she died, I asked whose house it was, where she had been. You and Dad would never tell me. But you are right. It's time. You can tell me now. Where was she?'

'In Pal Dezeffy's house. She sang for him. Then she was running. Then she drowned. That's what I know.'

Balthazar sat back, breathed out long and slow. Somehow this was not a surprise. Hungary in the 1990s had been ruled by the same dynasties as during the 1970s and 1980s – foremost among them the Dezeffys. They certainly were powerful enough to threaten a Gypsy family with the full weight of state if they did not do as they were told. 'Why didn't you tell me before?'

'Because I knew that as soon as you knew, you would start investigating. Even when you were a child, you were always asking questions: who, why, when, what happened, what might happen. And you could not ask questions about this. Not then. And then you became a policeman. By then he was the prime minister, the most powerful man in the country. We were worried that you would start investigating. It would have been dangerous. Not just for you, for all of us. You know the family business, what we do. We loved Virag and we mourned her. But she was gone and we were still here. Family first, Tazikam.'

'First before me? Before the truth? Even if I am part of that family? Although maybe I'm not any more. My father has disowned me.'

Marta looked down, traced the patches of faded blue ink on her knuckles for several seconds, then reached across the table and gripped Balthazar's hand. 'He loves you. He just wanted... different things for you.'

Balthazar smiled, his fingers still entwined with his mother's.
'And you, *Anyu*, what do you want?'

'Go to work, *fiam*. He is not powerful any more. Find out
what happened to my daughter. To your sister.'

Balthazar sat on his balcony and watched his mother get
into Fat Vik's black 7-series BMW. The car drove quickly
up Dob Street, towards the Grand Boulevard, back to Jozsef
Street and District VIII. His conversation with his mother
spun around his head. The air felt thick, hard to breathe.
The sky had turned dark grey, heavy black clouds on slow
manoeuvres over the city before they unleashed the brewing
storm. He glanced down at Klauzal Square. The dope-smoking
teenagers, the young mothers with their toddlers, had gone.
A sudden gust of wind buffeted the trees, sending their leaves
spinning outwards, making the Bubi bicycles wobble on their
stand.

To his surprise, he did not feel much more grief or pain
about Virag. He had loved her as much as he had loved
anyone. Of course it was a shock to learn that she was his
half-sister, not his third cousin. What was harder to process
was the knowledge that his parents had not told him the
truth, had concealed a secret for twenty years. On one level
Balthazar could see the logic: a few telephone calls from Pal
Dezeffy could have destroyed their lives, sent his father to
prison, seen the family home taken from them. But now Pal
was down, if not out, and he had a chance to start probing.
He glanced down at the news magazines on the small coffee
table: *168 Hours* and *HVG*, the Hungarian version of *The
Economist*. Both were full of articles about the migrant crisis,
the death of Mahmoud Hejazi, the ongoing chaos at Keleti,

and extensive coverage of Hungary's new prime minister. Balthazar picked up *HVG*: the cover showed a playground merry-go-round. Pal sat on the far side, a small Louis Vuitton suitcase at his feet, looking disconsolate. Reka Bardossy sat on the front side, a much larger Louis Vuitton suitcase by her legs, expensive rings on her fingers, a large diamond necklace around her neck, smiling widely.

Did Virag really come to his mother at night, in her dreams? Perhaps she did. Maybe there was a reason that Balthazar had recently been thinking so much about her, had taken her photograph to be framed and then placed it in the centre of his bookshelves. As long as someone was remembered they were never truly dead. Virag was not forgotten. For a moment Balthazar thought of Alex, his eager innocence, his zest for life and new experiences. Now Balthazar too was trapped in a web of lies. Should he tell him about Virag, that Alex had once had an aunt who had died, and he was going to find out who was responsible? Alex was quite capable of handling that knowledge, but he would then quickly ask how Balthazar knew, would learn that his family had deceived his father – and him – for years and become angry, none of which would help an already difficult relationship. But if Balthazar did not tell his son what he had learned, then he too would be guilty of deceit. Whatever Balthazar decided, for now he just needed to communicate with him. He quickly tapped out a text message that he loved him, missed him and would see him on the weekend. The reply came within a minute: 'Love u too Dad' with a stream of emojis of smiling faces and hearts.

Balthazar sat back and smiled for a moment. In all the chaos of his family life, at least there was one simple constant: his son. He looked down again at the cartoon of Reka grinning on the merry-go-round. Now was his chance to find out what had happened to Virag, and finally get justice. He took out his telephone and tapped out the number Reka Bardossy had given him. She answered his call herself. 'Detective Kovacs, a pleasure to hear from you. Have you made your decision?'

'I have. My answer is yes.'

'Thank you, I'm very happy to hear that.'

'When do I start?'

'Now, please.'

'What does Sanyi *bacsi* say?'

He could feel Reka smiling down the line. 'Sanyi *bacsi* says Godspeed and get to work. You are released from all other current duties and cases. I'll send a courier with your warrant immediately, and also a copy to your telephone.'

A few seconds after Balthazar ended the call, his handset rang. He looked down and pressed the green button.

Anastasia Ferenczy said, 'I need to see you.'

'When?'

'Now, please. I'm outside.'

FIFTEEN

'This is very sudden and leaves a large hole in our newsroom,' said Roland Horvath, his pale, jowly face pursed in a frown. 'And you are supposed to give me thirty days' notice. I won't hold you to that, but two or three days, rather than a few hours, would have been useful. Not to mention polite.' He fixed his beady eyes on Eniko. 'Are you sure this is what you want?'

Fairly sure, she thought. I'm human so I have some doubts about making a massive career change out of the blue on the basis of one conversation with no prior planning, but anyway I'm not going to discuss that with you and Kriszta Matyas. Even though you have a point. Leaving the same day as actually resigning was bad manners, although not unusual at news organisations where plans and stories were confidential. But there was nothing to be done about it. So Eniko smiled brightly and said, 'Absolutely. It's an amazing opportunity.'

'At least there will be someone in the PM's office to take our calls,' said Roland. His frown faded as he asked, 'You will take our calls?'

'Of course. What a question!'

Roland still looked puzzled. 'Is this because of our talk this morning about your coverage? I hope not. Because I am sure we could find a way to make things work here, Eniko. You own the migrant story. You have done amazing work. Traffic is up, revenue is up, advertisers are clamouring to get on the site. You've spread our name around the world.' He leaned forward, smiling now, his voice conciliatory. 'Eniko, this is a rough-and-tumble business. It's fast-paced, pressurised, and we have to take snap decisions. We demand XYZ, you give us ABC instead. Creative tension is the lifeblood of every newsroom. You know that. You're the most experienced reporter here. Rows, arguments, disagreements, that's in the nature of our business. And, yes, sometimes voices are raised. We are all passionate, creative people, aren't we?' he asked, turning to Kriszta, who nodded, her face a blank mask. 'It's all sortable,' Roland continued. 'There's no need to leave.'

Eniko, Roland and Kriszta were sitting around the small table in his office, as they had done that morning. But now a very different conversation was unfolding. Roland had looked shocked when Eniko told him that she had accepted a job with Reka Bardossy and wanted to leave immediately. Kriszta had remained stony-faced, but Eniko was sure she had seen a flash of pleasure in her eyes at the news.

Eniko said, 'Of course, there's no need. But this is what I want, really. Roland, honestly, it's not because of editorial or personnel issues. And thank you for the kind words, it's nice to feel appreciated. It's been an amazing opportunity and a real privilege working here. I've learned a lot, and I'm really happy my work has boosted the website. But my mind is made up.' She paused. 'I've accepted the position. It's official now. The announcement will be made in an hour or so. But of course I wanted to give you both a heads-up first.'

'Thank you,' said Kriszta, not sounding thankful at all. 'It's a natural progression from your recent work, some might say,' she continued, a thin smile on her face.

Eniko started to reply, to justify herself, then stopped. Kriszta was a talentless sycophant, like a party functionary of old, implementing the latest ideological reversal or advance, a loyal trooper in what was called the 'Parrot Commando', following orders from on high. There was no point arguing with her. The only aim now was to exit as smoothly and rapidly as possible. There would be enough time to ponder whether her new post was a darker or lighter shade of grey. Whether or not Reka's words about serving her country at a time of crisis were sincere, somewhat to Eniko's surprise, they had struck a chord. Either way, one thing was certain: her new job was on the other side.

Roland frowned, turned to Kriszta, 'This is the second time today you have raised these concerns, Kriszta,' he said sharply. 'All Eniko's copy passed through your desk before it was published. You are the news editor. If you didn't like what she was filing, then why didn't you do your job and edit it?'

Eniko watched, amazed at Roland's unprecedented defence of her. Kriszta seemed equally shocked. 'I... er, yes,' she stuttered, turned to look at Eniko, even tried to smile again, 'of course, you did amazing work. We are grateful. There will always be a place for you here, if you ever change your mind. And we are sorry to see you go. Very sorry.'

Roland continued, 'Perhaps, Kriszta, if you had tried hard to work together with Eniko, to encourage her, instead of making snide remarks, I wouldn't be losing my best reporter.'

Kriszta said nothing, her face bright red now. Eniko watched her pour herself a glass of water, her hand trembling as she raised it to her face.

Eniko had had enough. Leaving a job in which she had invested an incredible amount of emotion was like breaking up with someone, she was quickly learning. Now she just wanted to get away, as smoothly as possible. 'Roland, it's nothing personal. It's not Kriszta's fault, or anyone's fault. It's a decision I've taken. I am organising a leaving party tonight at Retro-kert.' She looked at Roland and Kriszta. 'I hope you can both come,' she added, although they were the last two people she wanted to spend her evening with.

'We'll be there,' said Roland. He turned to Kriszta. 'Won't we?'

She nodded. 'Absolutely.'

A minute or so later Eniko was standing in the women's toilet, leaning forward with her hands on the cracked white sink, staring at herself in the worn mirror, wondering why she had just ended one of the most successful and high-profile journalistic careers in the country. Because your prime source was about to dry up, your editors would, sooner or later, have put you on the celebrity beat, and your personal safety has been compromised, she told herself. And because now you will be sitting right by the hearth, instead of getting brief glimpses of the fire. More than that, you can pay for your mother to get the medical treatment she needs. Eniko exhaled long and hard, told herself doubts were entirely natural, ran the cold tap and put her hands into the flow. Just as she was splashing her face and neck Zsuzsa walked in.

Her friend stood next to her and stared at her in the mirror. 'You're leaving, aren't you?'

Eniko nodded. 'Yup. How did you know?'

'I had a good teacher. One who taught me how to look, how to watch. I saw you go into Roland's office for the second time today. The door stayed shut. There were lots of emotions playing on your face when you came out. And then you came straight in here. Did you jump or were you pushed? I can't imagine they sacked you.'

'They didn't. I jumped. You always had a good eye for detail. At least I did something right. Come here.'

The two women hugged, briefly.

Zsuzsa stepped back. 'Where are you jumping to? I heard Reuters and Bloomberg have been reading all your stuff with great interest. Or is it one of those glamorous international television networks that keep interviewing you about the migrants? BBC? CNN? London or New York?' She dropped her voice an octave, adopted a faux-American accent, *'Tonight, with Eniko Szalay, live from Keleti Station…'*

Eniko laughed. 'Neither. I'm not going very far. I'll be working at Parliament.'

'Politics. That makes sense, with your contacts. Who for?'

'Reka Bardossy. The prime minister.'

Zsuzsa frowned. 'I don't understand. You have a new job just covering the prime minister? I know she is a brilliant contact, but what if she stops talking to you?'

Eniko turned around and leaned back against the sink. 'I'm sorry, Zsuzsi. I'm not being very clear here. My new job is as Reka Bardossy's spokeswoman. From 8 a.m. tomorrow, I'm in charge of all government communications.'

'*What?* You won't be a reporter any more? You're changing sides?' Zsuzsa stared at Eniko in amazement, as though Eniko had just told her an alien spaceship had landed on Blaha Lujza Square. 'Why? Why would you do that?'

Eniko took Zsuzsa's hand. 'I'll tell you later; it's quite a long story. I'm going to announce it in a few minutes so keep it to yourself for now. I'm having a leaving party tonight at Retro-kert. You'll be there?'

'Of course.'

Eniko carried on holding Zsuzsa's hand, suddenly fighting to keep her feelings under control as they surged inside her. 'I'm sure I'll see you at government press conferences. And you can call me anytime for off-the-record briefings. We'll still be friends, of course.'

Zsuzsa stepped back slightly but squeezed Eniko's hand. 'Of course. You're not going to cry, are you?'

Eniko sniffed. 'Of course not.'

Zsuzsa was about to say something else when her telephone rang. She looked at the screen, glanced at Eniko, her head tilted to one side as if newly assessing her, and let go of her hand. 'Sorry, gotta take this. See you tonight,' she said and walked out.

Eniko watched Zsuzsa leave, suddenly guessing who was probably calling and why. The wide-eyed country girl was rapidly morphing into a smart city operator.

A couple of minutes later Eniko stood on her desk, tapping on the side of a mug with a teaspoon. At first the tinny clink was absorbed in the general clamour, but once the reporters and editors looked up at the spectacle they fell silent. She felt their eyes on her as she started to speak. The air was already electric with anticipation. It was almost impossible to keep secrets in a room full of journalists. Neither Eniko nor her editors had said anything, but several of her colleagues, not just Zsuzsa, had seen her twice walk in and out of the editor's office and close the door behind her. And after that she had disappeared into the bathroom for a long time, then Zsuzsa had gone in and out, while Eniko stayed inside. Something was up, that much was obvious.

At first Eniko had planned to give a quick speech, to talk about how much 555.hu meant to her, the valuable work they were doing, the importance of a free press at a time of national crisis. But when she looked around the room, at the worn, dull parquet, the grubby walls, the line of trophies lined up on top of the fireplace and the tatty poster of H. L. Mencken, her colleagues' silent faces looking at her – all except Zsuzsa, still ensconced with the editor – she swallowed hard, took a deep breath and said instead, 'It's my last day here. I start work tomorrow as the prime minister's chief of communications. But before that I'm buying you all a drink tonight at Retrokert. It's short notice I know but the bar tab opens at 7 p.m. Thank you.'

Eniko stepped down to scattered applause, looks of amazement and several cries of 'No!' A good-humoured chant started, 'Dark side, dark side, dark side,' until the whole newsroom joined in. Eniko swallowed again, wiped her eyes, suddenly overcome with emotion. Someone handed her a tissue and she blew her nose. A glass of palinka appeared in her hand. She gratefully knocked the shot back in one go, feeling the rough spirit sear her throat and the alcohol course through her. The door to Roland Horvath's office opened and Zsuzsa came out, followed by the editor. Zsuzsa glanced at Eniko, gave her a hesitant smile. The chant faded away and then stopped. Roland looked at Eniko still standing on her desk. 'We are really sorry to see you go, Eniko, but the show must go on.' Roland looked around the newsroom. 'Back to work, everyone.'

The atmosphere eased, the charge faded away and the reporters returned to their screens and keyboards. Eniko climbed down, sat at her desk for a few moments, gathered her thoughts and started to sort her stuff out. First on the list was one item in particular. She slid her hand into her desk drawer and took out the contents: piles of old press releases, handouts from conferences, publicity sheets about new companies, political parties, glossy flyers for new restaurants, worn and ragged reporters' notebooks. She placed the papers on her desk, made sure the drawer was emptied then eased her forearm into the space, her fingers tracing across the back of the desk. It was empty. A knot of anxiety sprouted in her stomach, but she told herself to be calm. Maybe the cartridge had got jumbled up with her papers, was caught in the spine of a notebook or something. She slowly and carefully sorted through the papers, double-checked the coils at the top of each notebook. All she found were several bent paperclips. Had she definitely put it there? She was sure that she had. Then where could it be? And had she wiped it? She had been in such a rush, she wasn't sure. And even if she had, there was probably DNA on it, or something.

She sat back, closed her eyes and retraced her movements since she had come down from the eyrie in the roof. There was the bad-tempered meeting with Roland and Kriszta that morning. She definitely had the bullet in her pocket then – she had still felt it pressing against her leg. And of course she had taken it out before going to Parliament, otherwise she would have set off the security scanners. She slid her forearm back into the drawer, methodically tracing her fingers along each edge, then sweeping back and forth. There was nothing there. Eniko took her arm out and dropped to her knees, crouched under her desk and started scanning the surrounds. There was nothing to be seen. The knot in her stomach grew in size and seemed to come alive. Somewhere in the 555.hu office, or anywhere, if someone had taken it, was a used cartridge, probably the one which killed Mahmoud Hejazi, with her fingerprints all over it. Unless she found it, and quickly, her new career – any career – was likely to be over before it even began.

Zsuzsa walked over and bent underneath Eniko's desk. 'Hallo, spokeswoman. I hope you aren't having second thoughts already. You can't hide from us under there. 555.hu will find you wherever you are.'

Eniko tried to laugh, not very convincingly. 'I'm still a reporter for another' – she glanced at her watch – 'three hours. And I'm not hiding. I'm sorting out my stuff.'

Zsuzsa said, 'Come out onto the balcony.'

That meant Zsuzsa wanted to talk about something in confidence. Eniko nodded and followed her across the newsroom. The two women stepped outside into the thick, warm air. By this time in the afternoon the office had turned into a heat trap, but Zsuzsa closed the door behind them anyway, ignoring the shouted protests from her colleagues. Eniko looked out onto Blaha Lujza Square, watching the crowds disappear into the metro station, clamber on and off the trams, the stream of traffic heading downtown towards the Elizabeth Bridge and north towards Keleti. Memories tumbled through her mind: watching Balthazar take down Mahmoud Hejazi, the line of international journalists waiting to interview her at Keleti, the look on the face of Maryam Nazir when Eniko showed her the photograph of her dead husband and the way she had fainted and slid off the sofa. This was her world, her corner, her place on earth. Journalism was her life, the only profession she knew, the only job she'd ever had. And she had surrendered it so quickly. For a moment she felt dizzy, almost nauseous. She leaned on the marble top of the balcony wall, her finger tracing a pattern in the cracked surface, then turned to her friend. 'Tell me honestly,

Zsuzsi. Do you think I am making a massive mistake? Maybe I should go back in, speak to Roland and Kriszta, get my job back. Or any job.'

Zsuzsa looked down at Blaha Lujza Square, did not reply for a moment. 'I'm not the one to give you advice any more, Eni. I'm sorry.'

'Why not?' asked Eniko, although she had already guessed the answer. Roland and Kriszta had moved quickly. So had Zsuzsa. But then, what did she expect?

'They've given me your beat. I'm going to Keleti later this afternoon. Any contacts you would like to share?' Zsuzsa asked, half defiant, half entreating.

Alkotmany Street, District V, 1.00 p.m.

Marton Ronay had finally arrived at his accommodation, where he was unpacking and arranging his clothes – white-and-blue button-down business shirts, pastel-coloured polo shirts and chino trousers – in the wardrobe of the flat that Pal Dezeffy's office had arranged for him. He put his soap bag in the bathroom, yesterday's *Wall Street Journal* and *Financial Times* on the coffee table in the lounge, walked into the small kitchen and dropped a bronze-coloured capsule into the coffee machine.

Today, he knew, was the toughest. Jet lag was always worst flying west to east. The last thing his body needed was more caffeine, but all he needed to do was get through the next six or seven hours then he could go to sleep. The bed, a large and firm king-size, beckoned from the other room. But he knew very well what would happen if he surrendered now. He would sleep for eight or nine hours then wake at two or three in the morning and be all messed up the next day and for days after that. The cycle had to be broken. The machine clicked, hissed and rumbled and he took his drink then strolled through the apartment. The place was huge, with two enormous bedrooms, and a lounge the size of his entire place in Washington DC. It was too big for a couple, let alone a single person, but was very centrally located on Alkotmany Street, on the corner of Honved Street, a couple of blocks from Kossuth Square.

Some company would be nice, he thought, his mind flicking back to the policeman at the airport. Mr 'Welcome in Hungary'. What was his name? Ferenc, that was it, Ferenc something. Could he find him? He couldn't see how. There must be dozens of policemen on duty at the airport. Ferenc was a very common name and he couldn't remember his surname. He could hardly go there and start asking questions. Pal's people, he was sure, could get Ferenc's details. The guy used to be prime minister so could doubtless find out anything. But that was the last thing he wanted, to give the client – especially that weird, creepy old guy – something personal on him. In any case, it was probably best to keep it zipped while he was here, avoid any potentially compromising situations, especially on a sensitive assignment like this one. So he told himself.

And even if the apartment was too big it was spectacular. The late-nineteenth-century building was certainly the most grandiose place he had ever stayed: the huge double doors to the building were at least fifteen feet high, the foyer was covered with black-and-pink marble and the lift even had a red upholstered bench along one side. The high-ceilinged rooms were decorated with ornate plaster cornices, and patterned roses in the centre of the ceiling, where chandeliers hung.

The furniture was all curved, gilded, lacquered wood with firm green-and-gold upholstery. The floor was extraordinary: wide slats of pale, gleaming parquet that looked as though it was about to host a ball and probably had.

He walked outside to the balcony. Even that was built like a mini-temple. Two ridged columns stood on the front corners, holding up a small roof above the space, while a gleaming, ornate black metal fence ran across the front. Curved buttresses underneath held the balcony in place. Marton felt as though he should be looking down on a military parade, or taking a salute or something. He looked down Alkotmany Street, towards the neo-Gothic splendour of the Parliament building. The size of the building was amazing, especially considering there were barely ten million people in Hungary, and only 200 members of Parliament. He looked again at the patches of grass on either side of the building. It looked as if two tents had been pitched there, one to the left and one to the right. For a moment he thought he must be seeing things. A tent by Parliament would be like someone camping on the White House lawn. He looked again, squinted into the afternoon sun. He was right: there were two small blue tents pitched on the grass. Whatever... every country had its quirks. Maybe camping out by the seat of government was one of them. Another was the white clouds of steam or mist that floated up from the square's stone slabs every half an hour or so, drifting across the square.

For now he needed to focus on the job at hand. His task sounded simple enough: provide 'strategic communications advice' to help replace the current occupant of the prime minister's office with the previous one. If only it was that simple. In the age of social media, the term 'strategic communications adviser' meant anything you wanted. In his case his job was to shred Reka Bardossy's reputation. The client was supposed to be a modern politician but was clearly years behind the curve, with his leaflets and monkey-like caricatures. Social media: fake Twitter, Instagram accounts for the younger target audience, Facebook for the older ones, could do the job quite quickly and efficiently. He was especially pleased with the hashtag #honestreportingHungary. Eniko Szalay's credibility was already dented. There was enough dirt on Reka Bardossy to bring her down. The problem was how to avoid collateral damage. Pal's career, and his fortune, was inextricably linked to Reka Bardossy's. They had been linked in other ways, too, if the rumours Marton had heard were correct, which made things even more complicated. Politics and the bedroom were never a good mix – especially among rivals for the same job. He sipped his coffee and watched a black Gendarmerie vehicle head towards Parliament, almost knocking over a cyclist in its wake. How to take down one without the other?

He drank the last of his coffee, put the cup down and leaned forward. Something pressed against his leg. He looked down, realising it was his passport, which he had left in his trouser pocket. That was slack, and could only be because of the jet lag. He stretched and yawned, hoping the oxygen and the coffee would rejuvenate him. Considering he was standing in the heart of downtown, the air was surprisingly cool and fresh. The biggest surprise was how quiet it was. This was the government quarter, with half a dozen ministries in walking distance, but apart from groups of Gendarmes on one side of the road, and police on the other, the wide streets and pavement were almost deserted. Compared to Washington DC, apart from the tourists taking selfies on Kossuth Square and the occasional government car, it was a dead zone.

Marton turned around, walked back into the flat, took his passport out of his pocket. He was about to put it away, when a slip of paper fell out. He bent down and opened it. The note said, 'Welcome in Hungary' next to a smiley-face emoji, the letter 'F' and a mobile telephone number underneath, ending in 53807.

Just as Marton picked up the paper his own iPhone rang. He glanced at the screen before he answered and saw with pleasure that the incoming number ended in 53807.

'Ferenc, is that you?' he asked, a broad grin on his face. 'I just found your note. But how did you get my number? You cops can find out anything, I guess.'

'Then I'm sorry to disappoint you,' said a male voice with a harsh New York accent. 'I'm not Ferenc. But I am someone you need to talk to.'

SIXTEEN

Balthazar sat in the front passenger seat of Anastasia's Skoda, the rain hammering on the roof like drumsticks, fat droplets smashing across the windscreen, thin, wet trails spidering across the glass. Thunder rolled and boomed under a carapace of dark clouds. The windows were open but the thick, hot air did not move. He put his hand out, palm up at first, felt the rain wash over his skin, turned his hand around until both sides were soaked, ran his fingers through his damp hair. Jozsef Street was the last place he wanted to be. He felt he could not breathe, would suffocate under the weight of what he was learning that afternoon. As if his mother's confession was not enough, there was this: the video clip he had just seen on Anastasia's iPad. Did anyone else have a collection of relatives like his? How could he protect his brother now? He closed his eyes for a moment, swallowed hard.

Anastasia turned to him. 'I'm sorry, Balthazar. But you needed to know. And it's better that you find out from me.' Her hand dropped down and squeezed his arm. 'Are you OK?'

'I'm fine. Please show it to me again,' he said.

Anastasia held her iPad in front of him. The film was about thirty seconds long. It was shot from a distance, but clearly showed two men talking to each other in a drab room. One was Mahmoud Hejazi. The other was Gaspar. Balthazar could see his brother's face, his heavy bulk, the way he leaned forward, his head jutting out from his thick shoulders when he talked business. The sound was muffled and rough but clear enough for Balthazar to recognise his brother's voice.

Balthazar said, 'I can't hear the conversation properly. Just a few words: Border, transport, euros. What exactly are they talking about?'

'Those, in essence. Our tech people tried to recover the sound but they couldn't get everything. But the gist of it seems to be Hejazi asking about some kind of VIP service, for him and two other people. How safe is it, how do they cross the border? Gaspar says he needs to meet the other two, Hejazi's companions, and then they can discuss everything. Hejazi says there is no need, they can arrange everything now. Gaspar says no, he needs to see the people he is moving, meet them in person first. Gaspar and Hejazi agree to meet, but we could not get the time or place. We don't know if that meeting took place. That's what we need to find out. Immediately.'

Balthazar leaned back and rubbed his eyes while he thought for a moment. Gaspar. How could he be such a fucking idiot? What the hell was he doing with Mahmoud Hejazi? Gaspar had promised, repeatedly, that all he was doing was dressing the migrants as Gypsies and moving them out to Austria. A straightforward business arrangement, he had said. But nothing was ever straightforward with Gaspar. He could never resist a chance to make more money, no matter what the risk, and how dangerous his partners were. He had no idea how out of his depth he was. Or maybe he did and just did not care. Or he even enjoyed the risk. Perhaps it was something in their people's culture and history. When you have been treated like dirt for centuries, then carpe diem, not just the day, but the hour, the moment, to leverage something, anything, turn a profit, put one over on the *gadjes*. Balthazar asked, 'Are you sure it's genuine? Maybe it's photoshopped or something.'

'Photoshop is for photos, Balthazar. Static images. This is a video clip. And we have had it analysed. It's genuine, raw and unadulterated footage.'

'When was it shot? What kind of camera?'

Anastasia shrugged. 'We don't know exactly, but recently, certainly. Hejazi was only here for a few days before he was killed.'

'Weren't you following him? That report you showed me last week was incredibly detailed. You were all over him.'

The previous Friday Anastasia had given Balthazar a copy of her ABS report on how Mahmoud Hejazi had crossed the Serbian border into Hungary. Hejazi had been monitored every step of the way to the hotel near Keleti where he had stayed. Anastasia herself had followed him down Rakoczi Way, following in the path of Simon Nazir, the Syrian migrant whom Hejazi had later killed.

Anastasia sounded rueful. 'We were. Then we lost him. We had him somewhere out in District X. He was in a white Opel in a car park of an abandoned industrial estate. Then six cars identical to the one in which he was travelling appeared, and all seven then went off in different directions. We only had two vehicles.'

'And the number plate?'

'All the cars had the same number plate, Balthazar, and a single passenger sitting next to the driver. It was very well organised.'

Balthazar thought for a moment, his hand back outside the window, the rain spattering against his palm. 'Six cars, all identical, with the same number plate and a passenger pretending to be Hejazi.' He turned to Anastasia. 'That's a lot of cars. And cost. Who's helping him?'

'That's what we're trying to find out. Pal is the obvious suspect. Maybe it was part of the deal with the Gulf investors. As prime minister he would have access to those kinds of resources.'

'Where was this film taken?'

'We don't know exactly. Somewhere in Budapest, we think. Near a main road. The technicians pulled out the sounds of background traffic. There are muffled sirens going quite regularly, so maybe there is a police station or hospital nearby. The metadata has all been scrubbed. It's quite easy to do that.'

'The source?'

'We don't know that either. It was left in my taxi some time this week, on a memory stick. We found it when we brought the car back from Keleti.'

Balthazar looked at the street. Two white vans were parked outside the front door of the family apartment building at number fifteen, enough to transport sixteen people or so. Big Laci and Little Laci, burly brothers who were distant cousins of Balthazar, stood nearby, leaning against the wall and smoking, one on either side of the street, mobile telephones in their hands. Both wore black vests and black jeans. Their arms were covered with intricate floral tattoos. The brothers both worked for Gaspar and were keeping a lookout for trouble. They had both immediately spotted the parked Skoda and began to walk over to investigate until they saw Balthazar and Anastasia inside. They acknowledged Balthazar with discreet nods and returned to their posts.

An elderly lady in a pink housecoat was carrying a bag of shopping, stopping every twenty yards or so to get her breath. She put the bag down and the clink of glass bottles sounded down the street. The rain was easing off now, a summer deluge that had passed quickly. A slight breeze blew through the car. He turned to Anastasia: 'So you don't know where Mahmoud Hejazi went when he escaped your surveillance, who he met or what he did. You don't where or when this video was shot. What do you know?'

Anastasia fixed him with her green eyes. 'That the other person there was your brother, Balthazar.'

Balthazar exhaled. Someone had hand-delivered this information to Anastasia. But who, and why? A business rival? Gaspar had enough of those. The streets around Keleti, the park on John Paul II Square, were thick with people-traffickers, fixers, hustlers, drivers offering a passage to the border. Or perhaps it was a rival pimp seeking to take over a chunk of the family business. But this footage was a different league of criminality. Pimps and people-smugglers were not usually working with terrorists.

Balthazar sat back. 'M and M.'

Anastasia shot him a puzzled glance.

Balthazar continued talking. 'Means and motivation. Who has the means to make the video and who has the motivation to pass it on to you?'

'The means to record a meeting like that: probably a state actor.'

'Isn't that you, or your colleagues?' asked Balthazar.

'Not me, personally. But maybe someone else in the ABS. I don't know everything that's going on. Pal still has his allies. He's down but definitely not out.' She paused for a few seconds, remembering how 'Access Denied' had flashed across her computer monitor that morning.

Balthazar glanced at her, saw that she was frowning. 'What's bothering you?'

'I tried to access Antal Kondor's file a couple of hours ago. I was refused. Even though I have the second-highest level of clearance.'

'Reka Bardossy's head of security. What does that mean?'

'Maybe that something else is going on. Something I don't know about.'

Balthazar smiled. 'Is there anything you don't know about?'

Anastasia shot him a look, half amused, half curious. 'The details of your new job?'

'I'm not sure about that yet,' replied Balthazar.

'But you'll take it?'

He thought of Virag and the photograph of her on his bookshelf. 'Yes, I think so.'

'Good. Let me know if I can help.' Anastasia, he saw, was wearing a light touch of mascara, the first time he had seen her with make-up on. She held his gaze, as if to say, 'Yes, a bit of make-up, and what of it?' Instead she said, 'I'll share if you will.'

'It's a deal. Meanwhile, talk me through Gaspar's plan again.'

Anastasia's voice turned brisk. 'Gaspar and Fat Vik are moving the next batch of migrants at five o'clock. They are from Syria and Iraq, about twenty people, mostly women and children. They are posing as a group of underprivileged Hungarian Gypsy families from Transylvania on an outing. From there it's a quick drive onto the M1, all the way to the Austrian border and the crossing at Hegyeshalom. There are still no proper checks on Hungarian vehicles. In any case, everything has been arranged at the crossing.' She gave Balthazar an ironic look. 'He's quite the businessman, your brother.'

'He is. Unfortunately he trades in people.'

'And he needs to stop. But for now the priority is to know everything about Mahmoud Hejazi and his two friends. Where Gaspar met Hejazi, who arranged it, who else was there, anything he knows about the two men that were travelling with Hejazi, *everything*.' She paused, remembering the new information she had about the men travelling with Hejazi, and for a moment laid her hand on Balthazar's arm. 'We have more on Hejazi's companions.'

'More information that you can share with me?'

Anastasia paused for a moment, took a decision. 'I'm not supposed to. But I will.' She gave Balthazar a quick recap of what she had learned earlier that day.

Balthazar looked out of the car window. This got worse and worse. He remembered watching a news report from Halabja, the dead bodies lying twisted in the dust. Not only was his brother somehow connected to one of the world's most wanted Islamic terrorists, he was also linked to a mass murderer and his bodyguard. Who had probably gone underground somewhere in Budapest. Balthazar asked, 'Do you think they are still here, in Hungary?'

'I don't know. But it's definitely possible. Both men know the city, speak Hungarian. Maybe Hejazi was planning something, either here, or somewhere else in the west. We need anything we can get on them. Adnan Bashari is a chemical weapons expert. His precise area of expertise is non-weapons-based unorthodox distribution systems.'

'What does that mean?'

'At Halabja they used bombs and shells. The bombs and shells exploded. The gas or nerve agent was released and the victims died. But Adnan knows how to release the nerve agent through air-conditioning systems, for example. This is as serious as it gets, Balthazar. We can send someone else to talk to Gaspar, if you prefer. Or I can go in.'

Balthazar yawned, the movement still sending small aches across his shoulders and chest. 'No. Gaspar won't talk to you, or anyone else. Only me.'

'If you need to persuade him further, you can show him this,' said Anastasia, as she opened a new file and handed him the iPad. 'Adnan's handiwork in Halabja. I'm sorry – they are pretty horrible.'

Balthazar glanced through several of the shots: one showed a mother cradling a baby, lying on her back in the room of a house, another several small bundles in the middle of the street. The bundles, he realised, were children, killed in the middle of a game. He closed the file. 'How do you want to do this?' he asked.

'We've changed the duty personnel and the protocols on the border. Gaspar's contacts have been sent home. We're monitoring their phones. They've already called him to let him know. The new orders are to check all vehicles and to specifically check for migrants travelling in Hungarian- or Romanian-registered vehicles. Gaspar will know that by now. He'll be anxious. He needs to get this group across. Word will quickly get out if he can't deliver. And he will have to give the migrants their money back.'

'And if he agrees to help?'

'Then we'll let them through. This time. But this is the last group. We've checked them all. Families from Syria and Iraq.

Nobody of any interest to us. I'm sorry – I know how difficult this is for you.'

Balthazar asked, 'Do you have a brother?'

'Two. One older, one younger.'

'But neither of them are pimps or people-smugglers.'

'One of them works for a Swiss bank in Zurich, managing accounts for non-tax-resident, high-net-worth customers. The other lives in New York and runs a hedge fund. It invests a lot in the arms trade.' She looked at him, a half smile playing on her lips. 'Is that better or worse?'

Balthazar laughed. 'Dunno. Tough call.'

She handed him an iPad mini and a Nokia burner. 'The video is there. So are the photos of Hejazi's companions.' Balthazar watched her as she leaned across him and opened the door, her ponytail sliding down the side of her neck. She looked at him, a rueful smile on her face. 'Keep the burner. I'll call you on it later. Off you go, then.'

Balthazar stepped out of the car and walked through the open front door and into the building. Every step was full of memories. Balthazar had grown up here and each return brought a sweet pain. His family had been poor. He wore hand-me-downs, often went to bed half hungry after a meagre dinner of *zsiros-kenyer*, bread and dripping. But what the Kovacs clan lacked in money, they made up for with a special kind of joie de vivre. His childhood had been happy, with an ever-present clamour of relatives, always celebrating a birthday, name day or Christian festival, praising, feeding, sometimes berating, shouting and laughing. Balthazar, his parents and siblings, had lived in a cramped three-room flat on the third floor, with a toilet in the courtyard. The apartment house was comparatively small, with four flats on each of the four floors, two on either side of a central staircase. The first and second floors had a balcony overlooking the courtyard, while the smaller flats on the third and fourth floor were reached directly from the staircase. The apartment house had been built at the end of the nineteenth century when Budapest was rapidly expanding. That was the city's golden age, when writers, painters and poets fuelled a flowering of culture, art and literature, and even everyday homes in District VIII had stained-glass windows on their staircases, granite tiles in their courtyards and fine metalwork along their balconies. But there was little money for renovation under Communism, unless it was for the plush Buda villas of the party elite. Over the years, Number 15 Jozsef Street, like its neighbours, steadily deteriorated. The stained-glass windows broke and were replaced by plain glass in ugly aluminium frames, the courtyard tiles cracked and shattered, the handrails on the balcony wore loose.

Then the one-party state collapsed and for a while nothing proper took its place during the early-1990s years of *vadkapitalizmus*. Laszlo, Balthazar's father, had started with a handful of joy girls handed on from his father. They worked out of a flat near Mikszath Kalman Square. The change of system, the opening of borders, suddenly brought an influx of money, especially hard foreign currency. Hungary, like its neighbours, was a sex-tourism destination. Laszlo realised that the new punters, coming in from Vienna and other Western European capitals, had money to spend and would pay for a more upmarket service. He bought a nightclub that offered strippers and clean, comfortable private cubicles for private dances and more intimate encounters. The money started to pour in, much of it in cash. One evening Balthazar had found $500 in $20 bills stuffed down the back of the sofa at home. Laszlo soon bought up every flat in the building

'Nobody is going anywhere, *ocsim*, at least for now.'

Gaspar's face darkened with anger. 'What? They've paid me thousands of euros. I need to get them out.'

Did you know, Balthazar wanted to ask Gaspar. *Did you know that we had a sister and our parents never told us?* Instead he held out the iPad mini. 'Come here. You need to see this.'

Gaspar stood closer to his brother, close enough that Balthazar could smell fresh sweat, cigarettes and the fruity odour of palinka. Gaspar rarely drank during the day. Underneath the bluster, his brother was under pressure. Balthazar pressed the play button. Gaspar watched the murky footage of the two men, then turned to his brother. 'Is that it? Is that why you're here? Because someone filmed me talking to someone? Is that why today is so *kibaszott*, fucked-up?'

'It's not just someone. It's Mahmoud Hejazi. What the hell were you doing having any kind of contact with him?'

'Who? I dunno. All these Arabs are called Mahmoud or Mohammed or whatever. Who is he?'

Balthazar grabbed Gaspar's arm, hard enough to make him wince. '*Eleg*, enough. You know full well who he is.'

Gaspar looked sulky. 'OK. So what? Lots of people talk to me. I told you, business is booming. Anyway, you said yourself, he's dead. You had your foot on his back when he was shot. So it doesn't matter any more.'

Balthazar spoke slowly and carefully. 'It matters.' He tapped the screen. 'This is proof you were talking to one of the world's most wanted Islamic radicals. What the hell were you playing at? Did you meet the other people Hejazi was talking about?' He called up the photographs of Adnan Bashari and his bodyguard and showed them to Gaspar. 'These men?'

Gaspar looked down at the photographs, then at his brother, resentment and a certain nervousness playing across his face as he began to understand what kind of trouble he might be in. 'Yes.'

'Where?'

'I don't remember. Really.'

Balthazar shot his brother a look. 'Try harder,' he said, his voice hard now.

'A flat. On Klauzal Square. Last week. Last Friday afternoon. All three of them were there. They wanted the new VIP service. We were supposed to launch it last week. Who are they anyway?'

Balthazar gave Gaspar an edited version of what Anastasia had told him about Adnan Bashari and his bodyguard. Then he showed him the photographs from Halabja. Gaspar scrolled through the photographs and seemed to slowly sag, as his bluster faded away. He looked at Balthazar, his red-rimmed eyes wide. 'Are they real? They did that?'

Balthazar nodded. 'Yes, *ocsim*. Like they gassed our relatives in the Poraymus.'

Gaspar looked across the courtyard at the migrants, the children laughing as they tugged their mother's new headscarves, tied around the face and knotted underneath, the mothers brushing them away affectionately, or looking at themselves in handheld mirrors. 'How can anyone do that to other people? To women and kids?'

Balthazar said, 'Tell me about the VIP service.'

'Government car. Official plates. Nice Audi A6, air-conditioned, driver, chilled mineral water, sandwiches, guaranteed smooth passage through the border, all the way to Vienna. Five thousand euros. Per person.'

Balthazar processed this. 'A government vehicle?'

Gaspar looked regretful. 'Yes, lovely car. V8 engine. Leather seats.' He exhaled long and hard. 'It was all set up with Pal's people. But it never happened. Never will.'

'Why not?'

'Change of government this week, *batyam*.' He smiled, revealing a mouth full of gold crowns. 'You did know that?'

'*Ocsim*, you need to come with me and talk to someone else.'

'I'll talk to you. Nobody else.'

'I'll be there.'

'Who? Police? Gendarmes?'

'No. Neither. Be happy it's the state security service. They won't arrest you. But they do need to ask you some questions.'

'Who is it? Your friend? The Duchess?'

Balthazar nodded. 'Yes. You can trust her.'

'When and where?'

Balthazar led Gaspar back across the courtyard and pointed at Anastasia's grey Skoda, where she was sitting in the driver's seat. 'There. Now.'

Gaspar asked, 'That's it? Just her?'

Balthazar nodded. 'That's all. So far.' He turned to his brother, stared at him. 'But you must tell the truth.'

Gaspar looked down at the ground, then back up at Balthazar, his eyes wide and entreating. 'Of course I will help. Am I in trouble?'

Balthazar sighed. 'Yes. But nothing we cannot sort out, if you cooperate.'

'OK. But you will be there with me, *batyam*?'

'Right beside you, *ocsim*.' Balthazar took his brother's arm, gently this time, and led him to Anastasia's car.

SEVENTEEN

Retro-kert, District VII, 11.00 p.m.

Zsuzsa looked down at her glass of wine, then back at Eniko, her face creased with worry. 'Are you sure you don't mind, Eni? It's a big ask, I know.'

Eniko said, 'Of course not. Why would I?'

'Because if you give me your contacts, you are helping me to be a better journalist, which means I can ask you more difficult questions about the migrant crisis once you start your new job.'

Eniko sipped her *froccs*, a white-wine spritzer, before she answered. *Froccs* was a Hungarian summer speciality with multiple variations, from the *hazmester*, two-thirds wine and one-third sparkling water, to the *hosszu lepes*, or long-step, which was one-third wine and two-thirds water. This was Eniko's third, or maybe fourth, *hosszu lepes* of the evening. It was a useful concoction that allowed the drinker to join in the alcoholic revelry with very little effect. Eniko felt quite sober. 'They will be more *informed* questions, let's say. And the better the questions, the more incisive the national debate on these vital issues. Which is good for Hungary, and good for all of us.' She stopped talking for a moment, started to laugh. 'God. Did I really say that? I haven't even started yet.'

Zsuzsa smiled and sipped her wine. 'You did, Eni. I think you are going to be a big success as spokeswoman. But we'll stay friends, even if I do ask you some tricky ones?'

'Of course. It's just a job. Jobs come and go. Friends don't.'

Zsuzsa looked relieved. 'I'm so happy you think so. I felt really guilty all day for asking.'

'Zsuzsika, stop worrying,' said Eniko as she clinked her glass against her friend's. 'It's no problem. Of course I'll share. I'll call my best sources, telling them you are taking over the story, ask them to help you,' she replied, knowing that she would not do that, and at most would share a couple of think tank analysts who would talk to Zsuzsa anyway. Eniko's best contact was Reka Bardossy and she was hardly likely to advise the prime minister to open a channel to Zsuzsa. She sipped her drink, smiling wryly to herself. You haven't even started work yet and you are already lying to your friend.

'Thanks so much,' said Zsuzsa.

'Now, let's talk about something interesting instead. Like cocktails at six.'

'And seven,' said Zsuzsa, turning a slight shade of pink.

'Did you try a Campari?'

'No. He ordered something for me. With fresh mint. A mojito. It was really nice. I had a couple. Adorjan was so easy to talk to.' She paused for a moment, looked down at her wine. 'I've never met anyone so interested in me or my work before. He wanted to know all about me and what I do, how 555 works, how I report a story. All Huba wanted to talk about was engineering or football.' She took another sip. 'And he's really good-looking,' she continued, her eyes wide with wonder.

Eniko and Zsuzsa were sitting in the front seats of a pale-blue Trabant with no roof that was resting on four piles of bricks in the middle of the courtyard of Retro-kert, the city's biggest and most famous ruin pub. Now a must-visit in every tourist guidebook, and for the stag parties that flocked to Budapest every weekend, Retro-kert was rarely frequented by Hungarians, especially urban hipsters such as the staff of 555.hu. There were newer, far cooler places on every corner of District VII and even District VIII. But Retro-kert had been the first ruin pub. Eniko had hung out here as a teenager when it had opened more than a decade ago. Even if the bar was jammed with drunken tourists, she still had a sentimental attachment to the place. She had brought Balthazar here a few times when they were together. Part of her wondered if he might still walk through the door. The Trabant was in keeping with the rest of the decor: old school benches and chairs, some still with wooden writing stands attached; office tables that had last been used before the change of system; raw brick walls covered with graffiti; a noticeboard bedecked in colourful flyers and handwritten notes. The slow sounds of Yonderboi, a chilled-out Hungarian musician and DJ, drifted across the courtyard.

'Great. I'm really pleased for you,' said Eniko. 'So when is date number three?'

Zsuzsa blushed again. 'Well, number two hasn't finished yet. He said he would come and meet here later. About now, in fact.' She looked around. 'And here he is.'

Adorjan Molnar weaved through the crowd until he arrived at the Trabant shell. Eniko watched Zsuzsa trying, not entirely successfully, to conceal her pleasure and surprise that he had turned up. As Zsuzsa and Adorjan kissed hallo, Eniko quickly scanned his near-white blonde hair, striking looks and gym-toned physique before she glanced at his watch and his shoes, in her experience the two most informative tells: in this case a blue TAG Heuer chronograph and a pair of tasselled suede loafers. The watch was probably worth a thousand euros and the shoes several hundred more. He also wore a black signet ring on one finger, set in thick gold. Eniko immediately recognised Adorjan's type: smart, smooth – too smooth – with easy access to the river of questionable money that flowed through Budapest, a charm that usually concealed a cold arrogance and ruthless determination. So what did he want with Zsuzsa? Her friend was certainly attractive and intelligent but she was a minnow swimming with sharks. Adorjan appeared to be pleased to see her, but his type usually went out with decorative, leggy models or the *plaza-cicak*, shopping mall chicks. Intelligence and an enquiring mind was not usually part of that girlfriend package. As for Zsuzsa – well, she was probably rebounding after her break-up, and still finding her way in the capital. She would, Eniko thought, be too easily impressed by someone like Adorjan, especially after Huba. Zsuzsa's words resounded in Eniko's head. *'We talked for ages... He wanted to know all about me and what I do, how 555 works, how I report a story.'*

Why would he want to know that? Something felt off here. Or was she just being too suspicious?

Adorjan introduced himself and he and Eniko shook hands.

Eniko felt him assessing her as he spoke, his smile revealing two rows of even, unnaturally white teeth. 'I hope you don't mind me crashing your leaving party,' he said.

Eniko smiled back. 'Of course not. Any friend of Zsuzsa's is welcome.'

'She told me about your new job. Congratulations. It's nice to meet you in person. You're in the news. Lots of websites are writing about you.'

'Really?' asked Eniko. The last time she had looked at the

news was three or four hours ago. It was a relief to switch off for a while. 'What are they saying?'

Adorjan held her gaze, for slightly longer than was polite, before he answered. 'All sorts of things.'

'Nasty or nice?'

'A bit of both. You know the Hungarian media, how polarised they always are. Take a look.'

'Later, maybe. I'm having a few hours off now before I start tomorrow. Budapest's a small town. A new government spokeswoman is news. It will pass.'

'Of course,' said Adorjan. Eniko glanced at Zsuzsa, who was looking at Adorjan. It was time to leave them alone for a few minutes. Eniko turned towards the bar, said to Zsuzsa and Adorjan, 'Can I get either of you anything?'

They both shook their heads. Eniko stepped away from the throng and walked over to the bar. She did not want any more alcohol, especially as she had an eight o'clock start the next morning, which she knew meant that she should be there at 7.30 a.m. Everyone had turned out to see her off, including, to her surprise, Roland Horvath and Kriszta Matyas. Roland had made a short but quite touching speech, praising her work, lamenting the loss of her unique reporting and voice, especially during the ongoing political and refugee crisis. There had been lots more jokes about Darth Vader and the dark side. Part of her was still full of regret that she was leaving. But another, larger part, was looking forward to being at the centre of the action in the ongoing political crisis. The question was, how long would she last? For a while in the hubbub and excitement and bonhomie she had forgotten about the missing bullet. Now it nagged at her. She looked down at her hands, once again feeling the smooth, cold metal between her fingers. She knew for certain that she had placed it at the back of her drawer. She could remember her fingers sliding over the notebooks and papers and placing it hard against the back of the drawer. She closed her eyes for a moment. That meant her fingerprints were definitely all over it.

But where was it? Maybe it had somehow rolled away in the confusion of moving out. That was bad enough. Or maybe someone had taken it, which was far worse, and looked more likely. Either way, there was nothing she could do about it now. She could hardly go back to the office now and start a midnight hunt for munitions. In any case she could not get back into the building as she had handed over her access card. Cheers and the sound of alcohol-fuelled bonhomie suddenly sounded, interrupting her reverie. She watched as a British stag party marched into the bar. The groom was dressed in a green fluorescent body suit over his chest and midriff, and a pink kilt. Half a dozen friends, all wearing pink-and-green T-shirts, emblazoned with their names, swarmed around him. Several shouted greetings at Eniko, offering to buy her a drink. She shook her head, laughing at the good-humoured spectacle. As she turned away, trying to catch the barman's eye to order a mineral water, her gaze roamed around the room. What she saw caused her smile to fade instantly.

Attila Ungar was walking towards her, squat, muscled, exuding a purposeful menace. The bar was crowded and he was not speaking but he seemed to exude a dark energy, enough to clear a path through the revellers who moved away from him instinctively. Eniko's stomach turned over but she stayed where she was as he came and stood next to her.

Attila smiled. '*Szia*, hi. We keep meeting in bars.'

'Do we?'

'Here I am.'

'So I see. You keep turning up where I am. First the Four Seasons last week. Now here. Why?' she asked, her voice cold. 'Are you going to arrest me again? Drag me off to some shit hole on Csepel Island?'

Attila waved a finger at her. 'Now, now, *lippy-lany*, Ujlipotvaros girl, don't be such a Pesti snob. I told you, I grew up on Csepel Island. Congratulations on the new job, by the way. Can I get you a drink?'

'No, thank you. Have you come to threaten me again? Or my mother? That was pretty low, even for you,' said Eniko, drawing strength from the knowledge of the announcement she would make the following day at noon.

He opened his hands, showed Eniko his empty palms. 'I come in peace. I'm off duty. *Kedves* Eniko, you really have the wrong idea about me.'

'I don't think so. What do you want?'

'Just a little chat.' He smiled again, his eyes glittering in a kind of triumph. 'And to show you something.'

Eniko felt a quick stab of alarm. 'What?' she asked, too quickly, suddenly guessing the answer.

Attila patted his trouser pocket. 'It's quite small. But definitely not for public viewing. Come with me and I'll show you.'

'No. I'm not going to do that.'

Attila stepped forward again, so near Eniko could smell beer and cigarettes on his breath. 'Oh, but I think you are. You really need to see this.'

As Attila moved closer to Eniko she took a step back without looking, banged into a chair and nearly fell over. He grabbed her arm to catch her. She righted herself and immediately shook his hand off. The stag party was nearby, still waiting to be served. Eniko saw that one of the groom's friends, a chubby, balding man in his early thirties, whose T-shirt announced his name as 'Tim', was watching the interaction between her and Attila.

Eniko gave her best smile before she spoke. 'Attila, can you do something for me?'

He smiled back. 'Maybe. What?'

'Fuck off and leave me alone,' Eniko said, her voice rising, in spite of her attempt to stay in control. At that very moment the music stopped and her voice carried clear and strong across the bar. Dozens of faces turned towards her.

Attila's face twisted in anger and he stepped nearer to her again. Tim muttered something to his friends and walked over, slightly unsteady on his feet. Eniko stared hard at him and shook her head, trying to make him understand that he should not intervene. Befuddled by drink, he did not pick up on her signals. Instead he came and stood next to her. 'Are you all right, love,' he asked in a Manchester accent. He turned to Attila. 'Is he bothering you?'

Eniko watched as Attila looked Tim up and down, like a butcher considering how to debone a particularly appetising joint of beef. 'Please don't hit him,' Eniko said in Hungarian.

Attila smiled. 'Nobody is hitting anybody.' Instead he leaned close to Tim and whispered in his ear for several seconds. Tim turned pale, trembled, apologised to Eniko and left.

Eniko asked, 'What did you say to him?'

'That he would have more fun in a different part of the bar.'

'In English?'

Attila nodded. 'I speak English. Not as well as you or our friend Balthazar. But enough.'

Suddenly Eniko wanted to be away from this place and from Attila most of all. But before that could happen, she needed to see the confirmation of what he had – although she already knew. 'Show me what you want to,' she said.

Attila smiled, reached into his pocket and took out a small, transparent, plastic evidence bag. Inside was a bronze coloured metal cartridge.

Balthazar's flat, 11.30 p.m.

Balthazar and Gaspar sat with their feet up on the coffee table, watching a rerun of a black-and-white Hungarian comedy from the 1980s, featuring a bumbling detective and his junior sidekick. The film unfolded in a world so different, so innocent, that it was hard to believe it had been made in the same country: the two cops were investigating the case of a party official at a wood factory in the countryside who was selling off lumber on the side. He denied everything but had used it to build a wooden holiday home on the shores of Lake Balaton. Each plank still had the mark of the factory franked on one side. The house had been built with the marks on the outside. When the investigating police officers asked him why, he replied, 'Because it looks nicer when we are at home.' Balthazar had seen the film many times. For a moment he was back at the family home on Jozsef Street, a ten-year-old boy with his family, staring in wonder at their first television, a small colour set, perched in the corner of the lounge. Balthazar was still smiling at the film when he turned to Gaspar, 'Do you remember the first time we saw it? We couldn't stop laughing.'

The answer was a soft snore. Balthazar turned to see Gaspar sitting back on the sofa, his mouth open and his eyes closed, an almost-empty bottle of Dreher beer in his right hand. His brother had called earlier in the evening and asked if he could come over. He had arrived a couple of hours ago, with three pizzas and half a dozen beers. The pizza boxes and beer bottles covered most of the table, leaving a small space for the brothers' feet. Balthazar had eaten one of the pizzas, and drunk a single beer. Gaspar had eaten the two other pizzas and sunk the rest of the beer. For a moment Balthazar thought of waking him, but he decided to let him sleep. He took the bottle carefully from his brother's hand and added it to the other empties on the coffee table. He was glad of the company, and it was comforting to have his little brother nearby, even if he was snoring. It had been a long day for both of them. Gaspar had talked at length with Anastasia. Balthazar had sat in, and, as far as he could tell, Gaspar had told her everything he knew: the date and time of his meeting with Mahmoud Hejazi, Adnan Bashari and Omar Aswan in the flat on Klauzal Square, the three men's manner and demeanour, the plan for the VIP service out of Hungary, which had been run by an official in the Ministry of Justice, although Gaspar did not know his name, and everything else he could remember. Anastasia had stuck to her word. Gaspar's migrants had been allowed to cross the border unimpeded. He had agreed with her request that there would be no more transports, at least until Omar and Adnan had been tracked down. In any case, border security at official and known illegal crossing sites was now on high alert in case the two Arab scientists tried to leave the country.

The credits rolled for the film and Balthazar switched channels to *Tonight*, the late-night news round-up on state television. He had noticed that so far the government media – television, radio and the news agency which fed stories to the local and regional radio stations and newspapers – had steered a fairly neutral line between Reka and Pal Dezeffy, probably because it was not yet clear who would triumph. But sooner or later they would come down on one side or the other. The news show started with the headlines. The newsreader, Erika Fekete, an attractive brunette in her late twenties, sitting behind a curved desk, seemed unusually excited, barely able to sit still. The reason became evident as soon as she started speaking: 'This is Erika Fekete, bringing you tonight's news. Our programme tonight has exclusive footage of Prime Minister Reka Bardossy and Eniko Szalay, her new spokeswoman who will start work tomorrow. Until today Eniko Szalay was the star reporter at 555.hu, known for her incisive reporting on the migrant crisis' – Erika stopped speaking for a moment, leaned forward to emphasise what she was about to say – 'and her unusual access to Reka Bardossy after she became prime minister.'

The show cut away from the studio to a still shot of Reka and Eniko sitting at a table in the corner of the bar at the Four Seasons Hotel. The newsreader continued talking, 'We can reveal that a week ago, she and the future prime minister met to plan how to manipulate future media coverage of Ms Bardossy's deep involvement in the passport scandal that has been used against the former Prime Minister Pal by his political enemies.' Balthazar sat up straight, fully alert now. The line had been decided, and not in Reka's favour. Gaspar murmured something, opened his eyes, looked at the newsreader, coughed, then went straight back to sleep. Erika continued talking, 'The meeting took place last Saturday night at the Four Seasons Hotel, where the two women enjoyed gin and tonics which cost 3,000 forints each.' In a country where many teachers barely earned 300,000 forints a month, that was a smart touch, thought Balthazar. 'The footage we have obtained reveals that while Eniko Szalay presented herself as an objective reporter on the passport and terrorism scandal, she had agreed in advance – with one of the main subjects of her reporting – to slant her coverage in a way that was advantageous to Reka Bardossy, in defiance of all norms of journalistic objectivity.'

The studio shot was replaced by footage of a waiter bringing Eniko and Reka their drinks and the two women clinking their glasses. The footage then showed Reka asking Eniko, 'As I understand it, the time to frame a story, to shape how it is covered, is when it is first reported. Is that correct?'

The camera then zoomed in on Eniko as she nodded. 'Broadly, yes. The way it is projected stays in people's memories. That is how they perceive it. But any story can go in different directions afterwards. Once it's out, it's impossible to control.'

The shot switched to Reka as she replied, 'Of course, but its *initial* impact, the first impression – that can be managed?'

Eniko replied, 'To some extent, yes.'

The report moved back to the studio, where a middle-aged man with receding grey hair, wearing a blue shirt, now sat facing Erika Fekete. She looked at the camera as she said, 'Gabor Novak is the editor in chief of *Magyar Vilag*, the country's best-selling daily newspaper,' then turned to Novak. 'Gabor, you are a veteran editor. What are your thoughts when you see this footage?'

Novak sat back, exhaled and slowly shook his head, revealing a substantial paunch pressing against his shirt. 'First of all, I'm shocked. Shocked and disappointed. Eniko Szalay is – was – one of Hungary's best reporters. I would never have expected this kind of ethical corruption.'

Erika nodded in agreement. 'And now she has a new job, as spokeswoman for our prime minister, Reka Bardossy. Can she last? Is it feasible for her to represent our new government?'

Novak looked doubtful. 'That's a question for Reka Bardossy. But I think we all know the answer.'

EIGHTEEN

Eniko stepped out of her building to face the scrum of reporters. The crowd spilled out on both sides of the entrance, in some places two or three deep. Several familiar faces stared at her. Theodore Nichols, the correspondent for the BBC, stood chatting to Gerald Palin, his counterpart at the Associated Press. She knew both men, had worked with them during the refugee crisis, admired their smart, well-informed reporting. Klara Fenyvesi, the Reuters television correspondent, waved with one hand as she immediately moved her camera to face Eniko. They all advanced as one as Eniko stepped forward, yelling questions – Will she resign? Did she agree to cover up for Reka Bardossy? How can anyone believe anything she says now? – waving microphones at her, telephones and television cameras recording her every move.

For a moment, Eniko stood still. She felt hunted, cornered, under attack. She had not even started her new job yet but somehow she had become the news. Would every day be like this? 'Just breathe,' she said to herself, forcing a calm, ready-for-anything expression onto her face. Kata Kiss, a lanky brunette in her late twenties, the star reporter of state television, was in prime position at the centre of the crowd.

As Eniko walked out onto the pavement, Kata advanced with her microphone in front of her, shouting questions. Kata, Eniko knew, was broadcasting live. Which meant that Reka would also be watching. A number-73 trolley bus lumbered past, drowning out Kata's voice, giving Eniko a couple of seconds to compose herself. Once the vehicle had passed Kata began again, 'Eniko, when will you resign? Will your first day at work be your last?'

That was a good question, Eniko thought, although she was hardly about to agree. She had barely slept all night, kept staring at her phone screen as it glowed in the darkness, bringing a stream of reports, gleefully linking to the footage of her and Reka, which was now up on YouTube as well as every Hungarian news site. Reuters, Associated Press and the BBC had also put out short stories about her, linking to the video, all quoting journalists and analysts who questioned whether she could take up her post, and if she did, how long she could remain. Not very long, was the consensus.

By any standard the video footage of her and Reka was a story, Eniko knew, but still she was an experienced enough reporter to sense that there was something, or someone, behind this. Many of the tweets, she noticed, used the same hashtag: #honestreportingHungary. Someone had thought that up, but who? Reka had called Eniko immediately after the story had gone out on the late-night bulletin, offering to send someone round to get her and put her up in a government guest house, but Eniko had declined. She knew the pack would be doorstepping her in the morning, and she needed to face them. Scuttling off to a safe house would send the wrong message and, in any case, she did not want to leave her mother alone. Several reporters, or people claiming to be reporters, had rung the entry-phone buzzer asking to speak to her the previous evening. Eniko had hung up on each one. Some time after midnight, Eniko had called Reka back and offered to resign. Reka had laughed, told her not to be silly. 'We're going to war, Eniko. Are you in?' she asked. Eniko replied, 'Of course.'

Reka had called again at 6 a.m. They had agreed the wording of a short statement, that Eniko now held in her hand. This time Eniko accepted the offer of an escort and a government vehicle to bring her to work. A black Audi A6 with tinted windows was parked on the corner of Radnoti Miklos Street. Antal Kondor stood leaning against it, wearing a black suit, a coil of white plastic wire dangling from one ear. He pointed at himself and then at her, asking if he should come and stand by her. Eniko shook her head. She did not need a bodyguard. She would do this on her own or not at all. She'd been here before, she told herself, many times, just on the other side of the scrum.

Eniko held her hand up, staring at the faces, the television cameras and telephones pointing at her. She stayed silent and the shouted questions faded away. Not saying anything, making the crowd of reporters wait, allowed her to take a measure of control. She made sure to keep her breathing slow and steady as she looked out over the faces, making them wait for several long seconds. Inhale through the nose, exhale through the nose. She felt her chest rise and fall. Today she had dressed in her only power suit: a black Donna Karan skirt and jacket she had bought in London when she was working for *Newsweek* and a fitted white blouse from Max Mara. The smart clothes helped, surprisingly so, and almost felt like a kind of armour. She saw that Theodore Nichols and Gerald Palin were looking at her expectantly. Kata Kiss was directing her cameraman how best to frame Eniko, the sun glinting on his lens. Theodore nodded and smiled encouragingly. Eniko looked down at the paper in her hand for a few moments. This was it, she told herself. Her new career would be decided in the next minute or two, if not the next few seconds. Either she would take control of the hack pack or they would take control of her, and Reka Bardossy would soon be looking for a new communications chief.

Eniko took a deep breath and started to speak. 'Last Saturday, Reka Bardossy and I met for drinks. At the time I was a journalist and she was minister of justice, a confidential source. We've all had those kinds of meetings. That meeting is no longer confidential.' She looked out over the crowd, the faces hanging on her every word, the cameras and microphones pointed at her. 'As you know. It's not only not confidential. It's all over the Internet.' She grinned. 'I guess I need to get used to making the news instead of reporting it.'

She paused again while the laughter faded away. The journalists were still staring at her, some with an almost rueful smile on their faces. There was no need for Eniko to spell it out: every reporter there was suddenly imagining that one of their meetings with a confidential source was suddenly in the public domain. Something shifted in the mood of the crowd, a lightening. Somewhat to Eniko's amazement she found she was almost enjoying herself.

We're going to war, Eniko, are you in?

Her voice strengthened, gained confidence as she continued speaking. 'As you well know, journalists meet sources all the time. I am now the spokeswoman for the prime minister. I will be – I am – one of your sources. That's how it works.' She looked over the sea of faces staring at her. 'That's it. We have no further comment on this. If you want a proper story, then I hope to see you all at noon for a press conference in

Parliament. We will be making a major announcement.' She paused for a moment. 'Trust me. It's going to be big. Much bigger than a couple of gin and tonics at the Four Seasons.' A small ripple of laughter sounded. Eniko glanced down at her watch, then out at the crowd. 'So see you in just over four hours.'

The journalists looked at each other for a moment, processing what Eniko had just said. A fresh barrage of questions erupted, some of them about the press conference. Eniko ignored them, spun on her heel and walked over to the Audi. Antal gave Eniko an appraising look, nodded slowly and opened the door. 'Nice work,' he said, as Eniko slid inside the car.

The vehicle smoothly pulled away and drove down Radnoti Miklos Street, towards the Danube, before turning left along the riverbank towards Parliament. For a moment Eniko closed her eyes and exhaled long and hard. Her phone beeped and she checked the text message, for a moment wondering if Balthazar too had been watching. The message said:

Welcome aboard. R

Whatever test that had been, she had passed, Eniko thought, pleased that Reka had bothered to write. But would every day be like this? She had expected a bumpy ride, indeed Reka had warned her that it would be difficult, but not this tough and not so soon. She glanced at her watch: 7.19 a.m. Only another twelve hours or so to go. And even then she would not be off duty. In fact she would never be off duty. Her iPhone glowed in her hand, its screen pulling her in as though she had lost all control over it. She surrendered, checked Twitter once again. A stream of commentators, analysts and journalists were still

ADAM LEBOR

firing off their opinions about the footage of her and Reka.
A handful were saying that it was too soon to judge, but the
overwhelming consensus was that she still had to resign.

Scattered among the criticism, she saw, were already a
couple of tweets about her encounter with the press a couple
of minutes ago. The BBC and Associated Press were reporting
that she had stood her ground. She smiled when she saw that
Palin had tagged his tweet #baptismoffire. It had been a clever
idea to turn the story back on the journalists, point out that
Eniko had simply done her job, as they did theirs. Once the
shock of the leaked footage, the media campaign against her,
had worn off, she realised to her pleasant surprise that she was
not intimidated. She understood that she herself was not that
important, merely collateral damage in the battle between the
former and current prime ministers. And she worked for the
prime minister now. She was not going anywhere, except to
her office.

Even so, someone was behind this, she was sure. The footage
had been leaked on purpose to force Eniko to resign and to
score a point against Reka Bardossy. The oldest question
was still the most useful – who benefits? That answer was
fairly obvious: Pal Dezeffy. What was it Balthazar used to
ask: who has the means and motivation? Pal had both. As
a former prime minister he would still have access to the
kind of operatives who could – who probably had – covertly
filmed her and Reka. Once the footage was gathered it was
simple to leak it to state television, where he doubtless still
had allies. The car approached the edge of Kossuth Square,
turned left into the underground car park. Several blue tents
were now pitched on the green area, near the Kossuth statue,
she noticed. She would have to ask Reka about that. The
prime minister wanted to put some distance between her

administration and that of her predecessor. Pal had banned demonstrations on Kossuth Square. Reka was allowing them. But an encampment of protestors around the seat of power did not look good, especially while Reka's government was still fragile. How could she control the country if she could not even keep the area around Parliament in order? Eniko watched a skinny man in his twenties step out of his tent, yawn and stretch. He wore ripped jeans and a T-shirt emblazoned in the red, white and green of the Hungarian national flag, with the words 'Magyar Szabadsag Mozgalom' – Hungarian Freedom Movement – whatever that was emblazoned underneath. He had something in his hand: a mobile telephone, she thought at first, but then she saw he was talking quietly into a walkie-talkie. Why was he using one of those? The Audi drove slowly down the ramp into the underground car park and she lost sight of him.

Budapest police headquarters, 10.00 a.m.

Balthazar passed Sandor Takacs a slim, brown cardboard folder. 'Kovacs Virag' was written on a white label on the top right-hand corner. 'Please open it,' he said.

Sandor placed the folder on the coffee table between them. He shook his head as he replied, 'I don't need to, Tazi.'

'Why not?'

'Because I know what's in it,' he said, his voice soft.

'Nothing. That's what's in it.' Sandor was his boss, so he had to keep his temper. But a boss who had kept a secret from him for more than a decade, for all the time they had worked together. A secret about his own family. Balthazar leant forward as he spoke, his voice tight with anger. 'It's empty, *sir*. I asked Agota, the archivist, where the contents were. You know Agota – she's been here forever, remembers when we used card indexes. A memory like an elephant. Agi knows everything. Or she usually does.'

'And what did she say?'

'She turned pink and looked away. Then she said she did not remember the case. Or know anything about it. She's a terrible liar. I asked her who had last asked for the file and when. She looked up the records. Nobody has touched this since 1996, when the case was closed. I asked her if she knew who that was. Because that had to be recorded.'

Sandor looked down for a moment, as if searching for a cigarette to shred, or a carrot stick to eat, but the desk was empty. They were sitting in the corner alcove of his office, on the brown fake-leather easy chairs, two cups of thick black coffee cooling on the table in between them. For once the air-conditioner was working, rattling out intermittent gusts of cold air. Sandor's stubby fingers, the tips brown with nicotine, twisted inside his palms as he spoke. 'And did she?'

'Yes, sir, she did.'

Sandor sat back for a moment, closed his eyes and slowly shook his head. 'I don't suppose there is much point reminding you that you are supposed to be investigating Pal Dezeffy, with a special warrant issued by the prime minister, on a matter of urgent national security.'

'I am,' said Balthazar. 'That's exactly what I am doing. Sir.'

Sandor said, his voice weary, 'Drop the "sir", Tazi. I get the message.'

Balthazar paused, looked at his boss for a moment. Sandor looked tired. There were sweat stains at the armpits of his white shirt. His thinning grey hair, usually neatly combed over his bald spot, was splayed in different directions and his brown eyes were dull and red-rimmed. 'OK. But when are you going to tell me what happened to Virag? And why the case was shut down.'

Sandor sat back for a moment, closed his eyes and slowly shook his head before reaching for his coffee cup. He looked down at the last drops of the tarry liquid and swallowed them before he answered. 'Do you want another one, Tazi?' he asked.

'No, thanks.' Balthazar shook his head, stayed silent, tried to let some of the tension drain away. There was no point getting emotional about this, even less in going to war with his boss, not unless he wanted to leave the police force, which he did not.

Sandor said, 'The case was not shut down. We have a pretty good idea of what happened to Virag. It was investigated and recorded. There is a proper case file.' He tapped the brown folder on the coffee table. 'It's just not in there.'

'Then where is it?' asked Balthazar.

Sandor said, 'Let's go outside, get some air.' He picked up the folder, walked across the room to his desk and locked it away. He picked up the telephone handset which had a direct connection to Erzsi, his secretary. 'Erzsike, please arrange for Gyuri to be in the car,' he asked, then replaced the handset. He gestured to Balthazar and walked to the door. Balthazar stood up and followed behind him. The two men walked to the end of the grey-painted corridor and waited for the lift, neither speaking as they travelled down to the basement. After a couple of minutes Gyuri drove up, at the wheel of the same black Audi A6 that had taken them to Parliament that morning. He steered the car through the car park to the exit, where a red barrier lay across their path. There he took out his car permit card and held it over the sensor. The barrier stayed in place. He tried again, twice more, but the barrier did not rise. After a minute he took out his telephone and made a call. Soon after that a man in his fifties shambled across, apologised, pressed a button on the side of the barrier, inserted a key and turned it, and the red barrier finally creaked upwards.

Two minutes later they were cruising down the far lane of the Arpad Bridge, heading west over the river towards Buda. The end of Arpad Bridge was flanked on both sides by glass-fronted office buildings, their walls of windows glinting in the bright summer sunshine. The traffic was thick on all three lanes on each side.

'Where are we going, boss?' asked Balthazar.

'I told you. For a little walk,' said Sandor. 'It's a beautiful day. I thought we could get some fresh air.' He turned to Balthazar, 'Margaret Island. Is that OK with you?'

Balthazar nodded. 'Fine.'

The car crossed the bridge, turned right onto the narrow slip road that let down towards the northern tip of the island. The Audi swept down the slip road as it curved sharply, first to the left, then to the right, all the while flanked by a high wall of grey cement blocks, before passing under a low, grimy ceiling, the underside of the bridge, and into the bright summer sunlight before pulling in by a bus stop. Sandor thanked Gyuri, told him not to wait. He and Balthazar got out of the vehicle and began to walk alongside the running track until they reached a green bench overlooking the water.

Sandor sat down, gestured for Balthazar to sit next to him. 'We have two things to talk about, Tazi. First work, then the personal stuff.' Sandor reached into his jacket pocket and handed Balthazar a burner phone, an obsolete Nokia candy bar model. 'I'm the only one who has this number. So if you get a call, you'll know it's me.'

Balthazar took the handset. 'Why do I need this?'

Sandor looked out over the water, watched a mallard duck drift by on the water, droplets shining on its wings. He turned to Balthazar, almost paternal affection in his eyes. 'She's going to war' – he glanced at his watch – 'in about twenty minutes. She has to. She has no other choice, but she might not win, Tazi. I don't want you to get caught in the crossfire. We need a safe means of communicating.' He looked down at the Nokia. 'That's it.'

Balthazar nodded, slipped the handset into his pocket. 'Thanks. The personal stuff?'

A light wind blew across the island, sending ripples across the wide expanse of the river. The breeze was fresh and clean, already scented with damp leaves, the first hint of autumn. The water glittered silver in the sunshine. 'I'm sorry, Tazi. I owe you an apology. More than that, actually. A confession.'

Balthazar looked at his boss, tried to read his mood. There was guilt, yes, a nervousness too, but also a kind of weariness, one that he had never seen before. Sandor was a survivor, one of the compromise generation. He had grown up under Communism, been nurtured by the system, given opportunities that many of his peers in the village could only dream of. But his glittering career in the Budapest police, the prized trips abroad when the borders were sealed, the luxurious dinners with foreign delegations, the family summer holidays at the police villa on the shore of Lake Balaton, all these came at a price: to know when to probe and when to back off, when to press for charges to be brought and when to let those charges fade away. And there were no more difficult or embarrassing questions under a one-party state than those involving politicians or Communist officials. Virag had died in 1995, five years after the change of system. The borders were open then, the economy was a free-market free-for-all. But the same people were still in power, reborn and renamed, and old reflexes, honed over generations, had not faded away. In any case, Balthazar asked himself, who was he to demand probity, ethical and honest behaviour? He was the son of a family of pimps. Only a day ago he had colluded in the cover-up of what was almost certainly a murder. Virag's death, however, he would not allow to fade away. 'No need to apologise, boss. But I'll take an explanation.'

Sandor wore a light summer suit jacket over his shirt. He scrabbled in the inside pockets until he found what he was looking for. His right hand emerged holding a half-crushed packet of Sopianae cigarettes. He took one of the cigarettes out, held it to his nose and breathed deeply before exhaling, then turned to Balthazar. 'Tell me what you know, and I'll try to fill in the gaps.'

'She was sixteen years old. She went to Pal's house to sing. She had an incredible voice. Once she started singing the whole room would fall silent. Her voice was like an instrument. She was a naïve young girl. She had barely been outside District VIII, had certainly never seen a house like that. I remember them washing her hair before the concert.' Balthazar paused for a moment, suddenly back in the kitchen of the family home on Jozsef Street, Virag bent over the sink while his Marta gently shampooed her long tresses then rinsed them. 'I remember wondering why my mother was washing Virag's hair as well.' He watched a long boat hotel as it headed downstream. Each room had large French windows which opened out. The sound of laughter and excited chatter carried across the water.

'And why was that?' asked Sandor.

'Because my mother was also her mother.' He turned to Sandor. 'Virag Kovacs was my half-sister.'

Sandor did not turn as he spoke. 'Your half-sister, Tazi,' his voice barely audible.

Balthazar looked at Sandor, glanced down at his hand where his fingers were twisting around the cigarette. Balthazar said, 'You don't sound surprised, boss.'

Sandor's face creased in a wan smile. 'That's because I'm not. I already knew.' Balthazar sat rigid, in a state of shock. His boss knew his deepest family secret. Sandor continued talking: 'I've always known.'

'Why? How?'

Sandor was staring far out, down the river, where the shores of the Obuda factory island loomed in the distance, his mouth slightly open, his eyes not seeing the vista, but locked on something, or someone, who had long vanished from his life. 'I'm sorry, Tazi, it was wrong to keep this from you. Wrong of all of us.'

'All of us? Us?' asked Balthazar.

'Yes, Tazi. Us.'

'What's your involvement here?' asked Balthazar, looking Sandor up and down. The cigarette was shredded, scraps of white paper and tobacco gathering at Sandor's feet. Sandor stood up. Balthazar followed.

Sandor gripped Balthazar's arm, swallowed hard before he answered, his voice cracking as he spoke. 'I was her father, Tazi.' He sniffed hard, wiped his eyes. 'Virag was my daughter.'

NINETEEN

Eniko walked quickly behind Reka Bardossy and her bodyguards as they strode through the long ornate corridor towards the Kossuth Hall, where the press conference was taking place. The journalists' clamour echoed through the hot, sticky air. Part of her asked what on earth she was doing here, trailing behind the prime minister. She should be with her colleagues, in front of her, preparing a series of sharp, devastating questions. Instead Eniko and Reka had spent the morning role-playing the press conference and planning their answers. The media gathering, they both knew, was much more than a forum for transmitting information to journalists. Unlike Pal Dezeffy, Reka had not won an election. She had taken power through his wrongdoings. That meant that Hungary's first woman prime minister urgently needed to assert her authority and legitimise her government. The next hour would be crucial: as soon as she took the podium and stood in front of the lectern she would expose herself. That meant she needed to take full control of the instruments of state. If all went well, she would banish the shadow of her predecessor, deal a fatal blow to his plans to return to power, and properly anchor herself in national life as prime minister. And if not? Eniko briefly shook her head, as though the movement itself would banish the idea from becoming reality. She glanced at her surrounds as she bustled onwards. Was there another building anywhere bedecked in so much gilt and marble? Gothic arches, trimmed with gold, reached across the ceiling. Both sides of the corridor were flanked by tall columns of dark-pink stone. The columns to her right were topped with statues, while those on the other side framed long, narrow windows that overlooked Kossuth Square, and each of those was topped in turn with a stained-glass panel. Plush benches with maroon padded seats lined one side.

For a moment she was a schoolgirl again, on a tour of the building. She could hear the guide's voice intoning statistics as though outlining the version of a five-year plan: almost seven hundred rooms, ten courtyards and thirteen lifts. Add to that today one nervous former journalist, hoping that her jitters did not show. As if reading her mind, Reka turned around and glanced at her, nodding reassuringly. Eniko nodded back, watching how the prime minister was flanked by four bodyguards, one on either side, one in front and another behind, marvelling at how they moved as though synchronised, keeping Reka boxed in, maintaining the same distance from each other as they headed towards the press conference. Eniko rushed to catch up and almost lost her balance as her formal dress shoes slipped on the thick purple carpet. In among the clamour of voices for a moment she thought she heard Zsuzsa speaking. But it was impossible to tell for sure. One thing was clear: Eniko was a long way from the offices of 555.hu.

She glanced quickly out of the last window before the ante-room. There were now half a dozen tents on the two patches of green that flanked the central square. A number of burly men were walking around and gesticulating, several holding what she now recognised as walkie-talkies. Eniko made a mental note to talk to Reka about the tents and men in Kossuth Square but the thought flew from her head as she walked into the crowded ante-room. There were more than a hundred people in the space, a mix of Hungarian journalists and foreign correspondents, gossiping and warily trading information in an excited babel of languages. In among the Hungarian voices Eniko heard English, Russian, French, Chinese and Arabic. Gerald Palin and Theodore Nichols, she saw, were standing slightly to one side at the back, near the tea and coffee jugs and cups laid out at the back of the room. Others were adjusting the headsets and small grey handsets that would provide simultaneous translation from Hungarian into English, French, Spanish, Russian and German. The chatter faded as the first bodyguard walked into the room, immediately followed by Reka and the three other protectors. Eniko paused for a moment as they continued into the hall, feeling the familiar buzz that a story would soon be breaking. The air itself seemed to be alive with energy. The familiar story-hunger surged again inside her but she damped it down. That was her old life, she told herself. Perhaps one day she would be back, but not today.

The journalists rushed to sit down or take their place behind their television cameras. Sensing movement to her right, Eniko turned to see Zsuzsa walking towards her, notebook in hand. Their eyes met. Zsuzsa mouthed, 'Are you OK?' Eniko nodded. Eniko could see that Zsuzsa was clearly about to ask another question, doubtless about the coming announcement. Part of Eniko wanted nothing more than to hustle her former colleague into a corner and give her the scoop ten minutes early. Instead she smiled, said, 'We'll catch up soon,' and walked on.

The chatter faded away as Reka walked onto the platform. Press conferences were usually held in the Delegation Hall. Eniko and Reka had discussed today's venue. They had agreed that the Delegation Hall, while decent enough, was not appropriately imposing for her first press conference. Eniko was about to announce a decision that would – if it worked – permanently alter Hungary's balance of political forces. They needed somewhere that was part of a historical continuum that reached back through the centuries, but could also launch a new kind of leader, firmly bringing Hungary into the twenty-first century. The answer, they decided, was the Kossuth Hall, one of the grandest rooms in Parliament, where the highest-ranking visiting politicians were received. One wall of long windows, overlooking Kossuth Square, gave a clear view over the main piazza, all the way up Alkotmany Street. The other walls were half lined with dark-wood panelling. But the rows of paintings of the usual men in eighteenth- and nineteenth-century dress that usually hung above the panelling had been replaced with photographs of young Hungarians: an Oscar-winning film director, several famous writers and artists, a fashion designer whose clothes were the talk of Paris and London, a particle physicist, a former student at Fazekas school – Balthazar's alma mater – who had just been awarded the Nobel Prize, and a female fencer who had won three gold medals at the last Olympics. The windows were open and the sounds of Kossuth Square drifted up, half muffled by distance: a number-two tram rattling around the corner towards the Ministry of Justice, shouts of excited tourists, the far-off revving of engines.

There were two light-wood lecterns in the room, each with a Hungarian flag on the front panel, facing out towards the reporters. Reka took her place behind one, Eniko the other. The four bodyguards fanned out, one to each corner. Eniko's early-morning flagging of the event had worked even better than she expected. She had never seen a government press conference as crowded as this: the room was jammed with reporters, sitting, standing, several even crouching on the gleaming polished parquet floor, notebooks in their hands, waiting expectantly.

In front of the two daises, a long table was crowded with microphones, each emblazoned with the symbol of their network, attached to a thick tangle of cables snaking back through the room. Behind the microphones were rows of television cameras: Eniko counted crews from the state and private Hungarian channels, as well as CNN, the BBC, French, German and Italian television, Russia Today and China's Xinhua. These were the lucky ones – chosen by Eniko on the understanding they would pool their footage. Budapest was crowded with international networks covering the refugee crisis at Keleti and the borders. Now that story – and its repercussions – had merged with the fall of Pal and Reka's rise, Hungarian domestic politics were suddenly international news. And not everyone in the room was a journalist, Eniko noticed. She had once been introduced to the striking tall black woman with buzz-cut hair sitting at the rear of the room. What was her name? Then Eniko remembered: Celeste Johnson, the British deputy ambassador. On the other side of the room sat a scruffy, unshaven American in rumpled chinos and a grubby button-down shirt whom Eniko had seen several times at Keleti. 'Brad', as he called himself, claimed to be a 'freelance reporter'. He had a strong New

York accent and took a lot of notes in a spiral notebook but somehow had never revealed a family name or which news media he worked for. Reka, Eniko noticed, glanced at both Brad and Celeste before looking away. For a second a cloud passed across her face before she slipped into a politician's professional smile.

Two thin, minimalist microphones reached up from the lecterns. Eniko looked at Reka. The prime minister was wearing a navy business suit with a cream silk blouse, a knee-length skirt and black slip-on shoes with a modest heel. A light-blue patterned silk scarf around her neck covered the scars of the assassination attempt the previous week. There was video of that footage, Eniko knew, which sooner or later would find its way onto the Internet and she would have to deal with it. But not today, please not today, she prayed. Eniko then looked out over the rows of journalists, the crowded aisles as the chatter slowly faded away, and tapped the microphone. The room fell silent.

Eniko began to speak. 'Thank you for coming today. As I explained this morning, and in the emails many of you have received, we have a major announcement to make.' The revving of engines sounded louder, as though the vehicles' exhausts were broken, or a squad of bikers was riding back and forth across the piazza, then faded away. Eniko decided to ignore the racket and continued talking, quickly looking across at Reka. 'Prime Minister Bardossy will make the announcement in a few moments. Then we will take questions. You may have noticed that Hungary has been in the news lately.' She paused while a polite ripple of laughter sounded. 'I'm especially pleased to see so many colleagues from the foreign media here. So we will alternate between foreign and Hungarian media. I ask all of you to please keep your questions brief and to stick to the topic of the announcement. We will have plenty of other press events and I look forward to working with many of you in the future.' She turned back to Reka and said, 'Prime Minister, the floor is yours.'

Reka looked out over the room, at the rows of faces staring at her. The engine noise started up again, noticeably louder this time. Several of the journalists looked back at each other, all wondering what the racket was, before it faded away. Reka began to speak. 'Six months ago, my predecessor, Pal Dezeffy, re-established a paramilitary police force, the Gendarmerie. At that time I was minister of justice. I opposed this decision, as did many of my political colleagues and adversaries in the opposition. The very name has a dreadful resonance. The Gendarmerie was responsible for rounding up Jews and Gypsies during the Nazi occupation and deporting them to their deaths. Everything about the force was designed to intimidate: its uniforms, its vehicles, its unprecedented legal powers, its headquarters at 60 Andrassy Way, above the former torture chambers of the Arrow Cross and the Communist secret police. Unfortunately all our fears have come true: the Gendarmerie has proved to be an arm of state repression. Its officers are brutal, violent and out of control. They do not enforce law and order. They disrupt it.'

Eniko watched the journalists: some writing, many recording Reka with their mobile telephones, others tapping at their keyboards, the black glass of the television cameras glinting as she spoke. All were intensely focused. It was not hard to guess now what was coming. Reka waited a few seconds then continued speaking, 'Which is why I have issued an executive order, backed by my cabinet' – she glanced at her watch – 'that as of noon today, ten minutes ago, the Gendarmerie is dissolved.'

Reka stopped talking, allowing the news to sink in. A loud, collective intake of breath sounded across the room, together with several 'Wows' and a single, drawn-out, 'Fuck, that is a story.' The reporters looked at each other, nodding, tapping, writing faster, hunched forward, totally focused. Reka continued talking. 'I have the power to do this, as the founding orders of the Gendarmerie make the force solely responsible to the prime minister. A previous prime minister re-founded this paramilitary force and, in effect, placed it above the law. *This* prime minister is dissolving the organisation and bringing it back within the reach of the law. All officers of the Gendarmerie are required to proceed to the nearest police station with their vehicles, and to surrender their uniforms and weapons within the next four hours. Any Gendarme who fails to comply with this order will be arrested. Thank you.'

The room erupted in a barrage of questions. Eniko tapped the microphone, until it quietened. 'We have a handheld microphone and I will direct it to whoever is asking a question.' She looked out over the room. Gerald Palin, the correspondent for Associated Press, had his arm up to get her attention. So did every journalist in the room, but Gerald had helped her out numerous times while she worked for 555.hu and she owed him a favour. One of Eniko's assistants, a skinny young man barely out of his teens in a too-tight suit called Leonard, walked across the room and handed Gerald the microphone. He stood up before he spoke, first introducing himself. 'I have a short and simple question for the prime minister.' The correspondent for Agence France Press, a rival, said, 'That makes a change.' There was scattered laughter as Gerald waved him away. 'Go ahead,' said Eniko.

Gerald turned to Eniko. 'You may have the legal right to dissolve the Gendarmerie, prime minister, but what if they refuse to be dissolved. How will you enforce this measure? The Gendarmerie are a very powerful paramilitary force, and have repeatedly proved themselves ready to use violence. You just said they will be arrested. What if they resist arrest?'

Reka nodded. 'That is a good question.' She leaned forward to emphasise her words. 'I can promise you that the full force of the state will be deployed...' The noise of revving engines sounded again, louder, faster, sharper now, drowning out her reply. Reka paused until the noise stopped, then continued speaking. 'As I said... will be deployed to ensure that the law is complied with.'

The journalists looked at each other, the same questions going through their minds. What was this racket and why wasn't it being stopped? How could she disband the Gendarmerie when she couldn't even hold a press conference without being disrupted? Eniko and Reka glanced at each other. They had not prepared for this scenario. Eniko looked out at the journalists. Zsuzsa had her hand up. Eniko directed Leonard to hand her the microphone. 'Who will arrest them?' asked Zsuzsa. Eniko nodded to herself. A good question, just like she had taught her former protégé. Short and simple. And very much to the point.

Eniko glanced at Reka. Just as Reka was about to answer, the engine noise sounded up again. Reka started speaking but her answer was drowned out by the racket. She stiffened and tried to speak over the noise, her authority draining away with every syllable. This time the sounds of the engines did not fade away and was soon joined by another sound: the quick-fire thump of helicopter rotor blades.

A voice asked, 'Are we being buzzed?' The journalists ran over to the large windows. Several television camera operators took their equipment down from their stands, hoisted the cameras onto their shoulders and rushed over to the window. Others kept their lenses trained on Reka at the lectern.

The noise of rotor blades sounded louder than ever. A black helicopter was swooping low over Kossuth Square, then banked sharply leftwards and soared up above the Parliament building. The excited chatter fell silent as the journalists watched a stream of black Gendarmerie SUVs drive down Alkotmany Street, towards Kossuth Square. The vehicles fanned out and parked all around the square, in front of the concrete blocks, and down the sides. Tourists stood staring, some open-mouthed, many holding their telephones in their hands as they filmed the spectacle. Reka stopped talking, glanced at one of her bodyguards who had already stepped towards the window in the corner to scan the scene unfolding. He quickly muttered into his mouthpiece as he turned on his heel and walked over to the lectern. The other three bodyguards quickly joined him and boxed in Reka again, directing her out of the room, several television cameras following her exit.

Eniko, too, walked over to the window. Her first press conference would likely be her last. This was a total disaster, it was clear. But an organised disaster. A very well organised one. She could see right down into the centre of the square and watched as a squat, familiar figure stepped out of the lead vehicle, leaned against the door and lazily lit a cigarette: Attila Ungar.

Gerald Palin turned to Eniko. 'They don't look very banned.'

★

Underground car park, Szabadsag Square, 12.20 p.m.

Marton Ronay turned to the man sitting next to him in the driver's seat of the scruffy Volkswagen. The car was parked in a distant, barely lit corner of the car park, a short walk from Kossuth Square. 'Brad,' as he called himself, said he was a diplomat but he didn't look like one. All the diplomats Marton had met were sleek and smooth, carefully shaven, wearing well-fitted suits. If they smelled of anything it was an expensive cologne or aftershave. They presented themselves well, watched their posture. This man sat slumped in the car seat. He wore chinos with a grease stain on the left thigh, a crumpled button-down shirt that had once, perhaps, been white, and scuffed white leather trainers. He had a paunch, his long greasy hair was streaked with grey, and he smelled of cigarettes. And American diplomats didn't drive cars like this, with Hungarian plates. So what was this about? Marton sat back, trying in vain to get more comfortable, feeling the worn springs of the seat give way underneath his weight, the hard metal pressing against his thigh.

'How can I help you, Mr... er,' asked Marton. He paused. 'Actually I don't even know your full name. What is it, may I ask?'

Brad laughed. 'You can call me Brad. That's enough.'

'And why are we meeting here?'

'Because it's near our embassy. And near to your clients.'

'OK, but how do I know that you even work for the embassy? I looked on the website. There are no employees listed who are called Brad. And nobody who looks like you,' Marton said, his voice rising in indignation as he looked around the grey concrete walls and pillars. 'Can I at least see some ID?'

'ID, yeah, good idea.' Brad pretended to rummage in his pockets, found nothing. 'Oops, looks like I must have left it in the office. We could take a walk over there; it's only a couple of minutes away but it takes forever to get through security. And all that time you would be visible to anyone passing by – who might wonder what the famous Marton Ronay, spin doctor extraordinaire, is doing there and who he might be seeing. Especially your clients, whose office is so nearby.'

Marton sighed. Brad, or whatever his name was, had a point. 'Media consultant, please. OK. No embassy. But give me something. Who are you? Who do you work for?'

'A government agency. Let's say that if it makes you feel more comfortable.' Brad turned to Marton, fixed him with pale-blue eyes that did not blink.

Marton looked away first. A black saloon cruised past on the other side of the car park as understanding slowly dawned. 'Oh. A government agency headquartered in Langley?' he asked, naming the township in Virginia where the CIA had its headquarters.

'You said that. Let's move on.' Brad sat up, his voice brisk. 'Now, we need your help, Marton. Or should I call you Marty?'

'I prefer Marton, thanks.'

'OK, Marton. You are a patriotic American? You will help us?' said Brad, although it was a statement more than a question.

'Sure. Of course.'

'You are meeting your clients in an hour. At their office, on the other side of the square.'

Marton nodded. There was no point asking Brad how he knew that. 'What do you want me to do?'

'Normally we'd put something in your phone. But they are upping security. They will put your phone in a secure bag at reception. You won't even be able to take it into the meeting.'

Marton sat back, blinked. 'What? You want me to bug the meeting? Why? They are clients. I'm working for them. I'm not doing anything illegal. I pay taxes. Everything is declared.'

Brad laughed. 'Calm down. We know that you are an honest corporate citizen. And you are very good at your job.' He fixed Marton with an appraising gaze, nodded slowly. 'That hashtag – #honestreportingHungary – that's pretty clever. There is no personal attack on Eniko Szalay. Instead we have a broad consensus issue that also keeps the pressure on the target. Who doesn't want honest reporting?' He nodded slowly. 'Subtle. I like it. Once this is all over, you and I should have another chat. We could use your talents, over there in Langley.' His voice hardened. 'Meanwhile, what your clients are planning, what they will be talking about once you have left, is definitely not legal. Not legal at all.'

'What plans?'

Brad rummaged in his pocket, took out a crumpled packet of Marlboro Light cigarettes. He looked at Marton. 'Do you mind?'

'Yes. I do actually.'

Brad opened the car window, wound it down before lighting a cigarette and blowing the smoke outside. 'How's that?'

'Fine. But what plans and why are you interested in them?'

'You been to Keleti?'

Marton shook his head. 'Should I?'

Brad looked at his cigarette, as though it held the answer. 'You should. You're a smart guy. Take a look. There are some genuine refugees there, families with kids. But look harder and you'll see lots of single, military-aged men from Afghanistan and the Middle East passing through with no or false papers. What does that suggest to you?' He drew on his cigarette, blew some more smoke out of the window. 'I'll give you a clue. It begins with the letter "T".'

Marton sighed. Becoming a CIA asset, getting mixed up in terrorism, was not what he had signed up for. Nor did he like the way Brad had played him at the airport and afterwards. 'OK. I get it. But that was a shitty trick you pulled with the telephone.'

Brad nodded sympathetically. 'Yeah. You're right. Sorry about that,' he said, not sounding sorry at all. 'But we needed to make sure you took the call.'

'What's this got to do with my clients?'

Brad smiled, revealing a row of nicotine-stained teeth. 'Well, Marton, that's where we hope you can help us.'

'And if I say no?'

'Then you might find that the Department of Justice, Homeland Security and the Internal Revenue Service will be taking a keen look at Marton Ronay Consulting. And your own personal tax returns as well. Which somehow don't mention your bank account in the Cayman Islands.'

Marton damped down his anger. There was nothing he could do except get this over with as quickly as possible. Whatever 'this' was. 'And my job is?'

Brad reached into his pocket and pulled out a small plastic box. He carefully took the lid off. Marton's smile faded when he saw what was inside: a metal object the size of a large pin-head with several wires extruding from the base.

'Seriously?' asked Marton. 'There's no other way around this?'

'None.'

'But you're... whoever you are. You have people for this stuff. People who know what they are doing. I'm not a spy. Why me?'

'Because that room is swept for bugs every morning. Then nobody gets in who does not work for Pal Dezeffy. Which is why America is calling on you, Marton, to do your patriotic duty. And because we don't have time to find anyone else. This kind of work is all about improvisation. Using whatever you have. And we have you, who in a couple of hours will be in that room.'

'But don't I need something to attach it to? Some putty or something, to make it stick under the table or wherever?'

Brad laughed. 'You've been watching too many spy movies. Just drop it on the floor somewhere. But not under the table obviously. Somewhere where it can't be seen.'

Marton suddenly felt exhausted. Waves of jet lag were hitting him. 'Sure. I'll just take a walk around the room when they are distracted. Find a good hiding place.'

'Sounds like a plan,' said Brad, his voice dry.

'No, it does not. And if I say no?'

'You can say no, of course. And then you can deal with the consequences which I believe I have outlined to you.' Brad paused, fixed Marton with a cold gaze. 'The truth is, Marton, you are in *way* out of your depth. And you are in danger of sinking hard and fast. These are seriously bad people. The less you have to do with them, the better.' He grinned suddenly, slapped Marton on the shoulder. 'But don't worry. You got yourself a lifeboat. As long as you follow the captain's instructions.'

'What if they search me, find it on me?'

Brad smiled, a genuine smile this time, 'Well, *Marty*, better make sure they don't.'

Kossuth Square

As Marton Ronay wondered how on earth he was going to bug his next meeting, a short walk away Kata Kiss and her crew were standing by a Gendarmerie vehicle. Her cameraman zoomed in on Attila Ungar as she asked her first question.

'Why are you and your colleagues still here, in your uniforms? Haven't you heard that the Gendarmerie has been disbanded?'

Attila sniffed and scratched the back of his neck, before turning to several of his colleagues. They, like him, were leaning on the doors of their black SUVs, which were now parked in the centre of Kossuth Square, ten yards from the main doorway to Parliament. 'Hear that, lads? Apparently we've been disbanded.'

The other Gendarmes shrugged. One lit a cigarette, another checked his mobile telephone. Attila turned back to Kata Kiss. 'News to us.'

The cameraman panned to a group of Israeli tourists passing by on electric Segways, then to a young Chinese couple posing for selfies with the Gendarmes and their vehicles in the background. The thud of rotor blades again sounded in the distance.

Kata replied, 'I was at a press conference a short while ago with Prime Minister Bardossy. Not only did she say that your organisation has been disbanded, but also that unless you surrendered your uniforms, vehicles and weapons within four hours, you would all be arrested.'

'Gosh,' said Attila, 'that's scary.'

The cameraman panned to several members of the parliamentary ceremonial guard. The guardsmen usually goose-stepped back and forth across the flagstones with military precision every half-hour, but now stood huddled by the doorway. Their Second World War rifles, complete with bayonets, were stacked in a corner. Several of the guardsmen stood smoking. Others watched disconsolately at the spectacle unfolding on their former parade ground.

Attila nodded, dropped his cigarette on the ground and ground it out with his boot. 'So we've got three hours, you say.'

'Not me, the prime minister.'

'Who's going to arrest us?'

'I don't know. The police maybe? The army?'

'The army.' Attila laughed, took his pistol out of its holster and looked it over as though checking for flaws. Kata looked alarmed. Attila said, 'Don't worry, sweetheart, the safety's on.' He stared at the camera, his gun still in his hand. 'Well, officers, you know where to find us.'

As if on cue, the sound of the rotor blades became a roar as the black helicopter swooped low over the square, scattering the tourists in every direction.

TWENTY

Balthazar sat back on his sofa, feet up on the low coffee table, flipping through the foreign news channels as he half watched the evening footage. All his telephones, the burners from Sandor and Anastasia and his iPhone were there, together with his wallet, a new Glock 17 pistol that he had been given by the Parliament security staff, a black leather shoulder holster and a cold cup of tea. The same clip was playing on both of them from the end of Reka Bardossy's disastrous press conference: the footage showed her walking out of the Kossuth Hall, surrounded by her bodyguards, Eniko trailing behind, while the world's press corps were huddled excitedly around the windows that looked out over Kossuth Square. And Kossuth Square, it was clear, was now the epicentre of the story. The white television vans that just a day ago had been parked at Keleti Station had now relocated to the space in front of Parliament and the patches of green to its sides. A reporter from CNN, a middle-aged American woman with dyed blonde hair and an over-eager smile, was interviewing an angry Hungarian man in his fifties, standing by a blue tent. He wore a black T-shirt and black combat trousers and claimed to be representing something called the Hungarian Freedom Movement. His long black hair, streaked with grey, was pulled back in a ponytail, under a bandana in the colours of the Hungarian flag. As a Gypsy, Balthazar kept a fairly close eye on Hungary's fissiparous far right, but he had never heard of this group.

'Why are you here and what do you want?' asked the reporter.

'Reka Bardossy is a traitor. She must resign,' said the man, jabbing at the camera with his right forefinger.

The reporter gestured for the cameraman to step back a little and continued talking. 'How is she a traitor? She is an elected MP and a former cabinet minister.'

The man paused for a moment, his face creased in concentration before he spoke. 'She is a *komcsi*. She turned our country into a staging post for terrorists. An army of migrants is on the march, using Hungary as a launch pad to get to the west. She must resign.'

'And if she refuses?' asked the CNN journalist.

'She will have no choice,' said the man.

Balthazar picked up his telephone and called Sandor Takacs. He answered on the first ring. 'Have you seen CNN?' asked Balthazar.

'Sure. He's also on the BBC and our television as well.'

'Who is he? What is the Hungarian Freedom Movement?'

'I don't know. But they have tents, walkie-talkies and matching bandanas. So they are organised.'

'Where are the police? What are our people doing? I thought we were supposed to enforce law and order. We weren't scared of the Gendarmes last weekend. Why are we now?'

Sandor said, 'Last week Reka looked like a winner. Now she doesn't. I can't pull that stunt again with their vehicles, Tazi. Attila's boys have since threatened all the officers who went to the Four Seasons. Some of their families as well. I can't give orders or make requests that will be refused.'

'What about the army? They could clear the square, get rid of the Gendarmes in a half-an-hour.'

'Do you want a civil war, Tazi? Nobody is going to fight for a prime minister who has not even won an election. The soldiers are like the cops. Watching and waiting.'

That left one other force. 'And the state security service?' asked Balthazar.

'The same. Except maybe for Anastasia and one or two others.'

'So where does that leave us?'

'Reka is a survivor. She'll think of something, I'm sure.'

'She might think about surrendering.'

'She might, Tazi. But she probably won't. Good night. We'll speak first thing tomorrow.'

Balthazar picked up his wallet and took out the government-issued ID with the warrant from the prime minister's office. He looked at his photograph, the wording authorising his mission, the request for assistance from all state bodies and authorities. He should be down at Kossuth Square, seeing for himself what was happening. In fact it was clear what was going on: an organised attempt at some kind of coup, doubtless being run behind the scenes by Pal Dezeffy. He put his wallet down and checked the 555.hu website on his phone. The site was running live updates from its reporters positioned across the city. The Gendarmes had not been disbanded. Instead they had deployed in force across downtown Budapest. They had set up checkpoints by the main interchanges, along the Grand Boulevard, the main metro and train stations. Most crucially of all, they had taken control of Kossuth Square and so now controlled entrance to Parliament. Balthazar scrolled

ADAM LEBOR

through the BBC and CNN. Both home pages featured a large photograph of Attila Ungar in uniform, lounging on his black SUV, with Parliament in the background. In the age of social media, the image was everything. Attila was in control. As for the actual prime minister, Reka had not been seen in public since the disastrous press conference. Her authority was draining away minute by minute. She could not control the patch of ground in front of her office. So how could she run a country? After the events of the day, it was looking more and more likely that Reka would be forced out of office, thought Balthazar. And if the prime minister did step down, where did that leave him?

But now family matters pressed down on him, not those of state. Balthazar leaned back for a moment and closed his eyes. He could still smell his brother on the sofa fabric. Had Gaspar known? There were many different ways to know things, especially in a family like his, with its rich – too rich – repository of secrets. But on balance, he thought that Gaspar had not known that he – *they* – had a half-sister, and a half-*gadje* one. Gaspar was quite hopeless at keeping secrets from him. Balthazar could read his younger brother like a book – luckily, as that skill had ensured that he got his brother out of trouble more times than he could count.

He glanced across the room, where Virag still looked out at him, frozen in time in her youthful beauty. How to process what he had learned today? He had once had a sister. A half-sister, in fact, but whatever their connection he could not have loved her more. No more pain accompanied this discovery. But there was amazement, amazement tinged with anger. His mother had kept this from him for twenty years. Not just the fact of his actual connection to Virag, but his mother's affair... fling, whatever... with his boss. Except his

290

mother did not have flings or affairs. She had fallen in love with Sandor Takacs all those years ago. In another world, Sandor Takacs might have been his father. Was that why he had taken him under his wing as his protégé, protected Balthazar as his career had steadily progressed? Because of guilt? No, not solely. There was some, how could there not be? But guilt alone was too simple an explanation.

Balthazar and his boss had sat on the bench and talked for some time after Sandor's confession. Balthazar had asked question after question. But the basic narrative was clear and simple. One night in the late 1970s, when Sandor was a young detective in the Budapest vice squad, he had been called to a fight in a bar in the backstreets of District VIII owned by Lajos Kovacs, Balthazar's grandfather. One of the hostesses, a seventeen-year-old Marta Kovacs, had been talking to a customer called Mishi. Mishi wanted to take Marta to a nearby hotel where rooms could be rented by the hour. It was explained to Mishi that the bar was not a brothel, but that service was available nearby, with plenty of girls to choose from. Marta, however, was not one of them and would be going home soon. Without Mishi. But Mishi, drunk and angry, refused to take no for an answer. He slapped Marta and insulted her.

This was a very bad idea. Marta's protectors, her uncles and brothers, instantly fell on Mishi and his friends. The fight did not go well for them. They were thrown out onto the street and given a serious kicking. Scared by the level of violence she was witnessing, Marta called the police. By the time Sandor Takacs and two colleagues arrived, the fight was over. Mishi had been taken away in an ambulance. Sandor and his fellow police officers did their best, trying to take statements, but eventually gave up after being continuously stonewalled. Nobody saw anything, nobody knew anything. Sandor expected nothing else but still went through the motions. In any case, they all – cops and Gypsies alike – knew that a fight in a bar in the backstreets of District VIII would never be a priority for investigation. But the young detective was completely beguiled by the girl who had phoned for the police, and she by him. They began to meet in secret. The danger of discovery – Sandor would have been sacked, Marta ostracised by her family, or worse – only fuelled their passion. Sandor was Marta's first boyfriend and she, his first serious relationship. They fell in love and began to talk of a future together. Then Marta became pregnant. After the initial shock – as far as her parents knew, she was still a virgin and would be when she soon married – it was decided that she would be allowed to keep the baby. On condition that she broke off all contact with Sandor and never saw him again. She agreed. She had no choice. A seventeeen-year-old Gypsy girl with a limited high school education had nowhere to go. Soon afterwards, Marta was married to Laci, Balthazar's father. Virag was absorbed into the family and her origins never spoken of.

The story of Virag's brief life, Balthazar realised, raised more questions than it answered. Had Sandor kept in touch with Marta? Had he followed Virag's progress to adulthood? Had he ever met his daughter? And did Virag know who her real father was? A simple deception about Virag's paternity had needed a whole web of lies around it to hold it in place. And what did he know about her death? But Balthazar knew that whatever answers he was looking for would not materialise that evening. This would be a long and slow investigation. He glanced again at the photograph of Virag, emotions surging through him. There was nothing to do except to let them flow. In time the shock would lessen and he could plot a course through the minefield of his family history. He picked up the warrant again and weighed it in his hand, once more looking down at his face staring out of the plastic laminate. He had accepted an assignment, which meant he needed to honour that commitment. Reka Bardossy might be a busted flush, but she was still prime minister, for now, at least. In any case, he reminded himself, he had a personal reason to carry out his mission of investigating Pal Dezeffy: Virag had died at Pal's house.

He glanced at his watch: it was one minute before nine. *Panorama*, the Hungarian state TV evening news bulletin, was about to start. Like every Hungarian who followed current affairs, Balthazar knew how to read the runes. The system of coded messages honed under Communism had outlived the one-party state. *Panorama*'s slant and bias would give a good sense of whether Reka Bardossy might yet weather the storm or if her power was already waning. The earlier news programme, with the footage of Reka and Eniko at the Four Seasons, was not a good omen for either woman. Balthazar sat up and watched as the lead story, shot earlier that day, showed Attila Ungar looking supremely unconcerned as he answered Kata Kiss's questions, and his mocking answer as he played with his pistol. A panning shot followed of the chaos on Kossuth Square as the helicopter roared overhead, scattering tourists and reporters alike, then footage of the two clusters of tents, which had now grown to half a dozen on either side of Parliament. The programme then switched to live footage of Kossuth Square. The Gendarmerie vans were all still in place, and numerous uniformed Gendarmes were nonchalantly strolling around, several smoking cigarettes or taking selfies in front of their vehicles. A voiceover noted that while Reka Bardossy had disbanded the Gendarmerie that day at noon, the message did not seem to have reached Kossuth Square.

The show then switched to the studio where Nandor Balogh, the youthful host, was introducing two familiar guests. Demeter Lazar, a pompous, pot-bellied man in his late sixties with thick grey hair that badly needed a trim, was introduced as a 'politologist', a Hungarian speciality which meant, more or less, a cross between a political scientist, commentator and analyst, and Kitti Karpati, an attractive young historian in her early thirties. Demeter had been a regular on the evening news for years, long before Balogh had taken the hot seat, and would doubtless be there once he had moved on. Demeter's politology largely consisted of apologia for the old system, under which he had also been a well-known analyst, and praise for Pal Dezeffy's reforms. Karpati had recently headed a commission of historians who had caused outrage on the conservative wing of Hungarian politics after authoring a new history textbook that positioned the Communist Party of the 1980s as far-reaching reformers who had intentionally brought down the one-party state for the greater good.

State television, Balthazar could see, had made its mind up. After days of equivocation, slanting the evening news one day in favour of Pal and the next to show Reka Bardossy in a good light, the broadcaster had come down in favour of the former regime. Pal was winning. In terms of viewers, that counted for little. Hungarians watched a lot of television, but most preferred the many commercial channels and streaming services such as Netflix and HBO. State television was the least-watched channel in the country, of interest only to politics geeks and junkies in the capital. But it was the perfect bellwether for judging political battles. It was clear that behind the scenes – and the studios – Pal was marshalling his forces.

The discussion, such as it was, was only of interest to confirm the new political line. Both Demeter and Kitti repeatedly referred to Reka Bardossy's role in the passport scandal, with frequent cut-aways to scenes of chaos at Keleti Station and on the border. The consensus was that if that was not enough, today's events on Kossuth Square were the beginning of the end for her administration. Demeter shifted in his seat, making sure he addressed the camera before intoning: 'We will not let Hungary be a staging post for terrorists. Nor are we a launch pad for an army of migrants to get to the west.' The same phrases, Balthazar noticed, that the angry man from the Hungarian Freedom Movement had used.

The ring of a telephone sounded, breaking his train of thought. Balthazar glanced down at the coffee table and saw his iPhone screen glowing. He glanced down at the screen: it was Eniko.

Headquarters of the Foundation for the Relief of Poverty, Szabadsag Square, 9.10 p.m.

Marton Ronay watched Pal Dezeffy as he turned towards him, a smile slowly spreading across his face. Pal's body language was relaxed and confident, quite different from their encounter that morning, as he started speaking. 'Marton, what a difference a day makes. Well done. I must admit I had some doubts when you presented your action plan. But it seems to have worked. So far, so good.'

Marton nodded warily. 'Thank you. I am pleased you are pleased.'

There were four of them in the room again: Marton, Pal, Adorjan Molnar and the old guy with the skin problem, all sitting back around the black mahogany table. The blinds were down and the lighting was muted. Trays of coffee, biscuits, fruit and muffins sat in the middle of the table. The large flat-screen television was showing four news channels simultaneously: BBC, CNN, NBC and Reuters. All were reporting from Kossuth Square, showing the now-familiar vista of Gendarmerie vehicles, blue tents pitched on the grass, protestors from the Hungarian Freedom Movement, and legions of tourists taking selfies. Marton and the others had been talking for twenty minutes or so, outlining Reka Bardossy's political position.

Adorjan looked around the table. Pal nodded at him and he started speaking. 'Let's recap where we are.' He looked at Marton. 'You emphasised this morning the words *doubt* and *confusion*. On both those fronts we are doing very well. Reka Bardossy's strategy was to portray her involvement in the passport scandal as a sting operation, aided by Eniko Szalay's reporting. Their credibility has been shredded by our release of the video of them drinking cocktails at the Four Seasons, as you recommended. In addition Szalay now works for Reka, which casts a backwards shadow over all her previous reporting. Your clever hashtag, #honestreportingHungary, is still trending here. The phrases that you suggested: "staging post for terrorists", Hungary as "a launch pad for an army of migrants" are now entering common parlance. And Reka Bardossy's first press conference, where she attempted to impose her authority as prime minister, was a disaster.'

'Thanks, Adorjan. But I cannot take credit for that,'

said Marton. Part of him was pleased at the praise, as any professional would be. But another was increasingly uneasy. He had been replaying his encounter with the mysterious Brad in his mind for much of the afternoon, before he had arrived at the client's offices. The more he went over it, the less he liked it. His own government had blackmailed him into a bugging a client. And what if it all went wrong, if they found the bug, or he messed it up somehow? Brad, whoever he was, would not be rising to the rescue, that much was clear. Marton was flying solo, without a parachute. He glanced at the television for a moment, where a reporter from the BBC was interviewing a group of men outside one of the blue tents. Just as Brad had predicted, his mobile telephone had been taken from him before he entered the conference room, although he had not been searched. The bug was in a small box that felt enormous in his pocket. How the hell was he going to get it out of the box and drop it somewhere, without being seen, and without the bug being discovered by these 'seriously bad people', as Brad had described them? He glanced at the jug of water and the vague outline of a plan began to form in his mind. Lost in his uneasy thoughts, for a moment he suddenly realised all three men were looking at him, waiting for him to say something. 'The helicopter was a master stroke,' he quickly said. 'Who's idea was that?'

Both Pal and Adorjan glanced at the old guy. He barely acknowledged their looks, briefly scratched the side of his neck where the skin was cracked and flaking, then pulled out another of his foul-smelling cigarettes. 'Mine,' he rasped. 'A prime minister who cannot control the space in front of her office, neither on the ground nor in the air, cannot govern a country.'

'True. So what comes next?' asked Marton. He reached for the jug of water, poured himself a glass and slowly drank it. The jug was almost empty now.

The old man lit his cigarette, blew out a plume of smoke, then coughed. 'Plenty. And when we need your input, we will let you know.'

Marton realised he'd been dismissed. But the bug was still in his pocket. Department of Justice. Homeland Security. The Internal Revenue Service. The list of government departments bounced around inside his head. It was now or never. He stood up to leave, then leaned forward, almost losing his balance, then lurched back, blinking rapidly and sharply inhaling. Pal and Adorjan watched Marton swaying back and forth, then glanced at each other, both looking alarmed.

Marton said, 'I'm sorry. It must be the jet lag. I don't usually get it like this.'

Pal quickly agreed, relief on his face. 'Yes, of course. You must be right. We brought you here virtually straight from the airport. You've had no chance to rest and gather your strength.'

Marton closed his eyes for a moment, gripping the end of the table, then opened them. Pal and Adorjan looked genuinely concerned. The old man was staring at him with an expression of irritation. Marton said, 'Jet lag, plus my stomach ulcer. Not a great combination. It flares up when I'm tired. Could I just sit down on the sofa for a moment? It's more comfortable. I just need to rest for a short while. Maybe even lie down. I'll be fine, I'm sure.'

Pal stood up and walked over to him. 'Of course. Take a little time out.' He turned to Adorjan and the old man. 'We can break for a few minutes, OK?' They both nodded.

Pal led Marton to the sofa. Marton sat back and closed his eyes for several seconds. 'Could you get me some water, please?'

Pal said, 'Of course,' walked over to the table, poured a glass of water and brought it to him. Marton sipped it slowly, once again feeling the box in his pocket pressing against his upper thigh. Pal and Adorjan stood nearby, watching him with concern.

'Are you OK?' asked Pal.

'I'll be fine, I'm sure,' said Marton. He turned to them. 'It's been a long day. Don't worry about me, please, grab a coffee, do whatever you need to do.'

Pal nodded. 'Thanks. We'll be back in a minute.' He and Adorjan walked back across the room and out of the door.

Two down, one to go, thought Marton. He looked across at the old man. He was reading something, then as if sensing Marton's gaze, looked up at him. 'Sir,' asked Marton, holding his empty glass in front of him, 'I hate to ask, but would you mind? I still feel a little wobbly.'

The old man stared at him for several seconds, then stubbed his cigarette out, stood up and took Marton's glass from him. He walked over to the table and picked up the water jug. There was barely any left inside. He stared at Marton once more, then walked out of the room. Marton did a quick mental calculation. He had about thirty seconds at the most, less if Pal or Adorjan returned before the old man. His heart thumping, he reached into his trouser pocket, opened the box, removed the lid, placed it on his trouser leg, lowered his arm down the side of the sofa and turned the box upside down before quickly bringing it back up. He glanced inside. It was empty.

At that moment Pal walked back in, the old man behind him with a full jug of water. They both looked at Marton holding a small box, the lid resting on his trousers. Pal frowned, but before he could speak, Marton smiled and shook his head. 'I'm so stupid. The one day I need my anti-ulcer medicine, I forget to put it in my pillbox.'

CIA safe house, Filler Street, 10.10 p.m.

Anastasia Ferenczy, Brad Miller and Celeste Johnson sat at one end of a heavy antique wooden table in a kitchen that pre-dated the Second World War. The floor was covered with cracked linoleum in a red-and-black pattern and the walls were painted a faded shade of green. There were no fitted units, only a free-standing cooker and chipped white enamel sink, with a small gas boiler above it. A Hungarian nobleman with a fine waxed moustache seated on a horse, stared out of a gloomy oil painting, flanked on both sides by a Vizsla hunting dog. A laptop stood in the centre of the table, together with half a dozen used or half-empty coffee cups.

Anastasia suppressed a shiver before she spoke. Even after two months of a long, sweltering summer, the house felt damp and cold. The villa, with its long corridors of unused rooms and dark, heavy furniture covered in dust sheets, was haunted, she was sure. She glanced at the nobleman on a horse. She did not know the full story of the house, only that it had once belonged to an aristocratic family, something like hers, before being appropriated by the Communists after 1945 and then somehow ending up in the hands of the American intelligence services.

'Shall we listen again to the crucial part?' asked Miller. The two women nodded. He scrolled back through the digital file, then pressed play.

Pal: 'It's all happened faster than we anticipated.'

The Librarian: 'Perhaps. But we can adjust to that.'

Adorjan: 'She's dead in the water.' He paused before continuing. 'How to finish off a government. Fly a helicopter over the Parliament while the prime minister is giving a press conference. Amazing.'

Pal: 'Then set a trap so she announces a policy she cannot implement.'

Adorjan: 'And have a paramilitary force occupy the seat of power, the symbolic heart of the country.'

The Librarian: 'You may finish the mutual admiration. We are not done yet.'

Pal: 'Are you sure? Is that really necessary? She'll be gone in a few days. Her authority is destroyed.'

The Librarian: 'Destroyed. Is it? Is it really? So was yours at the start of the week. And now it's Friday evening and here we are, plotting your return to power.' A pause. 'Assuming you still want to return to power.'

Pal: 'Of course. Of course I do.'

The Librarian: 'Then we must deliver the coup de grace. As planned.'

Adorjan. 'But so many? We could simply just… remove her. For good.'

The Librarian: 'And then, just after the totally accidental car-crash, or whatever else you dream up, Pal rides back to rescue Hungary. That would not look suspicious. Not at all,' he said, his voice heavy with sarcasm. 'No. That won't work. We need to destroy her authority, with her still alive. Once and for all. And we need to accelerate. For now, we have momentum on our side.'

Pal: 'When?'

The Librarian: 'Tomorrow night.'

Brad Miller stopped the file, turned to look at Celeste Johnson and Anastasia. 'That was earlier this evening, after Marton Ronay dropped the bug in the room.' He sat back, stretched his hands in front of him. 'What are they planning?'

Celeste said, 'Some kind of terrorist attack, I assume. But where, and what?'

Anastasia said, 'They want to destroy Reka Bardossy's authority. Make it impossible for her to govern.' She looked at Miller and Johnson. 'Where does her authority derive from?'

'Parliament,' said Johnson.

Celeste said, 'Which is in Kossuth Square. Which is already occupied by the Gendarmes and the Hungarian Freedom Movement. And being buzzed by helicopters.'

Anastasia nodded, glanced again at the painting. The nobleman seemed to be staring at her, willing her on. Maybe the house really was haunted. God knew, enough of Hungary was. 'Kossuth Square. The epicentre of the capital. That makes sense. And tomorrow night. It's already a massive attraction for locals and tourists. There will be hundreds of people there by tomorrow evening.'

'So what are they planning?' asked Brad. 'A bomb? A helicopter suicide mission?'

Anastasia gestured at the laptop. 'Let's take a look at it now. 555.hu has set up a live feed from Kossuth Square. Just Google it – you'll find it.' She glanced at her watch. Miller tapped away, then found the feed. He opened the browser window, then turned the laptop around so that the screen faced the two women.

The feed showed Kossuth Square from the left side, by the statue of the Hungarian for which it was named. The space was more crowded than ever but the atmosphere seemed almost festive. A group of Gendarmes lounged against their vehicles, eating slices of a pizza in a box on the bonnet. A teenage boy turned wheelies on his BMX. The regular police and the Parliamentary Guard were nowhere to be seen. Two young Chinese women wandered around, eating enormous ice creams. A few seconds later gusts of white steam erupted across the square, hissing upwards from tiny nozzles embedded in the flagstones, enveloping tourists and Gendarmes alike. The two Chinese girls happily ran through the mist as it swirled around them, coating their clothes and skin.

TWENTY-ONE

Balthazar's flat, 10.15 p.m.

Eniko Szalay cupped her mug of fruit tea in her hands as she looked down at the coffee table, staring at the Glock and the shoulder holster. 'There's a gun there.'

'Well spotted. I'm a cop,' said Balthazar. 'Hungarian cops carry weapons.'

She put the drink down, leaned forward, slid her forefinger under the holster's leather strap and raised it above the table, letting it dangle under her multi-coloured nails. 'I don't remember usually seeing a gun around. Or you having three phones.'

'These aren't usual times.'

'So I'm learning,' said Eniko, with a wry smile. 'It looks quite scary,' she said, reaching for the weapon.

Balthazar's hand was on hers in an instant. For a moment he felt the warmth of her skin under his fingers, then he let go. 'It's not a toy, Eni. It's a Glock 17.'

She smiled, started to say something, read his face and instead stayed silent. Balthazar sensed her emotions, but looked away and picked up the black pistol. He pointed it at the wall and looked down the square-shaped barrel. The Glock felt solid and reliable in his hand. It had sharp, modern lines, an indented non-slip handle and a trigger guard that ended in a curved point. The Glock was a state-of-the-art serious combat weapon, the same model carried by the Gendarmerie

Eniko asked, 'Are you in danger, Tazi?'

'I don't know.'

'Am I?' she asked, her voice suddenly strained, almost fearful.

This time Balthazar looked at her before he answered. Her hair was scraped back in a severe ponytail. She wore grey jogging trousers and a baggy sweatshirt. There was no trace of the confident, smartly dressed government spokeswoman who had taken the lectern in the Kossuth Hall that morning next to the prime minister. She looked pale, miserable and exhausted. Their history was a mess, of love found, hopes dashed, miscommunications, all the tangles of a relationship that had crashed and burned. But still, they had a history. Perhaps a future too, a part of him still sometimes hoped. But now she was here with him, asking him for shelter and reassurance, which he would provide.

'No, Eni. You are not in danger. Not while you are here with me.'

She put the holster down, then swallowed before she answered. 'Thank you.'

Eniko had sounded almost tearful when she had called and asked if she could come over. He had agreed, of course, but now he wondered if it was such a good idea. She looked in severe need of a hug, and if he knew her, she would welcome it. A surprisingly large part of him wanted nothing more than to take her in his arms and flow into whatever happened next. He was fairly sure that would lead them both into his bedroom. Another part of him told himself that that course of action, while momentarily pleasurable, would be an extremely bad idea. What might be a temporary moment of comfort for Eniko would trigger a large tranche of hopes and emotions in him that only now were finally fading. Maybe – maybe – he would explore that once this crisis was over. But for now, his emotions were the least of his priorities. There was the unfolding chaos outside, and there was his personal mission. He glanced over at the framed picture, staring out at him, a snapshot of Virag's youthful beauty and innocence, frozen in time. Now he had a lead. Virag had died at Pal Dezeffy's house. Reka's warrant gave him the means to pursue it. And if things got really dangerous, as he sensed they were about to, he also had the Glock. He put the gun back down on the table and moved away from Eniko, slightly, but enough to be noticeable. 'Don't touch.'

She gave him a wan smile. 'Don't worry, Tazi. No touching.' Eniko picked up her cup and took a drink of the tea. 'Tazi, what's going to happen? It feels like everything is out of control.'

'It's out of Reka's control. But it's very much under Pal's control.'

'I think you're right. Who benefits from all this chaos? He does, most of all.'

'You know I've got a special warrant from Reka Bardossy to investigate him?'

Eniko laughed. 'Sure. Reka told me. I'm not sure why, though. I don't think there's anyone who knows more about Pal than her. They've been lovers on and off for almost twenty years. He was her first serious boyfriend, when they were still teenagers. They used to go to parties together in the Buda hills, in the fancy villas that the Communists took and never gave back. There were all sorts of rumours about them, back in the day.'

Balthazar thought for a moment, processing what Eniko said. 'What kind of rumours?'

'They were the elite, Tazi. They could do whatever they wanted and get away with it. If any laws were broken, there would be no repercussions. That did not stop in the early 1990s. I'm a rep—*was* a reporter. There were all sorts of rumours about dirty money. We were thinking of doing a big investigation on Reka at 555 when she was appointed minister of justice.'

'Why didn't you?'

'Because our – the website's – owner, who went to school and university and who once sat on the same national committee of the Young Communist League with Pal and Reka, and who subsidises 555.hu for reasons that are still not entirely clear, said he would have to reconsider his investment if we did.' She put her cup down and gave Tazi a bright smile. 'So we did not.'

'Tell me about these rumours.'

'I don't know exactly, I just heard whispers. Doesn't mean they are true. You know what a snake pit Hungarian politics is. Full of people hissing and slithering.'

'Why don't you tell me, and then I can decide.'

Eniko picked up her cup and sipped her tea. 'Really, nothing specific. Money, corruption, the usual.' She paused, then frowned as she remembered. 'But there was something strange today.'

'I'm listening.'

'It was when we went back to Parliament after the disastrous press conference. I was sitting at my desk and the door to Reka's office was open. She was talking to someone and she sounded quite upset. At first I thought it was because of what had happened but then I could hear her, she was talking about something else.'

'What?'

'I don't know exactly, but she started raising her voice, saying, "Peter, this is a problem. You were there as well at that party. With me. Why the hell can't you come back? If they invest, they invest. If not, not. I don't care. I need you here now. Why is this coming up now, on top of everything else? It was twenty years ago. It was just a terrible accident. We were kids. This could derail everything." Then she stopped speaking. Her husband is called Peter. She must have been talking to him. Then she said, "They told me the case was closed, that the file had been lost. So what does he need it for now?" Then she realised the door was open and walked over and closed it. That was it. I couldn't hear anything else. You know these government office doors, they all have that thick padding on the outside so nobody can listen in.'

Balthazar sat up, alert now. 'You are sure that she said that, about the case being closed, the file being lost, then she asked "why is he asking for it?"'

'Yes. Completely. She sounded nervous. I thought it was strange, what with all the other things that are going on. Who cares about a police file from twenty years ago? Unless it's something that could damage her now.'

'And she said to her husband you were there, at that party as well?'

'Yes, Tazi, I told you. I know what I heard.' She blushed, reached into her black leather rucksack, took out a moleskin notebook and flipped through the pages before showing one to Balthazar. 'I took notes while I listened. Dated and timed. I *am* still a reporter,' she said, her voice a mixture of hope and defiance. He looked down at the page and the neat paragraphs of her handwriting, taking in the words.

Eniko glanced at him, taking in his focus, the familiar way

his eyes narrowed when he was concentrating. 'What's all this about, Tazi?'

'I'm not sure yet.'

'What file? What party? What happened over twenty years ago?'

He glanced inadvertently at the photograph of Virag. Eniko noticed. 'Is this something to do with Virag?'

'I don't know. Maybe.'

'Is that the file Reka was talking about? Did you ask for it?'

Balthazar looked at her before she answered. She looked a little less lost now. The old feisty determination to get to the bottom of a story, the tenacity that had also attracted him to her, was starting to show again. He half smiled. Should he tell her? Why not? 'Yes. I asked for Virag's file today. I got it and it was empty. That's all.'

Balthazar watched her face, which was creased in concentration, glance down at her notebook. 'I'm glad you still have your reporter's instinct.'

'Thanks. It doesn't go overnight.' She looked at him, her blue-green eyes open wide. 'Actually, I think I've made a terrible mistake, Tazi.'

Balthazar's stomach flipped. Was this it, the big confession of how she blew up a good and deepening relationship for no reason at all? He asked, 'Why?'

'Because I've thrown away a quite successful journalistic career to be spokeswoman for someone who will probably be Hungary's shortest-lived prime minister.' She sat back and sighed. 'This whole thing is a disaster. Did you see the press conference footage?'

Balthazar nodded, feeling a mixture of disappointment and relief. 'Yes. The same clip is all over the Internet. Reka walking out, you behind her, while the world's media are on the other side of the room, looking out over Kossuth Square. What did she say to you afterwards?'

'That she hadn't prepared enough. That she needed more backing. She is going to talk to her own party and to some of the opposition MPs. She also said she had another idea, but she needed to think about it first.' She paused for a few moments. 'Tazi, there's something else I wanted to show you.'

Balthazar nodded. 'OK.'

Eniko took out her phone and called up Twitter, showing it to Balthazar. He scrolled through a stream of tweets, read one out loud to himself. '*Buszatlan komcsi kurva*, unfucked Communist whore,' then handed the phone back to Eniko, his face creased in distaste. 'Jesus. That's hideous.'

'It doesn't even make sense,' she said, half smiling. 'Look Tazi, I'm not such a sensitive flower. I'm used to getting rude and nasty tweets. But this is a whole new level. There's lots more like that.'

'Does Reka know?'

'I showed her. It's nothing compared to what she's getting.'

'Sure, but she's the prime minister. Can't she get you some protection? There are lots of places she could ask.'

'She has. But she's being stonewalled. The Parliamentary Guard has more or less collapsed. Some of them have joined the Gendarmerie, or at least gone over to their side. The police say they don't have any spare manpower at the moment.'

'Wait. Let me call Sandor.' He dialled his boss. The conversation was brief. Balthazar asked for a squad car to be parked outside his flat, then asked what other news Sandor had. Sandor spoke for a while. Balthazar thanked him and hung up.

'What did he say?' asked Eniko.

'The consensus is that Reka is finished. The minister of the interior will resign tomorrow. He controls the police. He's told them to stand back, not get involved in the stand-off with the Gendarmes, unless there are actual incidents of violence or law-breaking. But as you can see on the news, at the moment the Gendarmes are being very friendly. Just parked on Kossuth Square, hanging out, smoking cigarettes and taking selfies with tourists.'

'They don't need to do anything else. The message is clear enough,' said Eniko. 'They control her front yard.'

'Precisely. But the chief still has allies, especially in the District V police station.' For a moment Balthazar remembered his drive to Parliament that morning, passing down Szalay Street, watching the stand-off between the police on one side of the street and the Gendarmes on the other. 'They hate the Gendarmes and the feeling is mutual, especially after the District V cops rescued you and Reka last week at the Four Seasons. They're sending a squad car. It will be parked here all night. So you're safe.'

'Thanks, Tazi. Thanks so much.' She glanced at the television, which was still tuned to the BBC. 'Oh, shit, look. Now what?'

Theodore Nichols was standing on Kossuth Square, illuminated under a standing floodlight, talking to a stocky, red-faced man in his late fifties wearing an expensive leather jacket.

'What?' asked Balthazar, also turning to the screen. 'Who's he?'

'Gyorgy Moscovitz. The leader of the Social Democrats parliamentary fraction. He can't stand Reka.'

Balthazar picked up the remote control and raised the

volume. Nichols asked, 'So when will you submit the vote of no confidence?'

'The first thing on Monday morning, as soon as Parliament opens for business.'

Nichols said, 'And you say you have cross-party support?'

Moscovitz nodded. 'We do. From left and right, and, of course, our own Social Democrats.'

'But why would you want to bring down a prime minister from your own party and topple the government?'

Moscovitz gestured around the area. Small bonfires now blazed by the side of the tents. Plumes of smoke rose over the square. The harsh chords of Pannonia, a Hungarian far-right metal band, sounded in the background. 'What government?'

Balthazar turned down the volume. 'Good question. Where is she?'

Eniko shrugged. 'Dunno. Gone to ground somewhere. Writing her resignation statement, maybe.' She put her teacup down and turned to him. 'Tazi...' she said, her voice uncertain. 'I want to tell you something.'

He sat still before he answered. 'I'm listening.'

'Going to work for Reka Bardossy was not the only mistake I made, Tazi.'

Not now, Eni, he wanted to say. Maybe once all this is over. But not now. Instead he said, 'Let's go out onto the balcony, get some air.'

Eniko followed him outside. He leaned on the railing staring out over Klauzal Square, hyper-aware of her presence, his gaze falling across the familiar scene: the row of green Budapest Bubi bicycles, the metal fence, the children's playground and the benches on each side. A large SUV was parked in one corner, its headlights on. The air carried the sound of the night-time city: the rattle of a tram trundling down the Grand Boulevard, distant laughter, revellers in the corner bar on the other side of the square. Carried the smell of her too, her perfume, heavier than he remembered, almost musky, the scent of shampoo on her hair. She looked at him, her mouth slightly open, her pupils huge in the semi-darkness. He felt his heart speed up. The air between them turned dense, charged with electricity.

She moved closer to him. 'You're missing your cues, Tazi.' She laid her hand on his right arm.

He willed himself not to turn to her, fully knowing what would happen next if he did. Instead he stared out across the Klauzal Square, suddenly alert at what he saw. The SUV was moving now, down the side of the square, towards the corner of Dob Street. It had black metal grilles over its windscreen and windows. It was a Gendarmerie vehicle. Balthazar turned to Eniko. She looked at him expectantly, a half smile on her face. Instead he said, 'We need to go inside.'

Her smile widened at first, then the tone of his voice – taut, brisk – registered. She looked down into the square and saw the Gendarmerie SUV slowly cruising around Klauzal Square. 'Oh. Yes. Of course.'

They stepped back inside and sat down on the sofa, this time keeping their distance from one another. Eniko asked, 'When will the police car get here?'

'Soon. A few minutes.' He turned to her, his voice reassuring. 'You'll be fine.' A telephone rang, interrupting him. Balthazar looked down: it was Anastasia's burner. He took the call, listened intently then said, 'OK, I'm on my way.' He turned to Eniko. 'I have to go. I'm sorry.'

Eniko's eyes widened as she watched Balthazar put on the shoulder holster, pick up the Glock and slide it in.

'Who is it?' she asked, her voice tight. 'Oh. Of course. It's her again.'

The two women had met the previous Sunday morning. After Eniko had been interrogated by Attila Ungar, Anastasia had arrived to talk about the plan for the operation that day against Mahmoud Hejazi, standing at the door with Eva *neni* who was carrying a plate of her famous pancakes.

Eniko turned to Balthazar. 'Look, Tazi, just tell me if you are seeing someone. I came here because I was scared. But you don't have to let me make a fool of myself as well.'

He tapped the grip of the Glock. 'I don't usually take weapons on dates. Eni, it's work. That's all. Pal Dezeffy is organising a coup. That's why your press conference was a disaster, why Kossuth Square is occupied by the Gendarmes, why Moscovitz is bringing a no-confidence motion and why Anastasia Ferenczy, officer in the state security service, is down there. We have to stop it.' He put his hand on Eniko's arm and gently rested it there. 'And now I have to go. Stay here tonight. You'll be safe. You can sleep in Alex's room, where you were last week.'

'Alex's room,' said Eniko, her voice flat.

You dumped me, he wanted to say. I introduced you to my son. I let you into my life and you walked away. But he said none of that. Instead he replied, 'Eni, stay inside and don't open the door to anyone.'

'Not even Eva *neni*?' replied Eniko, a rueful smile on her face.

'Her, OK. But only if she has pancakes.' He opened the door, and left.

TWENTY-TWO

Corner of Kis Diofa Street and Klauzal Square, 10.30 p.m.

'Thanks for coming so quickly. I'm sorry – it's bad news,' said Anastasia.

For a moment Balthazar's stomach lurched. 'Gaspar?'

Anastasia was sitting in the front of the Opel, Balthazar next to her. 'No. He's fine. All your family is fine, Balthazar. And before you ask, Alex is safe at home with his mother,' she said, anticipating his next question. 'We are keeping an eye on all of them.'

Balthazar exhaled with relief. 'Thank you. Then who?'

'Kinga. Kinga Torok.'

He turned to face her. 'Kinga? How?'

'A hit-and-run. She was on her way to work tonight. She lives quite far out, in District XV. She was walking down an unlit street to the bus stop. A car hit her from behind and drove away.'

'Intentionally? Or just a terrible accident?'

Anastasia sighed. 'There's no CCTV. A neighbour heard her scream but by the time the ambulance got there she was dead. There's no real pavement, just a rough track in front of the houses. And it's very dark, hardly any streetlights. But it's clear enough where the road is. I don't think there are any terrible accidents at the moment, Balthazar. Especially involving anyone connected to Pal.' She rested her hand on his arm for several seconds. 'I'm so sorry.'

Balthazar did not reply for a few moments, just looked ahead. He could see up Dob Street, all the way to where the thoroughfare bent, en route to the Grand Boulevard. As usual at this time on a Friday night, the pavements were crowded with revellers laughing, shouting, some holding bottles of beer. A wave of sadness coursed through him for the nights like this that Kinga would never know. She was barely in her twenties, had her whole life ahead of her. For a moment he saw her standing defiant, sweaty, tousled in front of him, explaining that she would do this for a year, until she had enough money put aside to leave Hungary and apply to university in England. 'So am I.' He turned to Anastasia. 'Why? Why would Pal have her killed?'

Anastasia took out her iPad mini. 'We found some footage.' She opened the video viewer and pressed play. The frame showed Kinga chatting with half a dozen other smartly dressed, attractive young women, waiting outside the Royal Salon at the Buda Castle. 'They are the hostesses for last week's government reception for Gulf investors. Pal was the host.'

Balthazar nodded. 'Yes. I know about that.' He watched Reka Bardossy walk by and greet the hostesses, head-turningly attractive in a dark, long-sleeved cocktail dress, with a light-coloured pashmina over her shoulders for modesty's sake. She looked calm and confident, utterly unaware, of course, that later that evening she would be fighting for her life and kill her assailant with the very high heel of one of the shoes on which she was walking. The footage jumped to another scene. Kinga was outside, leaning against the castle wall, talking to a striking young man. He wore a black polo shirt, looked to be in excellent shape, and had spiky blonde hair and wide-set, light-coloured eyes. The night-time illumination glinted off an expensive-looking watch. 'Who is he?' asked Balthazar.

Anastasia leaned over towards him. 'Adorjan Molnar. Director of communications at Pal's Foundation for the Relief of Inequality.'

'He doesn't look like he's suffering from inequality.'

Anastasia smiled. 'He's not. So, you see the foundation is working. Anyway, watch what happens now. There's no sound, but you don't need it.'

Adorjan handed Kinga a blister package. She shook her head. They argued for some time, then Adorjan pushed her against the wall and spoke in her ear. Her pretty face turned fearful. Adorjan stepped back, mouthed a question. Kinga nodded. He left first, and a minute or so later, Kinga slipped the pills into her handbag and went back inside.

'What did he say?' asked Balthazar.

'We lip-read his mouth. He told her to make sure that al-Nuri took at least two. She asked how. He said al-Nuri would turn up sooner or later at the brothel and ask for her. And then he said if she mentioned this to anyone, or failed to give him the pills, she would be killed and her little sister would disappear forever.'

'And then they killed her anyway.'

'Yes. Tidying up their loose ends.'

'We have some zoomed-in shots,' said Anastasia. She took the iPad from Balthazar's hand and opened a new viewer window. The frame showed the blister pack in Adorjan's hand, the small pills.

'Look familiar?' asked Anastasia.

'Very. I'm guessing that's not Viagra.'

'No. The forensic results have come through. They were
MDMA, super-high strength, just designed to look like Viagra,
but mixed with a sedative and anti-seizure medication to
prevent fits. The combination is a dangerous mix with cocaine.
Your heart doesn't know what to do, whether to speed up or
slow down. One of those and the coke would have been more
than enough to kill him.

'Al-Nuri was Reka's best hope. He liked it here,' said
Anastasia. 'His colleagues have already left. Took the first
flight this afternoon to Dubai. There's nobody else for Reka
to negotiate the investment with now.'

Balthazar felt a cold rage course through him. The life of
another young woman casually ended, for the convenience
of Pal and his henchmen. For a moment he thought of Virag,
alone and fearful in a house full of rich, powerful people. Nor
did al-Nuri deserve to die like that. They both watched as the
Gendarmerie SUV slowly drove past, breaking his chain of
thought. 'How long has that been here?' asked Anastasia.

Balthazar shrugged. 'I'm not sure. At least half an hour.
Just driving round and round.' He glanced across the street
at his flat. Eniko was back outside, standing on the balcony,
looking out over Klauzal Square. He watched her head turn
until she found what she was looking for: the white Opel
with Balthazar and Anastasia sitting in the front seat, parked
nearby on the corner of Kis Diofa Street. Go inside, he
willed her, it's not safe. She did not move. He reached for his
telephone, about to call, when she stepped back into the flat
and closed the balcony door.

Anastasia said, 'We don't have much time, Balthazar. The
Gendarmes are all over the city. We are in their comms. They
will start setting up more roadblocks soon, take complete
control of the major transport routes and intersections and

start shutting them down. The government will probably collapse tomorrow. They plan to arrest Reka. We still haven't found the two Arabs. We think Pal is planning something. Which is why we need to hurry.'

A young couple appeared, walking down Dob Street, then turning into Klauzal Square. The boy was in his late teens, his girlfriend around the same age. Both were laughing, happy to be going home together after a fun night out. They stopped laughing as they saw the SUV heading towards them down the side of the square. Two powerful beams of bright light erupted and for a moment both stood still. The driver had switched on the headlights and roof-mounted spotlights on full beam. Balthazar could see the fear on their faces. The boy and girl broke into a run, heading down Klauzal Street, away from the SUV as fast as they could.

But the driver was not interested in the teenagers. The SUV inched forward, then accelerated away, towards the corner where Anastasia's car was parked. He flashed his headlights and also put on the light inside as the SUV crawled past Anastasia's car, so Balthazar could get a good look at the two men. He recognised both of them: the driver shaven-headed, his companion with slicked-back black hair. The driver waved at Balthazar with a clenched fist, pointed at his head and laughed, before starting another circle of the square.

'Do you know them?' asked Anastasia.

'They were at Keleti, part of the group that attacked me,' said Balthazar. 'Now what?'

Anastasia took out her iPad mini and called up the photos of the two Arab men who had been travelling with Mahmoud Hejazi. 'We need to find these two. They are the key. Whatever Pal is planning.'

Balthazar looked at his watch. 'It's almost eleven o'clock.'

'We need to find them now. There's something planned for tomorrow, we think.'

'Where? And who is we?'

'We don't know. We is me and our American and British friends.'

'What leads do they have?'

'Only one, I'm afraid.'

'Which is?'

'Gaspar.'

Bardossy home, Remetehegyi Way, 10.30 p.m.

Sandor Takacs walked over to Reka and took the television remote control from her hand. She was watching the same footage on the BBC that Balthazar and Eniko had just viewed, of Gyorgy Moscovitz, her erstwhile party ally, announcing the forthcoming no-confidence vote. Sandor pressed the off button and the screen went dark. Reka turned and looked up at Sandor, her face a mix of anger and resignation. 'Is it over?'

'How long have we known each other, Prime Minister?' asked Sandor.

'Reka, please, Sanyi *bacsi*.'

'How long, *kedves* Reka?'

'Since my grandfather plucked you from obscurity and brought you to the big city,' said Reka, her voice affectionate.

Sandor leaned in, sounding mock-pompous. 'The village of Kunhalom is not obscure. It is a regional metropolis. Of 722 people.'

'Absolutely. Maybe I will move there. Next week.'

Sandor shook his head and sat down next to her. 'I think you know that if we don't win, you will be moving. But not to Kunhalom. To somewhere a lot less pleasant, at least if you stay in Hungary.'

'I'm not going anywhere. Whatever happens will happen here: in Hungary, in Budapest, in Kossuth Square.'

'Good. What did you say, yesterday, to Eniko, Prime Minister?' He did not wait for her to answer. '"We're going to war. Are you in?" So are you? Or are you giving up?'

She shrugged. 'Is there any point? I can't govern the space ten yards in front of my office. How can I run a country when I cannot control Kossuth Square?'

'You've lost a battle, Reka. Not a war. Did you think this would be easy? That Pal would say, "OK, I lost, step this way for the PM's office, Reka, and here's how the coffee machine works?"'

Reka laughed, the first time that evening. 'Maybe not. And the coffee machine is in the ante-room, not my office.' She ran her hand through her hair, sat back and exhaled hard. 'To go to war, we need a strategy.'

'That's why we are here,' said Sandor. 'Prime Minister,' he added, emphasising each word.

Reka looked around at her remaining allies. There were three of them: Sandor Takacs, Akos Feher, her chief of staff, Antal Kondor, her chief of security, all sitting in the front room. Beneath the banter ran an undercurrent of tension. All three had nailed their colours to Reka's mast. Sandor because he believed in her – and because he was the archetypal survivor. He had a genuine affection for Reka and her family. He also had extensive files on both the Bardossy family's wealth and its sources, as well as a similar dossier on Pal. If Reka went down, he would, they all knew, find a way to avoid going down with her. Akos was there because, while he had grown to admire Reka in her brief week in power, he had nowhere else to go. The former point man for the corrupt passport scam run by Reka and Pal, he was thoroughly tainted. The tension was highest between him and Antal Kondor. Just a week earlier Antal had ordered Akos to take the fall for the passport scam, and to go to prison. When Akos protested, Antal had threatened his family. Events had overtaken both of them, but neither man had forgotten. Which was why just after Sandor had finished speaking, Reka gave her security chief a pointed look. Antal and Reka's family too had their own history, which reached back to the early 1990s and the era of *vadkapitalizmus*. There were reasons why Antal had fled Hungary and joined the international brigade of the Croatian army, and none of them were good.

Antal nodded, turned to Akos, extended his hand and said, 'I owe you an apology. I should never have said what I did about your family. It was inexcusable. But I hope you can forgive me.'

Akos leaned forward for a moment and took a long swig of his beer. He put the bottle down and said, 'I can. And I suppose I will.' The fact that Antal was a messenger for Reka, that she had decided he would go to prison, was left unsaid. Akos and Antal shook hands, and the atmosphere eased.

'Thanks, gentlemen,' said Reka. 'Now let's get to work.'

The Bardossy home was a large early 1940s villa on Remetehegyi Way, a residential road in District III, on the Buda side of the river. The house like many in the Hungarian capital, had once belonged to a Jewish family and had been nationalised after the Second World War, like most of the property of Hungary's once-thriving bourgeoisie. The Bardossys had lived there since the 1950s when Reka's grandfather, then the minister for heavy industry, had acquired it, simply by asking the state property agency to hand it over. Ministers' requests then were not usually denied. Reka had recently employed a Swedish interior designer to remodel and redecorate the villa. The designer had executed her task with taste and style, working around the panoramic picture windows and long, curved balcony that looked out over the Danube and the Pest side of the city. The clean, minimalist lines were accentuated by the abstract works of art by modern Hungarian painters that hung on the pale cream walls.

Reka and Sandor were sitting on a black leather armchair, while the other two were perched on a matching sofa, all grouped around a 1980s Philippe Starck coffee table, a square of thick smoked glass resting on four legs, each topped with a black rubber ball. The table was one of Reka's favourite pieces. At the moment it was crowded with two coffee pots, half a dozen empty or half-empty cups, bottles of beer, mineral water, a fruit basket, and several trays of gourmet sandwiches. The table was much stronger than it looked and the rubber balls gave it extra stability and resilience. It was, Reka thought, as good a model for her next moves as any. She looked around the room. All three were watching her expectantly. She had a choice to make: surrender or fight. If she fought, she still might lose, but at least she would be able to look herself in the mirror the next morning. Reka continued talking, 'And to do that, to go to war, we need to understand what forces are in play, and which are available.'

Sandor said, 'That's more like it.'

Reka looked at the three men, one by one, before she spoke. 'Sandor will brief us on the police, Antal on the security services and Akos on the political situation. Sandor, if you could start, please.'

Sandor leaned forward as he spoke, blushing noticeably. 'I'm sorry to say that most of my colleagues, apart from the District V station, have decided to sit this one out. The guidance from the minister of the interior is that the police are neutral and will not intervene in a political dispute.'

Reka frowned, her voice tight with annoyance. 'Even though laws are being broken?'

'So far, they are quite minor. Civil transgressions.'

Akos said, 'An illegal paramilitary force occupying Kossuth Square is a civil transgression?'

'There's no violence. Nobody is being beaten up. It's all very Hungarian,' said Sandor. 'And the Gendarmerie has issued a statement that its members are simply doing their job and protecting the organs of state. In any case, as you know, the interior minister has issued an opinion that the executive order dissolving the Gendarmerie needs to be ratified by Parliament.'

Reka turned to Antal, who began speaking. 'The security services are divided. Pal has plenty of allies on Falk Miksa Street. But so do you. They are like the police. They won't come down on one side or the other until they see how the crisis is unfolding. The consensus is that they let your ally Anastasia Ferenczy and a couple of her colleagues try to help you. If Anastasia's operation works, and it looks like she can bring down Pal, the rest of the security service will come out for you. If not, they will go with Pal.' Antal picked up his coffee and took a long drink, before nodding appreciatively. 'This is very good. Where's it from?'

'It's blended for me in a small shop around the corner,' said Reka. 'I'll get you a lifetime's supply if we win. And the army?'

Antal put his cup down. 'I put some feelers out, to see if they would come out for you. They could surround the Gendarmes on Kossuth Square quickly and easily, and disarm them.'

'So why don't they?' asked Reka. 'We could wrap this up tonight.'

'Same as the police. They want to back the winning side. And they are not sure who that is yet.'

Reka nodded, turned to her chief of staff. 'Give us the political perspective, Akos.'

He nodded, leaned forward as he spoke. 'It's not good, I have to report. You've obviously seen all the media reporting, the Gendarmes on Kossuth Square, the far-right activists camping out. The optics are not favourable. Your own party is preparing a vote of no confidence on Monday. Most of the opposition, from the far right to the centre-left will vote with them. They want a new election. Everyone thinks they can win it. Everyone except the People's Alliance.'

The People's Alliance, a coalition of environmental, liberal and social activist groups, was the fifth largest in Parliament with twenty-seven MPs out of 199. It was not strong in parliamentary politics, but was strongly supported by voters who were heartily sick of the old left–right divide and the way the establishment of both sides sliced up politics and the economy between them.

Reka raised an eyebrow. 'The People's Alliance will vote for an old *komcsi* like me?'

Akos said, 'Not exactly. You have some support there because you are a woman. They will abstain.'

Reka laughed. 'So the police, the army and the security services are all sitting on their hands, waiting to see which way the wind blows, while all of Parliament will either vote to no-confidence me or abstain.' She turned to the three men, 'Gentlemen, if you want to leave now, I completely understand and no blame will be attached to any of you.'

Sandor said, 'I'm not going anywhere.'

Akos said, 'Me neither.'

'Nor me,' said Antal.

'That's good,' said Reka. 'Because I do have a plan.'

All three stared at her expectantly as she began talking.

TWENTY-THREE

'Really? That's it?' Balthazar turned to Anastasia, his voice mildly incredulous. 'Gaspar?'

Anastasia shrugged. 'Yup.' She raised her eyebrows and tilted her head to one side. 'And al-Nuri did die in your brother's... establishment. In normal times that would be enough to bring him in for a lengthy interrogation. There are some other leads, but Gaspar is our best chance. He met Omar Aswan and Adnan Bashari here in Budapest, and recently.'

'But he has already told you what he knows, which is not very much.'

'There must be more. He probably doesn't even know what he knows, or how important it might be. We'll try again. We have to find these people, Balthazar. Gaspar's at home now. Call him, please, and tell him we are coming over and he should stay there.'

Balthazar dialled Gaspar's number. Anastasia was correct. Gaspar was at home. The two brothers chatted briefly. Gaspar informed Balthazar that Laszlo, their father, was also there. Balthazar hung up. He would deal with that once they got to Jozsef Street. 'OK,' he said to Anastasia. 'Let's go.'

Anastasia switched the engine on and glanced in the mirror. She and Balthazar both saw the Gendarmerie SUV speed up and pull in directly behind the Opel as she pulled out and turned right. The route to Jozsef Street took them to the very end of Klauzal Street, where it met Rakoczi Way, across onto Blaha Lujza Square via a circuitous turn through a car park, then right again onto the Grand Boulevard, past Rakoczi Square, then a final turn onto Jozsef Street. It should be a fifteen-minute drive, perhaps less in favourable traffic conditions.

Klauzal Street was a narrow, one-way thoroughfare, barely wide enough for three cars. Like its neighbours, the street was in a rapidly changing state of flux as legions of hipsters moved in. They drove past several blocks of drab grey-fronted pre-war apartment houses. The paint was peeling from grubby window frames, the ground-floor shop fronts locked up for the night, protected by rusty metal bars, the walls covered with graffiti. On the next corner, on the ground floor of a carefully restored art nouveau apartment building, the newly-opened Boho bar beckoned. Its retro 1970s typography offered several dozen craft beers while a blackboard listed six types of *zsiros-kenyer* – lard-bread, the cheapest snack available – on as many types of bread, including gluten-free. The *zsiros-kenyer* was ironic, of course, but there had been plenty of times in Balthazar's childhood when that had served as supper for the whole family. Still, even he had to smile when he read that the lard was sourced from organically reared animals and there was also, somehow, a vegan option. Perhaps he could bring Sarah and Alex here on Saturday to stop by for a quick snack. But when he looked in the driver's mirror, he stopped smiling. The Gendarmerie vehicle was still right behind them.

'You know we're being followed,' Balthazar said.

'Yup,' said Anastasia, sounding unconcerned. She quickly glanced at the new GPS screen attached to the dashboard. A blue dot represented her car slowly moving along Klauzal Street. She looked ahead. The end of Klauzal Street, leading onto Rakoczi Way and the southern end of Blaha Lujza Square, was just visible, a few hundred yards or so ahead.

Anastasia slowed as they approached the corner of Wesselenyi Street, the first of two cross-streets before they reached Rakoczi Way, losing more speed than seemed necessary to Balthazar. She then stopped the Opel just before the crossroads. A dirty blue Nissan saloon with a very noisy engine coughing out plumes of exhaust smoke pulled up at the end of Wesselenyi Street. Anastasia revved the engine of the Opel. As soon as the Nissan indicated to turn right onto Klauzal Street, she jammed her foot down on the accelerator. The Opel skidded forward, the Nissan jumped out then slid in directly behind the Opel. The black SUV was now behind the Nissan, engulfed in grey clouds of exhaust fumes.

'Interesting move. Who's in the blue car?' asked Balthazar.

Anastasia said nothing, slowed down, reached into the driver's-side door pocket and took out a burner telephone. Balthazar looked down. It was primed to send an empty text message. 'Press the green button,' she said.

'That's it?' asked Balthazar.

Anastasia glanced at the GPS screen. There was one more cross-street to go, Dohany Street, about thirty yards ahead, a few seconds away. 'Please, Balthazar, just do as I ask.'

Balthazar shrugged and pressed the send button. He looked in the mirror as a couple of seconds later the blue Nissan's engine sounded even louder, there was a crunch of missed gears, and the car juddered and shook, then stopped amid great gusts of oily smoke. The Gendarmerie SUV stopped a few inches behind the Nissan, barely in time. The parked cars on either side of the vehicles blocked any passage forward. The bald Gendarme opened the door of the SUV and marched up to the Nissan and began knocking angrily on the window. The driver, tall, pale and stooped from too much time spent in front of computer monitors, sat inside, supremely unconcerned, then called up a number on his mobile phone. A couple of seconds later Anastasia's telephone rang. She put it on speaker.

'Sorry, boss. I think the car's gone for good.'

'Nice work, Szilard. Don't worry. It was a write-off anyway.'

Anastasia drove along Klauzal Street, passed Dohany Street, then pulled out into Rakoczi Way, a six-lane thoroughfare that reached from Keleti Station, through downtown, onto the Elizabeth Bridge. She looked left and right and made a sharp left turn, her tyres screeching. Rakoczi Way was near empty, giving her a clear run to Blaha Lujza Square. Then they both saw why. The crossroads, one of the most important in downtown Budapest, had been closed. A line of Gendarmerie vehicles blocked the whole width of Rakoczi Way and both sides of the Grand Boulevard where the two roads intersected. On each side of the square, there was enough space for a single car to pass through, flanked by uniformed Gendarmes checking drivers' papers and identities. Balthazar turned around and looked down Rakoczi Way in the other direction towards Astoria. The same line of black vehicles was clearly visible on the corner by the Astoria Hotel.

'We're blocked at both ends,' he told Anastasia.

She nodded, slammed the brakes on so hard the Opel skidded, then executed a perfect three-point turn, driving the wrong way down Rakoczi Way in the face of oncoming traffic, barely missing a number-seven bus, whose angry driver hooted long and loud. Balthazar braced himself as she spun the wheel around and sped across the car park, tyres screeching as the car turned into Somogyi Bela Street, a back road as narrow as Klauzal Street. Balthazar glanced at Anastasia, her face locked in fierce concentration, then at the GPS screen. Somogyi Bela Street ran parallel with the Grand Boulevard and from there they would cross Gutenberg Square, then turn onto Jozsef Street. They sped past the second-hand clothes store, the 500-forint shop where everything on sale was marked at that price, the dark, narrow *borozo* where wine was served by ladle from aluminium tureens, and the cheap lunch place where locals filled up on starchy noodles and *fozelek*, flour-thickened vegetable stews.

They did not notice the grey, dirty Volkswagen parked near the end of Somogyi Bela Street, just before Gutenberg Square, and nor was there any reason for them to do so. Anastasia's was a decent plan and might have worked had not Somogyi Bela Street been blocked at the entrance to Gutenberg Square by three Gendarmerie SUVs. As soon as she saw the line of black vehicles parked by the curved pavement around the Rabbinical Seminary, Anastasia slowed the car. The street was too narrow to execute a three-point turn, so she slammed the Opel into reverse. At that point, just as the Opel started to move backwards, a short, stocky man stepped out of the grey Volkswagen and threw a spiked chain across the road. Anastasia was moving too fast to stop in time. She drove backwards onto the metal prongs, which shredded the car's tyres. The Opel skidded to the left, the metal wheel rims screaming as they met the pavement, then hit the side of the kerb, where the vehicle finally stopped. For a second she watched the Gendarmes running down the street towards them. She pulled out her phone, sent a text message, then deleted it.

Balthazar took his telephone out and called Gaspar. 'Listen, *ocsim*, we're on the corner of Somogyi Bela and Gutenberg Square. The Gendarmes are here. They will take us. Don't come here.'

Just as Gaspar began to answer, both passenger windows exploded, showering Balthazar and Anastasia with shards of broken glass. Two Gendarmes, one tall and wiry, the other shorter and stocky, stood on either side of the car, holding their pistols in their hands like a hammer. Both wore fine black leather gloves. They brushed the pieces of broken glass from the stock of their weapons and stood on either side of the Opel, now pointing their guns at Balthazar and Anastasia.

'Phones,' said the tall Gendarme. Balthazar and Anastasia surrendered their handsets. The Gendarme looked at Balthazar's phone.

Gaspar's voice was sounding in the tinny speaker: '*Batyam, mi a fasz van*. Brother, what the fuck's happening?'

'This,' said the Gendarme. 'This is happening.' He dropped Balthazar's phone on the ground and stamped down on it, shattering the screen. He gestured to his colleague, who immediately did the same with Anastasia's phone.

'Get out,' said the Gendarme. 'You are under arrest.'

Balthazar ignored the Gendarme and looked at Anastasia. 'Are you OK?'

She was carefully shaking her hair, one hand over her eyes, and pulling at her clothes to shake the pieces of glass off. 'I guess so. You?'

'I'm fine.'

There was, he saw, a small cut on the side of her face. 'You're bleeding. By your nose.'

She looked him up and down. 'So are you, above your eye.'

'Shut it,' said the Gendarme, still pointing his weapon at Balthazar. 'I told you. Get out. Both of you. Hands on your heads.'

Balthazar looked at him, then glanced at his hand on the trigger. He was young, still in his early twenties, with buzz-cut blonde hair, standing very still as he held the gun in his hand. Like all the Gendarmes, he was dressed in full uniform: black trousers, stab vest, shin and shoulder pads and shiny riot helmet with a rear neck protector, and a yellow taser on his belt. But beneath the violence and the bluster, Balthazar sensed that he was not completely sure of himself. It was not only the police, army and security services that were waiting to see who triumphed. The Gendarmes had aligned themselves with Pal Dezeffy. They were organising his coup, blocking streets, setting up checkpoints, arresting people. But what if Pal lost?

'Are you sure about this?' asked Balthazar. 'What you are doing is called treason. It brings a life sentence.' Balthazar watched the muzzle of the Glock waver for a second or two. 'A whole life sentence.'

The Gendarme blinked for a moment, then decided. 'I told you to shut it, *budos cigany*, stinking Gypsy.' He pushed the muzzle into Balthazar's cheek. 'And get out. Hands on your head.'

It was an amateur's move that brought the gun too close to the prisoner. For a moment Balthazar considered grabbing the weapon with one hand and smashing the Gendarme's arm up against the window frame at the elbow, to shatter the joint. But there was no separate safety catch on the Glock.

Instead the trigger safety was built into the firing mechanism as a separate, parallel trigger. That meant it was impossible to discharge accidentally. It also meant a sustained, deliberate pull on both triggers would fire the gun. The Gendarme had both triggers pulled back. A fraction of an inch and the weapon would discharge. Still, it might have worked if Balthazar was alone, and any bullet fired went wide. But Anastasia would almost certainly have been hit. In any case there was another Gendarme standing on the other side of the car, pointing his weapon at Anastasia.

'Yes, officer,' said Balthazar, stepping out of the car. 'We are doing exactly what you say. Slowly and carefully.' He glanced at Anastasia and saw that she too was obeying the Gendarme's instructions. Balthazar looked up the street as he and Anastasia stood on either side of the Opel with their hands on their heads. The door in the middle of the black SUV blocking the road at the top of Somogyi Bela Street opened.

Attila Ungar stepped out. He walked towards the Opel, shoved his hand inside Balthazar's jacket, took his weapon from the holster, then slowly slid the barrel of Balthazar's Glock down the side of his chin. 'Nice gun, Tazi. We've got the same. Much better than that crap they gave us in the police.' He paused, laughed for a moment. 'Oh, I forgot. You still are in the police. Well, I think I told you that our offer still stands. You can join up whenever you like.'

'I serve my country. I'm not a traitor.'

Attila smiled. 'You do, it's true. Never more than last weekend.' He paused, walking around Balthazar. 'But you must have wondered why your country has so little interest in serving you. And the rest of your people.' He gestured at the surrounding streets. 'Remember when we were on the beat here, together? Back in the good old days. When life was much simpler.' For a moment his voice softened. 'You showed me parts of this city I had never seen. Backstreet tenements with families living ten, twelve in a couple of rooms, sleeping in beds on a rota, almost nothing to eat, electricity and gas all cut off, no money coming in. Like stepping back to the nineteenth century.' He stepped closer to Balthazar. 'All your people, Tazi. Who let them live like that? Who enriched themselves while half the country slid deeper into misery and poverty?'

They were good questions, thought Balthazar, ones he had often asked himself. But he was not about to start discussing social exclusion and Roma rights with Attila. Instead he smiled. 'Gosh, Attila, I've never heard you make a speech before. It's quite impressive. To answer your question, Reka and Pal and all the other *komcsis*. They enriched themselves. You work for one, I for another. Two sides of the same coin.'

'Where were you going, Tazi?' asked Attila. He frowned for a moment. 'Of course. You're back in the 'hood. You must be going to see Gaspar.'

Balthazar said nothing. Attila continued speaking. 'Next time you meet, you can ask him a question: How did your family get that nice house on the hill?'

Now Attila's words hit home, as he knew they would. And that was a question Balthazar intended to ask Gaspar. The revelation from Marta, that Virag had died in Pal Dezeffy's house, Eniko overhearing Reka Bardossy talking about a file, these were not yet evidence but they were the slow start of a pattern forming, of connections being made. And one possible conclusion that would change his relationship with his family forever. But none of that was for sharing with Attila. 'You'll go down for a long time for this, Attila. Is that where you want to meet Henrik? In a prison waiting room?'

Attila's face tightened at the mention of his son's name. Back when they were partners the two men had spent much time talking about their sons. After the second disciplinary procedure against Attila for beating prisoners, his wife had left him, taking Henrik with her. Balthazar knew that Attila longed to be a doting father, missed his son more than anything, but could not find a way to connect with the boy.

Behind the brutal facade was an intelligent, street-smart mind. Attila too knew he was taking a massive gamble. If Pal lost, Balthazar was correct. He would be arrested and this time the Gendarmes would be disbanded for real. He hardly saw Henrik anyway and could not imagine that his mother would let him anywhere near a prison. But it was what it was, and by this stage, there was nowhere else for Attila to go. He gestured to the stocky Gendarme. 'Cuff them. Nice and tight.'

Anastasia said, 'I am an officer in the state security service. You have no jurisdiction over me. You are a uniformed criminal in an illegal, disbanded organisation.'

Attila laughed, shook his head. 'I keep hearing this. Illegal. Disbanded.' He stepped closer, stopped laughing. 'Listen, Duchess. It's over. You lost. You backed the wrong horse. Your kind always does.' He gestured at the stocky Gendarme. 'I told you to cuff her. Are you deaf or stupid?' The Gendarme reached for Anastasia's arms and quickly plasticuffed her wrists in front of her. Attila then stood at right angles to Anastasia, pressed his left hand on the front of her left shoulder, then quickly swept his boot behind her knees. She instantly collapsed onto the ground, landing on her side, before scrabbling up and righting herself.

Balthazar said nothing as he watched, tried to keep his emotions under control and his reserves of energy in place.

For now at least, there was nothing he could do. They were outnumbered and outgunned and they had no phones any more. He held his hands in front of him, tried to keep his elbows wide. A sharp twist and yank could snap a plasticuff, if done with enough leverage and strength, or at least damage the ratchet so it could be levered free.

Attila watched. 'Nice try, Tazi.' He brought Balthazar's elbows together and produced a roll of duct tape from his jacket pocket. The Gendarme slid the plasticuff over his wrists and pulled it tight. Attila then taped Balthazar's elbows together, walked over and did the same to Anastasia. Attila stood very close to Balthazar, so close he could smell the cigarettes and coffee on his breath. 'You going down, Tazi, or do I have to do it for you?'

Balthazar looked across the street before he answered. An elderly lady in a worn brown coat was passing by on the other side of the road. She glanced at the scene and quickly scurried off. He crouched low, his cuffed, outstretched arms now resting on his knees. Attila turned to Anastasia. 'You too, Duchess.'

The two Gendarmes stood guard over them as Anastasia manoeuvred herself into the stress position. Balthazar watched Attila step away to make a telephone call. The position was bearable for a minute or so. After five, the pain in Balthazar's thighs radiated from his calves to his thighs and up into the small of his back. For a moment he wondered if he could get inside the Rabbinical Seminary, hide somewhere with Anastasia and summon help. Balthazar knew the building reasonably well. There was a maze of tunnels underneath that dated back to the Second World War, when Jews had hidden there from the Nazis and their local Arrow Cross allies. The seminary had once been part of his beat. Over the months he had become friends with the Rabbi, David Stern, a Hungarian-born Jew who had been raised as an atheist by devoutly Communist parents, then rediscovered his heritage after the collapse of the old system. There was a synagogue inside the building but the Friday-evening services had ended several hours ago. Or maybe he could somehow make a run for it, across the square.

Attila saw Balthazar turn his head to look at the seminary gates. 'There's nobody there, Tazi. Especially not tonight. Anyway, it's the Sabbath. Your friends have all gone home for Friday-night dinner. You should have, too.'

A second Gendarme SUV arrived, discharging another four men. 'Now, Tazikam, I'll ask you one last time. Are you joining us, or do we have to give you a taste of our hospitality?'

'Join what?' asked Balthazar. 'Your organisation doesn't exist.'

Attila laughed, turned to the other Gendarmes. 'And yet, here we are.' His voice hardened. 'And there you are.' He looked down at Anastasia. 'What about you, Duchess? We could use a class act like you.'

Anastasia spat on the ground. '*Kocsog.*'

Attila's face creased in anger. This could not be laughed off. He had been humiliated in front of his men. He stood over Anastasia. 'Stand up,' he ordered.

'I'm fine down here,' she replied.

Attila gestured to the Gendarme who had arrested Balthazar and Anastasia. They picked her up, held her steady on her feet while the blood supply slowly returned to her legs. A third stepped forward, unclipped his taser, pointed it at her shoulder and squeezed the trigger. A sharp snap sounded and her eyes opened wide as a projectile on a wire raced towards her. She clamped her mouth closed, determined not to shout or scream as the barbs sliced through her denim jacket and touched her skin. Her legs gave way and her eyes rolled back in her head. Just as she collapsed, the two Gendarmes on either side caught her and lowered her prone body to the ground.

Attila turned to Balthazar. 'Now then, see how gentle we are? We can be gentle with you, Tazi. Or rough, if you like.'

Balthazar braced himself. He and the entire murder squad, as well as several other specialist units, had been put through taser training when the weapons had been introduced to the Budapest police force. The training had included the experience of actually being tasered, albeit with a five-second charge, the weakest of the shocks the machine could administer. He still remembered it as one of the most unpleasant experiences of his life, worse than being knocked unconscious at Keleti the previous week. There he had gone down fighting, giving as good as he could until the knockout blow landed. There was nothing to do against a taser, just wait for the hammer blow of total body pain to hit after the snap of the projectile as it flew forward. At least he, unlike some older colleagues, had not lost control of his bladder.

Balthazar looked at Anastasia, crumpled and moaning softly on the pavement, her hair in disarray. For a moment he saw Alex's face, heard his son's voice saying 'Hi, Dad' while they hugged. He imagined Sarah and Alex at his front door the next morning, Sarah eventually giving up when there was no answer. Unless Eniko stayed. He hoped she had the sense to call Reka for help and get out, once he did not come home or answer his phone.

Attila said, 'Still waiting for your answer, Tazi.'

He turned to Attila, a cold anger surging through him. 'Like she said.'

Attila gestured at the blonde Gendarme. He aimed the taser at Balthazar. Just as he pulled the trigger, Balthazar jumped up, raised his hand and shoved Attila into the path of the flying probe. It hit the middle of his stab vest, then fell to the floor, the four prongs still sparking uselessly. For a second Attila looked down in surprise. That was enough time for Balthazar to pivot on one heel and swiftly kick Attila in the groin with full force. Had the kick landed properly it would have felled Attila. Instead he skipped sideways, dodging most of the blow, but receiving enough to reel backwards.

Balthazar dived forward. His right hand grabbed the barrel of the Glock, his left its stock. He raised the weapon and pointed it skywards in case it discharged. Even with his wrists bound together in the duct tape there was a small amount of room to manoeuvre his hands. He kneed Attila in the groin as hard as he could, making contact this time, and twisted hard. Attila grunted in pain. He wobbled, his grip on the gun loosened, then broke. Balthazar pulled the weapon away and out of Attila's hand and let it slide into his as he spun around. Keeping the pistol trained on the Gendarmes, in a two-handed grip, he walked over to Anastasia. She groaned and opened her eyes, trying to process what she was seeing. Balthazar watched as she shakily stood up, all the while sweeping the pistol back and forth between the Gendarmes as he headed towards the square. But they and Balthazar both knew that six against a single gunman are poor odds, especially when he is helping a partner whose limbs barely worked.

As the Gendarmes began to advance, one of their number peeled off to the side. Anastasia staggered alongside Balthazar into Gutenberg Square, while he was still covering the

Gendarmes. Just as he noticed that there were only five now, the sharp snap sounded again. A sledgehammer hit him in the shoulder, the pain exploded through him. His muscles stopped working and he collapsed. The Gendarme fired again; daggers tore at his other shoulder, his body shuddered and he passed out.

Under Kossuth Square, 11.45 p.m.

Omar Aswan turned to Pal Dezeffy. 'The money has been deposited?'

Pal nodded. 'Check your account. One million dollars for you.' He turned to Adnan Bashari, 'And the same for you.' Pal handed both men burner telephones. 'Call your people. One million each now, and the rest once the work is finished. Please, check.'

Both men did as he bade, speaking in rapid Arabic. Satisfied with what they heard, they both cracked open the telephones, took out the SIM cards and crushed them underfoot, before removing the batteries, then smashing the handsets.

The two Arab men, Pal and Attila Ungar were standing in a large chamber that stretched for twenty yards in each direction under Kossuth Square. The room was brightly lit and silent apart from the distant humming of an air-conditioning unit. The walls were bare grey concrete, the floor covered with granite tiles. The air was damp and chilly and the room illuminated by neon striplights. A few yards away, in the centre of the room, stood a large yellow metal box, about two yards long, three yards wide and four yards tall. Tall brass pipes extruded from each end, each with a pressure dial a foot or so from the box. The pipes extended out into a web of fine tubes that were attached under the ceiling. The yellow box was an industrial-strength pump that converted plain water into a mist, the mist that every hour during daytime in the hot summer months gusted up from the ground on Kossuth Square, delighting and cooling the hordes of tourists. A computer-controlled timer panel on the side of the pump controlled the delivery time. It all ran automatically. The timer had a manual override switch in case of faults in the programming.

'You can make this work?' asked Pal, his voice slightly uncertain.

'For four million dollars we can make anything work,' said Aswan.

Omar looked at Adnan, who followed him as they walked over to the yellow pump. On top of the metal covering was a wide plastic cap. Omar stood staring at the machine for several seconds, then gestured at Adnan, who unscrewed the cap. Omar peered down into the water chamber, then waved his fingers at the opening. Adnan replaced the cap.

Omar shrugged. 'It is simple. We add the mixture to the water. We adjust the timer. The mixture combines with the water. The mist is pumped out over Kossuth Square.'

'When?'

'We will come back tonight. We need to wear proper suits and masks.'

Attila shifted uneasily. Half his mind was on his encounter with Balthazar and Anastasia. He still felt sick from taking Balthazar's knee in his groin and furious that Balthazar had taken control of his weapon, in front of his men. By now the prisoners should be safely locked up. But nothing was ever certain with those two. Meanwhile he was cold, his balls ached and these two men gave him the creeps. Attila had also done his research, called in some favours at the Ministry of Defence and had managed to access the files on the two men. He knew who they were and what they had done. Pal had assured him that nothing serious would happen. But the photos he had seen still haunted him. 'Can you please remind me what the effect of your mixture will be?'

Omar, Attila noticed, glanced at Pal for a fraction of a second before he answered. Pal nodded, almost imperceptibly. 'Nausea, vomiting, dizziness. It will last an hour or two. That's all.'

Pal rested his hand on Attila's shoulder. 'We've talked this through, Attila. No permanent harm will be done. It's the final nail in Reka's coffin. Not only can she not control her front yard, she cannot even keep the people there safe. She'll have no choice but to resign. I'll be back behind my desk, and then we dissolve the police into the Gendarmerie, just as we discussed.'

Attila turned to Omar. 'Can you guarantee that? No serious after-effects or worse?'

Omar scratched his beard before he answered. 'Of course. I can guarantee whatever you want.' He handed a small black control panel to Pal. 'Here it is. Radio-operated, as you requested. You need to be nearby, within fifty yards or so. The mixture needs sustained exposure, several seconds, for full effect. It will be coloured green. Just press the button and move away. And you, Mr Dezeffy, can guarantee that we will leave Hungary safely?'

Pal looked down at the control panel. 'That's all I need?'

'Yes. Shall I explain it again?'

'No, no need. Once the job is done, I can guarantee your safe passage. The exit plan is ready for tomorrow evening.'

Omar's black eyes flickered for a moment. 'Good. Because you know that if anything happens to us, our friends have long arms, and longer memories.'

TWENTY-FOUR

The queue to get through the Gendarmerie checkpoint at Nyugati Station reached back fifty yards on the Grand Boulevard, down towards Margaret Bridge, but the line of cars was at least slowly moving. Sarah lowered her hand back into the side pocket on the driver's door and took out her driving licence and the car papers again. The boulevard sliced through downtown, a long, sweeping curve of road and tramlines from Margaret Bridge to Petofi Bridge, further along the river. It was four lanes wide, two on either side. The number-four and -six trams usually ran back and forth between the traffic but today the service was closed. Both the Nyugati tram stops were empty. Instead, three stationary yellow trams lined up back to back. Two black Gendarmerie vehicles were parked at an angle across each lane, leaving enough space for a single car to pass through.

Sarah watched the Gendarmes stand in front of each vehicle as it stopped, walking around, peering inside, checking the drivers and their papers. Her unease grew. Normally at that time on a Saturday morning it would be a fifteen-minute drive from her flat on Rose Hill, on the Buda side of the city, to Dob Street and Balthazar's place. But today the journey had already taken her over thirty minutes just to get across the river to here. Then they had to get past Oktogon and turn down into the backstreets of District VII. She glanced at her watch again. They were already late. They would be lucky to get there by nine o'clock at this rate, and she couldn't get through to Balthazar on the telephone.

The car in front, a grey Nissan Micra, moved forward a yard or so. Sarah moved her Toyota SUV after it, then tried calling Balthazar again, her phone on speaker. The ringing tone sounded inside the car, followed by a burst of Hungarian. 'What is that, Alex? What are they saying?'

Alex frowned. 'I told you, Mum. It's the same as before. This number is no longer available.'

'How can it be not available? It worked fine yesterday. Maybe there's something wrong with mine. Try him again on your phone.'

Sarah had already been stopped by Gendarmes on both the Buda and the Pest side of Margaret Bridge. Each time, the checks had been swift, almost cursory, but the message was clear enough: we control the city. She had not seen a single police officer. The pavements were almost deserted, the shops all closed or shuttered, even the cafes and Turkish kebab houses that were usually open all hours. Her driver-side window was open and a cool breeze blew through the car. She watched the Gendarmes, wondering if she and Alex should have cancelled and just stayed at home. She was not sure what was happening here, but one thing was clear: it was nothing good. She glanced at Nyugati. The station was one of her favourite buildings, but today its elegance brought her no pleasure. Gendarmes stood at the entrance, checking the papers of everyone going in and out. Even the drunks and homeless people that usually congregated on the steps had gone.

'Same as yours, Mum,' said Alex, as he put his phone down. 'Why isn't he answering? He's never done this before.'

'Don't worry, honey. I'm sure it's just a problem with the telephone networks. We'll be there in a few minutes and we'll all head off on our trip,' she said, trying hard to convince herself. Hungary was blanketed in mobile coverage. There were multiple national networks. Mobiles worked perfectly here in every part of the country, far better than when she went home to New York. There was something wrong, she knew.

The Toyota moved forward to the checkpoint. A Gendarme approached, stocky, thickly muscled, with a tattoo of talons up the side of his neck. Sarah watched, feeling increasingly nervous as he looked at the car, walked around, peered inside on both sides. 'Hallo, Sarah,' said Attila Ungar. He looked at Alex. 'Hi, Alex.'

Alex's eyes widened. 'Hi,' he said, uncertainly.

Sarah flinched at the mention of their names. 'Hallo, officer. How do you know who we are?'

Attila said, 'We've met before, Sarah. Don't you remember?'

She looked at him again, taking in his hard, intelligent eyes, muscular build, intensity of movement, the way he seemed to simmer with an unspoken anger. Then it came back to her. Years ago, when Balthazar first joined the police and she had once visited him at work. This was Balthazar's former partner. She had never liked him, but had always tried to be courteous. As she was now.

Sarah tried to smile, cover her nervousness. 'Of course. You're Attila Ungar, you and Balthazar worked together.'

Attila nodded. 'You remember my name. I'm impressed.'

Now she smiled with more confidence. 'Of course. Balthazar was so excited to have a partner. He talked about you a lot.'

'Did he? But now we've gone our separate ways.' Attila turned to Alex. 'Remember once, you came over, and had a play date with my boy Henrik? We went to the park and had pizza and ice cream. You probably don't. It was a long time ago.'

Try and remember, Alex, Sarah thought, sensing that this was somehow important, wondering if she could send her son a telepathic message. She watched with relief as Alex nodded enthusiastically. 'I do, there was a castle in the playground that we climbed on.'

'Good boy. We should do that again sometime, once all this is over,' said Attila. 'You can meet Henrik again.'

Alex nodded enthusiastically. 'Sure. That would be great.'

Oh, you clever boy, thought Sarah.

Attila's air of menace seemed to soften, Sarah saw. She asked, 'Attila, perhaps you could help us.'

He shrugged. 'I'll try.'

'We're supposed to be meeting Balthazar this morning. But we keep getting stopped. It takes a long time when they check all the car papers, our IDs and my driving licence. So now we are running late. We're going on a day trip but it will take hours to get out of the city. Could you call ahead or something to the next checkpoints?'

She watched Attila as she spoke. Something flickered in his eyes, a shadow that for a second looked like regret. There was something else going on here, she was sure. None of this was a coincidence. Attila knew they would be here. But how and why? For a moment she thought about calling the American ambassador, whose number she had on speed dial. The ambassador was an old friend of Sarah's mother. The two women moved in the same circles in New York, of charity galas and fundraising. Sarah watched the news, had seen the reports from Kossuth Square. The government was under extreme pressure, that was clear, and might even collapse. Attila and the Gendarmes were part of that. But whoever took power next would not want to make an enemy of the United States.

Attila nodded. 'I can help with that.' He reached into his pocket, took out several sheets of headed A4 paper. The documents were topped with an impressive letterhead from the Gendarmerie headquarters, had a couple of lines in Hungarian and a large stamp underneath. He handed it to Sarah. 'It's a *laissez-passer*. There's another checkpoint ahead, at Oktogon. Show them this and you won't have any trouble. You can travel freely around the city.' He tapped the bonnet, waved at Alex.

Sarah thanked him profusely and drove off. Ten minutes later, she had parked the Toyota in front of Balthazar's building. Attila had been as good as his word. The stamped paper worked like magic. One glance at it and the Gendarmes at Oktogon had waved her through. They had not even checked the wording. But there was still no sign or sound of Balthazar.

Now she and Alex were standing in front of his building, her anxiety growing by the second. She pressed the door buzzer for the third time. No answer. She looked at her watch: they were almost twenty minutes late, but that was no reason for Balthazar not to be at home.

'Where is he?' asked Alex, his voice tight.

'Try calling him again, honey,' said Sarah.

Sarah glanced up at Balthazar's balcony then looked around Klauzal Square, as if Balthazar might suddenly appear. The square was almost empty at this time in the morning, the rows of Bubi bicycles standing waiting. Beer cans, wine bottles and scattered cigarette ends evinced last night's partying. But now it was clear that the Gendarmes were taking control of the city the air was thick with tension. The corner ABC, usually open all hours, was also closed and shuttered. A black Gendarmerie SUV was parked on the other side of the square, but so far had remained stationary.

Maybe Balthazar had gone out for some breakfast, or to another shop further away, to get supplies for their trip. Her ex-husband was not the most organised or domestic person. Except, she knew, when Alex was involved. Then he was ready ten minutes early, keen to maximise every moment he could spend with his son.

The front door of the building opened and Eva *neni* came out. Her face lit up when she saw Alex, who ran towards her for a hug. Eva greeted Sarah more formally and the two women exchanged polite greetings in Hungarian. As neither spoke the other's language, that was the extent of their exchange. Alex and Eva then began a rapid-fire conversation in Hungarian, which Sarah was unable to follow. Eventually, exasperated, she turned to her son. 'What's all that about? Does she know where he is?'

'No, Mum, she doesn't.' Alex's face twisted with worry. 'What's going on, Mum? We were talking about this all week.'

Eva continued speaking in Hungarian. Sarah could understand one word that Eva said several times: Eniko.

Sarah asked Alex, 'What is she saying?'

'That Eniko was here yesterday evening, but she thinks she left around midnight.'

To her surprise, Sarah felt a stab of jealousy. Budapest sometimes seemed a small town. Sarah had known all about Balthazar's romance with Eniko and its messy end. Part of her was sad for him, that he was alone again. Another part, she was surprised to discover, was still pleased that there was no other woman in his bed.

Eva turned to Alex. 'Come in, both of you. Let's go upstairs and see for ourselves. He's probably overslept.'

The three of them stepped inside, Sarah for the first time. Balthazar had always invited her up for a coffee or tea when she dropped off Alex, but she had always declined. Once inside the foyer, she was impressed. The apartment house had been built in the 1930s and had retained its art deco style: a spacious foyer with pale marble walls and clean, curved lines. She glanced at the marble plaque on one side commemorating Rezso Seress. Why had she never stepped into the building before? The truth was, part of her felt guilty for divorcing Balthazar. Feeling guilty made her feel angry with herself, anger which she then dumped on Balthazar. None of which was good for Alex, she knew. He had adjusted well enough, as children do, to his new situation and enjoyed the novelty of having two mothers. But not all her feelings were complex. She was seriously worried now. Balthazar was a doting father. Wherever he was, at any time of day, he left his mobile telephone on so Alex could contact him. Strictly speaking, they were not supposed to have unsupervised phone calls or contacts. But she knew all about their SMS exchanges and did not interfere.

The three of them stepped into the lift and travelled up to the fourth floor. It was a small space and nobody spoke, but Alex held her hand tightly. They stepped out into the corridor. There were three flats on each floor, each with the original 1930s dark wooden door with a small panel that opened behind a black metal grille. Alex ran forward and banged hard on Balthazar's door, shouting, 'Dad, where are you?'

The door flew open and Alex fell forward, almost tumbling to the floor. Sarah rushed to catch him. All three of them stepped forward. Sarah turned with her arm out and said, 'Wait,' guiding Alex and Eva back out to the corridor. 'Alex, you stay here with Eva,' she told him.

Sarah took out her iPhone and called Amanda on Facetime video. 'Listen, Mandy. I need you to record this call.' Amanda immediately started firing off questions: where was she, what was happening, was she safe? 'I'm fine, honey, just please do as I say. I'm going into Balthazar's flat. He's disappeared and his door is open. If there is someone in there, then we'll have a record of whatever happens next. Can you record this?'

'Yes, but maybe you should call the police. It might be dangerous. Why you?'

'Because I'm here,' Sarah said, and she stepped inside the apartment, her iPhone held out in front of her as though it might save her from the bad news she knew was coming.

Apostol Street, Buda, 8.40 a.m.

As his ex-wife stepped into his flat, three miles away across the city, in the basement of a 1920s villa perched on the crest of a hill with a sweeping view of Buda, Balthazar awoke. He blinked several times, then fully opened his eyes. His mouth felt like someone had vacuumed it dry. His eyes felt dry and gritty. His joints and muscles ached as though he had been beaten unconscious again. Where was he? He felt weak, groggy. His brain took several seconds to start processing information. His phone had been smashed and his watch taken from him, so he had no idea what time it was. But a weak light filtered into the space from a small barred window recessed into the wall, just under the low ceiling, so he knew one night at least had passed.

And why was there a deep burning pain on each shoulder? Then he remembered the taser probes ripping through his light summer jacket and T-shirt. He tried to raise his arms to take a look at the marks. But something heavy was clamped around his wrist, dragging on his hands, and then he could not move his arms any more. He looked down to see his arms in two large manacles, both on the end of a heavy black chain that was attached to the wall. The sight triggered a rising sense of panic. He was trapped here. Nobody knew where he was. He was an irritant, an ant to be crushed as Pal and his allies stepped closer to taking power. He closed his eyes for a moment, saw Alex's boyish face twisted with anxiety as he wondered where his dad was. He pushed his son's image aside, tried to focus on a plan to free himself. Firstly, he needed to understand as much as possible about his situation.

He was a prisoner, but his legs at least were free, although clearly he was not going anywhere soon. And there was another ache, in the side of his neck, a different, dull pain to the soreness he still felt after his fight last weekend at Keleti Station. He rolled his left shoulder. A sharp pain shot through the base of his neck on his left side. It felt sore and tender. He turned his head from side to side. The dagger shot through the side of his neck again, but the pain was localised. A taser could knock someone unconscious, and he had taken two. But not for more than eight hours. If it was daylight now he must have been drugged, probably with an injection in his neck, which would account for the soreness. And where was Anastasia? He looked around the room. It was a cellar with raw brick walls, and a rough, cracked concrete floor that was slightly sloped on both sides, leading to a narrow channel in the middle with a drainage hole at the halfway point. Brown stains and patches spread across the concrete. He felt a sudden chill, and not only because the room was damp and cold.

There was a set of manacles on each wall around the room. There was writing on the walls, he realised, graffiti in Hungarian and Russian. As his eyes adjusted to the gloom, he looked again at the second set of manacles on the facing wall. There was something there, by one of the chains, crumpled, made of fabric. He narrowed his eyes. It was a dark-blue denim jacket, Anastasia's jacket. So she had been here, and was at least alive when they'd arrived. Not far from his right leg were two crumpled, empty cigarette packets showing a space satellite against a dark-blue sky. He recognised the brand from his youth: Sputnik, as smoked by Russian soldiers. Next to the packets was an empty bottle of sweet Russian champagne. He frowned for a moment, did a quick calculation. The Russians had left in the summer of 1991. It was now 2015, twenty-four years later. The air was stale and his head was starting to ache. The place had been untouched for more than twenty years. Then he realised he was in a *mokkry haz*. The phrase was a mixture of the Russian word for wet and the Hungarian word for house. The cellar, he guessed, was underneath one of the numerous fine villas in the Buda hills that had once been owned by an aristocratic or rich industrialist family and appropriated during the Communist era. Some had been taken by the families of the party elite as residences – Reka and Pal both sprang to mind – others were used as offices or by the secret police. They had taken a special delight in working with hands, fists and other tools in the basements of the mansions of the former ruling class to bring about the classless society. All the *mokkry hazak* were haunted. He looked again at dark patches on the concrete. This place certainly was.

The fear coursed through him again. His heart started pumping, jumping, missing a beat. It was the after-effect of the tasers, he assumed. Would he die here? For a moment he saw Alex's face again. Maybe he would, but if this was the end he would not go passively. He sat back against the wall, pulled hard on the right chain at the wall bracket. It did not move. He turned and pulled on the left. Was there a tiny shift? He pulled harder and felt the wall bracket give a little more. He looked closer. The brickwork was damp and crumbling, untouched for decades, the manacle housing pockmarked with rust. He extended his right arm to his left, breathed in as deep as he could, ignored the starbursts of pain around his upper body, grabbed his wrist above the manacle, exhaled suddenly and pulled as hard as he could. He sat back for a moment with his eyes closed as the pain juddered away, then pulled again, slower and more steadily on the manacle bracket. It was definitely looser. He raised his arm again, pulled the chain taut, trying to widen the gap, when the door opened.

Balthazar's flat

Sarah, Alex and Eva stood in the middle of the lounge, looking around, deeply puzzled. The flat was empty. The bed in the spare room – Alex's room – was unslept-in. The large, open-plan lounge was moderately untidy – a couple of rumpled cushions, two teacups on the coffee table, a half-eaten cheese sandwich on a plate. There was no sign that anyone had been here, searching for something or wanting to leave a message.

Nothing was damaged, everything seemed to be in its usual place, only a faint smell of shampoo and perfume, the residual scent of a woman.

Sarah looked around the room with interest, taking in the bookshelves, the rows of historical works about the Poraymus, some classics of Hungarian literature, several airport thrillers, copies of *The Economist* and *Newsweek* on the table. So this was where her ex-husband lived. It was a bachelor pad, to be sure. The walls needed repainting, the parquet a sanding and a thorough polish. But it had potential. The light streamed in from the large windows overlooking Klauzal Square. She walked out onto the balcony, looked over the square. For a second she imagined herself and Balthazar having a glass of wine here, discussing their days. What was she thinking? She banished that vision from her head. In any case there were more urgent matters, like where was Balthazar?

Sarah walked back inside and turned to Alex, asked him to ask Eva *neni* again when Eniko left. Alex did as she requested, and translated Eva's reply. 'She told you. Around midnight. But Eniko would surely have closed the door. So why was it open?'

Sarah shrugged, watching Alex look around the room, his face creased in concentration. His gaze stopped on the bookshelf. 'That's weird – why would they want that?'

'What?' asked Sarah. 'Is something missing?'

'The photo of Virag, Dad's cousin. It's gone.'

TWENTY-FIVE

Apostol Street, Mokkry haz

Balthazar dropped his arm and sat very still, watching as Pal Dezeffy walked into the cellar, Attila Ungar at his side. Pal was casually dressed in jeans and a black polo top, a brown leather messenger bag over his shoulder, while Attila was wearing his Gendarmerie uniform, without the stab vest and body armour. A Glock 17 pistol and a yellow taser were holstered on his belt.

Pal walked around Balthazar as he spoke. 'Detective Kovacs, what are we going to do with you? I admire your persistence.' He shook his head, sighing loudly. 'But you keep getting in the way.'

'In the way of what?' asked Balthazar.

'Our plans.'

'The only plans you should be making are how you will spend the rest of your life inside a maximum-security prison cell.'

Pal laughed. 'I don't think so.'

Balthazar asked, 'Where is Anastasia Ferenczy?'

Pal said, 'Oh, don't worry, she's perfectly safe.' He paused, tilted his head to one side and looked Balthazar up and down. 'Safer than you, perhaps. The disappearance of an officer in the state security service would cause a lot of... ripples. We will need the ABS once all this is over. But a police officer, the brother of a troublesome pimp, going missing? Who knew what he was really mixed up in? We'll leak the footage of your coke-tasting session with Black George. There will be a media furore for a day or two. It's true you are this week's hero for taking down Mahmoud Hejazi. But what with everything else that's going on, it will fade away very soon. Then a sparsely attended memorial ceremony in a month or so. A plaque on the wall at headquarters. And after that...' Pal brushed his palms against each other, as though washing them. 'Meanwhile, I have something for you. At least you won't die ignorant. Or alone.'

Pal opened his messenger bag and took out a large photograph in a silver frame. He pulled out the back support and placed the frame on the floor, just out of Balthazar's reach. 'Poor Virag. I never knew you were related. She was your...?'

'Cousin. You've burgled my flat.'

'Your cousin.' Pal smiled. 'If you say so. If that makes you feel better. We know all sorts of things about you, Detective Kovacs. And your guilty mentor, Sandor Takacs. And yes, we borrowed the photograph. I thought it might be a comfort to you.'

'Did you kill her?'

'Not directly, no. There was no murder.'

'But you let her die.'

Pal looked Balthazar up and down. 'You might as well know. It won't make any difference now. For what it's worth, I'm sorry. She panicked, ran out of the house, fell in the pool and drowned. She couldn't swim. But I think you know that.'

'I do. But I don't know what happened before, why she ran?'

Pal smiled regretfully. 'Why would a young woman run from a man?'

Balthazar felt the anger stir inside him. 'Because she was frightened.'

'Yes, she was scared of me. But she didn't need to be. The room was prepared, clean sheets, perfumes, soft music. I would have been gentle. She was beautiful, exotic. A voice like an angel. Even Reka said so.'

'Reka Bardossy? She was there, at the party?' Pal had just confirmed what Eniko had overheard outside Reka's office, Balthazar realised.

'Of course she was. We were the masters of the universe. Our fathers had handed us a whole country to play with. It was 1995. I had just been appointed chairman of the Social Democratic Party. I was barely in my early twenties. Reka was nineteen. But we were the future. We could do whatever we want.' He stopped talking for a moment, lost in memories. 'There was nothing wild about wild capitalism, nothing at all. It was all perfectly thought out, years in advance. We all knew that the system would collapse. And when it did, we were there to help ourselves to what was left. And there was plenty: houses, businesses, factories, holiday homes on Lake Balaton. It worked more smoothly than any Socialist five-year plan.'

'You can swim. Why didn't you rescue her? She was a young girl. It would have been easy.'

For a moment regret flickered on Pal's face. 'I wanted to. In fact I stripped off and was about to dive in. Then Reka stopped me.'

'Reka? Why?'

'There would have been a scandal. Virag would have made all sorts of wild accusations. Some of the mud would have stuck. There was too much at stake...'

'For a Gypsy girl to mess up your plans,' said Balthazar.

'Yes. Exactly. If she died, it would be a tragic accident. There are lots of Gypsy girls. Nobody would make a fuss about her. There are worse ways to die than drowning. You just slip away. And the family, *your* family, were richly compensated.'

'How?' asked Balthazar, suddenly feeling sick to his stomach. He already knew the answer, realised that he had known it for years.

'The house. Your brother's brothel. That's the house where Virag died. The pool has been filled in. Some of it has been remodelled. But it's the same place. That was the deal. The villa for your family's silence. The place is worth two or three million dollars now, I would guess.' He looked around. 'Still, we're not short of houses. The Budapest property market is booming. I think it's time, once all this is over, to renovate this one.'

Pal bent down and lifted up the chain attached to the manacle on Balthazar's left arm. 'So you see, you picked the wrong side, Detective Kovacs. Not only did Reka Bardossy persuade me not to save Virag, she will also be out of power in' – he looked at his watch – 'it's almost nine o'clock now, so in about three hours.'

Balthazar felt the anger turn to a cold fury, a wave rising through him, a surge of energy that started in his stomach and spread up through his chest. He knew this feeling. It also brought a wild strength, the kind he had seen at family weddings and celebrations when overweight, middle-aged men danced for hours, spinning and turning on long-vanished reserves of energy, fuelled by the love of life itself. A strength that had a dark side too, bringing a power to absorb blows and punches and keep striking back long after most men would have been felled. It was that strength he felt now, that if he pulled hard enough on the left chain, he could finally yank it from the wall, and wrap it around Pal's neck, pulling and turning it until the flesh tore and his throat cracked. But that would not work, not with Attila standing there, and the other men that he presumed Pal had brought with him. 'And Kinga Torok, and Abdullah al-Nuri? They did not pick any side. But you killed them all the same.'

Pal shrugged. 'Collateral damage. It happens.'

'Kinga was twenty-two years old. She had her whole life ahead of her. A hit-and-run. From behind. A coward's way to kill someone.'

Pal smirked. 'I understand that was her favoured position. And al-Nuri's.'

Pal was in control. The best way to break his composure was to provoke him, and then he might let something slip, thought Balthazar. 'And what was yours, with Reka? Is that what this is all about? Because you are a loser and she dumped you?'

For a second a cloud passed across Pal's face. He walked across to Balthazar and back-handed him across the face. It was an amateur's blow and Balthazar rolled with it, although it still sent shockwaves of pain around his skull. 'On my desk,' said Pal. 'In the prime minister's office. That was her favourite position. When she wasn't on her knees.'

'Where you will be, once all this is over. *Kocsog*,' said Balthazar. He braced himself as Pal raised his hand again, then dropped it, shaking his head. He walked away, as though he realised Balthazar's plan.

Balthazar closed his eyes for a moment, tried to put aside the pain in his head and the rage he felt about Virag and

ADAM LEBOR

focused on what Pal had revealed. There was something
planned for later in the day. Something that would destroy
Reka Bardossy's government, such as it was. It must be
connected to the two Arab men, the butchers of Halabja.
Could it be some kind of chemical attack? And if so, where
and how would it be delivered? For a moment he heard
Anastasia's voice: *Adnan Bashari is a chemical weapons
expert. His precise area of expertise is non-weapons based
unorthodox distribution systems.* Was Pal was planning
some kind of chemical attack? And if he was, where?
At the airport, or a train station? Perhaps at a shopping
mall. Any of those would further shred what was left of
Reka's authority, deal a probably fatal blow to her position
as prime minister. But terrorism was about spectacle,
about inspiring fear, destroying trust in institutions, in
governments' ability to keep people safe. If he was Pal,
where would he try and deliver the coup de grace to Reka
and her tottering administration? At the epicentre of the
political crisis, the site of Parliament, the symbolic heart of
the country, he realised. At Kossuth Square. But how? For a
moment Balthazar was back in the car with Sandor Takacs,
driving into the car park under Kossuth Square, watching
the clouds of fine mist roll across the open space, enveloping
the crowds of laughing tourists. That had to be it. Pal was
planning to launch a gas attack on the square, through the
mister system.

Balthazar looked at Attila for a moment. His former
colleague was a brute and a traitor. He may even have tried
to have Balthazar killed the previous weekend when two
Gendarmes, posing as policemen, attempted to arrest him and
Goran Draganovic. But was Attila really prepared to sanction
mass murder? He needed to get Attila alone.

Balthazar asked, 'And how many people are you planning to kill this afternoon?'

Pal held his hand up, his voice conciliatory, 'None, of course. I am not a mass murderer.'

'But you are a murderer.'

'That's enough,' said Attila, stepping forward. 'Shut it.' He tapped the taser. 'Unless you want another dose.'

Balthazar fell silent. He watched Pal walking around the room, peering at the graffiti in Russian and Hungarian. One part of him was trying to work out how he might get out alive, another marvelled at Pal's cool, entitled arrogance. Every society had a ruling elite, he supposed. It was Hungary's misfortune to have one like Pal and his allies. Pal started reading out the names chiselled and scratched into the wall, 'Vladimir from Vladivostok, 1972. Csaba from Pecs, 1969. Ivan from Moscow, 1964. Z.U. from Csepel Island, 1984. Poor Z.U. I wonder what his name was. Zoltan, probably. He must have done something really bad to end up here in the 1980s. My uncle Kende used to run this place then. He told me the *mokkry hazak* weren't used much after the 1970s.'

Pal looked down at Balthazar. 'Shall we add a B.K., District VIII, 2015? Everyone deserves some kind of memorial.'

Balthazar ignored the barb. He had watched both men as Pal spoke. At the mention of the names, Attila seemed to stiffen for a second or two. Pal, absorbed in the sound of his own voice and dreams of coming power, did not notice. Z.U., Balthazar realised, could also stand for Zeno Ungar, father of Attila, who had raised his family on Csepel Island. Who, Attila had once confided over a few beers, had once been arrested, taken away for six months and had never really recovered. Could it be him? The dates fitted. Balthazar looked at Attila, held his gaze, flicked his eyes to the wall where the letters Z.U. were scratched into the brickwork. Attila said nothing, but a distant look fell across his face as though he was somewhere else for a moment. Had Pal's uncle imprisoned and tortured Attila's father?

Attila blinked, looked at Balthazar, seemed to nod his head, a microscopic movement that most people would never notice. The two men had served two years on the backstreets of District VIII together, had learned to read each other's body language, anticipate the other's moves. Would Attila understand what he wanted? At least listen? There was one way to find out. Balthazar turned to Pal. 'Could I at least have some water, please?'

Pal shrugged. 'Sure. We are not sadists. You won't die of thirst.' He turned to Attila. 'Attila, could you please? There's a kitchen somewhere upstairs. I asked Kende *bacsi* the other day. He's still alive, by the way, comes here every now and then to check up. He told me that the water's still switched on. You never know when you might need the place again, he said.' Pal looked down at Balthazar. 'How right he was.'

'Water? Please?' said Balthazar.

Attila looked hard at Balthazar, at Pal, then back at Balthazar. 'I think I should stay here, sir. Keep an eye on him. We know he's dangerous, even manacled. And you know your way around better than me. Don't you think? If you wouldn't mind. It would be much quicker, sir.'

Pal nodded. 'Perhaps you are right. Soon it won't matter anyway,' he said as he walked out of the room.

Balthazar spoke quickly. 'Z.U. from Csepel Island. It wasn't a Zoltan. That was your father, wasn't it? Zeno.

Zeno Ungar.' Zeno was an unusual name, and Balthazar remembered.

Attila nodded, his face suddenly taut with emotion. 'He was a broken man. Never recovered, never worked again. I saw him in the bath once, after he came home. His back was covered with dozens of tiny round scars. I asked my mother what they were. She said insect bites. But I knew they were cigarette burns. Six months later he died, then soon after that my mother had her... sudden accident.'

The phrase, they both knew, was often a euphemism for suicide. 'Doesn't Pal know?' asked Balthazar.

Attila shrugged. 'No. Why would he? He's never asked me anything about myself or my family. I'm just the hired muscle. You've got another minute, I guess, so make it quick. And convincing.'

Balthazar spoke rapidly, outlining what he knew about Omar Aswan and Adnan Bashari, their role in the Halabja massacres, their specialist expertise, and his belief that Pal was planning to use them to deliver a chemical or biological weapons attack on Kossuth Square. To Balthazar's surprise, Attila listened without interrupting or arguing. He stood still for several seconds, thinking, before saying, 'I know. I was there. Under Kossuth Square where the misting equipment is. The Arabs said it would just cause nausea and vomiting. Nobody would be seriously hurt.'

'And you believe that?'

'Maybe. Maybe not.'

'You're many things Attila, but you are not a mass murderer.'

'Who's talking about mass murder? A bit of green smoke, some puking tourists, that's all.'

'Which is more likely to bring down Reka Bardossy? A few people feeling a bit queasy? Or a lot of dead ones littering Kossuth Square?'

Attila said nothing, tapped his right foot.

Balthazar said, 'Decision time, Attila.'

Corner of Verhalom Street and Apostol Street, 8.50 a.m.

Fifty yards away, just out of sight of the *mokkry haz*, Szilard Szabo was sitting in the passenger seat of a parked white Ford Transit van. Gaspar had driven, while Fat Vik sat next to Szilard. All three were armed, Szilard with a Glock 17, Gaspar and Fat Vik with FAG pistols that Gaspar and his relatives had, over the years, paid several police officers to 'lose'.

The three of them had been up all night. Anastasia had texted Szilard with Gaspar's address before she and Balthazar were taken away by the Gendarmes. He had then taken a long and circuitous route to Jozsef Street, going around the outskirts of the city to avoid the Gendarme checkpoints, before cutting down into the backstreets of District VIII. The paramilitary force was only a few hundred strong and did not have the manpower to seal off large parts of the city outside the crucial downtown areas. Away from the centre, public transport had continued to run as normal, the pubs and bars had been as crowded as any other Friday night. For most people, the Gendarmerie checkpoints were a minor inconvenience.

Szilard had been tense and nervous as he arrived at the Kovacs family building. He had grown up not far from where they were now parked, in the leafy streets of Rose

Hill, another world to the back alleys and courtyards of District VIII. He realised that he had never interacted with a Gypsy before, apart from tipping the occasional violinist at a restaurant when the family celebrated a special occasion. The Laci brothers had searched him in the courtyard, were about to rough him up when they found his gun. Then Gaspar had appeared. He fired off questions about Balthazar: what did Szilard know, where was he, what was the plan, what was happening with these fucking Gendarmes? Szilard's answers were satisfactory and he was ushered into the family salon, where, despite the stress and anxiety over Balthazar's disappearance, or perhaps because of it, everybody, including the largest number of children he had seen in one place outside a school classroom, seemed to eat and drink non-stop.

Gaspar and Fat Vik had been all for getting into the van straight away, finding his brother and busting him out. Szilard – and an older man called Laszlo, Gaspar and Balthazar's father – had been more level-headed. They needed to think this through and plan things out. Szilard agreed. They had one chance and they needed to make it work. First of all, they needed a list of likely locations. Szilard had made some calls to colleagues working on communications intercepts. They had picked some chatter from Pal's phone when he had let slip a mention about the *mokkry hazak*, but had not revealed which one. The six *mokkry hazak* were all sited in a fairly small part of Buda. Szilard, Gaspar and Fat Vik had left shortly before dawn, looped around the city to avoid the Gendarme checkpoints, then drove back in through the distant suburbs. The white van was a perfect disguise. They had been stopped twice, each time Gaspar talking them through by pretending that they were Gypsy labourers heading to Szell Kalman Square, where employers had their pick of would-be workers every morning. Szilard kept a baseball cap pulled down over his face and pretended to snore loudly.

'This must be it,' said Szilard, pointing at the house. 'It is the last one on the list. And the only one with Gendarmes posted outside.'

'Great,' said Gaspar, reaching for the door handle. 'Let's go.'

Szilard put his hand on Gaspar's. Gaspar and Fat Vik's determination to rescue Balthazar was impressive – and touching. But this was not a time to be headstrong. 'Wait a moment. We can't just go in and start shooting.'

Szilard had been dreaming of becoming a field operative for months. Yesterday's little outing with the Nissan had gone very well. But this was something of a very different magnitude. And he had imagined that once in the field, he would have all the resources of his service to back him up: communications, research, reinforcements, the full force of the law. He had received a smattering of intelligence from a couple of colleagues, and the chatter from Pal's telephone, but his request for operational support was, he had just learned, 'still under consideration', even though Anastasia was likely held here as well. The process of consideration, he knew, could last for days. He had hours at most, if not minutes, to deal with this. So instead he was out with a pimp and his chief enforcer. Who both wanted to rush into the house, would probably start shooting and in all likelihood end up shooting each other or even Balthazar. But that was the mark of a good field operative, he remembered the instructor telling the class: he could work with what was available.

'You said he is in there,' said Fat Vik. He yawned and rubbed his eyes. 'So what are we waiting for?'

'For me to have a look, and then we'll know what to do next,' said Szilard. He took his telephone out and called Gaspar's number. 'Comms check.'

Gaspar's phone rang. 'It works fine.' He looked at Szilard, who said, 'I'm going for a little walk. I'll call you.'

Mokkry haz, 8.45am

The door to the cellar was a thick slab of grey mottled steel in a metal frame that turned on rusty tubular hinges. Balthazar watched as Attila stopped tapping his feet, turned around, walked over to the entrance and closed the door. There was a simple bar by the handle that slid into a metal holder. The door was still loose and not completely soundproof – distant voices echoed - but it was impossible to open from the other side. Attila dropped the bar into place and walked over to the channel in the floor. He dropped down to his knees and looked at the dark stains.

'These people,' he said. 'I don't know exactly what they did to him. The burns healed but he never really recovered. He asked for an operation to fix his broken nose, but the doctors said it was "non-essential" and he would have to wait. He waited until he died. My mother went soon after him. Maybe that's why I'm so angry.'

'Maybe it is, but Attila, we don't have much time.' Balthazar lifted his arms. 'Can you get me out of these? And where's Anastasia?'

'Anastasia is in a room upstairs, being interrogated.'

'Will they kill her?'

369

'I don't know. Pal said they won't. So probably not. But as you can see, he's half out of his mind.' Attila looked hard at Balthazar. 'Do you really think he's planning some kind of massacre at Kossuth Square?'

'Yes. Of course. And you know it. That's what those two Arabs do. They kill people.' Balthazar turned leftwards and started pulling hard on the chain, which loosened further. 'Help me get this out of the wall.'

'No need.' Attila walked over, took something from his pocket, slipped it into the manacle, and turned. The metal loop sprung open. 'I put you in these,' he said as he released the other one.

Balthazar tried to stand up, but the room spun around him. He sat back down, feeling the cold bricks against his back, slowly rubbed his arms as the circulation returned, sending waves of pins and needles through his muscles. He gingerly touched his neck, wincing at the pain and soreness. 'What did they give me?'

'You both got a sedative. Nothing toxic. They wanted you both alive. Anastasia to question and you... well, you saw why.' He looked down at the floor for a moment, then back at Balthazar. 'I'm sorry about what happened to Virag. To let a kid die like that.'

'Thanks. We need to move fast,' said Balthazar. 'Then we can stop a lot more kids dying.'

The sound of banging, of a muffled voice, carried through the door. Pal shouted, 'Attila, what's happening, are you OK?'

Attila turned, his voice confident, 'I'm fine, sir. The prisoner tried to escape. I'm just securing him now. Don't come in yet, until the room is safe.' He turned to Balthazar, spoke rapidly, sotto voce. 'OK, here's the sitrep. He's got a radio signal device. The Arabs gave it to him. There's a remote timer release device on the pump under Kossuth Square. He has to be near enough to set it off.'

'Why doesn't he just use a mobile phone?'

'By that time there won't be any mobile coverage within several miles of Parliament. It's all been arranged.'

'So now what?' asked Balthazar.

Attila bent low, spoke rapidly for a few seconds, walked across the room and opened the door.

TWENTY-SIX

Corner of Verhalom Street and Apostol Street, 8.47 a.m.

Szilard walked towards the front of the *mokkry haz*, his heart racing, feeling the weight of the Glock in his waistband, the suppressor pushing against the small of his back each time he took a step. The villa, an ornate turn-of-the-century pile with long, curved balconies, was set back from the road in a tongue of land that ran between Verhalom Street and Apostol Street. Low stone walls ran down both sides of the plot, topped with a spiked black sheet-metal fence. There was a large garden in the front and substantial grounds in the back, all of which were overgrown with weeds. Seven circular stone steps led to the ornate grey metal gate, each smaller than the previous one.

Two Gendarmes stood outside the house on either side of the steps; one tall and rangy, the other shorter and stocky. The tall Gendarme was playing with his telephone; his companion was leaning against their vehicle, smoking a cigarette. They looked relaxed – who would bother them up here, in the middle of Rose Hill? Both Gendarmes, he was glad to see, wore bulletproof vests. Szilard had no desire to kill anyone. He had spent many hours on the ABS shooting range, focusing on leg and shoulder shots on moving targets. But leg shots would be no use here, as the Gendarmes would still be able to draw their own weapons and fire back if they were not disabled by the pain. And shoulder shots were very risky, just a few inches off and the bullet would hit the heart.

The Gendarmes noticed him as he walked towards them, and suddenly turned alert. 'Hey, fuck off,' the tall one shouted, waving his hand at Szilard as though he was a fly or other irritant, 'Or we'll—'

But he did not get a chance to finish his sentence. In one swift move Szilard drew his gun from his back, dropped into a two-handed stance, swung a little to the left, fired, swung to the right and fired again, the Glock making a noise each time like a loud cough. The first shot hit the tall Gendarme in the centre of his chest. As the bullet embedded itself in his Kevlar vest, rather than entering or passing through his body, the kinetic force did not dissipate but spread out, driving the Gendarme backwards. He lost his balance, tripped, and went sprawling over the curved stone steps, banging his head as he went down. He stayed down. The second shot hit the stocky Gendarme a little lower in his vest, instantly winding him. He flew back then sat down in the middle of the street, gasping for breath, his face red with disbelief and fury.

Szilard quickly took in the scene. The tall Gendarme was no threat at the moment but the second was still in the game, wheezing and breathing raggedly but about to get up. Szilard walked over, swallowed hard, grimaced with distaste at what he was about to do then swung his right hand out in a horizontal hammer punch. The stock of the Glock slammed into the side of the Gendarme's head; he groaned, his eyes rolled back and he slid sideways, unconscious.

'Not bad, for a *gadje*,' he heard a gravelly voice behind him.

He turned to see Gaspar standing behind him, flanked by

Fat Vik, both with their guns in their hands, both breathing hard. Gaspar asked, 'Are they dead?'

'Of course not,' said Szilard. 'And I said you should wait for me.'

Gaspar walked over, poked the stocky Gendarme with his foot. Blood seeped from the side of his head, but his breathing was regular. 'Yeah, you did, but you know us Roma, we're not very good at following orders. What do you want to do with them?'

Szilard handed Gaspar two sets of plasticuffs.

'Sure,' said Gaspar, 'and then? You want to leave two trussed-up Gendarmes on the street?'

'Oh,' said Szilard. 'Good point.'

Gaspar shook his head, turned to Fat Vik, and said, 'Bring the van here. We'll get them inside.'

Fat Vik nodded, walked back and drove the vehicle over, bumping over the pavement so that the rear doors rested almost on the round stone steps. The three of them quickly dragged the two Gendarmes inside the vehicle. Gaspar made sure both were in the recovery position, then stepped out and closed the door. Fat Vik then parked the van nearby and walked back.

'Now what?' asked Gaspar.

'I'm going in,' said Szilard. 'You wait here. Cover me when I come out.'

Gaspar laughed and gestured to Fat Vik, 'I told you once, my *gadje* friend. We are not waiting for anyone. We're coming with you.' Szilard nodded, then led as the three of them slowly moved forward through the thick weeds, Gaspar and Fat Vik wheezing audibly from their efforts.

★

As soon as Pal stepped back into the cellar, carrying two plastic bottles of water, he realised something had changed. The scene looked the same as when he left: Balthazar sitting with his back against the cellar wall, his legs outstretched, his arms in manacles, Attila standing by him as though watching a prisoner. But his sixth sense told him otherwise. There was a subtle charge in the air, a sense of anticipation of something about to happen. It was the mood of a cabinet meeting about to turn on an errant minister, of an inner-party cabal about to take power. Pal had not survived in politics for this long without being able to sense such changes.

As Attila walked towards him to take the bottle of water, Pal spun on his heel, aiming to step out into the corridor and call for more Gendarmes. But Attila was faster, positioning himself in less than a second behind Pal. One hand slammed the door closed, the other was instantly clamped over Pal's mouth. Pal coughed and struggled. Attila gave him a fast, light jab to his left kidney, then released him.

Balthazar opened his manacles, stood up and walked over to Pal. He was coughing now, pale and bent over, his hand on his left side as he took deep breaths. Attila drew his pistol with one hand, pushed it against the side of Pal's head and handed a plasticuff to Balthazar. Balthazar guided Pal's hands behind his back and yanked the plastic tie into place.

Pal winced, stopped coughing, recovered enough strength to stand up and turn to Attila. 'Attila, are you out of your mind? Firstly, you will never get out of here alive. And even if you do, you will be spending the rest of your days in prison.'

'Shut it,' said Attila.

Pal said, 'Whatever he's offering you, Attila, I'll double it. Triple it. And make you overall commander of the Gendarmes and the police.'

Attila said, 'Do you really think this is about money?'

'In my experience it usually is. How much do you want?'

Balthazar shook his head. 'Wait a minute.' He checked the plasticuff, saw there was still a little bit of give and yanked even tighter.

Pal gasped. 'Ah, that hurts.'

'So will this,' said Attila. He turned to Balthazar, his meaty fists now clenched. 'One each. Do you want to go first?'

'Be my guest. But we need him conscious.'

'Sure. A grade one. That's all.' He turned to Pal. 'You remember the manual that you insisted we use? The ex-KGB instruction book for dealing with prisoners. Five grades of beating, from light to terminal. All laid out, page by page, complete with illustrations. I wonder which one my father took from your uncle and his *komcsi* friends.'

Pal's eyes widened. 'Your father?' His body seemed to sag as he spoke, realising why Attila had changed sides and that there was no inducement he could offer to save himself.

Attila handed his gun to Balthazar, walked over to the graffiti, ran his forefinger over the etched initials. He turned to Pal. 'Z.U. Csepel Island, 1984. Zeno Ungar.'

Pal's eyes widened in fear. 'Oh. Attila, I'm so sorry, I had no idea.'

Attila walked back. 'Of course not, because in all the months I have been working for you, you've never once asked me anything about myself, my family or my background. I'm just the hired muscle.' He stopped talking, walked around Pal, sizing him up. 'They broke my dad's nose. And that was just the start.' He ran his finger down Pal's nose, then stepped back. Attila turned to Balthazar. 'Hook or cross?'

Balthazar looked Pal up and down as he considered his response. 'Right cross, I think. Although a left jab would probably do the job, if it's fast enough. A hook might break his jaw. And don't knock him out. We need him to talk.'

Attila smiled. 'Right cross it is. Brace yourself, Prime Minister.'

Balthazar said, 'And mind you don't hit his teeth. You can get blood poisoning from that.'

'Thanks. I have done this before.'

'Then you will know how it works,' said Balthazar as he stepped behind Pal and held him up, a hand on both of Pal's forearms.

'Attila, no please,' shouted Pal. Attila pivoted on his right foot, his hips driving the punch forwards as his fist smashed into Pal's face. The crunch of snapping cartilage sounded. Pal's plea turned into a howl of pain as the blow landed. Attila's eyes turned distant and cloudy, a look that Balthazar knew too well from their time in the cells of the District VIII police station. He swung back for another blow.

Balthazar said, his voice sharp, 'Attila. We agreed. One is enough.'

Pal rocked back and forth on his feet, dazed and moaning, his nose splayed to one side. Attila blinked, focused and returned to the room. He looked at Pal, satisfied with his work. 'I'll search him.' He quickly ran his hands up and down Pal's trousers and shirts, checking the pockets. He extracted an iPhone and a wallet. 'It's not here.' He turned to Pal, 'Where is the radio controller?'

Pal had turned white, made paler by the gouts of blood seeping from his broken nose. 'What are you talking about?' he said, his voice thick and shaky.

Balthazar said, 'The radio controller that will set off the gas attack on Kossuth Square. Where is it?'

'I have no idea what you are talking about.'

Attila gestured to Balthazar. 'Your turn. Where now?'

Attila took Balthazar's place, holding up Pal as Balthazar walked around him. 'I'm thinking about it,' said Balthazar. He swung around with a right hook to Pal's midriff, winding him. He sagged, groaning loudly.

'I'll ask again,' said Balthazar. 'Where is it?'

Pal grimaced in a half smile. He turned to the side and spat a crimson gout of blood. 'Somewhere safe. Somewhere that you won't find it. And it won't matter if you do. You are both dead men.'

Balthazar said, 'Lie down. On your back.'

'Fuck you,' said Pal.

Balthazar nodded at Attila, who stepped away from Pal. Balthazar swept his legs from under him. Pal crashed to the floor. Balthazar walked across the cellar to where Anastasia's jacket lay crumpled on the floor, picked it up and walked back to the two men. Attila looked at him, puzzled. Balthazar straightened out Pal's legs then dropped Anastasia's jacket onto his face. Pal shouted in pain as the jacket made contact with his broken nose, started coughing and protesting.

Balthazar told Attila. 'Bring one of the water bottles.' He did as Balthazar asked. Balthazar bent down and said to Pal, 'Where is the radio control?'

Pal muttered something unintelligible. Balthazar lifted Anastasia's jacket from his face. Pal said, 'I told you, somewhere safe.' Balthazar replaced the jacket, gestured at Attila for a bottle of water. The two men stood on either side of Pal, jamming him between their legs. Balthazar opened the water bottle and starting pouring it over Anastasia's jacket. Pal coughed and shouted, tried to slide out from under the deluge but was trapped between Attila and Balthazar.

Balthazar gestured to Attila, who handed him another bottle of water. He stretched out his arm, held the bottle over Pal. To Balthazar's surprise, his anger had faded. Instead he focused on the task: to find the radio controller and save the lives that Pal planned to take. For a moment he remembered reading about the psychology experiment at Stanford University where some students pretended to be prisoners and others prison guards. Many of the guards quickly turned into sadists. It was surprisingly easy to move from prisoner to jailer. Balthazar looked down at Pal, prone, in pain, red rivulets of blood mixing in with the water around his head under Anastasia's jacket. He felt no sympathy, none at all, just a desire to get the job done. Perhaps it was this place. Or the memory of Virag. In the end it didn't matter. Muffled grunts sounded under the wet clothing. Balthazar tipped his hand to the side, watched half the water pour over Pal's head. The grunts got louder, more desperate. Pal tried to wriggle away. Balthazar and Attila both moved closer, jamming him tighter between their legs.

Balthazar lifted the sodden clothing from Pal's face. Pal shouted, 'I'm sorry, I told you. I wanted to rescue her. But Reka stopped me.'

Balthazar said nothing, dropped the wet jacket back on Pal's face and tipped the rest of the bottle of water on top of him. Pal thrashed and gurgled until the water stopped. Balthazar said, '*There are worse ways to die.* You won't actually die from this, but your brain thinks you will. So at least you get to experience the terror she felt.' He lifted the jacket once again. 'Where's the radio control?'

Pal lay panting and coughing, blood still seeping from his nose, crimson tendrils floating in the water as it pooled around him. 'OK. Stop, please stop. It's in my office. At the foundation, on Szabadsag Square.'

Balthazar asked, 'Are you lying? Because if you are...'

Pal was half sobbing now, 'I told you. It's in the office.'

'Al-Nuri. Why did you have him killed?'

Pal tried to compose himself. 'He was in the way. If Reka got the money from the Gulf she would stay in power. But if she doesn't, she won't. It's simple.'

'Is that it? A man died.'

Pal shrugged. 'Coked-up, on the job with a hooker in your brother's brothel. I'd keep quiet about that one if I were you.'

Just as Balthazar was about to answer, a muffled sound, something between a sharp crack and a bang, echoed in the room, followed by the thump of something, or someone, falling.

A muffled voice shouted, '*Batyam, batyam*, where are you?'

Balthazar gestured at Attila, who quickly unholstered his pistol and gave to it to Balthazar. He rushed over to the door, pulled up the bar and opened the door, the Glock trained. Gaspar stood outside, together with Fat Vik and a tall, skinny man he recognised as the Nissan driver yesterday. All three had pistols in their hands. They lowered their weapons and the two brothers embraced.

'This is all very moving,' said Attila, 'but we need to get out of here.'

Gaspar's eyes widened when he saw Attila. He moved to raise his gun when Balthazar put his hand on Gaspar's arm. 'He's with us.'

Gaspar said, 'If you say so.' He and Attila glared suspiciously at each other.

Balthazar said, 'I do say so. *Mondd ocsim*, tell me little brother, where's Anastasia?'

'Here,' she said as she walked into the room.

'Are you OK? Did they...' asked Balthazar.

'I'm fine. And no, they didn't touch me. They shouted at me a lot, that's all.' She turned to Balthazar, gestured at Attila. 'And now he's on our side? Are we supposed to trust him? What brought that on?'

Attila walked over to the far wall. He pointed at the spot where his father's initials were carved into the brickwork. 'Z.U. Csepel Island, 1984. Zeno Ungar My father. A prisoner of the state security service. The predecessor to your employers. They even had the same name.'

Anastasia blushed, looked down for a moment. 'I'm sorry. That was a different organisation. In different times. We don't torture people.'

Attila laughed. 'But *we* do, don't we, Tazi?'

Anastasia frowned, walked over to the other side of the room, where her jacket lay on the floor near Pal, a bloodied, sodden mess, and picked it up. 'What did you do with it?' She looked at Pal, sitting slumped against the wall, saw that he had been drenched, the blood still dripping from his broken nose. 'Oh,' she said, realisation dawning. She reached into her jeans pocket, pulled out a handful of tissues and handed them to him. 'Here – clean yourself up.' She dropped the jacket, turned to Balthazar. 'You'll buy me a new one, once all this is over.'

'Sure. We'll go shopping.' He turned to Gaspar. 'Tell me what happened.'

'There were two Gendarmes in front, guarding the gate,' Gaspar said excitedly. He turned to Szilard. 'He shot them both. Boom, boom, one to each chest and down they went. Just like in the movies.'

Anastasia closed her eyes for a moment, reopened them and said, 'Szilard, please tell me you haven't killed two Gendarmes?'

Szilard said, 'Of course not. They had body armour on. They are alive, although they will have sore ribs and awful headaches when they wake up.'

'Where are they?' asked Anastasia.

'In the van,' said Gaspar.

Balthazar asked, 'And in the house?'

'Only two more,' said Szilard. 'They thought that would be enough.'

'And those two?'

Szilard smiled proudly. 'Same. Close-range chest shot. Body armour. Target is winded, may have broken ribs, can't stand up. Is then knocked unconscious.'

Anastasia smiled. 'Busy weekend you're having, Szili. But nice work.'

'Let's go,' said Balthazar. He pointed at Pal. 'And we need to get him out of here.'

TWENTY-SEVEN

Marton Ronay's flat, Alkotmany Street, 10.00 a.m.

Marton surfaced unwillingly from a deep slumber, turned in his bed and tried to ignore the noise. Finally, he had managed to sleep through the night. His jet lag was fading and he had been looking forward to a lie-in, then perhaps a visit to one of the city's famed Turkish baths. And now this. Whatever this was. Muffled chanting, shouting and laughter sounded through his windows. What the hell was going on at ten o'clock on a Saturday morning in the middle of the government quarter? Some kind of street party, or something more significant? If it was here, on Alkotmany Street, it was almost certainly heading to Parliament. Which meant this was something *political*. But now the crowd sounded like it was passing under his window, yelling something about the Gendarmes and democracy. This was definitely political. He grabbed a pair of trousers and a T-shirt, put them on, walked over to the balcony and peered out. The crowd reached most of the way down Alkotmany Street and was slowly heading towards Parliament. Half the city seemed to be here. He watched a group of elderly pensioner couples, dressed in their weekend best, walk arm in arm, waving Hungarian flags; a platoon of groggy-looking hipsters stopping momentarily to peer longingly into the window of the artisan coffee shop, a gaggle of tough-looking men in shiny tracksuits.

He turned to look in the other direction and did a quick calculation – Alkotmany Street was about a third of a mile long, extending from Parliament to Bajcsy-Zsilinszky Way, by the Nyugati Station, and four lanes wide, two in each direction, with a bicycle lane on the other side of the street. It was full. There were easily twenty or thirty thousand demonstrators heading towards Kossuth Square. Marton and Pal's people had discussed organising a demonstration here earlier in the week, to show the strength of feeling against Reka Bardossy's government. But this protest seemed to embody the opposite sentiment. He watched a middle-aged man in a brown coat hold up a home-made cardboard placard proclaiming: 'Down with Pal. Up with democracy'. Marton tried again to call Adorjan Molnar, but his phone was still on voicemail, had been since yesterday. In fact, his clients seemed to have disappeared. He had called and texted several times to see when they next wanted him to meet, saying he was available over the weekend – rest days were also paid at full day rate – but nobody replied or called back. He also sent emails to say he was available – it was important to leave a data trail in case there were disputes later about the bills – but when he checked his bank account his full fee had been paid in advance.

He turned back around to watch the first protestors reach Kossuth Square. The Gendarmerie vehicles were still parked in front of Parliament, the blue tents remained pitched on the green verges. Marton had seen footage of the 2006 protests. The square and its surrounds, including Alkotmany Street, could hold more than 100,000 people. What if the Gendarmes and the blue tent dwellers started fighting? Perhaps that was part of Pal's plan, some secret battle order for chaos that Marton was not to be trusted with. Well, that was their choice. He'd been paid.

Marton turned, went back inside and switched the television on, frowning as he stared at the screen. Every channel was blank, showing the same wording: 'This channel is not available for technical reasons.' Impressive work by Pal and his people. That creepy old guy had a hand in this, Marton was sure. So how had all these people known to come to Kossuth Square? Television channels could be blocked but it was impossible to switch off the Internet. He grabbed his telephone and checked his Twitter feed: it loaded slowly, but eventually he saw that #saveHungarydemocracy was trending, and a video of Reka Bardossy had gone viral. He clicked and watched it. It was not very professional and appeared to have been filmed in what he guessed was her home, probably on an iPhone. She looked pale and drawn. But she got her message out. The clip lasted for about a minute:

'My fellow citizens and guests in our country. We Hungarians are good at dividing among ourselves and fighting each other. But today is a time to unite. Our democracy is under attack. Pal Dezeffy and the Gendarmes are attempting to mount a coup. Yesterday morning I dissolved the Gendarmerie by executive order. But its commanders and officers have defied that. They are an illegal organisation, operating illegally. They are criminals.' The clip switched to the Gendarme checkpoint at Blaha Lujza last night, and the long lines of vehicles waiting to pass through, then went back to Reka. 'As you know, I assumed the office of prime minister after Pal Dezeffy resigned due to his involvement in facilitating the movements of terrorists through Hungary. But this is only a temporary measure. I am now calling a general election to take place as soon as possible. I may win or I may lose. But this is how we transfer power in this country. Not by an illegal organisation of armed paramilitaries taking control of the streets. I call on all loyal democrats – left, right, and centre or none of these – to come to Kossuth Square and show their support for democracy, not a dictatorship.' She paused, stared at the camera and blinked. 'Hungary will be a democracy, not a dictatorship. But we need you to make that happen. Please come now to Kossuth Square. Thank you.' The video ended with a plain white screen and the hashtag #saveHungarydemocracy.

Marton nodded and put his telephone down. Reka's impassioned speech was impressive for a home-made broadcast. She was sincere and passionate. In a way the rough and ready feel made it seem more honest and appealing. Would it work? He walked back onto the balcony. By now the front of the crowd was spilling into Kossuth Square, and the protestors were still pouring in from the top of Alkotmany Street. Whatever was going on here was more interesting than a trip to the baths. He grabbed his telephone, quickly brushed his teeth and went downstairs to take a look for himself.

Sarah held tightly onto Alex's hand as they walked down Alkotmany Street. They were on the edge of the crowd – she hated large gatherings, felt trapped and claustrophobic when she was surrounded. Once she and Eva realised that Balthazar had disappeared and his flat was not a good place to be, they had quickly left. Eva had gone back to her apartment and loudly locked the door. Sarah decided to head home, wondering which route to take back to Buda. But just as they sat in the car Alex started checking his telephone. His Instagram feed was full of excited messages from his school friends, many of which linked to Reka's video appeal. Sarah and he had watched it together after which he had pleaded to go on the demonstration. She was torn between being a protective mother, keen to shield her child from any potential conflict or trouble, and letting him experience something memorable. And there would be safety in numbers, she was sure.

She had parked the car on Kalman Imre Street, which ran parallel with Alkotmany. She had the *laissez-passer* that Attila had given her at the ready, but the Gendarmes had waved her, and the other vehicles, through. The pavements, empty an hour ago, were now crowded with people heading to the demonstration. The Gendarmes who had previously stopped her at Nyugati Station were nowhere to be seen and there the traffic was flowing freely again. Government coercion, she remembered studying in a class at Central European University, rested on consent. That consent could be either active or passive. But no government could control its population if they chose, en masse, to take to the streets. Fear was the greatest weapon an oppressive regime had in its armoury. But the fear was in people's heads and once they banished it, they could take back control of their country. Violence, even shooting protestors, would merely fuel a greater determination.

She looked around, trying to get the measure of what was happening. After five minutes' slow walking they were on the corner of Bihari Janos Street, three long blocks from Kossuth Square. The atmosphere was tense, the faces of the protestors focused and determined, as though they understood what was at stake. A grey-haired lady in her sixties proffered a bag to Alex, looking at Sarah for permission. '*Pogacsas,* home made – take some, please,' she said.

Alex also glanced at his mother. She nodded and he took a couple of the savoury pastries, and gave one to Sarah. The layered, salty pastry was delicious. Just as they both thanked the lady, the chant went up again, 'No to dictatorship, yes democracy'. The grey-haired lady joined in, shouting lustily, as did everyone around them.

Alex was wide-eyed with excitement, looking around, drinking it all in. Sarah felt him tug hard on her hand and he pointed rightwards. 'Look, Mum – there's Henrik. That man's son. With his mum – I think her name is Monika.'

Sarah's gaze travelled through the crowd until she saw a tall, skinny teenager with floppy brown hair, sixteen or seventeen years old, chanting and waving a rainbow flag. He was perhaps ten yards away, with a middle-aged woman with short brown hair.

'Let's go over there,' said Alex. 'I want to say hallo.' He smiled at Sarah. 'I really do remember him. We had fun that day. Don't worry, Mum – he's much nicer than his dad.'

Sarah nodded and they eased their way through the crush of people. The boys greeted each other. They smiled with their arms around each other. Henrik took a selfie of them together. 'Shall I send it to Dad?' he asked his mother with a mischievous smile. 'With the flag?'

'Sure,' she replied. 'Why not?'

Budapest looked the same as ever from the tinted windows of a Gendarmerie SUV, thought Balthazar, but the vehicle seemed to be surrounded by a force field. Cars pulled over to the side of the road to make way, pedestrians stepped back or rapidly turned to walk in another direction, and when the black SUV stopped at a corner or ran a red light, other vehicles kept a healthy distance.

Attila looked at Balthazar as they raced down from Rose Hill onto the Margaret Bridge as though reading his mind, two saloons in front of them almost banging into oncoming traffic as they swerved out of the way, 'Fun, eh? Much better than a cop car.'

'Enjoy it while it lasts, Attila,' said Balthazar. He winced as Attila yanked the SUV sideways and onto the tram lines, skidding until he righted the vehicle. There were four of them in the car: Attila drove while Balthazar sat next to him. In the back Anastasia sat next to Pal, who had been recuffed and now had his hands in front. Gaspar and the Fat Vik had gone home. The four injured Gendarmes had been left on the pavement after two ambulances had been called for them.

Balthazar stared at the panorama of the city as they crossed Margaret Bridge, swerving at the sharp bend in the middle where, on the other side of the road, a spur led down onto the island. Budapest looked magnificent, spread out along the riverbank, the water for once almost blue, shimmering in the bright autumn sunshine. Parliament was visible in the distance on the Pest side of the river bank, a gothic concoction of needle-sharp spires, long rows of windows set in pale stone, topped by a brown dome. The pavements were unusually crowded, he realised, and not with the usual gaggles of tourists and teenagers taking selfies against the backdrop of the river. This was a crowd on the move, calm and determined, walking en masse to a destination. Many carried placards and home-made banners all with the same message: 'Democracy not dictatorship'.

'Something's happening. Put the radio on,' said Balthazar.

Attila flipped a switch on the steering wheel. Bartok spilled from the speakers, the sweeping music full of yearning.

'I never would have guessed you were a classical music fan,' said Anastasia.

'I'm not,' said Attila, flipping through the stations, as they came off the bridge and turned right, towards Parliament. Now the roads were jammed with people and the traffic crawled. 'I'm looking for the news.' Attila flicked through half a dozen different stations. All were either broadcasting white noise or Hungarian classical music. Eventually Reka Bardossy's voice sounded through the speakers, distant and crackly, '… Hungary will be a democracy, not a dictatorship. But we need you to make that happen. Please come now to Kossuth Square. Thank you.'

A male announcer said, 'This is Budapest Kaloz, pirate radio, broadcasting on the move to evade the Gendarmerie. All commercial stations have been closed down. State radio is broadcasting classical music. But we are still on air. Catch our live feed on the internet. Kaloz.hu. Here again is Prime Minister Reka Bardossy.'

Balthazar, Anastasia and Attila fell silent as they listened to her broadcast in full. Balthazar watched the crowds gather and thicken as they walked along the embankment.

Pal laughed as Reka finished her broadcast. 'Do you think that's enough? Some students and *nenis* walk to Kossuth Square, Reka makes a plea on the Internet and pirate radio? You cannot stop us. You have no idea what or who you are dealing with.'

'Tell me, then, Mr Dezeffy,' said Balthazar, 'who are we dealing with? Your Arab friends, the terrorists that you let pass through this country? Or the Gulf investors that want to turn us into a colony so they and their families can get Hungarian passports?'

Pal coughed and wiped the blood from his nose before he answered. 'Don't ask me. Ask Reka. She knows all about them. She invited them here in the first place. Arab money is just a tiny part of this. There are forces here, in this country, that you have no idea about. Reka and I, we are two sides of the same coin. We go back a long way. We fight, then we ally, then we fight again. In bed and out. This isn't your war, Detective Kovacs, and I am not sure why you are in it.'

Balthazar said, 'But it is. We know you plan to release some kind of poison gas onto Kossuth Square. A lot of people will die.'

Pal shrugged. 'No they won't. A lot of people will feel sick and go home and Reka Bardossy's last tiny bit of authority will be finished.'

Balthazar said, 'And that's why you engaged two of the men who were responsible for the Halabja massacre? To make people feel sick and go home? You could do that yourself, just tip something into the machine that pumps the steam out. But only they know how to kill people. Once that gas is rolling across Kossuth Square nobody will be going anywhere, except to the morgue, or maybe the hospital if they are lucky.'

'What nonsense,' said Pal. He leaned forward, said to Attila, 'Attila, did you really think I would kill hundreds of people? I told you once. I will tell you again. Nobody is going to die. They are just going to throw up a lot. And that will get the job done.' Pal laughed again. 'And Reka, poor Reka. She thinks she will win by bringing the people onto the streets. She has done exactly what we expected her to.'

Balthazar looked at Anastasia in the mirror. Their eyes met and both silently asked the same question: Was Pal lying?

ADAM LEBOR

There was one way to find out. They needed that radio controller. Balthazar said, 'Attila, can you speed up?'

'Not much more, but I'll try,' said Attila as he yanked the steering wheel to the right and the SUV lurched down Honved Street. They were now half a mile from the edge of Szabadsag Square where Pal's foundation had its office. Attila heard his telephone beep. The handset was in a well by the gearstick. 'Tazi, get that please,' he asked. 'See what it is.'

Balthazar took out the handset and opened the messages. A photo appeared of two teenage boys in the demonstration, a block or so from Kossuth Square, Parliament rising high in the background. He closed his eyes for a moment, hoping that the image might somehow become something else when he reopened them. It did not. It showed Alex and Henrik, with their arms around each other, Henrik holding his rainbow flag.

TWENTY-EIGHT

Eniko checked her Twitter feed once more then put her telephone down. #saveHungarydemocracy was trending now internationally, #kossuthsquare not far behind it. #honestreportingHungary, she was pleased to see, had all but vanished, overtaken by events. All the major international news organisations were reporting from the square, even though cable television networks were not available, flooding the Internet with coverage. CNN had set up from a balcony on Alkotmany Street, panning back and forth between the junction with Bajcsy-Zsilinszky Way at the top and Kossuth Square at the bottom. The street was completely full with people and more were pouring in from the side roads. The small speaker on her phone blared out the crowd's chant, 'Democracy, not dictatorship'.

Eniko turned to Reka. 'It's time, Prime Minister. We need go to Kossuth Square, now. There's a critical mass. We can win this.'

'We can. But from here,' said Sandor. He turned to Reka, 'You're not going anywhere. It's not safe. Pal has planned something. We don't know what exactly, but nothing good.'

Reka sat back and took a drink of her coffee. 'Sani, if fifty thousand—'

Eniko looked down at her phone again, checked her browser. 555.hu had set up a live feed from the square, fronted by Zsuzsa, and a real-time ticker giving an estimate of the numbers of protestors, 'Sixty-two, sorry to interrupt,'

Reka nodded, continued talking, '... a thousand people are walking into an uncertain situation to support me, I really think I ought to be there, don't you?' She turned to Antal. 'Antal, you're my security chief. What do you think?'

He thought before he answered. 'The situation is unstable. Possibly dangerous. We don't know enough about the nature of any threat to properly assess it. But you'll be in much more danger if Pal returns to power. I would say, Prime Minister, that you don't have a choice. You need to be there.'

Eniko smiled. 'As your communications chief, I totally agree.'

Akos nodded, 'And so do I. Eniko is right. This is the moment. You really need to take ownership of the square. Otherwise it will all fizzle out and we will still be sitting here in this room, wondering what to do next.'

Reka looked at Sandor, an indulgent smile on her face. 'It seems you are outnumbered, Sanyi *bacsi*.' He was about to reply when her telephone rang. Reka looked down at the screen, glanced at the others, mouthed 'Peter' and left the room. Eniko knew her husband was in the Gulf, on a business trip, had been there all week. Eniko was somewhat mystified as to why he had not flown home earlier, once it was clear that Reka's grip on power was slipping. But Reka had intimated that they led somewhat separate lives. She focused on her political career, he on business, and when they could, they enjoyed weekends together. But not this one, even though Reka's political career hung in the balance and would likely be decided by the end of the day.

Eniko stood up and started gathering her bag and her jacket. However cautious Sandor was, it was inconceivable that Reka would remain at home. Politicians, she knew, lived for moments like these. Reka was probably already imagining the roar of the crowd when they saw her walking among them. Eniko yawned as a wave of tiredness hit her, mixing with the caffeine and adrenalin that she was running on. She, Sandor and Akos had all spent the night here. The guest bedroom had its own bathroom and was extremely comfortable, but she had barely slept, her mind churning over the last couple of days. Eniko had left Balthazar's flat around midnight the previous evening. Scared as she was, there was not much comfort in sitting alone in someone else's apartment. In any case she was annoyed with herself for turning up there in the first place. She had virtually offered herself to Balthazar when they were standing on his balcony. Instead he had driven off into the night with Anastasia Ferenczy.

Soon after Balthazar had left, Eniko had called Reka. She had insisted on sending a government car, an Audi driven by Antal Kondor, to come and get her. The car had arrived ten minutes later. They had driven up Dob Street onto the Grand Boulevard. When they approached Blaha Lujza Square, and the Gendarmes' checkpoint came into view, Eniko's reporter instinct kicked in. She asked Antal to park on the side of the road, just before the crossroads with Rakoczi Way. He was reluctant – the situation was unstable and his orders were to bring Eniko straight to Reka's house. But she had insisted and when the car slowed right down in traffic, she had opened the door, got out and filmed the night-time scene, ignoring the repeated requests from the driver to get back into the vehicle. That was the footage that Reka had used in her broadcast. Two Gendarmes had come over to question her, and probably detain her. At which point Antal had stepped out of the vehicle, his weapon clearly visible. The Gendarmes had glanced at him, his pistol, the government number plates on the car, turned on their heels and waved the vehicle through their checkpoint.

Reka came back into the room, holding her coat. She looked drawn and preoccupied until she realised the three of them were all looking at her and instantly broke into a bright, professional smile. 'What are we waiting for? Let's go, people.'

Szabadsag Square, 11.35 a.m.

Balthazar stared at the text message on the screen of his telephone as Attila skid-parked the SUV on the corner of Square and Sas Street, narrowly missing three teenage girls walking arm in arm to nearby Kossuth Square.

> Alex Sarah Henrik Monika – get out of Kossuth Square NOW and get as far away as possible. This is NOT a joke u r in danger. Balthazar

Written in smaller type, underneath was the single word: 'Undeliverable'

Balthazar tried calling Sarah again, then Alex. Neither call went through. He looked down at the top left-hand corner of the screen again. The space where there were usually three or four bars was empty, apart from even tinier lettering: 'No network available'.

He looked around, as though the surrounds might provide a solution. What should have been a five-minute drive from Margaret Bridge had taken more than twenty. The streets around Parliament, all the way back to the Great Boulevard, were jammed with demonstrators and almost impassable. And with Pal a prisoner, walking was not an option. The Hungarian National Bank stood on one side of the road, a grand monumental building in pale stone, its walls decorated with ornate sculptures of toiling, busy workers. On the other side was a small park lined with hedges and a low metal fence. Two young women in their early twenties had set up a stall on a ping-pong table, selling drinks, snacks and sandwiches to the steady flow of people heading towards Parliament. Many of those walking through were staring at their phone, frowning, or handing them to their friends to check. Nobody was using them to talk.

Attila switched the engine off and glanced at Balthazar, who said, 'Nothing. There is no coverage. We might be able to get a wi-fi connection to send it, but there's no guarantee that it will arrive or even if it does that they will see it. And they would need one to get it.' He turned to Pal. 'Did you do this?'

Pal smirked. 'Not personally.'

Attila nodded, turned around in the seat and addressed Pal. 'I want to explain something to you, Comrade Pal.' Attila's voice was low and even as he spoke, but his eyes were wide, his nostrils flared and his body coiled like a spring ready to leap forward.

Pal shrank back. 'Are you going to hit me again? I told you where it is. It's in the drawer of my desk. It's not locked. You know what it looks like. You'll find it. I can come with you if you like. There's still time. You just to need to get to the edge of Kossuth Square. That will be near enough.'

Attila shook his head. 'Nice try. But there are security guards and CCTV cameras in the office building. The sight of you, a former prime minister, will raise the alarm. I'll go with the duchess here, and Detective Kovacs will look after you. Is that OK?' he asked, turning to Balthazar and Anastasia.

'Sure,' said Balthazar while Anastasia nodded, rolling her eyes.

Pal asked, 'Is that what you wanted to explain to me? Or is there something else?'

'There is,' said Attila. He reached for his telephone, showed the photograph on the screen to Pal. 'This.'

'Good-looking boys,' said Pal. 'Who are they?'

'My son, and his son,' said Attila, pointing at Balthazar. 'Both now on Kossuth Square.'

'Oh,' said Pal. 'That might be unfortunate. But very progressive, to be waving a rainbow flag. Is that a big thing in your family, Attila? Gay rights?'

Attila refused to rise to the bait. 'The big thing in my family is not killing any of us.'

Pal's tone changed. 'Meaning?' he asked, no longer flippant.

Pal leaned forward, grabbed Pal and jammed his forefinger into the wreckage of his nose. Pal yelped in pain. Attila said, 'That's nothing to what will happen to you if something happens to either of our boys. Nothing at all. I will kill you. I will break each of your limbs one by one with a hammer, then your joints until you are screaming to be put out of your misery. And nobody will find your body. You will vanish from this planet.'

Pal coughed and swallowed. 'I've got a son as well.'

'Where is he?' asked Balthazar.

'New York.'

'He should stay there,' said Attila.

'Do you think so?' asked Pal. He glanced at his watch. 'I guess we'll find out in a few minutes.'

Anastasia asked, 'What do you mean?'

Pal smiled. 'You are all misinformed. The radio controller stops the gas emission. There is a code for the controller's keypad. Only I know it. The timer is set automatically. I don't have to do anything. It's all going to happen. At 11.45 a.m. On the dot.'

'What is the code?' asked Balthazar.

'Take a guess.'

Attila extended his forefinger and moved towards Pal's broken nose.

'Wait,' said Balthazar. 'Let's ask him again.' He turned towards Pal. 'The code?'

Pal said, 'The year I first took power, Detective Kovacs. The year our revolution started. You remember when that was?'

Balthazar nodded. '2006. Fifty years after the 1956 uprising. How do I know that you are not lying?'

Pal stared at him. 'You don't, Detective Kovacs. But Attila here has made the consequences very clear if I don't help you. And as I don't wish or plan to be dismembered, I am telling you the truth.'

Balthazar thought for a moment. Pal's answer made sense. In any case they had to move forward.

Attila looked at Balthazar and nodded. 'OK. He should stay there,' said Attila. 'I'll tell the Gendarmes on the square to stand down,' he said to Balthazar as he stepped out of the car and strode rapidly through the small square, Anastasia rushing to catch up with him, not noticing that her phone had fallen out of her pocket and was now lying on the car seat.

Pal saw the handset on the edge of his field of vision. Balthazar was watching him closely, he saw, in the rear-view mirror, but had not looked down and seen Anastasia's handset. Pal raised his arms and stretched forward. Balthazar snapped, 'Sit still.'

'Sorry. My muscles are seizing up,' said Pal. 'Actually, I don't feel very well. I think I am going to be sick,' he said, his arms falling to the side of his right leg, inching towards Anastasia's telephone.

Balthazar frowned, exhaled. 'Then stick your head out of the window. Throw up there.' He looked back in the mirror. The street was filling slowly with protestors heading to Kossuth Square. He watched an elderly couple, hand in hand, chatting with a lanky student, waving an EU flag.

'I just need some air, Detective,' said Pal as his fingers closed over Anastasia's iPhone. The handset was a small 5e model and had a hard metal case. He slipped it between his palms and glanced down. With both hands extended, his fingers were just long enough to cover the handset from view.

'Can we step outside? Just for a minute. I really don't feel well. I've got a broken nose and I think I have a concussion as well.' Pal started inhaling rapidly and deeply and rocking back and forth. 'Detective, I really think I am going to throw up. It will go all down my front. I can't sit here in my own puke.' He lifted his hands. 'Look, I'm cuffed. You've got a gun. Even if I wanted to I'm in no state to make a run for it, and where would I go?' He stopped talking, heaved convincingly.

Balthazar exhaled loudly, stepped out of the car, walked around the back to the rear passenger door and looked inside. Pal did look like shit, it was true. There was dried blood all around his upper lip. His nose was red and swollen. Sooner or later there would be an inquiry into all of this. Refusing a prisoner air, making him vomit in a vehicle, would not look good, whatever he had been planning. Balthazar opened the door, helped Pal out, stood next to him as he leaned on the SUV. 'Are you OK?' he asked.

'Much better, thanks,' said Pal. 'By the way, your friends are wasting their time. The radio controller's not in the office. Although it is nearby.'

'What?' asked Balthazar.

'You heard,' said Pal.

He twisted on his left foot, whirled towards Balthazar and smashed the edge of the iPhone into the side of his head. Balthazar felt the pain mix with fury as he stumbled backwards against the car, before the edge of the iPhone slammed into his head again. The world wobbled, was filled with pain. He pulled his gun, but the weapon was useless as he watched Pal run forward weaving in front and behind the protestors and disappear into the crowds walking across Szabadsag Square.

As Balthazar set off in pursuit of Pal, a black Audi A6 with government plates came to a racing halt at the other end of Szabadsag Square, just behind the large obelisk monument to the Soviet liberators of Budapest.

Reka and Eniko got out first, ignored Antal's protests and stepped into the crowd. They were immediately swept up in the flow of people heading down Vecsey Street to Kossuth Square, a hundred yards away. Antal Kondor pushed his way through and quickly caught up with them, Sandor Takacs and Akos Feher trailing in their wake.

Reka was quickly recognised. The word spread quickly that the prime minister had joined them. Someone pressed a Hungarian flag into Reka's right hand, which she gladly accepted and loud cheers soon echoed across the street, together with the now-familiar cry, 'Democracy, not dictatorship'. A light rain, an autumn flurry, began to fall but did nothing to dampen the crowd's enthusiasm. The sky was a light grey, shot through with blue as the sun struggled to break through the crowds.

A camera crew from the BBC filming on the edge of Kossuth Square quickly scurried over and started filming. Theodore Nichols, the BBC correspondent, thrust his microphone towards Reka, and asked, 'Prime Minister, your government is collapsing and you face a no-confidence vote on Monday. Will you resign?'

Reka stopped walking for a moment, about to answer, when a familiar figure appeared in the corner of her vision. Was it… could it be? 'Prime Minister, will you resign?' asked Nichols again.

It was him, Reka could see. She put her shock aside, suddenly remembering she was live on international television. 'You can see yourself how much support I have. Not now, and not next week. But in my own good time, once the situation has stabilised, I will call a general election.'

Eniko said, 'OK, Theodore, you've had your interview. We need to move on.'

Nichols nodded, turned away and began speaking to the camera again.

Eniko whispered in Reka's ear, 'On the steps. That would be best.'

Reka nodded, the protestors steadily swelling in number in her wake as she walked forward, Antal Kondor at her side, steadily sweeping the square for signs of threat or danger.

TWENTY-NINE

Balthazar forced a path through the crowd, ignoring their protests and the pain in his head as he sprinted after Pal. He held his Glock in his right hand and with his left he wiped away the trickle of blood that ran from his forehead into his eyes. Pal, he could see, was about twenty yards ahead. The black SUVs were still parked in clusters on the square but there was no sign of the Gendarmes themselves, although in the distance, on the left side, he could see some figures in black uniforms walking past the statue of Ferenc Rakoczi on his horse, in the direction of the Ministry of Justice. There was no sign of Attila or Anastasia but there were thousands of people here, so they could be anywhere. There were some police officers walking around, though, the first he had seen since the crisis started. One was female, with red hair. It was the officer he had seen yesterday, on nearby Szalay Street, giving the Gendarmes the finger, he realised. She was already following the commotion, had registered Balthazar's presence and that he was in pursuit of somebody.

'Vera,' shouted Balthazar. 'It's Pal, stop him.'

Vera whirled around as Pal approached. She looked at Balthazar, then at Pal, and tried to grab him. He lashed out, caught her on the side of her head with a lucky blow and she staggered backwards. A tall, well-built man was standing by the tents, wearing a Hungarian Freedom Movement T-shirt and holding a walkie-talkie to his ear. A voice crackled from the handset as he scanned the crowd. He nodded and replied. When he saw Pal advancing through the crowd, he lowered the walkie-talkie and started moving towards him. A few yards later, the two men's hands brushed past each other. Pal slipped something into his trouser pocket. The man with the walkie-talkie raised the handset to his mouth again and spoke quickly before moving back into the crowd.

By now Balthazar was just a few yards away. Pal turned around, quickly smacked his palm against his broken nose. He gasped at the pain, tried to ignore it as his nose immediately started bleeding again, and shouted, 'Help, help, this man is attacking me. He's beaten me up. Help me. I am Pal Dezeffy. He is beating me.'

The protestors nearby turned, trying hard to see what was happening. Pal started yelling again, shrinking back in fear from his pursuer. Some in the crowd recognised Pal and began to form a protective ring around him. Balthazar took out his police ID, pushed forward. 'Make way. This man is under arrest.'

Pal smiled for a moment, turned to the spectators, pointing at his nose, proclaiming, 'What kind of policeman does this? Please, I beg you, protect me. I am the rightful prime minister. This criminal and his associates kidnapped me and assaulted me. They are organising a coup against us, against our democracy.'

The protestors looked at each other uncertainly. The mood of the crowd was already tense, almost febrile. It could turn in a second, Balthazar sensed. Law and order was collapsing.

The fear had gone, both of the Gendarmes and of the regular police. Plus he was a Gypsy. Some of the protestors advanced towards him. 'Look at him,' said one lady in her fifties with purple dyed hair, waving her hand dismissively at Balthazar. 'How can he be a policeman? We know his kind. They break the law, they don't enforce it.'

A thin, bald man with thick horn-rimmed glasses nodded in agreement, his companions gathering around him, starting to circle around Balthazar. None of them were particularly dangerous or even fit-looking, but they could crowd him in, certainly delay him. He thought back for a moment to what he had just seen. Or thought he had seen. Had the man in the Hungarian Freedom Movement T-shirt handed something to Pal? The radio controller? He thought so, but it was impossible to be sure. Pal was moving off now, Balthazar could see, and another thick-set man, also in a Hungarian Freedom Movement T-shirt, was helping him. Balthazar looked back at his immediate surrounds to see that around twenty people had gathered around him. The atmosphere was turning hostile.

Balthazar pulled out the Glock 17 and fired twice into the air. The crowd scattered instantly. The sound of the gunshot resounded over the square. The protestors started running in all directions. Pal too was running, towards the Ferenc Rakoczi statue on the far side of the square, trying to escape. Now the red-haired police officer was in pursuit, sprinting after him, her pistol in her hand, shouting at him to stop. At that moment the bulky man in the HFM T-shirt stepped out in her way, barged into her and she went flying. Her gun skidded across the damp flagstones, towards Pal. He picked it up and pointed it at Balthazar, then swept it back and forth across the square. The bulky man put Vera in a bear hug from behind, above her elbows, trapping her arms, or so he thought. She grabbed his hands with her left hand to hold them in place, stepped sideways, slid her right hand up towards her left shoulder then out of his bearhug, pivoted on her left foot and slammed her open palm down into his groin. He groaned in pain. Just as his grip loosened, she delivered the same blow again, even harder. He staggered backwards and she stepped away.

Balthazar watched as Vera advanced on Pal from a side angle, out of his line of sight.

'You are going to let me go, Detective Kovacs,' said Pal. 'I'm not a good shot. If I miss you, I might hit anyone. You don't want to be responsible for anyone's death, do you? Think of that nice photo your son sent you. He's having such fun with Henrik.'

For a second Balthazar was back on the firing range. The chest offered the biggest and most lethal target. He aimed the gun at Pal's leg and fired. Pal quickly stepped sideways, dropped the gun down. The bullet went wide and smashed into the base of the Rakoczi statue. Pal raised the gun and took aim again. At that moment Vera launched herself onto Pal, grabbing his gun. He let go of the weapon and started running again, in a straight line towards the end of the square.

Balthazar lowered his Glock and aimed at Pal's legs. He fired once. Pal flew forward, landed face-down on the grass.

Balthazar ran over to him and turned his prone body over. The bullet had passed through his leg, and the exit wound was clearly visible. It was only a flesh wound, the kind that healed quite rapidly. But the shock of the wound, after the waterboarding and beating, was too much for Pal. He was semi-conscious now, his eyes rolling back in his head, his eyeballs fluttering.

Balthazar shouted at the nearest protestors, 'Find an ambulance.' He quickly slid his hands through each of Pal's pockets, simultaneously glancing at his watch. It was 11.43 a.m. The pockets were empty. There was no radio controller. He looked around, scouring the surrounds in case it had fallen out. There were cigarette ends, sandwich wrappers, empty bottles of mineral water. But no small black box with a keypad. He shook Pal, tried to wake him, asking urgently, 'Where is the controller? Where is the box?' But Pal had slipped into unconsciousness.

Balthazar closed his eyes for a second, forced himself to think. Heart pounding, he checked the pockets again. They were still empty. He ran his two hands up and down Pal's body, as though he were a suspect who had just been arrested. Arms, legs, armpits, waist, small of the back. Nothing. Until he reached his ankles. There was something inside his left sock, square and hard. Balthazar pulled out a small black box, perhaps two inches long, his hands sweating so much that he almost dropped it, looked again at his watch – 11.44 a.m. – forced himself to control his breathing, tapped in the numbers 2006. Nearby, he saw that several small metal grilles embedded in the flagstones were now sliding open. Had he entered the numbers incorrectly? Balthazar tapped in 2–0–0–6 again, slowly and carefully, glanced sideways. The metal grilles stayed open. Small black nozzles were slowly moving upwards.

Then it came to him. He could hear Pal's voice again. 'The year I first took power, Detective Kovacs, the year our revolution started. You remember when that was.' Pal had lied. But he had also given Balthazar a hint. He was not talking about his election victory. He had first taken power not in 2006 but in 1995, when he took over the leadership of the Social Democratic Party, disposing of the old guard who had made him their protégé. The year that was seared into Balthazar's brain. The year that Virag had died.

Balthazar prayed, for the first time in many years, then tapped in 1-9-9-5.

The nozzles moved back down and the grilles slid shut.

He collapsed onto the grass, closed his eyes and took great gulps of air, until he felt a shadow move across his face.

He looked up to see Alex and Sarah standing over him. Alex said, 'Hi, Dad. We were on the other side of the square, then we heard the shooting, so we hid behind the Kossuth statue till it stopped. It was scary but kind of exciting as well. What are you doing down there?'

THIRTY

Parliament, six days later, 4.00 p.m.

Balthazar stood by the window in the ante-room to Reka Bardossy's office, watching a police launch bump along the water towards the Chain Bridge, wondering how much longer he would have to wait. He was wearing his black Zara suit, which still fit, just, a white shirt and grey tie which Eva *neni* had knotted and adjusted for him. It was Friday afternoon, the start of the weekend and most Hungarian workplaces were already closing up. But here there was no let up in activity. A stream of officials and aides bustled up and down the corridors outside and in and out of Reka's office. The door opened again and Balthazar turned around. He looked expectantly but Akos Feher walked in. He smiled broadly at Balthazar, crossed the room and shook his hand vigorously.

'The man of the hour. That's twice you have saved us from something very unpleasant indeed, Detective Kovacs. Thanks so much for coming in today. The prime minister will be with you very shortly.'

Balthazar felt himself redden. He hated this kind of attention. Once again the footage of him in action, this time taking down Pal, had gone viral. The former prime minister was now recovering from his bullet wound in hospital, under armed guard. He was facing charges of attempted mass murder and terrorism. Adorjan Molnar had also been arrested and Pal's foundation closed down. This time there would be no quiet departure and comfortable life of think-tanks and consulting. Pal Dezeffy was going to prison for a very long time. Perhaps for ever. The water tanks under Kossuth Square had been decontaminated by specialist chemical units from the Hungarian military. The liquid had contained a new compound, heavier than water. Had it been sprayed over the epicentre of Kossuth Square, the area directly in front of the Parliament's entrance, everyone in the immediate vicinity would have died or at least become very ill, but it would have been extremely localised. Those on the edge of the square, where Pal had been trying to reach, would likely have been OK, or only suffered minor side-effects. It was a very precisely targeted new type of chemical attack, being studied with great interest by all sorts of agencies.

As Balthazar said goodbye to Akos, he sensed Kati Tolma, Reka's personal assistant, watching him closely. 'Are you sure you won't have something to drink, Detective Kovacs?' she asked, a hint of a smile on her face. 'Coffee, tea, perhaps something stronger?' Was she flirting with him? She was not really his type, pale and skinny with a bob of black hair, but her face was finely sculpted with delicate cheekbones. And her almond-shaped blue eyes fizzed with confidence and intelligence. Kati tilted her head to one side so her hair slid across her face, then flicked it aside. 'Go on. Be a devil, detective. It is Friday afternoon. The prime minister won't mind. She might even join you.'

Balthazar smiled, despite his nerves. She was flirting with him. This was happening ever more frequently. So why not enjoy it? Not everything had to be agonised over.

Kati continued speaking, glanced at her watch. 'I'm finishing in half an hour.' She looked back up at him, her eyes alight. 'Or maybe I can buy you a drink, Detective? Once you're done in there.'

He was about to say no, reflexively, when the door opened. Eniko Szalay walked out. He and Eniko looked at each other for several seconds. She wore a navy business suit and a pale blue blouse, and carried an oversized iPhone in her hand. Her nails were painted with a uniform clear varnish, her hair had been cut back to half its former length and the hoop earring was gone. She smiled uncertainly, then she greeted him. 'Taz... Detective Kovacs, what a pleasure to see you. How are you?' she asked.

He nodded slowly. She was a long way from the pale, frightened woman on his balcony just a week ago. 'Fine.' He sensed Kati Tolma watching their interaction with more than professional interest. The air turned heavy with his and Eniko's history. Then she broke the spell. 'It's nice to see you, look after yourself, Detective,' she said, her voice brisk and professional. Just as Eniko started to move towards the door, Reka Bardossy walked in.

A minute later Balthazar and Reka were sitting in the corner alcove of her office. The Beidermeyer furniture had been replaced by modern pieces by young Hungarian designers, and the whiskery men had been banished to a far corner. Most of the walls were empty, and there were dust marks around the spaces where the portraits had hung. The Zsolnay coffee set stood in the centre of an elegant, light-wood table. A plastic folder lay nearby, next to a catalogue for an art gallery.

Balthazar started with surprise when he saw the name of the gallery: Rainbow. 'That's my sister Flora's place.'

Reka smiled. 'I know. I'm redecorating. She has some really nice pieces by young Hungarian artists. I'm thinking of buying quite a few.'

'Good. She'll be really pleased. So will the artists.'

'I hope so.' Reka poured Balthazar a cup of coffee without asking. He accepted the drink and took a sip. It was very good coffee.

This was the second time they had met this week. The first was on Monday, two days after the dramatic events on Kossuth Square. They had discussed what had happened, the charges that would be brought against Pal, and Balthazar's future. Reka had offered him a job in her security detail, working with Antal Kondor at double his salary. He had refused. Few things seemed more welcoming than simply going back to his desk at the Budapest police headquarters and dealing with the back-log of murder cases. They had also discussed his medal ceremony and the reception for under-privileged children to take place next month at Parliament. Balthazar had not then raised Pal's claims that Reka too had been at the party where Virag had died. It was too soon and there were many other things to talk about. But it hung in the air, and Reka, he thought, could sense something. Two days later he had asked for this meeting and she had immediately agreed.

Reka sipped her coffee as they exchanged greetings and pleasantries. 'My door is always open, Detective Kovacs. How can I help you?'

He looked down at the table for a moment, considered how to answer. Hungarians appreciated the direct approach. 'Prime Minister, Pal told me that you were there when Virag died. You were at the party. He said you stopped him from diving in to rescue her.'

Reka put her cup down. Her hand, he saw, was still. 'Why would I do that?'

'Because Pal tried to sleep with Virag. She was scared and she ran away. She would have made accusations. They would have messed up his political career.'

Reka looked at him. She was no longer pale. The marks on her neck and scratches on her hand were fading. Her posture was straight, her voice confident as she replied without hesitating. 'This is a very hard thing to say, Detective Kovacs, but think back to 1995. Pal would have denied everything, of course. Who would have been believed? A young Gypsy girl from District VIII, or Pal, a scion of one of the country's most powerful dynasties?'

The answer was obvious to Balthazar. And would not be very different in 2015. 'Pal. But were you there?'

'Yes and no.'

'That's a politician's...'

'...answer, I know. Except it's not.' She held her hand up for a moment, before she continued speaking. 'Please wait a moment. Yes, I was there at the party. No, I did not see Virag drown and I certainly did not stop Pal from diving in to save her. I would have dived in myself.' She lowered her hand and her eyes turned distant for a moment. 'It was a big party, Detective Kovacs. I was in another part of the house entirely.'

'Doing what?'

Reka blushed. 'Do I have to spell it out? I was nineteen. Pal was supposed to be my boyfriend but he slept with anyone he could. I thought he was about to dump me. You know our phrase, "Don't let yourself fall between two benches?"'

Balthazar smiled. 'Yes, of course.'

'So I didn't. And no, I had no idea about Pal's plans for Virag. I thought he brought her to sing, nothing more. I would have stopped him immediately and sent her home in a taxi, if I had.' She rested her hand on Balthazar's for a moment. 'Detective Kovacs, I am truly sorry for your loss. I can only imagine how much Virag meant to you. And how much you still miss her.'

'Can you?'

'I hope so. And I hope this will at least preserve her memory.'

She slid the file forward. Balthazar opened it and removed the sheets inside. They outlined plans for the Virag Kovacs College of Music, to be sited in a former school not far from Mikszath Kalman Square. There would be numerous scholarships and grants for under-privileged children.

Reka asked, 'Do you approve? At least in principle? I do hope so. We can discuss the details later. I want you, and your family, to be consulted at every step.'

For a moment he felt his stomach lurch. A voice in his head, female, he thought, said, yes, Tazi, we approve. Tell her that we do. Was it her, or his imagination? Perhaps it didn't matter. 'Thank you, Prime Minister. This is a lovely idea. I will need to speak to my relatives, but I think we should be able to give it our blessing.'

Reka smiled, widely. It was a genuine smile, that lit up her face. 'Wonderful news, Detective Kovacs. Perhaps we can talk more about it one evening over dinner at Kadar.'

'I'd like that,' said Balthazar. Was Reka telling the truth about the party? He had watched her closely as she answered. Her voice did not quaver, she did not look left or right, or touch her mouth. There were no tells that she was lying. But then she was a highly experienced politician. It was, he thought, at least a version of the truth, and nowadays in Budapest that was as much as he could expect.

A few minutes later, after Reka had outlined the plans for the music school in more detail, Balthazar was back in the ante-room. Kati Tolma, he saw, was still there, idly playing on her computer.

She looked at him expectantly, raised a single, carefully sculpted eyebrow. 'You didn't reply to my invitation yet, Detective.'

'I'm sorry, I got sidetracked by the prime minister.'

'That happens around here. So?'

Balthazar smiled. 'Let's go.'

EPILOGUE

Margaret Island, a month later

Winter was coming soon, Sandor Takacs could feel it. The bench's wooden slats were cold; the river was no longer blue-green but a muddy grey. Leaves and twigs floated on the water, bobbing and weaving in the currents. The autumn breeze was not balmy, but brisk, gusting hard with a chilly undertow. It was mid-October and there was no sign of an Indian summer, only the coldness to come.

Sandor shivered as he turned to the man sitting next to him. 'Will she win the election?'

'Of course,' he replied, his voice rasping, ruined by decades of smoking. 'For now, we are working together. In any case there is no functioning opposition. But she wants to break out, go her own way.'

'And will you let her?'

The man did not did not answer. Instead he pulled a packet of Sopianae cigarettes from his coat pocket, offered it to Sandor. 'But only if you smoke one. I'm down to my last twenty packs.'

Sandor laughed, shook his head. 'You keep them. I've given up. I won't waste yours.'

The two men were perched on a bench at the very tip of Margaret Island, the same bench where, just over a month ago, Sandor had sat with Balthazar and confessed that he was Virag's father. Sandor had known the man next to him for decades, ever since he had come to Budapest and made his career as a policeman, enforcing the law of a now long-vanished political system. They were both bundled up against the cold, Sandor in a police-issue winter coat, thick and padded, and a winter hat with ear-flaps. The man next to him wore a long, grey woollen overcoat, its collar spattered with flakes of dandruff. He peered out through thick glasses; his straggly grey hair poked out from under a brown peaked cap, his flaking skin raw red in the wind.

'Apart from Reka, who else is there?' asked Sandor. 'Pal is gone.'

The man they called the Librarian gave Sandor a sideways look. 'Yes, poor comrade Pal. A most mysterious death, as the newspapers reported it. The first time he had recovered enough to go for a walk on the riverbank by his penthouse apartment. A shove from behind, police, bodyguards, nowhere in sight, CCTV not working. A fast current, sucked under Margaret Bridge, still weak from the bullet wound and that's that. Drowned.' He lit his cigarette, drew deeply, looked hard at Sandor. 'Some might call that almost poetic.'

Sandor held his gaze. 'Some might. Let's focus on the election. There's nobody on the right or in the centre. Only her. It would be better to keep her under control.'

'Pal was a fool. He had everything and he wanted more. He was too greedy. She is much smarter. She knows she has enough.'

'And the material we have, on her and her husband?'

The Librarian smiled. 'She doesn't care. She says we can leak whatever we want. Now they are sick of leaks, she says. People want a government, one to bring Hungary into the twenty-first century. They don't care about *kompromat*. The whole country is compromised. There were 800,000 people in the Communist Party when everything collapsed. People did what they needed to survive. To live as best they can. They still do.'

Sandor nodded. 'She might be right.'

'She says she will win, with or without us. Eniko, the PR girl, is turning out to be rather good at her job. Public opinion is swinging right behind Reka.'

'*Kompromat*,' said Sandor thoughtfully. 'We have the video of Reka killing the Gendarme with the heel of her shoe and getting rid of the body. Anything else?'

The Librarian nodded then coughed, a long, wet rattling sound. He turned to Sandor, muttered 'Excuse me', and spat out at the side of the bench. The phlegm was streaked with blood. He was dying, Sandor realised.

The Librarian pulled out a small plastic bag from his coat and held it up. A long brass cartridge was inside.

Sandor nodded. 'Good. I wondered where that got to.'

'The girl's fingerprints are all over it. The murder investigation into the death of Mahmoud Hejazi is still ongoing. It's enough for her. Losing Eniko would be a serious blow to Reka. But in the long term... we still need someone we can control. Reka refuses to take orders. She is wilful. Now Pal is gone, she thinks she is untouchable. The fear is gone. And I don't have much longer. There are only a few of us left, now.'

Sandor nodded, watched a grey barge slowly move upriver, towards Slovakia. It was almost as long as a football field, piled high with coal. A Hungarian flag fluttered in the wind, mounted high on the bridge. He asked, 'Do you have someone else in mind?'

The Librarian took another drag of his cigarette, blew the smoke out over the water. It vanished instantly in the wind. The barge's horn sounded, a long, mournful low note that carried over the river. 'Yes,' he said. 'We do. Someone very close to Reka. Someone back in her life after a long time away. And, someone, we are pleased to see, getting closer to Eniko.'

'Who?'

'You will learn, when the time is right.'

'And Balthazar, and his boy? They are safe? I have your word?'

The Librarian turned towards Sandor, his rheumy eyes locked on his. 'Don't worry, Takacs *elvtars*, comrade Takacs. I give you my word. Nothing will happen to them.'

Across the river, on the top floor of a drab nineteenth-century apartment house, far out of sight of the two men, a tall, stooped man in his twenties, who had spent too much time playing video games, peered through the viewer of his video camera. The telephoto lens was powerful enough that he could see every movement of their lips. He watched the two men stand up, shake hands, go their own ways. A few seconds later the footage was sitting in a corner office that overlooked Falk Miksa Street.

ACKNOWLEDGEMENTS

My thanks, as ever, go to my agents Georgina Capel and Simon Shaps for their steadfast support and their faith in Balthazar Kovacs and his adventures. Thanks also to Rachel Conway and Irene Baldoni for all their help. It has been a pleasure to continue working with the team at Head of Zeus, especially my editors Nicolas Cheetham and Sophie Robinson. Their encouragement and their incisive comments were invaluable. Thanks also to Claire Kennedy, Rights Director, for securing multiple translation deals and to Louis Greenberg for his sharp copy-editing.

I remain grateful to the Society of Authors for its generous grant when I started writing *District VIII*, the first volume in the Balthazar Kovacs series. I am very pleased to be working with Kindle Entertainment, a London-based production company, as they develop a television series from the Balthazar Kovacs books. Special thanks to Ross Murray for his belief in Balthazar's television potential, Steve Bailie for his creative ideas and to Melanie Stokes. Thanks also to the many friends and acquaintances who shared their knowledge of Budapest, Roma society, police matters and the city's underworld. Readers wishing to learn more about Roma culture and society may visit the European Roma Rights Centre website at: errc.org. I am especially grateful to Clive Rumbold, a great lover of Budapest, for his insight and editorial suggestions and for sharing a chilling anecdote about the basement of a Buda villa. Special thanks to Monika Payne for her diligent reading of the first draft of *Kossuth Square* and her eagle-eyed list of suggestions and corrections, and also to Akos Gergely Balogh for his thoughts on *District VIII*. An honorary shout-out goes to Hannah Wood, my former editor at HarperCollins US, now at hannahwoodedit.com, who helped so much along the way with *Kossuth Square*. Last but not least, thanks, as ever, to Justin Leighton, Roger Boyes and Peter Green, fellow veterans of the 'hood.